COMET BOMB

On the screen they saw the sequenced charges inside the comet mass doing their job. A lump flaked off one side of the comet and then another. Then the main mass split in two, and the demolition charges inside each section blew up. The comet became a mass of rubble falling toward the Martian surface.

"I hope it works," Dekker's mother said.

"I hope we can pay for it," Tinker Gorshak said.

The myriad chunks of rubble turned dazzlingly bright as they hit the thin Martian atmosphere, the heat of the friction producing a thousand blinding meteors.

Then the fragments hit. They were not tiny, and they made H-bomb-size fountains of cloud . . .

By Frederik Pohl
Published by Ballantine Books:

BIPOHL
      The Age of the Pussyfoot
      Drunkard's Walk

BLACK STAR RISING

THE COOL WAR

THE HEECHEE SAGA
      Gateway
      Beyond the Blue Event Horizon
      Heechee Rendezvous
      The Annals of the Heechee
      The Gateway Trip

HOMEGOING

MINING THE OORT

NARABEDLA LTD.

POHLSTARS

STARBURST

THE WAY THE FUTURE WAS

THE WORLD AT THE END OF TIME

With Jack Williamson
      UNDERSEA CITY
      UNDERSEA QEUST
      UNDERSEA FLEET
      WALL AROUND A STAR
      THE FARTHEST STAR

With Lester del Rey
      PREFERRED RISK

THE BEST OF FREDERIK POHL
      (edited by Lester del Rey)

THE BEST OF C.M. KORNBLUTH
      (edited by Frederik Pohl)

MINING
THE OORT

Frederik Pohl

A Del Rey Book
BALLANTINE BOOKS • NEW YORK

A Del Rey Book
Published by Ballantine Books

Copyright © 1992 by Frederik Pohl

All rights reserved under International and Pan-American Copyright Conventions. Published in the United States of America by Ballantine Books, a division of Random House, Inc., New York, and simultaneously in Canada by Random House of Canada Limited, Toronto.

Library of Congress Catalog Card Number: 91-58639

ISBN 0-345-37200-X

Manufactured in the United States of America

First Hardcover Edition: August 1992
First Mass Market Edition: July 1993

For Harry Harrison

who made me do it

1.

THERE ISN'T ANYTHING much wrong with Mars that a decent atmosphere wouldn't fix right up. Unfortunately the place hasn't got one. Looking at Mars's situation from a human point of view—and how else have humans ever looked at anything?—the mean little atmosphere Mars does have has a number of serious things wrong with it. The most important of these is that there isn't enough of it. The air pressure at the surface of the planet is a pitiful nine or ten millibars. That's so tiny that people on Earth would probably call it a vacuum, but it isn't—quite.

That's bad news for would-be ecopoiesis engineers, as the people who practice the fledgling science of transforming other planets into acceptable imitations of Earth have come to call themselves. The fact that Mars is desperately short of atmospheric gases makes their job tough, but there's good news for would-be Martian immigrants, too. The good part is that there happens to be a place in the solar system where all those volatiles that Mars so conspicuously lacks are floating around in vast quantities, going to waste.

That place isn't very handy, but that's all right. Distance doesn't matter much in space, where if you just start a thing off with the right kind of shove, sooner or later it will get where you want it to go. The source of these potential Martian gases is way out in the fringes of the Sun's family of satellites, far beyond even Pluto; it is where comets sail forever in slow, cold orbits—at least until one or two happen to twitch themselves out of orbit and begin to slide down toward the Sun. The name of the place is the Oort cloud.

2.

WHEN DEKKER DEWOE was eight years old—that was Mars-years, of course, because Dekker was a Martian and they didn't use the Earth calendar on Mars, or indeed anything else from Earth that they could possibly get along without—well, when Dekker was eight, the first comet came plunging down on Mars at the end of its weary journey out of the Oort cloud.

That was a wonderful time. It was also a scary time for young Dekker, because nothing like it had ever happened before in his life. But mostly it was wonderful because, as everybody had been saying for as long as Dekker could remember, it meant that Mars would be alive again—some day—as soon as those comets began arriving in the large numbers they surely would—some day. These days, though, the comet strike was not only wonderfully exciting, it was also a great pain in the butt. It meant turning his life upside down, because Dekker was going to have to pack up and move out of the comet's way.

Not just Dekker DeWoe and his mother, either. The whole population of the Martian deme named Sagdayev was moving, all forty-three men, women, and children, and that was definitely something for an eight-year-old to think about. It didn't *frighten* Dekker, of course. There wasn't much that frightened Dekker DeWoe. He was at an age that doesn't frighten very easily—the Earth equivalent would have been nearly fifteen—and anyway he had inherited courage from his pioneering parents. There were some things that Dekker treated with prudent respect, though—things like air leaks, or getting lost, or the Bonds—and moving his whole town belonged in that category in his mind.

The move wouldn't be permanent, though. Evacuation was just a precaution, Dekker's mother said. The comet's impact point was supposed to be way up in the Chryse Planitia, a thousand kilometers east and north of the underground mining settlement of Sagdayev, but for cautious people that wasn't quite far enough away to be safe. You didn't live long on Mars unless you made a habit of being cautious. So the Martians of Sagdayev deme weren't going to take any chances. "We don't want to be anywhere near ground zero," his mother explained, fretting over what to pack and what to abandon out of their sparse possessions. "Their aim might not be that good."

"You mean the comet might hit *Sagdayev*?" Dekker asked, his eyes opening wide.

"Oh, no," his mother said, touching him, "or at least I don't think so. Well, no, I'm sure. Really. It's just that if it came too close it could shake the town up—maybe even breach the pressure integrity." She sighed, looking fretfully around their single room. "Sometimes I think we shouldn't have built Sagdayev way out here on the edge of the Bulge, but how were we supposed to know?"

Dekker didn't answer that rhetorical question, only the one that lay behind it. "The copper's here," he pointed out.

She said absently, looking around at the clutter of possessions, "I suppose. Dekker? What about leaving Brave Bear here? You don't ever play with him anymore."

And of course Dekker admitted that he didn't. He was awed by the ruthless way his mother was discarding her own second-best shoes and his long-absent father's spare worksuit—kept only for sentiment, its air pump was old and leaky, and surely Boldon DeWoe was never going to come back to wear it again. She even threw away the little hot plate they had sometimes used to make midnight treats of cocoa or even fudge in their own room, when Dekker was little. "We can come back for some of these things later," his mother explained. "Maybe. *Probably*, Dekker. I think Sagdayev will be all right, but for now we aren't supposed to take more than twenty kilograms apiece."

It wasn't just personal possessions they were leaving behind, it was the whole underground town that had been carved with great effort out of the Martian soil. They closed down the little metal refinery and domed over the entrance to their precious copper mine. They even abandoned most of the solar mirrors and photovoltaic generators that kept all the Martian settlements powered up and alive. They harvested everything that was ripe, or nearly ripe, from the aeroponic gardens down in the deme's lowest level, but left the growing plants behind. They did not bother with the three hectares of glass-headed mushrooms that were doing their best to survive out on the slope of the long-dead volcano they had built on. They didn't even take the central kitchens and baths. There wasn't room. Four cargo carts had been dragged over from Sunpoint City, plus one pressurized cart for people. What could not fit in the carts had to stay behind.

The adults were still loading the carts up when Dekker's mother ordered him to bed on his last night in Sagdayev. Dekker certainly didn't cry. Eight-year-old Martians were much too grown-up to cry, but he had bad dreams that night, and when his mother woke him up before dawn he was bleary-eyed. She hustled him into his clothes and settled him in his metal-lath seat in the pressurized cart and left him there. Gerti DeWoe had been assigned as a relief driver, and so she had to ride in the big tractor that pulled the train of carts instead of sitting with her son.

It was a long trip to their haven in the metropolis of Sunpoint, more than eight hundred kilometers in a straight line, and they couldn't travel in a straight track. The area between the peak called Tharus Tolus, where Sagdayev had been built next to its rich vein of copper ore, and the far more impressive mountain at Sunpoint City, Pavonis Mons, was fissured and uneven. They had to take endless detours, and they didn't travel very fast at best. The solar-powered tractor was slow by nature, even with all the extra photovoltaic accumulators on the carts. And, of course, when the sun went down no more electrical power accumulated. After sunset the tractor could keep on going only as far as the stored power in its batteries would take it, leaving enough of a prudent reserve of energy to keep everyone alive and breathing until daybreak the next morning.

All in all, they were five days en route.

It was a long five days. Most of the time Dekker had little to do except sit there and eat when the meals were passed around, hand over hand, and three or four times a day get up to take his turn at the cramped little toilets. They had installed four virtuals, and when Dekker got his turn at one he could call up any kind of entertainment in the store. That was pretty good, watching old stories unroll all around him, or even catching up on his schoolwork. But that only happened for an hour or two a day. All in all, the trip was a test of their training for all the Martians from Sagdayev. If they hadn't all been schooled from birth in Manners and Consideration and Nonaggressive Interaction there might even have been fistfights. There almost were anyway—more raised voices, or angry, hissing ones, than Dekker was used to hearing, at least. But he himself was not involved in any of the petulant near-quarrels among the grown-ups.

Dekker wasn't entirely alone. Three or four times a day his mother would call him on the phone line from the tractor cab, just to chat, and between times one of her friends was right there with Dekker, because the man had taken the next seat. That was Tinker Gorshak, of course. Dekker still didn't like him, but he was glad enough to have the man's shoulder to fall asleep against sometimes.

Dekker didn't do much talking on the trip. He read his school texts when he was awake. He slept as much as he could. And, although he was really much too old for such things, he was always aware of the comforting presence of the earless, eyeless stuffed toy he had slipped into his suit at the last minute, when his mother was looking the other way. Because when push came to shove, even the nearly grown Dekker DeWoe had not been willing to let Brave Bear face the comet alone.

3.

T HE BEST THING Mars had—at least, so the Martians mostly thought—was the Skyhook at Sunpoint City, and that didn't come with the planet's original equipment. It had had to be built—by Earthies, as a matter of fact, so they weren't all bad. The Skyhook had a kind of interesting history. It was one of the two critically important human inventions— the other being the Augenstein antimatter drive that made possible the fleets of spaceships that made a Skyhook worth building in the first place—which had been invented long before there was any need for either of them. In fact, the Skyhook had been invented long before there was any possibility of actually building one. The man who devised the first "space elevator" was an engineer from Leningrad named Yuri Artsutanov, and he had done it way back in 1960.

That was pretty far-sighted of Yuri Artsutanov. No human being had managed to reach even the fringe of space in 1960, and the kind of materials that you could possibly build such a thing with didn't even exist then. But it was Artsutanov who proposed that if one were to position a satellite in geostationary orbit right over a planet's equator, and hang a cable thirty-six thousand kilometers long from it, the whole lash-up would amount to an "orbital tower." Then you could run elevators up and down the cable to lift ships and cargoes and people from the planet's surface right into orbit for damn near nothing—or at least for much less than trying to do the same thing with rockets.

It all worked out just the way Artsutanov thought it would. Once the Augenstein antimatter drive came along and made spaceships fast and fairly cheap themselves, it became feasible to junket all around the solar system—once you got into orbit. But that first step was the hardest, and that was what the Skyhook was for.

Not that that first Skyhook itself had been all that cheap. The Earth one had been strung from Nairobi on the surface to geosynchronous orbit, and its construction had cost about as much as an average war. But when they came to do the same thing for Mars the price was slashed way down. The reason for that was that they didn't have to hoist all the materials that went into it from the surface of the planet to space. Mars's Skyhook *started* in space: ores from the asteroids, fabricated in orbit, made the whole thing, and then Mars was only an elevator ride from the rest of the universe. Those first daring, dedicated Martian colonists, needing everything, could then import just about anything they liked. All they had to do was pay the import bills.

4.

SUNPOINT CITY WAS a settlement of a whole different order from Sagdayev. Sunpoint City's mountain was the truly impressive Pavonis Mons, topping out at twenty kilometers and startling to look at, even for Martian-born Dekker DeWoe. The city sat right on the Martian equator—that was of course why it was called "Sunpoint." Therefore it was the point where the Skyhook touched down, and therefore the metropolis of the planet.

The other impressive thing about Sunpoint City was that, by Martian standards, it was *vast*. There were more than nine hundred people living in its nearly three kilometers of underground tunnels and chambers, all carved out of the soil under the Martian surface caliche and doubly sealed to keep the precious atmosphere inside.

Dekker DeWoe was awed. He had never seen so many *strangers* before. Some of them were really strange—in fact, some were not Martians at all. Sunpoint was where off-planet visitors arrived, and where many of them stayed. It held several dozen Germans, Americans, Ukrainians, Japanese, Brazilians— whole families of them—people from *Earth*! As they strolled together down one of the passageways Dekker's mother pointed a group of the Earthies out, three or four grown-ups and a couple of children. "Take a good look," she whispered. "You won't see them very often." Dekker knew why. The Earthies kept pretty much to themselves, in their own luxurious quarters.

"Can we see where they live?" he asked.

"Well, we can walk by their section," his mother said, after a moment's thought. "We haven't been invited in, though." But when they got to the Earthie quarter, a level down from the— slightly—risky top sections of Sunpoint, there wasn't much to see. It looked pretty much like any other part of the city, just

7

another corridor, though conspicuously marked DIPLOMATIC AREA. Loud music was coming out of it, though. That was certainly strange; people didn't trespass on other people's hearing, did they? It did not look any grander than the corridor that held the DeWoes' own borrowed cubicle—not from the entrance, anyway—though Dekker did notice something strange about it. A dozen small rectangles of patterned, colored fabric hung from sticks in the walls. "They're pretty," Dekker said, to be polite.

"They're *flags*," his mother explained. "The one with the red stripes, I think that's the flag for America." And as they walked back to their own place she startled him by telling him that, down that corridor, the Earthies had private rooms for each person, as well as such other unimaginable luxuries as bathtubs and even *pets.* "Two of the Earthie families have cats," his mother sniffed when they were back in their own quarters, "and Tinker says there used to be a parrot, but it died." And when he asked how the Earthies could afford such wanton waste, she said somberly, "Earthies can afford *anything*, Dekker. Especially because, you know, we're the ones who'll be paying for it."

"Oh, right," he said, enlightened. "The Bonds."

"The Bonds," Tinker Gorshak growled from the doorway, surprising Dekker, who hadn't known he was there. "Earthies and the Bonds," he said, moving his mouth as though he wanted to get rid of the words.

He wasn't alone, either. A little kid was hanging on one of Tinker's legs, thumb in his mouth, staring at Dekker. "This is my grandson, Tsumi," the old man said proudly. "We came by to see if you needed any help. You boys are going to have fun together, Dek."

Feeling his mother's eye on him, Dekker put out his hand to shake the kid's. He pulled it back quickly; it was the one Tsumi had had in his mouth, and it was still spit-wet, but Tinker, not noticing, went back to his subject. "The Earthies say they're here to supervise their investments, but they're really tourists. They came to watch the fireworks show! And we're paying a thousand cues a day for each one of them. Do you know what cues are, Dekker? Their money. *Hard* money."

Dekker's mother shook her head at him. "Dekker knows what currency units are, Tinker," she said.

"And does he know that we have to borrow the goddam

things *from* them, so we can use the funds to pay *for* them? Because they don't want the things we have here, you know. What they want has to come from Earth, and it has to get paid for in Earth currency units."

Gerti DeWoe sighed. "Tinker," she said, half joking, "I think you need docility training more than the kids do. Anyway, as long as you're here, let's get some work done. Help me get everything put away."

That didn't take long for the refugees from Sagdayev—even with Tinker's pesty little grandson getting in the way—since they didn't have many possessions to stow. The funny thing was, Tinker told them, that all over Sunpoint the locals were engaged in the same activity. The refugees from Sagdayev thought it was pretty comical that the Sunpointers should be worrying about the comet impact for themselves. There could be no doubt that Sunpoint City was far enough away to be safe from even ground tremors. Mars was too old to suffer much seismic activity, even when some tens of millions of tons of cometary material smashed onto its crust. All the same, since the refugees were guests of Sunpoint City, it was only good manners to help their hosts. So they all turned out to get everything battened down, books off the shelves, walls braced, breakables stowed away, and to help emergency crews practice damage control with sealant in case the outside walls sprang a leak.

The trouble with everybody being busy was that Dekker had to be busy, too. Not with anything *useful*. With *baby-sitting*. It was Tinker's idea, but Gerti DeWoe endorsed it. "Of course you can keep an eye on Tsumi," she said reasonably. "You'll be a big help. Tinker's got all he can do, and so does Tsumi's father." So did she. She didn't say that, but she didn't have to, so Dekker resigned himself to the company of the brat.

The trouble was that the brat wasn't interested in showing Dekker around Sunpoint City, which could have been interesting. He wanted Dekker to play with him, and Dekker got pretty tired of playing little kids' games. Tsumi didn't even want to use the virtual-reality hoods, or at least not the kinds he was old enough to be permitted, although it was a heaven-sent opportunity for kids. With everyone else so busy, most of the time the hoods were idle. The brat wouldn't sit still, either.

Nearing desperation, Dekker suggested, "How about reading a book?"

"A book." Tsumi sneered. "Screw books. If you want a book, you can have mine." He fumbled in his belly pouch and pulled out a book cartridge. "This is old butt-face's idea of a good book," he said, throwing it at Dekker. "I didn't want this crap. I wanted a book about *war.*"

Dekker caught the book and turned it over. Its title was *The Adventures of Huckleberry Finn*, and according to the jacket it was written by somebody named Mark Twain. "Don't be an idiot," he told the boy. "Who wants to read books about war?"

"I do. You see wars, don't you? In the eights-and-up docility? So if it's all right for you, why for Jesus' sake can't I read about them?"

"Because you're too young."

"That isn't *fair*," Tsumi said spitefully. Well, Dekker thought, maybe it wasn't. But it wasn't his fault. He hadn't made the rule that the under-eights couldn't see war clips and, come to that, it wasn't fair for him to be stuck with this nasty little piece of work all day, either. His mother had been wrong, Dekker decided. Maybe old Tinker Gorshak did need some docility training, but *nobody* needed it more than his grandson.

Then the world's pressures eased for Dekker, because suddenly it was time for Tsumi's actual docility class; because, of course, it never mattered how busy things got or how little spare time anyone had. There was *always* time for docility training, because the world, the *worlds*, had long ago passed the point where they could survive their own internal stresses without something like it.

Dekker, at eight, didn't have to attend the little kids' class. Once he had succeeded in getting Tsumi in the room he was free. He found a quiet place to sit. He took out the book Tsumi had thrown at him and thumbed the "start" button to see what it was going to be like.

He hadn't hoped for much. But as the words flowed across the screen, he glanced at them, then read them more attentively, and then was hooked.

When he was finally permitted to return Tsumi to his grandfather's care, Dekker kept the book. As time allowed he read in it, marveling at such outré concepts as "slaves" and "guns" and, perhaps most of all, "rivers." When he came to the part where Huck feigned his own suicide—suicide!—to escape from his drunken father's beatings—beatings!—he went back and reread it twice to make sure he was understanding what the author meant to say.

So Dekker was not the only boy in human history whose father hadn't particularly cared for him.

Dekker tried to regard that as a comforting thought, but it wasn't.

Every night on the flat screens there were pictures of the approaching comet, a big, dirty snowball, ten kilometers through.

Its temperature was no longer at the icy cold of its birth out in the almost-interstellar Oort cloud, because it had already swung around close to the Sun to slow itself down before climbing back out to intercept Mars. It was warming up. Some of its gases were making its spectacular tail, and even its core was growing fuzzy.

Watching the thing grow on the news screens didn't satisfy Dekker. It was not anything like being up on the surface itself, in facemask and thermal suit. So when Dekker's mother was detailed to go outside to help secure the city's all-important solar power cells, Dekker invited himself to join the work party. The brat would certainly not be there. It was going to be fun to be out with the workers, even though Tinker Gorshak would be there, too.

5.

MARS ISN'T ENTIRELY without water. But neither is the sand of the Sahara Desert, if you are willing to work hard enough to get the bound water of crystallization out of the sand grains, and if you're content with a tiny reward. Most of the accessible water Mars has is frozen in the polar ice caps—much good may that do anyone. There's also a certain amount of water that is frozen in mud, under the surface caliche, but it

stays there because the distant Sun isn't able to heat the surface
enough to melt much of it out; Mars gets only about half
Earth's sunshine. Some parts of Mars are marked with the
evidence that there once was real flowing water there, namely
such scarring as floodplains, and the dendritic riverbeds called
lahars. Perhaps streams once did flow in the lahars, when some
brief volcanic flurry melted some of that frozen mud and forced
it to the surface, so that it flowed downhill until it evaporated
into the parched air. It doesn't do that anymore. When people
first came to Mars some of them tried to melt out the icy mud
under the hardpan. If, they thought, you could drive out some
of those volatiles you could increase the density of the atmosphere, which would warm things up, which would help drive
out more volatiles. Or, to put it in another way, if you had some
eggs you could make ham and eggs, if you had some ham.

6.

THE GROTESQUE, RUSTY landscape of Mars was the only
landscape Mars-born Dekker DeWoe had ever known.
He would not have tried to tell anyone it was beautiful. Few
youngsters think of such things as the beauty of a landscape in
the ordinary course of their lives, and Mars was very ordinary
to Dekker. He found the scenery he lived in unsurprising and,
actually, quite homey.

Going out with the work party onto the rubbly plain was a
welcome break from the tunnels of Sunpoint City, especially
since Tsumi Gorshak hadn't been allowed along. Tsumi's
grandfather Tinker, though, kept getting on Dekker's nerves.
Tinker insisted on *helping*. Every time Dekker picked up one
edge of the great sheets of protective film, Gorshak materialized
beside him to lend a hand, grinning silently through the faceplate of his suit. Dekker hated that. The old man treated him
as though he were a *child*.

Dekker generally spent a lot of time trying to stay away from

Tinker Gorshak, and it wasn't only because of his pesky grand-kid. Tinker had faults of his own. To begin with, he was an old, old man. He was nearly forty in Martian years, or over seventy by Earth's standards; after all, he even had grandchildren. Tinker Gorshak was, in fact, one of the very earliest Martian settlers. For that reason, Dekker had a certain amount of re-spect for Tinker, but he was wary of the man, too, because he knew why the old man was always trying to be his friend. Gorshak kept on doing things for the boy—taking him along on survey trips, or to check the slow growth of the crystal mushroom plantations; bringing him little presents of apples and strawberries as the aeroponic crops grew in the hothouses; asking him how he was doing at school. Dekker wasn't flat-tered. He didn't want Gorshak's gifts, and he didn't think Gorshak specially cared about how he was doing. What Tinker Gorshak actually wanted was to marry Gertrud DeWoe, and Dekker really didn't want his mother getting married again—even if his father had been actually dead instead of only di-vorced.

What made it hard to rebuff Gorshak's offers of help was the fact that, although Dekker did his best in struggling with the covers for the photovoltaic cells, the job really called for adult muscles. It required wrestling huge sheets of film over the long mirrors and the troughs of photocells that turned the sunlight into electrical power. It was also, the people from Sagdayev muttered to each other, pretty much a waste of time. True, it was only common sense to protect your power supplies. If anything happened to the photovoltaic cells, the city of Sun-point would be in desperate trouble. But what could happen to them? No pieces of the comet would stray so far as to destroy Sunpoint City's mirrors. There might well be some hellish huge dust storms, but those were always a problem on Mars, and every deme's photovoltaic arrays had survived plenty of dust storms before.

So Dekker wasn't much help to the suited, sweating men and women unfurling the great film sheets, and it didn't make things easier when he could hardly keep his eyes on the ground be-cause so much was fascinating in the sky. There was the great comet itself, its glowing, milky tail spreading almost from hori-zon to horizon even in the bright midday sunshine. Even more exciting for the boy from the back hills, there were the skinny spiderweb cables that stretched up to invisibility where the

Skyhook did its work of lifting capsules from surface to orbit.

It was also true that the heat of the Martian day sapped much of what strength Dekker could muster for the job. Where Sunpoint sat on the Martian equator, in the middle of this summer day, the temperature was over twenty degrees Celsius. When Dekker dropped his end of a sheet for the third time, Tinker Gorshak hand-signaled to him angrily, and his mother came over and pressed her facemask against his own.

"Better give it up, Dekker," she advised, her voice thin and faint. "Go find something else to do. We'll finish this without you."

Dekker signaled agreement gladly enough. There was indeed something else that he preferred to do, and he had only been waiting for the chance.

Deceitfully, he started back in the direction of the city lock, craning over his shoulder to see what the work party was doing. When he was sure they were too busy to be bothering with him anymore, he changed direction, hurried along in the shelter of the mirrors, and headed out for the open plain.

The scenery before Dekker's eyes was all brand new to him. What he saw when he looked around the Martian surface were shadows like ink, boulders colored rose and rust, and a pink sky with the small, bright Sun overhead. It not only wasn't like Earth, it wasn't much like Dekker's familiar backyard, either. Sagdayev's soil was browner and grayer at this time of year; here at Sunpoint it was all pink windblown sands over the caliche. An Earthie might not have seen a difference between the two, but Dekker did.

Of course, that was only natural. All Martians knew that no one but the Martians knew what Mars really looked like. The mudsuckers could never understand. There was an Earth TV show that Dekker and the other Martian settler kids sometimes watched, because it was funny. It wasn't *meant* to be funny. It was supposed to be a kind of soap opera about passions and perversions among the Martian colonists, but any Martian could see that it was a fake. The whole thing had been computer-shot in studios somewhere on Earth. Good enough to fool the mudsuckers, but an obvious fraud nevertheless.

When Dekker had put a kilometer's worth of hillocks between himself and the work party, he stopped. It was as bright as daylight ever got on Mars, and the Sun as hot. Dekker turned down the heating coils in his suit and looked up at the sky.

The comet was majestic above him.

The thing was immense. Its tail now was forked into two streams of milky light, hardly dimmed by the sunlight. It spread from the western horizon, up past the midday sun and the spindly cables of the Skyhook, almost to the top of the mountain to the east. Dekker could hardly take it in all at once. The facemask wasn't built for sky-gazing. Although it gave nearly 360-degree vision in all horizontal directions, it wasn't made for looking up.

So, being well away from any interfering grown-ups, Dekker did what he had to do to observe the spectacle. He lay down on the rusty, pebbly Martian soil. He leaned against the side of a little boulder that wore a reddish yarmulke of dust on its top and gazed straight up. He slipped his arm out of the sleeve of his suit, fumbled in his waist pouch for a biscuit, and with two fingers eased it past the stiff helmet collar. He nibbled the biscuit thoughtfully while he admired the comet.

Dekker was feeling happy. It wasn't just the comet that Dekker wanted to find, out on the barren plains of the dead planet. There was something else there for him, and its name was "privacy."

Dekker didn't spend much time thinking about whether he disliked living in an underground town, where everyone was always in everyone else's pocket. He had no other life to compare it with; he had lived in Sagdayev deme since he was born. Dazzlingly huge as Sunpoint was to him, it was only a larger Sagdayev. There was no chance in any Martian settlement for the solitude a young boy needs. So as soon as he was old enough to be trusted out by himself, Dekker had spent a lot of his free time roaming out of sight among the barren dunes. Out there, he had seen the comet almost as soon as the naked eye could detect it at all, more than a year earlier, when it was only a minute pearly blotch in the nighttime sky. He had followed it down toward its rendezvous with the Sun until it was lost in the solar glare, and picked it up again as it began its return toward Mars orbit. Now it was certainly a spectacular sight. It didn't really look like green fields and rainstorms and cloudy sunsets, but that was what it was supposed to turn into—though of course Dekker knew that this comet was only the first and tiniest beginning of the long effort to make Mars live.

And out there in the Oort, where this comet had been born and had lived its billion-year incidentless life until some Oort miner had zapped it and threaded it and sent it falling in toward the Sun—out there in the Oort, right this minute, some other Oort miners were picking other comets for the harvest.

Just as Dekker's father had done, once.

Dekker wrenched his thoughts away from that subject. Dekker didn't want to think about his father. Dekker had spent too many hours already thinking about the man—yes, crying about the man, too, sometimes when he was little—in all the long Martian years since Boldon DeWoe had lifted him up and kissed him good-bye and given him a stuffed animal to remember his father by, and set off for the Oort . . . and never come back.

Oh, the man was alive still, no doubt, somewhere on Earth— Dekker's mother had told him that, on the one of the few times she ever talked about her former husband. But Boldon DeWoe had never come back to see his son.

Dekker wanted something better than that to do with his precious solitary time, so he fumbled in his suit pouch again and pulled the *Huckleberry Finn* book out. He forwarded through to the part about the feud between the Grangerfords and the Shepherdsons and read it over again. How baffling it was! How *awful.* People causing death to each other, and not for any crazy impulse of passion but deliberately, because of some matter of *pride* . . . yes, and other people applauding them for it, as though that sort of beastlike behavior were the most natural, and even the most *proper*, thing for them to do!

He could not understand. He gave up trying after a while and read on. He was back on the safety of the raft with Huck and the runaway slave, Jim, when something made him stop reading. He snapped off the book and blinked, squirming around in his suit. He became aware that he was feeling a slithery, clattery vibration from the soil under him. He jumped to his feet to look around.

A buggy was coming toward him, heading in the direction of Sunpoint City.

He couldn't hear it, of course. No one could hear much in the scanty Martian atmosphere, but he could see the buggy clearly as it topped a rise. Evidently the driver saw him. The vehicle hesitated, then made a sharp turn. Rusty pebbles flew like spray from one set of its great mesh wheels; then all wheels spun together and it rolled rapidly to his side. It stopped with the nearest wheel almost touching him, and a young girl looked down at him from the enclosed control seat.

Dekker realized he had seen her before. She was one of the Earthies his mother had pointed out, and he had even heard her name. Anna? Annette? Something like that. There was no question that she was an Earthie, anyway. Dekker didn't have to recognize her face to know that, because no Martian child would have been allowed a buggy of her own just to wander around in.

The Earthie girl was gesturing for him to climb up and join her inside the buggy.

Dekker scowled up at her. He hadn't come out onto the plain to talk to some spoiled Earth brat! But she had already ruined his solitude, and anyway it was easier for him to do what she wanted than to try to argue about it in sign language. He gave in, stepped between the metal mesh wheels, each one twice as tall as Dekker himself, and climbed the spike ladder into the little entrance.

When the air hissed in and the inner door clicked he opened the door and unsealed his facemask to look at her.

"Are you lost?" the girl asked. "You shouldn't go out here by yourself. What would happen if you fell or something? Your father's going to give you hell, boy!"

"I'm not lost," he told her. He didn't bother to tell her all the ways in which she was wrong. If he fell! He supposed she meant if he broke a leg or something—imagine breaking a leg here! Where there was nothing high enough to fall from, and only the gentle Martian gravity to speed the fall. Even if he had somehow managed to knock himself unconscious the suit radio would immediately send out a distress signal and someone would be out to rescue him in minutes.

There was one other thing she was very wrong about. His father was certainly nowhere around to punish him, but he wasn't prepared to talk about that to this young female mudsucker from Earth.

"I guess you just wanted to look at the comet, like me," she said, studying his face. "My name's Annetta Cauchy."

He shook her hand, mostly to show that he knew Earth customs. "I'm Dekker DeWoe." And, to show that he recognized her, "You're Mr. Cauchy's daughter."

She nodded graciously, as though he had given her a compliment. "Isn't the comet pretty?" she asked, making polite conversation.

"I guess so."

She nodded again, satisfied with his concurrence. Then she advised him, "You ought to like it. It costs a zillion dollars to bring those things here, and my daddy is one of the people paying for it. He's an underwriter for the Bonds."

Although Dekker wondered for a moment what an "underwriter" was, he didn't answer that. He had heard all he wanted to hear about what the Earthies were paying for, and what they were going to want in return. Anyway, she didn't seem to expect an answer. She was pointing out the window to the Skyhook cable, where a capsule was sliding swiftly down toward the touchdown on the far side of Sunpoint. "My daddy's firm helped pay for that, too," she told him. "It's nice. I rode down it when I came from Earth with my parents. I'll be going up it again when we go home. Would you like to go into space some day?"

"Of course I would. I will," Dekker said sternly, "some day."

The girl looked skeptical but polite. She sighed to show she was changing the subject, but without prejudice to her own opinions, and frowned as she looked around at the mountainside. "Tell me, Dekker," she said. "Don't you think all this stuff is pretty, well, creepy? It looks like somebody's just thrown rocks around."

Dekker gazed at the landscape, puzzled. "How else should it look?"

"But it's *boring*. Doesn't it ever change?"

Dekker said defensively, "I don't know about here. Around Sagdayev it's pretty in the winter."

"You mean snow?"

"Snow?" He stared at her, marveling at her ignorance. "There isn't any *snow*, but sometimes there are frost shadows around the rocks, and things."

She looked unconvinced, and smug about it. "Was I right? Were you watching the comet?"

"Actually," he said, glad of the chance to show her she had been wrong, "I was reading a book."

"You shouldn't read in an airsuit. It's bad for the eyes."

He ignored that. "It was an Earth book called *Huckleberry Finn*. Did you ever read it?"

"Read it? No. We had it in school once, I think. Anyway,"

she added practically, "it's getting late. I think I'd better take you home. Are you hungry?"

"No," he said, but when he saw that she had picked up a little gilt candy box to offer him he changed his mind. He took one. That was just good manners, but then he discovered that it tasted really fine. It was chocolate! And it contained something fruity and sweet and wonderful inside; and, since she had left the box out, he took another. Dekker didn't think his mother would have approved of that, but he knew Earthies didn't have the same standards of manners as Martians.

The girl put her hands on the controls. "Take off your suit," she ordered over her shoulder as she advanced the speed levers on both sets of wheels. She didn't ease them gently forward as a proper buggy driver would have done but just thrust them almost to full-out. Naturally the buggy wheels spun, wasting energy.

"You're going to wear your treads out that way," he informed her, meaning to add that he didn't want to be driven back to Sunpoint anyway, as he was perfectly capable of walking.

But she had left the box of chocolates out, and didn't seem to mind when he took a third, and then a fourth.

7.

EVEN IF YOU managed to pump Mars's atmosphere up to the thousand-millibar pressure of the Earth's, you couldn't breathe the stuff. It simply doesn't contain what people need for breathing.

The first thing you think of wanting is oxygen, of course. Well, actually, there's oxygen in Mars's air. In fact, more than half of what atmosphere there is on Mars is oxygen—kind of. The trouble is, that oxygen is already tightly locked up into carbon dioxide. Only 5 percent of the negligible quantity of air Mars possesses is anything *but* that useless carbon dioxide, in fact, and a lot of that remaining 5 percent is equally useless stuff like argon. No, that won't do to support human life. What Mars needs to make it green is hydrogen, to react with some of that oxygen to create water, and nitrogen, to mix with the rest of the oxygen in order to reduce the air to something people could breathe without burning out their lungs—and, oh, yes, so that you can eat, because plants won't grow without nitrogen.

8.

WHEN THEY GOT back to the Sunpoint entry, Dekker watched critically as the girl mated her crawler with the city lock. All in all she did it fairly skillfully, and Dekker found little to criticize. He followed her inside, sealed the door himself, and turned around to see that someone was watching them. It was another mudsucker, male, a few years older than Dekker, and as short and squat as any Earthie; he was, of course, looking amused. Annetta greeted him warmly. "Dekker," she said, "I'd like you to meet my friend Evan."

"Hi," Dekker said politely, shaking the young man's hand. "But I have to go, there's something I have to do. Thanks for the candy."

The one named Evan didn't seem to mind that at all. He was already turning away from Dekker, talking to the girl. "Listen, Netty, about the party tonight—" he began, but Dekker was rapidly moving away.

It wasn't entirely true that there was something he had to do. The fact of the statement was accurate enough, of course. Sooner or later; because even though they were in a strange deme, and in spite of the fact that the comet was due to strike in a matter of hours, and regardless of all the effort involved in protecting Sunpoint's destructibles against possible harm—in spite of all these things, the essential functions of life on Mars went on. For Dekker, one of them was the compulsory daily class in Getting Along.

But he had an hour or so to go before he had to be there, and he spent it roaming around—blessedly alone, for Tsumi was, no doubt, grumpily tending the capybara meat animals by himself.

Nothing was the same here as in Sagdayev. The place was not only bigger, it was laid out funny. Mostly it was *huge*—six levels deep, against Sagdayev's three—and Dekker had a satisfying hour or so just roaming it, always remembering to look as though he had some important errand so that no one would ask him why he wasn't doing anything useful.

He cut the time a little fine. When it was time to get to docility he suddenly realized he didn't know where to go. He asked directions; but with all the preimpact excitement nobody seemed to know where anything was happening, and so he arrived in the classroom just when the Pledge of Assistance was about to begin.

The room was crowded. There were at least sixty or seventy young men and women there, and Dekker was startled to see that Tsumi Gorshak was among them. What was the kid doing in a session meant for eights-and-ups? For that matter, why was Tsumi nodding satisfiedly to the proctor and pointing at Dekker at the same time?

Dekker slid into a seat on the floor next to Tsumi and joined the recital:

> "I pledge my life
> to those who share it,
> to the safety and well-being of my planet,
> and all who live in it.
> One world,
> with liberty and justice for all,
> through sharing."

But everybody was looking at him, and as soon as they were finished Tsumi whispered, "You're late."

He wasn't alone. The proctor was pointing at him. "Punctuality," the young man, a ten-year-old with a sparse beard, said, "is the courtesy of kings. What's your name?"

"Dekker DeWoe," he admitted.

"Dekker DeWoe. Well, Dekker DeWoe, lateness steals time from other people. It is as bad to take someone's time as to take his property."

"I meant no offense," said Dekker, looking around to see if, by any chance, that Annetta Cauchy person was in the room. She wasn't. There weren't any Earth children at all in the class. Perhaps Earthies didn't need to be taught to be nonaggressive. Or perhaps they didn't care.

"And meanwhile," the proctor was going on, "your young nephew was worried about you."

"I meant no—" Dekker began again automatically, and then realized what the man was saying. He turned a glare on Tsumi, who shrugged blandly.

"I said you told me to meet you here," Tsumi whispered.

"You had no *right*," Dekker whispered back, but stopped there because the proctor was addressing his audience. Dekker subsided as the proctor spoke:

"Let's begin. I haven't met all of you before, so let's get back to basics. This is docility training. What do we mean by 'docility'?"

He looked around. A Sunpoint eight-year-old in the first row had her hand up already. "Docility is learning to consider the needs of society and other people," she said.

"That's right. That doesn't mean being passive. We're not passive, are we? But we're docile; which is to say, we're civilized. And, being civilized people, we just made our Pledge of Assistance. Does everybody do that?"

"Everybody on Mars," the same girl said at once.

Another put in, "Everybody in space, even, the Loonies and everybody. But not the Earthies."

The proctor nodded in satisfaction. "That's true. When you see our Earth guests here you have to remember they're a little different. Of course they have their own kind of training—well, they have to, don't they? Or they'd still be having wars there. But they make a different kind of pledge in their schools; they pledge 'allegiance.' What does that mean?"

Dekker knew the answer to that, and it was a good time to regain a little favor. "It means they pledge to be loyal, and that kind of means you'll do what someone tells you."

"Exactly," the proctor said, looking surprised. "They pledge allegiance to a flag. Do we have a flag?"

The class sat silent for a moment—Dekker, too, because he was interested in hearing the answer. Finally a girl almost as old as the proctor put her hand up. "No, because we don't need one. We have each other."

The proctor nodded. "Right. What flags are for," he went on, settling into his lecture for the day, "is so you can see which side is which when you're fighting. So you know who to *kill*." He waited for the little gasp of shock from his audience. He got it. He went on, "Yes, they killed people for their flags, and the terrible thing, friends, is that the people doing the killing *liked* it. Oh, they didn't like getting killed themselves—or burned, or paralyzed, or blinded—but they thought that fighting gave them a chance to be *heroes*. What's a 'hero'? Anybody?"

Beside Dekker little Tsumi's hand shot up. He didn't wait to be called, but shouted out: "Somebody very brave who does great things!"

The proctor gave him a measuring look. "That's one way to look at it, yes," he said, in a tone that showed he thought that way was the wrong way. "But that depends on what you mean by 'great,' doesn't it? People used to have a different idea of heroes. They used to think they were like gods—and what they thought about gods, those days, was that the gods always did whatever they wanted to. They didn't question themselves, they shoved people around any way they felt like, and they always thought they were right. That's what a man named Bernard Knox wrote once; he said heroes were like gods, and he said, 'Heroes might be, usually were, violent, antisocial, destructive.' Now tell me, friends. Would we call people like that heroes? Or would we see anything heroic in a *war*?"

Resoundingly the class roared, "No." Even Dekker. But not, he saw with surprise, little Tsumi, who was sitting next to him with his thumb in his mouth and a thoughtful expression on his face.

They never did finish the class. Just as the proctor was getting into the main work-together docility activity—it was a cooperative project, building a geodesic structure out of struts and cords, impossible to do unless every member of the group held and lifted and pulled just at the right moment in his turn—there was a harsh alarm beeping for a blowout drill.

It was only practice, of course. It was always only practice—except the one time when, maybe, it would be real, and that was the one they always had to be ready for. So they never fooled around, even when they were sure it was just practice. Everyone scattered to check the automatic corridor seals and the room doors and vents, making sure everything was closed off and airtight, all over Sunpoint City, in a matter of a minute or two; and then there was nothing to do except to sit there, in a little room with the air motionless and almost beginning to stale, for a few more minutes until the lights blinked three times and the long wailing beep sounded "all clear."

Then the docility class had disintegrated, the proctor long gone to his duty post for the drill. Dekker looked around for a while for Tsumi Gorshak, but not very hard, and then went back to the room he shared with his mother for a nap.

His conscience was clear, and his hopes high: he wanted to stay awake as much as he could that night, so as not to miss a moment of the comet's final approach and strike.

He woke when he heard someone coming in the door, and sat up quickly, hoping it would be his mother. It was only Tinker Gorshak, though, looking surprised. "So there you are," he said. "Your mother wondered. She had to go to a meeting, but she said we might as well eat here tonight, so we could watch the comet together. She's a wonderful woman, Dek."

Dekker nodded resignedly, measuring out enough water in the bowl to wash his face and run a comb through his hair. "We're going to eat here?"

"We're going to cook our own dinner," Tinker said, offering good news as a gift. "Just the three of us—I wish Tsumi could have been along, but he has to be with his dad tonight. Now, give me a hand while I braise the cappy for the stew."

Dekker did as he was told, helping get the dinner ready. The killed-animal smelled good as it began to sear, which left Dekker with mixed feelings. It really was a treat for him and his mother to cook something up together instead of going to the community dining hall—but not necessarily with Tinker Gorshak sticking himself in. Dekker would have been almost as happy to go to the hall. Their tiny room was somewhat gloomy—everywhere in Sunpoint was gloomy now, with only one light allowed per room to conserve power in case of accident, and hot, too, with all the climate machines turned down to barely tolerable levels—but it was an occasion, and so they were allowed to have the news screen on.

Naturally the screen was relaying the satellite observations, as they followed the comet. When Dekker looked up to the screen he could see the comet's core; it was the grayish-yellow color of old Tinker Gorshak's beard, lumpy as a Jerusalem artichoke. It was spinning slowly, with the drive jets now spitting out slow-down correction burns every few seconds.

He checked the time. There was still a long way to go. The actual impact was scheduled to take place in midmorning—midmorning according to the time it would be at the impact point, that was, though it would be nearly noon at Sunpoint in its position to the east. "That's so it will be a kind of grazing hit," Tinker Gorshak informed the boy as they were preparing their meal. "There'll be less kinetic energy released that way, they think, so maybe less ground shock. How are you doing with those onions?"

"They're almost chopped," Dekker reported, rubbing at his stinging eyes with the back of his hand.

Gorshak dumped the chopped onions into the stew, stirred it, sniffed it critically, then put the lid on. "It'll be ready in twenty minutes," he declared. "Gerti ought to be back before then, and if she isn't, it'll just get better the longer it simmers. What do you say, Dekker, do you want something to drink? Tea? Water?"

Dekker shook his head, and watched the old man carefully measure out a "highball"—straight alcohol, diluted with water one to three, flavored with a little mint extract. Dekker wrinkled his nose. That was one of the other things Dekker didn't like about Tinker Gorshak. Dekker's father had never been known to drink alcohol, or at least as far as Dekker remembered he hadn't. Nor had his mother, as long as his father was around. "So," said Gorshak, swallowing the first half of his drink. "Have you been thinking about what you want to do when you grow up?"

"Not much," Dekker admitted.

"I mean," Gorshak explained, "it's all going to be different, now that it looks like the crystal plants are a dead end." He got that discontented look he always had when the subject of the purpose-built Martian plants came up. "I always hoped—"

He stopped there without saying what he had hoped, but he didn't have to. Dekker knew what it was. As a geneticist, Tinker Gorshak's main job on Mars had been tending and crossbreeding the artificially produced photosynthetic plants—well, organisms: you could hardly really call them "plants," because they certainly didn't look like anything that had ever grown on the Earth—that the Martians had hoped would produce some sort of natural crops for them. They were pretty little things, mushroom shaped, with parasols of ultraviolet-opaque crystal on their tops. The crystal let the light necessary for photosynthesis in, but screened out the deadly ultraviolet—a very necessary precaution on Mars, where there was no ozone layer to protect them. The mushrooms were most wonderful simply in that they grew there at all.

That was where the wonderfulness stopped. As a crop, the glass-headed mushrooms were hopeless. They had to have long taproots to get down to the little frozen water under Mars's hard-crusted surface, and so much of their metabolic energy had to go into the work of sinking their roots and building their sunscreens that there was nothing to speak of that was worth harvesting.

But that had all been Tinker Gorshak's fantasy, anyway. It certainly hadn't been Dekker's. As far as Dekker had thought about his grown-up career, which wasn't very far, he had leaned more toward what his father had done—even, maybe, going out into the Oort some day—than to following the career of the man who wanted to usurp his father's place.

Tinker lifted the pot lid, sniffed, and then sat down, gazing at Dekker. "Tsumi says you've got his book," he said.

Dekker was suddenly flustered. "Oh, that. The *Huckleberry Finn*. I guess I ought to give it back to him."

"Have you read it?"

Dekker debated with himself for a moment, but saw no reason to deny it. "Well, yes."

Tinker nodded with an appearance of satisfaction, then got up to refill his glass. "I really wanted Tsumi to get something out of it, but the boy's not much of a reader. You are, though, Dek, aren't you?" Dekker nodded cautiously. "Tell me, then. What did you think of the Law of the Raft?"

Dekker searched his memory. "The Law—?"

"—of the Raft, right. What Huck says about getting along together, Dek. Didn't you get to that part?"

"I'm not sure what part you mean."

"It's when Huck and Jim are floating down the Mississippi River, and all these bad things are happening on the land— lynchings and thievery and so on. And Huck thinks about how people get along on the raft and he says—I think I remember the exact words—he says, 'What you want above all things on a raft, is for everybody to be satisfied, and feel right and kind toward the others.' Do you remember that?"

"Oh, right," Dekker said, energized. "Then they go on down the river and they come to—"

"No, that's not what I'm after, Dek. I didn't want to talk about the story itself. Just that one thing that Huck says. Do you see, that's what docility training is all about. Not just getting along, but wanting everybody to be satisfied, and to feel good about the other people. Not just on the raft, everywhere. On our planet, too. That's what we do here on Mars, while the Earthies are always grabbing whatever they can grab and competing with each other—"

He stopped, laughing at himself. "Well," he said, "sometimes I don't remember the Law of the Raft myself, I guess. I suppose I should be more charitable to the Earthies. It's hard, though. Anyway, that's what I wanted Tsumi to understand. Do you follow me?"

"I think so," Dekker said doubtfully.

"I wish Tsumi did. That boy hangs out with a lot of the wrong people, I'm afraid, and his father—well, I shouldn't say anything against his father." He looked at his watch. "Anyway, Dekker, I'm going to finish up the cooking. If you want to read the book, go ahead. It's a fine story, isn't it?"

Dekker nodded agreement, and did as he was told. But, although the novel was as interesting as ever, he was glad when his mother arrived, looking both amused and surprised. "I've got a message for you, Dekker," she told her son at once. "You're invited to a party."

That startled Dekker. He blinked at his mother. Who in Sunpoint did he know well enough to invite him to anything? And the surprise was bigger still when his mother told him, "It's an Earth girl. Annetta Cauchy. She says her parents are having a preimpact dinner, and she wants you to come."

Dekker opened his eyes wide in astonishment, but he was nowhere nearly as astonished as Tinker Gorshak. "You've been getting around in a hurry," the old man grumbled.

"I'm glad you're making friends so fast," Gertrud said. She waited to see if her son was going to say something. When he didn't she asked, "What about it? Do you want to go?"

"Now, wait a damn minute," Gorshak said, scowling. "I thought we were going to have a little private party right here. Just family." He reached over to pat Dekker's knee and didn't notice when Dekker, who didn't consider Tinker Gorshak any part of his family, pulled stiffly back. Gorshak went on,

"What's the use of him getting mixed up with those people? All they want to do is suck our blood. I think he should tell this girl to take her invitation and stuff it."

"Tinker. It isn't going to hurt him to see how the other half lives," Gertrud said, "if he wants to go. What about it, Dekker?"

Dekker said, "I probably ought to go, I think. I mean, it's kind of like the Law of the Raft, isn't it?"

Tinker scowled, then grinned. To Gerti he said, "It's something we were talking about. Maybe he's right."

"All right, then," Gerti DeWoe said, not bothering to try to understand the allusion. "Then what about a present?"

Another surprise. Dekker gave his mother a puzzled look. "A present?"

"That's right, a present. Earthies are always giving presents to each other. You can't go to a party without bringing something along to give your hostess."

"But I don't have anything to give away," Dekker protested.

Tinker Gorshak said sourly, "Who does? But that doesn't stop the mudsuckers from always wanting something anyway." He thought for a moment, then shrugged. "Well, if you're sure you want to do this— Tell you what, Dek. Let me make a couple of calls and see what I can do for you."

9.

A GOOD-SIZED COMET can mass more than a hundred billion tons, and in the richest comets as much as four-fifths of that mass may be water—not liquid water, of course, but ice is just as good.

Water's the first thing you want to grow crops. Old Earthie farmers used to calculate that it took about seven million tons of irrigation water to lay one inch—in modern measures, two and a half centimeters—of water on a hundred square miles ("miles"!) of farmland. The other figure to remember is that you need about ten "inches" a year to make most crops grow, even with trickle irrigation.

What that adds up to is that you could wet down nearly a million and a half square miles with one decent-sized comet, sort of.

In practice it's harder than that. You can make those sums work only if you could keep the water contained in one place—which you can't. And also if most of it didn't get blasted right back into space by the impact—which it does. And if that was all you wanted. . .

But of course the Martians wanted much more than that. They wanted water to keep, and air besides. So they needed a *lot* of comets, because what they wanted was to make the whole old planet bloom.

What a lucky thing it was for all of them that the Oort had literally trillions of the things.

10.

WHEN DEKKER DEWOE, gift in one sweaty hand, turned up at the home of the Cauchy family, the first thing that surprised him was the walls.

Dekker knew what walls were supposed to look like. All Martians lived within walls all their lives, and all the walls in Sunpoint City, as in every Martian settlement, were made out of the same material. The stuff looked like poured concrete but, since there certainly wasn't enough spare water on Mars to waste on such water-intensive processes as pouring concrete, certainly wasn't. What the walls were made of was the cheapest and most convenient material available on Mars: rock. Rock was cheap to obtain and easy to deal with—as long as you had plenty of solar heat. You just dug up some of the bare rock that lay all around the surface, and then you crushed it, pressed it, and heated it until it sintered into flat construction panels.

Of course, most Martians then did as much as they could to

decorate those monotonous walls. They painted them at least—"crayoned" them might have been a better word, because the pigment was in waxy sticks that you just rubbed on. Or they hung pictures on them when they had any pictures to hang. Or they lined the walls with shelves and cupboards, which was usually a necessity anyway, living space being as scarce as it was.

But that was about as far as any Martian could afford to go with wall decorations, and Dekker had never before seen walls hung with draperies. They weren't just any old kind of spun-rock draperies, either. These were *fabric* draperies—woven out of organic fabrics, probably even out of real cotton and silk and wool, natural-fiber textiles that had to have been shipped all the way from Earth. At, as Tinker Gorshak would have been sure to point out, the expense of their Martian hosts.

Dekker's consolation was that at least he had a worthy gift for his hosts, for Tinker Gorshak had come through for him. The old man had not stopped disapproving of Dekker's socializing with the Earthies, but all the same, he had postponed his own dinner long enough to escort Dekker down to the Sunpoint hothouse, and there he had wheedled an actual rosebud from his colleague, the amiable Mr. Chandy. When Dekker entered the Earthies' apartment—more than one room, obviously, since there were no beds in this one, although it was easily three times the size of the single room he shared with his mother—his eyes were popping as he held his flower before him like an ambassador's credentials, staring at everything around.

It wasn't just the drapes on the walls, it was everything. Even the lights. There wasn't any one-dim-bulb rule here; the room was flooded with brilliant light. He had never seen people dressed like these, either—filmy, silky drapes on the women, puffed shirts and ruffled shorts on the men, nothing that would keep you warm or fit under a hotsuit. Nor had he ever seen a table longer than he was, and every square centimeter of it covered with *food*. Dozens of varieties of food. Dishes of spicy little balls of hot killed-animal. Fresh raw celery. Carrots slivered into pencil-thin strips (they had to be on even better terms with the hothouse geneticist than Tinker Gorshak was). Bowls of yellow or pink or green pastes to dip the vegetables in. "So glad you could come, Dekker," said the tall, yellow-haired Earthie woman who let him in. "Oh, a rose! How kind of you," she finished, sniffing it and offering it to her daughter. "Look, Annetta, Dekker has brought us a rose."

"I'll put it with the others," the girl told her mother, and took Dekker's arm. "Come on, Dekker, let's hit the chow line. You must be starving."

It was annoying to Dekker that this girl should always assume he was hungry. It was even more annoying, in fact embarrassing, when he observed that on the buffet table there were half a dozen vases of flowers, all kinds of flowers, and when Annetta thrust his lone contribution into one of the vases he could hardly find it again.

But the fact was that as soon as she handed him a plate he found that she had been right. He really was hungry, his salivary glands flowing at the smells and sights of all that remarkable food. And Annetta was devoting herself to him. "Some lobster, Dekker? You've never *had* lobster? Well, these are only irradiated, you can't get live ones here, of course, but still— And try the guacamole! My mother made it herself, grew her own avocados in the aeroponics."

The stuff called "guacamole" looked too much like the algae paste the cooks added to soups and stews, and Dekker certainly wasn't going to touch the funny-looking red-shelled stuff Annetta said was lobster. But there was plenty of other food to choose from. He let her guide him to the salads, and the killed-poultry legs in barbecue sauce, but when he took a good look at the display behind the table he stopped short.

Across the top of the wall was a banner that read CAUCHY, STERNGLASS & CO. CELEBRATES THE TRIUMPH OF ECOPOIESIS. And under it was a row of pictures, the fake-3D kind that almost looked as though they had depth: a grove of fruit trees in blossom; some people with long boards strapped to their feet, sliding down an immense snow-white slope; laughing nude men and women, all young, all beautiful—all distinctly *Earthie* in their proportions—diving and swimming at the edge of an immense blue lake. The startling thing was that they all looked somehow oddly almost familiar, though of course he had never seen anything like that in the flesh. "Is that Earth?" he asked.

She was laughing at him. "Silly. That's *Mars.* The way it's going to be. Don't you recognize Olympus Mons, for heaven's sake? Those pictures are what they call renderings. They aren't meant to be *real.* Daddy's company uses them to encourage the investors when they underwrite a new issue."

"Issue?" Dekker said, and then realized. "Oh. The Bonds."

"Of course, the Bonds. Have you got everything you want? For starters, I mean? Then come on, I'd like you to meet some people."

It was not exactly what Dekker would have liked, but he was determined to be a good guest. Annetta herself was not now the girl in the plain brown hotsuit he'd met out on the slope. Somehow she had grown up in a few hours. She was dressed in white, and what she was wearing was not shorts or even pants but a *skirt,* ankle length, filmy as her mother's. She wore a necklace of sparkling stones, with a large red one that lay close above her very nearly significant young breasts, and her pale hair was upswept with something like gold dust sprinkled on it.

Dekker was dazzled—by the food, by the surroundings, by the girl, maybe most of all by the company. *All* these people were dressed like characters in a video play. All of them were Earthies, too—or almost all. He did recognize one elderly Martian couple as high-ups in the Sunpoint City administration. They seemed to be painfully on their best behavior, and Dekker saw that they were treated with elaborate courtesy, but no real concern, by the Earthies whose party it really was. Dekker also saw, with some scorn, that a large American "flag" was standing on a pole in one corner of the room, and then discovered that, even so, these people weren't all Americans. As he was introduced, catching none of the names, he learned that there was a German couple, and some Japanese and a handful of Brazilians. Some he couldn't identify at all. Altogether there were twenty or thirty people in the room, probably the whole Earthie population of Sunpoint City, Dekker thought.

There were not very many children; Dekker was pretty sure he was the youngest person present.

Annetta, he supposed, was not much older, and there was another Earthie girl and a boy a little older still; no one else under full adult age. Annetta introduced him all around. That was an ordeal in itself, because he had a plate of food and his mouth usually full, and hardly any of the names stayed with him long enough even to say hello. Still, he did get the names of the other kids: Evan, shorter than he but with a glass of wine in his hand, and Ina, with more makeup on her face than even Annetta. He remembered that Evan was the one he had met in the entry lock, and noticed that Evan and Ina were holding hands, and that when Annetta saw them doing it she bit her lip.

"How old are you, Dekker?" the boy asked, looking him up and down with amusement.

"Eight," Dekker said shortly, looking down at the Earthie boy. Evan was barrel-shaped; Dekker thought the boy looked as though he could break Dekker in half—what a strange notion, Dekker told himself reprovingly; just a few minutes with these mudsuckers and he was forgetting all about his nonviolence classes.

"But that's almost fifteen, Earth years," Annetta put in quickly.

"Oh, really?" Evan said, pursing his lips. "Then I suppose you're old enough to have a glass of wine with us?"

Dekker knew what wine was, had even had a sip of his mother's now and then. "Of course I am," he declared. "We drink alcohol often." And then was stuck with this incredibly fragile-feeling crystal glass with this sour-tasting liquid in it. He swallowed it down anyway and managed to say, "Good wine," appreciatively.

"It's really a pity," Annetta was saying warmly to him, "that we won't be seeing each other much, Dekker. My father's going to take us home, you know, as soon as we see the comet impact is going all right."

"Home to Earth, that is," Evan supplied, grinning as he refilled Dekker's glass. "You've never been there, I suppose? No, of course not. You really should, if you ever can, I mean. Paris, Rome, San Francisco, Rio—Earth is just wonderful, Dekker. The scenery! The culture! The women! Here, let me fresh your drink up a little."

"I think Dekker would rather have a soft drink," Annetta said worriedly.

"Why do you think that?" Dekker demanded. "No, I like to drink this wine very much." And in fact he discovered that he did—not for the taste, of course, because who could enjoy swallowing weak vinegar?—but it did warm him up in pleasant ways.

It wasn't just the wine, either. People more mature than Dekker DeWoe found intoxication in moving in the society of their betters. It was fascinating to Dekker to watch the Earthies dealing with each other—always smiling, but always, he thought, serious and even—what would you call it?—yes, *punishing* behind the smiles. And what things they said! He caught bits and pieces of phrases and discussions, no more comprehensible to him than ancient Etruscan: What were "double-dip securities"? Or "self-licky debentures"? Or "off-planet tax-frees"? And always there was Annetta, worriedly keeping an eye on him as Evan, grinning sardonically, kept refilling Dekker's glass, making conversation, always patronizing. "Pity you've never been in a spaceship; it's so broadening. Three weeks en route, with the whole universe spread out before your eyes—"

"I bet," Dekker said belligerently, swallowing a sip of the wine, "you've never been in an airship."

"A what?" the Earthie asked tolerantly, one eyebrow raised.

"A dirigible airship. We use them all the time—for mass lifting, you know. They're hot-air. You cruise over the Valles Marineris for the mines, say, and you're looking right down into the crevasses—"

Annetta appeared from nowhere. "Here, let me take that for you," she said, tugging the glass from his hand with a glare at Evan. "Dirigible, you say? That sounds really fun, Dekker."

"It is," Dekker affirmed, and went on describing the raptures of lighter-than-air flight on Mars—well, not really out of his own *personal* experience, of course, but they didn't have to know that; he'd seen it often enough in the virtuals, and it had been just as his mother had described it to him.

"So you have virts," the girl, Ina, said. "Virtuals," she added helpfully, when he looked surprised.

He blinked at her. She seemed a nice enough girl, short and squat, but too nice for that snot, Evan. "Did I say anything about virtuals?" he asked, trying to remember.

"Of course they have virtuals, Ina," Evan said, his hand on her shoulder. "Only sight and sound, of course. On Earth," he informed Dekker, "we have full-sensory virts. Of course—" He gave Dekker an unexpected wink and poke in the ribs. "—they're not very convincing unless you dope up a little first."

"Dope up? You mean like this wine stuff?"

Evan laughed. "Oh, a lot better than that. I mean serious dope."

"Oh," Dekker said. "I know. I saw it in the plays, but it's against the law."

"Of course it's against the law. Who ever lets that stop him?"

Dekker looked around to see what Annetta Cauchy thought of that, but the girl had disappeared. He did see his nearly empty wine glass on the table where she had left it. He picked it up and drank the remains while he thought over what it meant to deliberately break laws. That struck him as preposterous. What were laws for, if they were broken?

But the Earth boy was still pressing him. As he refilled Dekker's glass he said, "What about games?"

"Well, of course we have games. All kinds of games. Prospecting's good, and there's Blowout, and Building—"

"I mean *competitive* games. War games. Crime games."

"I don't think I've ever seen anything like that," Dekker confessed.

"I didn't think you would have," Evan said comfortably, stroking Ina's back in a leisurely, self-confident way. "What do you do? I mean your father."

"Oort miner," Dekker said, omitting the verbs in order to avoid bringing up the subject of whether his father was still with him.

"Oort miner," the Earthie boy echoed, transparently pretending to be impressed. "How very interesting, Dekker. Mine's nothing so glamorous. Just an ordinary investment-fund portfolio manager, if you know what that is."

Dekker was getting pretty well fed up with people supposing he didn't know what things meant. Especially when he didn't. "It's connected with the Bonds," he guessed, supposing that it must have something to do with them since everything these Earthies were involved in apparently did.

"Yes, more or less. Someone has to buy them, you know, I mean with real money. We're the ones who make it easy for them to do it, and that's how your bonds get sold. That means," he went on modestly, "that we're the people who did all this for you. Oort miners are all very well, but it takes money—*cue* money—to get all those comets down here. Without us this whole planet would stay a permanently useless desert. But," he added, twinkling, "you don't have to thank me. Have some more wine."

"I think he should have something solid," Annetta said. He hadn't noticed that she had returned. "What have you been eating, Dekker?"

He tried to remember. "I had some of the killed-meat things, I think."

There was a quick, hushed titter around the group, and Evan laughed. "Oh, Dekker! You're just too precious. Why do you

say 'killed-meat'? Do you think we'd be likely to eat it while it
was still alive?"

Dekker concentrated for a moment until he remembered the
answer to that—it had come from so many docility classes, so
long ago, that it was buried in his subconscious now. "Because
we always say that. It's to, you know, remind us that in order
for us to eat ki—to eat *meat*, something has to be slaughtered."

Evan opened his eyes wide in an imitation of surprise. "But
that's what they're *for,* boy. No, don't worry about things like
that. Here, give me your glass."

The thing about wine was that it made you feel nice and
warm and rather cheerful, although it also seemed to make you
feel as though your skin were tightening up on your face, and
the floor didn't seem as solid as it ought.

Dekker decided, though, that he was conducting himself
rather well. Evan had finally left him alone—Dekker saw him
off in a corner with Annetta Cauchy, looking tolerant as the girl
scolded him about something—and Dekker just wandered
about, talking to whoever seemed to want to talk to him. Not
everyone did. Some of the people, especially one of the sallow-
skinned women with the straight, jet-black hair, didn't seem to
understand him very well, and when she spoke to him he was
startled to find that he was being addressed in some other
language.

But others were quite nice. Annetta's mother, for instance.
He didn't quite understand the worried look in her eyes as she
spoke to him, but when she asked him about his home he was
glad to tell her all about Sagdayev deme. He described the
landscape, and the rooms, and the copper mine; he told her how
they concentrated solar heat so that the molten copper flowed
out of the ore, and how the oxygen that had bound it was
usefully added to the deme's supply. He was going on to explain
some of the differences between Sagdayev and Sunpoint City
when he discovered that she was no longer listening. That surprised him, because he didn't remember her turning away. Nor
did he remember how he came to have a filled glass in his hand
again, but he cheerfully lifted it to his lips. It was astonishing
how the taste had improved.

He was, he felt confident, holding his own in this strange
party, where people kept trying to impress other people rather
than make them feel partyishly happy. The most striking thing

was the established pecking order: the richest deferred to by the not-quite-as-rich, and the one Martian couple among the guests condescended to by all. That bothered Dekker. Yet even the Martians were smiling as though they were enjoying all this opulence and laughter.

And the blocky young Earthie, Evan, kept refilling Dekker's glass, and everything around him seemed even brighter and more beautiful and exciting . . . right up to the time he felt himself being picked up and carried.

"Where'd you come from?" he croaked, twisting around to stare into the face of Tinker Gorshak.

"Came to get you, you idiot," Gorshak snarled. "I knew you'd make a fool of yourself. Shut up. What you need is a good night's sleep."

11.

NO MATTER HOW badly you want water and air, there are limits. You certainly don't want a hundred billion tons of anything crashing into your planet in one lump. That would cloud the skies with more dust than even Mars has seen for a very long time, not to mention shaking up everything around.

So you have to take some precautions. Before your approaching comet gets that far, you site demolition charges in its core, carefully placed to shatter it into the tiniest pieces you can manage. (The pieces won't be all that tiny, anyway, but still.) Most of the fragments will burn up or at least volatilize from air friction—even Mars's thin air is enough to do that—and the seismic impacts of the residues as they strike will be, you hope, tolerable.

You don't want them crashing into the surface at an excessively high velocity, either. So you navigate your comet to come up on the planet from behind, so that both are going in the same orbital direction around the Sun and the combined speeds are minimized. Then, at that last moment, you fire the decelera-

tion jets from the Augenstein drives you have forethoughtfully
already installed in the comet in order to slow it still more—so
that your impact velocity isn't much more than one or two
kilometers a second. Then you jettison the Augensteins, cross
your fingers, and hope.

12.

DEKKER DIDN'T GET a good night's sleep after all, or at least
not as much of it as he really wanted; it seemed only
minutes had passed before his mother was shaking him awake.
"Are you all right, Dekker?" she was asking anxiously. "I
didn't think you'd want to miss seeing the impact."

He fended her off, wincing. Someone was pounding nails into
his head. Tinker Gorshak was standing over him with a cup of
something hot. "Strong tea," Gorshak muttered. "Go ahead,
drink it. You'll be all right in a while, hangovers never kill
anybody."

And after a few scalding gulps and an eternity of throbbing
temples, it began to seem that Tinker Gorshak was right. When
the pounding behind his eyes began to subside Dekker bundled
up in a robe before the news screen and watched what was
happening. The time was impact minus thirty minutes, and on
the screen he could see the comet's drive jets detaching themselves and hurling themselves away, bright and tiny shooting
stars, to be captured and salvaged by the workers in the tender
spacecraft. There weren't any additional burns after that; now
the comet was purely ballistic.

Dekker sipped his tea and began to feel almost human
again—human enough to begin replaying the scenes of the
party in his mind. "You know," he announced, astonished at
his discovery, "she didn't really like me. She only invited me to
make that other guy jealous."

"Earthies," Gorshak grumbled, looking at his watch. "In
about two minutes now—"

"I don't think they even like each other," Dekker went on, thinking it through. "Evan was always making jokes about the Japanese and the Brazilians, and they were mean kinds of jokes, too."

"Of course they don't like each other. Don't you know yet what Earthies are like? They used to have *wars*," Gorshak informed him. "They probably still would, except nobody dares anymore. Now they just try to take each other's money."

"Oh, yes, the money," Dekker said, remembering. "What's an 'underwriter,' Tinker?"

"An underwriter! An underwriter is somebody who sucks your blood, and wants you to thank him for it."

"Tinker," his mother said gently. "Dek, it's how they do things on Earth. We borrow money by selling bonds—you know what the Bonds are. But we don't sell the Bonds directly to the people who want to invest in them. That would take too long and, anyway, we don't really know how to do that sort of thing. So somebody 'underwrites' the bonds. He buys the whole lot from us, and then he sells them, a few at a time, to the people who really want them."

"Stealing part of the money along the way," said Tinker Gorshak.

"You know it isn't stealing, Tinker," Gerti DeWoe said crossly. "There's no Earthie law against it. Besides, we agreed to it. If the bond is supposed to sell for, say, a hundred of their cues, then the underwriter gives us, say, ninety. So every time he sells one he makes a ten-cue profit."

Dekker puzzled that over for only a moment before he saw the flaw. "But what if he can't find anyone to buy it?"

"Then," Tinker said, "he has our bonds at a bargain rate. But don't worry about that, Dek. They'll always find somebody to buy. Any way they can."

The boy nodded, thinking about the glamorized pictures on the Cauchys' wall, deciding not to mention them to Tinker. He thought of something else. "Ina said . . . was saying something to Annetta. It was really quite unpleasant, about 'unloading' their bonds if the comet impact was successful—"

"*If* it was successful!" Gorshak said indignantly. "What a way to talk! And *if* it's successful, then you know what will happen. We're going to be swamped by immigrants from Earth."

"We're all immigrants from Earth," Gerti DeWoe reminded him, "or our parents were."

"But our roots are here! It isn't just *money* with us. It's *freedom.*"

Dekker refused to be distracted into that familiar argument. "But what did they mean about unloading?"

"It's just another thing they do, Dek," his mother said. "They have a kind of saying, 'Buy on bad news, sell on good.' A successful strike tonight will be good news, so that means the price of the Bonds might go up a little."

"But everybody already knows the comet's going to land. Why would just seeing it happen make the Bonds worth more?"

"It wouldn't really, Dek. It might make people *think* they were worth more, though, and that's how Earthies act. They go by what they *think* things are worth. So if any of the people that owned the Bonds now wanted to get out—I don't know why; maybe because they want the money to invest in something else—I suppose this would be when they'd sell."

"That's foolish," Dekker pronounced.

"That's Earthies for you," Tinker Gorshak said. "Hey, look! It's going off!"

And indeed it was. On the screen they saw the sequenced charges inside the comet mass doing their job. A lump flaked off one side of the comet, then another. The main mass split in two, then the demolition charges in each section blew up, all at once, and the comet became a mass of rubble, all falling together toward Chryse Planitia. The scene shifted swiftly to a quick shot from the surface cameras atop Sunpoint City. The churning mass of the comet was now visible to the naked eye, moving perceptibly down and to the east. The comet didn't have a tail anymore. Rather, they were now *inside* the tail. All they could see was a general unnatural brightness of the sky.

"I hope it works," Gertrud DeWoe said prayerfully.

Tinker Gorshak grunted. "I hope we can pay for it," he grumbled. "Those bloodsuckers from Earth are charging us plenty for the capital. Do you know what it costs, Dekker? I'm not talking about the whole project. I'm just talking right now about that party you went to—who do you think is paying for it? And all they're doing is watching to see it fall—at a thousand cues a day apiece, and we have to pay—"

"Look!" Dekker's mother cried.

Because—back to the cameras in orbit—all those myriad

chunks of rubble turned dazzlingly bright at once as they struck the thin Martian atmosphere, the heat of friction producing a thousand blinding meteors. Switch again, this time to the remote ground-based cameras in their dugouts on the slope of Olympus Mons. . . .

And the fragments hit.

They were not tiny. The biggest was more than ten million tons. Even some of the smaller ones were the size of a skyscraper. When they struck, they made H-bomb–sized fountains of cloud, red-lit and white-lit and yellow, with all that kinetic energy transformed at once into impact heat.

The people in Sunpoint City never did feel the shudder of that impact—they were too far away—but the needles of their seismographs jumped right off the tapes.

When Gerti DeWoe tucked her son in bed at last he said drowsily, "I guess we won't see any difference right away?"

His mother didn't laugh at him. She just shook her head. "Not right away, no. It'll be years before Mars has any decent atmosphere. And then we won't be able to breathe it directly, you know. There'll be too much carbon dioxide, not enough free oxygen, not much nitrogen at all. We'll have to find the nitrogen somewhere else. And then we'll need to seed the blue-green algae, and some kind of lichens, to start photosynthesis going so we'll have free oxygen, and then—But, oh, Dekker," she said, looking more excited and young than he had ever seen her, "what it's going to mean to us! Can you imagine crops growing under the naked *sky*? And the climate getting really *warm*?"

"Like Earth," he said bitterly.

"Better than Earth! There aren't as many of us, and we get along better!"

"I know," Dekker said, because he did know. Everyone on Mars had been told over and over why they needed to borrow all that money to get all those comets—water for the crops, water to make oxygen for animals and themselves. *Lakes.* Maybe even *rain.* The warming greenhouse effect that the water vapor would provide. The kinetic energy of each cometary impact transformed to heat, doing its part to warm the planet up.

He asked, "Do you think we'll live to see it?"

His mother hesitated. "Well, no, Dekker. At least I won't, or at least not to see the best part of it, because it'll be a lot of years. But maybe you will, or your children, or your children's children. . . ."

"Hell," Dekker said, disappointed. "I don't want to wait that long!"

"Well, then," his mother said, grinning fondly, "then when you grow up you'd better get out there and help make it happen faster!"

"You know," Dekker said, beginning to yawn, "I think that's what I'll do."

13.

THE FUNNY THING was that Dekker DeWoe meant it. He did what he said he was going to do—sort of—though it didn't work out exactly the way he had planned, and it certainly didn't look as though it would work out at all for a while.

He started out well enough. Right that very week, before the Sagdayev people went back to their quite-unharmed home, Dekker took the first step. He made a trip all by himself to the Oort Corporation headquarters in Sunpoint City; but when he told the clerk he wanted to fill out an application for training at the academy on Earth, she naturally said, "You're too young."

"I won't always be," he said.

She shook her head. "But you are now. There's no point. Come back when you're—what is it?—" Because, of course, the clerk was an Earthie, too, and so she had to calculate. "—when you're twelve or thirteen, anyway."

"I will. But I want to fill out the application now."

"You're not supposed to do it until you're of age," she said, snapping her lips shut at the end of the sentence as though the subject were closed. It wasn't. Dekker didn't give up. He stayed there, reasoning patiently with the woman, and finally, maybe because she was just in a good mood or maybe because even an

Earthie woman might have a soft spot for a determined young kid, she took his name and entered it in a "hold" file. She even gave him a study list—all the subjects he would need to know to pass the academy's entrance test—and, though she told him several times just how bad the odds against his acceptance were, she wished him luck.

That surprised him. "Why do I need luck?" he asked. "If I pass the test, they ought to let me in."

"But I thought you knew. They give the admission test at the academy itself. Back on Earth."

"So?"

She laughed, almost affectionately. "So how are you going to get there to take the test, Dekker DeWoe? Are you going to pay the fare yourself?"

That, of course, was the question. Dekker thought about it all the way back to his room, and talked about it with his mother as soon as he saw her.

The problem at root—like almost all Martian problems, at root—was money. The Martians didn't have it. They didn't have Earth currency units to pay for an applicant's fare to Earth except by diverting the price of the fare—the highly *exorbitant* price of the fare, far higher than the operating costs of a spacecraft justified—from other things that the planet needed even more.

It wasn't that Gerti DeWoe—and Dekker himself, when he got old enough to do anything about it—couldn't save the money, it was that the money they saved wasn't worth anything for that purpose. Their money wasn't Earthie currency units. If they had been allowed to buy cues at the official exchange rate they could have managed it, but there were far more important uses for every cue Mars could get its hands on than sending one more young person out to work in the Oort.

"But when I'm there I can pay my way!" Dekker complained. "They pay the Oort miners in cues. They even pay an allowance at the academy itself—I could even send money home!"

"They do," his mother agreed. "You would. It's the getting you there that's hard, Dek."

"The fare, right. But I don't understand. Look, we're supposed to pay off the Bonds by shipping food to Earth, right? So why does it cost less to ship, I don't know, fifty tons of wheat to Earth than to ship me?"

She said somberly, "It's simple. The Earthies want the wheat, Dek. They don't particularly want you."

The one loophole in that otherwise impenetrable barrier was that Mars itself did want Martians in the Oort, and not only because their earnings there would help the balance of payments. So there were scholarships available. Not many, but enough for someone who was bright enough, and willing enough to work hard enough.

So Dekker studied twice as hard as anyone else, and his grades showed it. The scholarship that meant the Oort looked possible, and meanwhile he had his job—for even a would-be Oort miner had to work his way on Mars.

Dekker's job was as third pilot on an interdeme blimp, though he didn't actually do much piloting at that stage. "Flight attendant" would have been a more accurate job description, because his biggest task was making sure the passengers stayed in order and caused no trouble, but he was qualified to take the controls if the pilot and copilot both suddenly dropped dead in flight. Still, it was a very worthwhile job to have: it paid well, if only in Martian currency; it took him all over Mars, from the North Polar Cap to the outpost demes in the freezing southland; and it let him meet a lot of interesting people, many of them young women who were happy to get to know him better.

That was a benefit Dekker enjoyed. He could not have been said to have a girl in every port, but he went to a lot of ports. Besides, the job was good background experience for piloting a spotter ship in the Oort.

And then that prospect receded almost to invisibility.

The thing that happened was a little glitch in Earth's financial markets. It wasn't anything severe, at least for most of the Earthies. A few speculators were ruined, a few others got suddenly very rich, but those things happened every now and then.

But when Earth sneezed, Mars got pneumonia. The break came at a bad time. A new issue of the Bonds was just due out, and in the temporarily queasy market climate they were undersubscribed. Earthie cues had always been sparse; now they had all but dried up entirely. Imports were slashed, luxuries disappeared from the Martians' own market—though the Earth colonists still did themselves as well as ever—and that one most valued luxury, the scholarship program, was abolished.

What Dekker was good at—what all Martians were good at, because how else could anyone survive on Mars?—was making the best of what he had and not spending a lot of time grieving over what he didn't.

Losing the hope of the Oort had been a blow, but Dekker had a whole other life to live, and he spent his efforts on living it. By the time he was eleven—nineteen or so, by Earth standards—he not only had a promotion to second pilot, he had a medal. At least as close to a medal as Martians ever gave each other. It was a little green rosette, and it was for courage.

There weren't many medals for courage on Mars, for two reasons. The first was that it took so much courage to get by there that there was hardly any point in making a fuss about a little extra bravery. The other reason was that any time someone was called on to display that little extra bit of courage, it was generally because someone else had done something particularly dangerous and dumb. Such as failing to secure the LH_2 valve on Dekker's dirigible before takeoff. So there they were, sailing along at three thousand meters above the Valles Marineris, with their precious reserve hydrogen bubbling away. Apart from the possible danger to the ship, there was the hydrogen itself: hydrogen was too hard to come by on Mars to waste.

So what else was a third pilot, desirous of making second pilot, to do? It cost him an ear, while he was clinging to the outside of the bag and the damn freezing-cold stuff was seeping out right past his vulnerable head, but the ear could be replaced. It got him the promotion and the rosette—a reasonably good trade.

But the Oort was still far away.

Sometimes on night flights, when the passengers were quiet and the captain was letting another pilot take a turn at the wheel, Dekker would crawl up into the skyside bubble and just look at the comets, the dozens and dozens of comets that had begun to fill the heavens and blur the stars. He didn't feel sorry for himself, he didn't brood about his missed chances; he just looked at the comets and wondered what it would be like to be out there, capturing some prize ones and sending them falling in toward Mars.

There were plenty of comets landing on Mars every week now, sometimes twice a week. There wasn't any real atmosphere on Mars to show for it yet, though the dust storms were certainly denser and a lot more frequent, but every once in a while Dekker's blimp would pass over a recently comet-struck area and he could see the great craters the impacts had gouged out. More than once he was able to persuade himself that, yes, there really was a kind of a faint haze that was visible, or almost visible, at the crater bottoms. The pilots claimed the blimp rode higher these days, too. The worldwide pressure was certainly up a millibar or two.

Then one day, while Dekker was talking to a pretty passenger in the lounge at a little Ulysses Patera deme called Collins, he got the call from his mother. "I need to talk to you," she said. "Come on home."

And would say no more.

So Dekker took a five-day leave and headed for Sagdayev. He hadn't seen his mother very often recently, because she had been stuck with the job of representing Sagdayev in the Commons—dull work, and hard work, too, trying to keep the planet's affairs running smoothly—and that meant she was never home. He hoped she would meet him, but the first person Dekker saw at the passenger lock as he came out was Tinker Gorshak. Old Tinker was looking worried, but as soon as he saw Dekker he broke into a welcoming grin. "Hello, boy," he said. "Your mother wants to talk to you."

"I know that. What about?"

Tinker looked mysterious. "She's got a right to tell you herself. Listen, what I wanted to ask you, Tsumi isn't on your ship, is he?"

"Tsumi? No. I haven't seen him for months. Isn't he here?"

"If he was here, would I be asking you? The little bastard's supposed to be in school in Sunpoint, but the school called the other day to say he was missing his classes. He's hanging around with a bunch of people I don't like, Dek. I called all his friends—all the ones I knew about, anyway—and told them to tell him to get his ass back here so I could straighten him out, but—"

The old man sighed. Then he brightened. "But go see your mother, Dek. She's waiting for you."

Dekker did. By the time he got to Gerti DeWoe's little room Tinker had already called her to say he was on his way, and she was waiting for him. She even had a pot of cocoa on the stove.

He flung his arms around her and she kissed him fondly, then pushed him back to look in his eyes. "I've got some news for you, Dek," she said. "Do you still want to work in the Oort?"

"Well," he said, "sure." Then he took it in. "Is there a chance? Have they loosened up the scholarships again?"

"No such luck," she said, shaking her head. "Haven't you been watching the news? The Earthies are screwing up again—strikes, and banks failing, and—no, we're going to have to find some more cuts to make, in fact. No, it's something else." She hesitated, looking at him almost apologetically. "The thing is, I got in touch with your father."

He blinked at her. "My father?"

"Well, why shouldn't I?" she asked, sounding defensive. "I let him know about what you were doing a long time ago, as soon as they canceled the scholarship program. Dekker, I didn't beg him for anything. I couldn't. He's living on his disability pension, and he didn't have much money to spare. But he said he'd try. It took him a long time, but—"

Dekker felt his heart suddenly pound. "You don't mean he's going to pay my way to the academy, do you?"

"That's what I do mean, Dek. The money for your fare to Earth is here, and he'll put you up while you take some refresher courses before you take the entrance exam and—well, Dekker. That's the way it is. The rest is up to you."

14.

THE FIRST THING a visitor to Earth discovered was that Earth didn't have just one Skyhook, like Mars. Earth had three of them. The reason was that there was a lot more ground-to-space traffic for Earth than for any other planet, and all three of its Skyhooks were kept busy.

They all, of course, had to touch ground at Earth's equator, because it is only over the equator that a geostationary satellite can stay in position. The one in Ecuador was the busiest, although the mountains around Quito made transshipment a problem. The one at Pontianak was the newest, and maybe

some day it would be the best because its location right on a
coast made the transshipment of bulk goods very practicable—
or at least it would do that whenever the Martians finally
succeeded in growing enough produce to ship to Borneo to
matter. Until then, Pontianak had so little traffic that it still
used only a single cable. But the one in Kenya was in some ways
the best, not least because it was handy to all the businesses and
industries of that very big African city called Nairobi.

Nairobi was so big and busy that people forgot that it was
only accidentally a city. It didn't have most of the things that
cities grow up around. It had no river or port or anything else
to distinguish it from all the highland plains that surrounded it.
It existed simply because it happened to be a convenient place
for the developers to put a station stop when, long ago, the first
railroad was built from the heart of Africa to the coast. Now
that same place was still a station stop—though of a markedly
different kind—and it was prospering therefrom.

15.

GETTING TO EARTH was a blast for Dekker DeWoe, all of
it. It was a dream come true.

First there was the little Skyhook capsule screaming up the
cable from the Martian surface to the transfer point, with all of
Sunpoint City falling away beneath him and his heart dragged
down into his belly with the acceleration—but buoyant, too,
because he was *on his way*. Then there was the ship itself and
the private cubicle they had given to him for his own—no
bigger than a bathtub, maybe, but on a *spaceship*, with all the
wonders that that entailed to thrill the heart of a quite mature
twelve-year-old. No! Earth years, now! A twenty-year-old.

Just to make it more exciting still there was even a solar flare
alarm eleven days out. A solar prominence erupted, and its
violent outpouring of particles radiated out from the Sun,
which meant that everybody was stuck in the shielded core

chamber for twenty-two hours until the ruddy loop of the prominence collapsed back on itself and the solar radiation died back down. The experience wasn't dangerous, really, but it was certainly something to tell Tinker's grandson and the other kids back in Sagdayev—if he ever got back to Sagdayev, and if, whenever that might be, the kids were still kids.

Of course, Dekker himself wasn't really a kid anymore. But even a young adult like Dekker DeWoe could feel a special tingling in his heart when he was getting into a spaceship for the hundred-million-kilometer flight to Earth. By any standards at all, that was really *special*.

But it took twenty-some days to traverse those hundred million kilometers, and with nowhere to go inside the ship and only the same eighteen people, passengers and crew, to talk to, the experience got old pretty fast.

Being on Earth, though—that was something else entirely.

Once Dekker had come down the vastly bigger Skyhook and first stood on Earthie soil, it didn't take him long to realize just how different it was. It was not going to be all fun. Earth *hurt*, hurt his bones at every step with its cruel pull. Earth was *dirty*. Earth was hostile—or the people were; or so it seemed to a skinny Martian kid who couldn't run or jump very well, and had a loser for a father besides. All the advice and warnings, all the calcium milkshakes and polysteroid injections, all the shipboard indoctrination hadn't prepared Dekker for the many ways in which Earth was nastier than Mars, but the thing he was least prepared for of all was Dad.

When Dekker limped out of the customs hall at the base of the Nairobi Skyhook, pulling his wheeled duffel bag behind him like a puppy on a leash, he looked for his father, but didn't see him. Instead, he saw a stooped, slow-moving old man hobbling toward him, and knew before the man spoke—but only half a second before—that this wreck of a man was indeed Boldon DeWoe.

The man stopped to regard Dekker, half a meter away. When Dekker looked at him closely he could tell that the man had been a Martian once, because he had the slender, stretched Martian physique. But now he was bent almost to Earthie height, and he was leaning on a thick cane, besides. He did not look well. His shoulders were hunched forward, but his head was bent back and his chin thrust out as he squinted at his son.

They didn't kiss, hug, or even shake hands. Boldon DeWoe
nodded, as though he were getting just what he had expected
and hadn't expected very much, and said, "Well. You're here.
What's the matter with your ear?"

Dekker saw no reason to go into the complicated story of the
hydrogen leak on the dirigible and the pain of the transplant.
He just said, "Frostbite."

His father didn't comment on that. "That's all the baggage
you've got?" he said. "Then come on. We've got a train to
catch." He was turning away to limp down the ramp before he
thought to add, over his shoulder, "Son."

Dekker followed, moving not very much more quickly than
his father with his luggage cart to pull. They probably should
have kissed, he thought, but he had been unwilling to make the
first move.

They descended a moving staircase to a platform where eighteen or twenty little cars, not joined together like a train, were
waiting. Boldon DeWoe led the way to the first car in line.
When he got in he punched out a code on the keypad and
inserted a shiny, pencil-thick thing that he wore around his
neck in a slot. He looked at his son.

"That's how you pay for things, with your credit amulet.
You have to pay for things here."

"We pay for things on Mars, too," Dekker said. "Of course,
you probably wouldn't remember."

His father didn't comment on that. He lowered himself to a
seat and said, looking at Dekker, "Why is your face so red?"

"They give you whole-blood transfusions before you land,
to help build up the red cells. That's plus all the other shots
and—" He held up one leg to show. "—the braces."

"Hold on tight, then," his father said, just about in time. At
that moment two or three other cars smacked into theirs, finally
forming a train. When it moved off the acceleration was a good
deal more violent than Dekker expected. He thought for one
unhappy moment that he might get sick, but didn't. None of the
other passengers seemed to be bothered. There were only four
others in the little car, all apparently Earthies, and when the
train stopped three of those got off.

The other cars uncoupled themselves, too, and their car
lurched away. In five minutes it stopped and Boldon DeWoe
got out.

"This is the neighborhood," he said over his shoulder.

It wasn't much of a neighborhood: Little cars and bigger vans were whining along the streets, trailing clouds of steam from their exhausts; people, most of them black, were cluttering the sidewalks; the buildings were astonishingly tall, by Dekker's Martian standards—eight to ten stories, some of them—but they seemed old and not particularly well cared for. Even the air had a funny sort of smell—smoky, perhaps, or *spoiled.* Dekker sneezed as his father turned and painfully began to climb some brick steps.

There were four or five tall black men lounging on the stoop, drinking beer. Most of them were wearing shorts and brightly—or formerly brightly—colored open-necked shirts. Some of the garments were faded, most were sweat-stained. The men themselves seemed friendly enough: they moved aside to make room, and all of them nodded amiably to Boldon as they approached.

This was not what Dekker had expected, none of it, and the man who was his father was not what he remembered. What Dekker remembered of Boldon DeWoe was a string-bean thin, smiling man, tall and skinny even for a Martian. Not this twisted, scrawny old guy, so bent that he was no taller than the black Earthies on the stoop. But when Boldon DeWoe introduced Dekker around he said, "This is my son." Then things began to look up a little for Dekker, because his father sounded actually proud when he said it.

Then they were in the lift, which took back some of that momentary optimism, because not only did it smell of stale sweat and worse but it jolted Dekker's troubled legs so that he staggered. But he was glad the elevator was there, because the alternative would have been worse; his father's apartment was on the top floor.

Then he saw the place where his father lived, where *he* would live. It wasn't just that it was small—Dekker was used to small—this place was also *dirty.*

"You get the couch," his father told him, limping over to a sink and beginning to rinse out a glass. "It's short, but you're young. I'm going to have a drink."

"No, thanks," Dekker said, though he hadn't been offered one. He picked a half-empty case of bottles off the couch and brushed the cushions off before he put his duffel bag on it. Then he began picking up dirty dishes from around the room.

"Leave that," his father ordered, sitting down heavily with

the drink in his hand. "I want to find out what you know. What's an Augenstein?"

Dekker blinked. "What?"

"An Augenstein drive. What is it, how does it work?"

He was evidently serious.

Dekker put his collection of dishware on a sideboard, pushing a stack of clean, but unsorted, laundry out of the way to make room. He sat down. "Well," he began, "an Augenstein is what drives spaceships. Basically its power chamber is a porous tungsten block in a hydrogen atmosphere. There's a pipette through the block that admits antiprotons to the central chamber; the antiprotons react with the hydrogen, *blam*, and the heat propels the working fluid out the rocket nozzle. Mostly they use powdered rock for the working fluid, but it could be—"

His father stirred. "Don't say 'they,' Dekker. 'We.' Say 'we.' "

"I beg your pardon?"

"Get in the habit of saying it. I want you to think like an Oort miner so you'll *act* like an Oort miner. *We* use powdered rock for the working fluid, only, of course, out in the Oort we don't. What do we do there?"

"We use comet mass."

His father nodded, swallowing a sip of his drink. "Comet mass, right. We tank up with frozen gases from a comet. What about the antiprotons that fuel the Augenstein?"

"The antiprotons?"

"Where do they come from? How do they make them?"

For a moment Dekker was tempted to point out to his father that he had said "they," but it didn't seem like a good idea. This sudden pop quiz looked to be very important to the old man. Instead, Dekker said, as though called on in class, "Antimatter is made on the Moon, because of the vacuum environment, the ready availability of electric power, and the danger of accident. The photovoltaic power from the sunlight is used to run a ring accelerator that's about forty kilometers across, inside a big crater, and the accelerator produces antiparticles. Do you want me to write out the reaction?"

"I do," Boldon DeWoe said, and pointed to a memo screen under the piled clothing on the sideboard. When Dekker retrieved it, his father watched carefully while Dekker wrote the equation out on the tiny screen. When that was finished, he wanted to know how Dekker would go about determining the deltas for an orbit from Mercury to Mars, what sort of comets were the most valuable, and how their orbits were controlled. He didn't comment on any of the answers. Finally he said, "All right, now what kind of shape are you in?" He wouldn't settle for an answer but ordered Dekker to pull out his record cartridge and display the results of the tests for his physical parameters—reaction time, depth perception, concentration factor, and the rest. Then Boldon DeWoe leaned back thoughtfully in his chair, stared at the ceiling for a moment, and sighed. He levered himself erect and stumped over to the refrigerator. "You want a beer?" he called over his shoulder.

Dekker didn't, particularly; he'd never really enjoyed alcohol since Annetta Cauchy's party so many years before. Still, he said yes anyway, simply because drinking beer with his father seemed like a bonding kind of thing to do. He could feel the stuff bubbling ticklishly behind his nose. Then his father said, "I guess you're tired."

Dekker nodded, reminded to notice that he was.

"So let's get some sleep. You'll need all the rest you can get, Dek. There's a good prep school here in Nairobi. I know some of the teachers. The school isn't particularly aimed at the Oort, but they can brush you up on the theoretical stuff." He paused to sip from his drink. "The school isn't cheap, Dek, and I don't have much money. Do you have any cues?"

"Earth cues? No. You sent the money for the fare, but there wasn't anything left over."

"I didn't think there would be. Well, I'll get you an amulet—that's what you need to pay for things—and I'll transfer a hundred cues or so to your account, just for walking-around money. There won't be much, though, and I can't afford to keep you in the school forever. But you don't have forever, anyway. In about seven weeks you're going to have to take the tests for Oort training, and they're a bitch."

"I've already taken all the preparatory courses," Dekker said proudly.

"Sure you have. On Mars, a long time ago. Anyway, it's going to be harder here; just physically, you're not used to the gravity. It wears you down. I hear you can work hard when you want to, is that right?"

"I guess so."

"Then want to, Dek. It's important. All I can give you is the one chance."

* * *

After a week Dekker decided the school was just as hard
as Boldon DeWoe had predicted, and that was a surprise to
him. In spite of what his father said, he hadn't expected it.
He had been of the comforting Martians' opinion that, since
everything on Mars was naturally better than anything on
Earth—physical-environmental problems notwithstanding—anybody who could get along well in a Martian deme
school would naturally jump right to the head of the class
in any school Earth had.

He didn't, quite. The other students turned out to be
damnably quick and smart. They were almost all black, too,
a fact that surprised Dekker at first. To be sure, the existence
of black people was no surprise to him; there were plenty of
black people on Mars. But nowhere on Mars was there any
place that was so overwhelmingly *all* black—or all white or
all anything else—as this.

The major visible exception was the teacher, Mr. Cummings. He was a good deal paler than anyone else in the
classroom, but his skin was still milk chocolate rather than
cocoa powder, and a good many shades darker than Dekker's own. So Dekker stood out. Not only for his skin. Not
only for his height, either, though he towered above the rest
of the class. The other conspicuous difference was in the way
they were dressed. Male and female alike they wore brightly
colored tailored shorts and tailored shirts—both of which
always seemed to stay neatly pressed no matter what sports
their owner was in—as against Dekker's own scuffed poly-
denims, and they all wore shoes made out of what Dekker
was astonished to find was *leather.* It wasn't just a single
kind of killed-animal skins, either, for some of them wore
pigskin on their feet and some wore cow, and there was even
a couple whose shoes were made from ostrich hide. It had
never occurred to Dekker that anyone would ever wear
anything that had been taken from a killed-animal.

There were other surprises, too. Not so much in the cur-
riculum, though Dekker was dismayed to find that he was
required to memorize a good many dates from histories that
had never received much attention in Sagdayev. Still, most
courses were easy enough for Dekker DeWoe to deal with.
Mathematics was mathematics, no matter what planet you
were on, and so were physics, chemistry, and astronomy.

The biggest surprise was in the fact that Nairobi's students did not have compulsory docility classes. What they had, instead, were the perplexing twice-a-week sessions they called shove-and-grunt. They were, the teacher explained when he saw the bafflement on Dekker's face, designed to reduce tensions so that people could get along with each other better, and the shoving and grunting were real—and very *physical*.

It was also, for a Martian newly arrived on Earth with his bones and sinews still making the adjustment, fairly dangerous. The first exercise they did was called "breaking in." All but one of the students formed themselves into a tight ring, arms locked around each other's bodies, pressed hard against each other, while the one student left out was charged with getting inside the ring. At first Dekker thought he might actually enjoy it, because the student next to him was an unusually tall young woman named Sally Moi. Holding her warm body pressed against his own was interesting in ways that were by no means unpleasant. But then Mr. Cummings signaled to begin, and the left-out student selected Dekker as the weakest link. He put his head down and came butting against Dekker's kidneys, hard and serious, and the wind went out of Dekker with a whoosh.

That was enough for Mr. Cummings. He excused Dekker from the exercise and in the next session, a kind of wrestling, paired him with the young man named Walter Ngemba, who promised to go easy. Going easy wasn't easy enough. Walter Ngemba was as careful as he had promised, but still when he flopped Dekker over onto his back and pinned his shoulders to the mat Dekker winced from the impact. Mr. Cummings intervened again. Dekker was retired to the side of the room, glad enough to save his Martian bones from splintering, but sorry to be found unfit to participate—and regretful to be giving up the chance to wrestle with Sally Moi. Women had no great place in his immediate plans, not when they might interfere with the prospect of getting into the academy, but her warm body had felt interestingly good within his arm.

Then Mr. Cummings blew his whistle. He gave Dekker a good-natured glance, and said, "I think we'll move along to the verbal phase a little early today. Dekker, since you didn't get much out of the physical part, this is your chance to get a bit of your own back with Walter. Perhaps you'd care to start by calling him some names."

"Why?" Dekker said.

"Why, in order to *offend* him. Don't you have hostility management on Mars? All the bad things you've ever thought, this is a chance to get them out of your system. Call him race names. Say something like, 'You stupid kaffirs aren't even human,' for instance."

Dekker looked at Walter Ngemba, who was waiting with an expectant grin, then back at the teacher. "What's a kaffir?" he asked.

"Call him a jungle bunny if you prefer. Or a wog, perhaps? Really, Dekker, you must have heard some ethnic slurs at some time in your life, haven't you?"

Dekker thought for a second, then remembered. "Dirtsucker," he said experimentally. "Walter, you're a dirtsucker, aren't you?" And was astonished when the whole class, Walter Ngemba included, broke out in laughter; and more astonished still when Mr. Cummings, to show Dekker how the process worked, allowed the whole class to insult Dekker himself at once, and he found out just how many scurrilous terms Earthies knew to express the simple concept of "Martian."

It was a long way, he thought, from the Law of the Raft.

After two full weeks on Earth, Dekker's body had begun to accept the fact that extra efforts were required of it on this planet. It still hurt to walk, or even to stand up; it just didn't hurt quite as much. Earth, Dekker DeWoe decided, wasn't really a bad place. It might actually be a good one if it were just a little less noisy and crowded . . . and if the Earthies had ever learned the Law of the Raft.

But, he concluded, they hadn't. Earthies didn't try to make each other comfortable and happy and satisfied with the world. They didn't even like each other, and the best they could do in their hostility-management sessions was to find ways to keep from showing it.

It was, Dekker thought, pretty childish of them.

It seemed to Dekker that his fellow students acted like children because they were treated like children. The worst part was that he felt as though the same thing was happening to him. For instance, every afternoon when Dekker got out of school there was his father waiting in his dumb little three-wheeled car to drive him home. The other students came hurrying purposefully out of the schoolyard, with the old Peacekeeper lady at the corner vainly trying to keep them from dodging traffic as they crossed the busy street, and Dekker was being met like some five-year-old. He wasn't the only one. Walter Ngemba, too, was picked up every day at the school—though in a pale blue limousine six meters long instead of a trike—but Dekker DeWoe, a full adult with a medal for heroism, resented it.

When Dekker was inside the wobbly little car, climbing in clumsily because of his leg braces, his father reached over him to snap the door lock and stared at him for a moment before he started the car. "Didn't your mother teach you to say thanks?" he asked. There was whiskey on his breath.

"Thanks," Dekker said, to save time, but then he said, "I wish you wouldn't come for me, though."

"Bullshit. It's Thursday, did you forget? Anyway, you're not strong enough to walk all the way home."

"I want to *get* strong enough," Dekker said. He nodded toward the Peacekeeper, who was squinting at them under her sun hat. "She wants you to move on, Dad."

"Screw her." But the old man stepped on the speed pedal and the trike pulled away. The Peacekeeper, Dekker saw as they went through the intersection, had a funnily mixed expression on her face. Half of it was a smile, for Dekker himself—she always had a cheerful hello for him—and the other half was not smiling at all. Dekker was pretty sure that part was for his father. Dekker was pretty sure that all the Earthies had that kind of not-very-admiring feeling about his father, even the neighbors who greeted him so warmly from the stoop—because none of them spent *all* their time drinking beer and sitting around the stoop, since they had jobs to go to.

Boldon DeWoe didn't have one, and he never would.

Because it was Thursday, which was shots day and exercise-machine day, Dekker's father didn't make the right turn toward home but scooted right through the intersection, faster than the Peacekeeper lady would have preferred, and headed for the clinic. Dekker didn't like any of the shots, not even the fairly painless polysteroids, but he purely hated the calcium boosters, which left his thighs bruised and painful all day. When that nastiness was over, the two of them took the elevator up to the next ordeal in physical-therapy rooms on the top floor. There Boldon DeWoe limbered up his text screen while Dekker fitted himself into the whole-body exercise machines. The old man waved the attendant away, because he didn't trust anybody but himself to run the machine slow enough for his son, and while Dekker's Martian muscles were getting flexed and stretched in the iron grip of the machine, his father, with one hand on the speed controls, was reading study guides to the next day's lessons aloud for his son. "There'll be a history test tomorrow," he said. "You'll need to know about the Wars of the Roses, so let's review."

"Ouch," Dekker said, as the machine twisted his knee. "Dad? How come you know what's going to happen tomorrow?"

"I have friends, how do you think?" his father said, turning back the speed control a hair. "Here, is that better?"

Dekker didn't answer, partly because the slower speed wasn't any "better"—just a little less likely to crack his fragile Martian bones—and partly because he didn't want to admit that he needed any special care. "What kind of friends?"

"*Good* friends. Now shut up. Now, let's hear what you remember about the Wars of the Roses. That was York against Lancaster—?"

Dekker rebelled. "That's all old stuff from the crazy times, Dad. Why do I have to learn about *wars*?"

"Because the school requires it, and that's all the reason you need. Now what about it?"

Dekker gave in to logic. "It was in England," he said, panting. "Both sides wanted one of their people to be king, and the reason the wars were called that was that emblems for both sides were roses, white on one side and red on the other. They fought over it for a hundred years, and—" And so on, until they came to the time of the battle that killed King Richard and brought on the Tudors. Then, satisfied, or as nearly satisfied as Boldon DeWoe was likely to get, his father turned off the text machine and began to get that faraway, absentminded, *thirsty* look that Dekker had begun to recognize. He didn't cut the exercise session short, though. He let it go to the tick of the sixtieth second of the sixtieth minute of the hour, and then he released Dekker, limp, rubbing his sore limbs, and hurried him down and into the trike again.

Dekker noticed that his father drove even faster than usual on the way home. He didn't comment on it. He didn't say anything at all, much, until they were already in the apartment again and his father had pulled a beer out of the little refrigerator and, glancing at his watch, sat himself down in front of the old flat-plate video.

Dekker knew the routine by then. There was an hour's study time before his father would start assembling dinner, so Dekker said, "I'll get on with it," and started to sit down before his own screen without being told.

"No, not this time," his father said. "You can do that later, Dek. There's a special on Mars starting in a minute. You'd probably like to watch it."

"All right," Dekker agreed. He got up to stand behind his father's chair, but busied himself with picking things up around the room while the opening credits for the program rolled. That was a duty Dekker had taken on himself. Sacrificing sleep to make time for it, he had long since put away everything he could find a place for and scrubbed everything that could be scrubbed. The place was nowhere near Martian standards, of course, but at least it had become less offensive. His father had not seemed to notice, and every day there was a new fallout of socks, bottles, and dirty dishes to greet him when he came home.

Then, as the program began, Dekker stopped his housework and focused his attention on the screen.

Most of what the report had to say he already knew. Still, it was good to know that the Oort controllers could now get better than 99 percent of the fragments in a narrow ellipse no more than six or seven hundred kilometers long; there was no longer any need to evacuate whole demes. Of course, that remaining 1 percent could still do a lot of damage where it struck. But if Mars was rich in anything, it was plenty of barren space where there was no real damage to do. Not once, the program's narrator pointed out, in all the six hundred-odd strikes so far, had anyone been killed or any real damage done, and in one of the deeper parts of Valles Marineris they had actually measured a pressure of nearly forty millibars one day.

Then Dekker made a discovery. When the screen·was showing the giant craters left by comet impacts, when it switched to some of the new demes with their windmills and bubble-farms actually on the planet's surface—when it was showing Mars as it was, his father's face was drawn and weary.

Dekker thought it over carefully, but there was really only one conclusion to be drawn. His father was homesick.

Dekker cleared his throat and started to speak, but his father hushed him. "Hold it," he said. "They're just getting to the important part."

"But it's over."

"The *show* is over. Now we get the experts commenting on it. That's what I want you to see."

Dekker shrugged. "All right." But his legs were protesting the long standing period, so he crossed the room for a chair, and while he was there got himself a drink of water, found a couple of overlooked dishes that needed rinsing off, and got back to the screen just in time to hear a middle-aged woman with a mop of golden hair say, "It just doesn't add up. Making Mars into a kind of national park is a sweet, do-goody kind of thing to do, but the cues aren't there. The farm habitats can deliver food faster, and in the long run cheaper."

"What's she talking about?" Dekker asked in alarm.

"If you listened," his father said grimly, "you'd hear."

So Dekker did listen, in alarm, then disbelief, then anger. A pale young man in a pale pink sweater protested that it was humanity's destiny in the long run to settle every piece of real estate that *could* be settled, so why not Mars? Then a darker, older, bearded man scoffed, "That's the kind of airy-fairy thinking that started the Oort project going in the first place." And Boldon DeWoe, grunting irritably to himself, snapped the set off and limped to the refrigerator for another beer.

Dekker followed him over. "What the hell was that all about?" he demanded.

His father shrugged. "You heard. It's what I've been trying to tell you. If you're going to get into the academy, you'd better do it now, because there are a lot of people who want to cancel the whole project."

"They can't do that!"

Boldon DeWoe considered that proposition for the length of time it took him to get back to his chair and sit down again. "No," he said at last, "they probably can't. At least I think they can't. But not for the reasons you think, Dek. I think they'll keep it going because they just have too much invested in it already, and they won't want to write it all off. But they can cut back, slow it down—"

"That's stupid!" Dekker flared.

"Sure it is, boy. Did I ever say Earthies weren't stupid? But it's a real possibility, so you can't fool around. You have to take the psychological test in a few weeks, and that's in Denver, so you're going to have to get everything you can out of the school here as fast as you can. What does that mean, Dek?"

"It means I have to study."

"Right. Now I want to watch the ball game."

He switched on the set again and started to put the earpiece for private listening in place, but Dekker tarried. He was remembering the expression on his father's face as he looked at the Martian scenes. He ventured, "Dad?"

His father dislodged one earpiece to hear his son. "Is there something you don't understand?"

"No, I just wanted to ask you. Why didn't you come back to Mars, after . . . ?"

His father gave him a hard look. "After I got hurt, is that what you mean?"

"Why didn't you?" Dekker persisted.

His father made a gesture of annoyance. "Hell, Dek. What would I do on Mars?"

"What do you do here?" Dekker asked, pressing his luck.

This time Boldon's look was actually angry. Then slowly it evolved into a grin when he decided it was a fair question. "Since you ask, I'll tell you. Here on Earth is where I have to be. This is where I draw my pension—"

"They'd give it to you on Mars, wouldn't they?"

"They'd give it to me in Martian funds. Here I get it in cues. Do you know the difference?"

"Sure I do."

"Then don't ask dumb questions." He hesitated, then added, "And there's another reason. Here I have repair shops handy, too."

"Repair shops?"

"They call them hospitals, but—" He slapped at his thigh. "—it's all electronics here, Dek, and when the system goes out they have to open it up and take the components out and fix them. Yes, they have repair shops on Mars, too, but they have to import the components from Earth. That means they have to be paid for in cues. I may not be much use anymore, Dek, but I don't want to be a liability, either. And anyway, here's where I've got my friends." He put the plug decisively back in his ear to show that the conversation was over.

Dekker couldn't let it go at that. "When you say 'friends,' " he said obstinately, "what you mean is drinking buddies, right?"

His father took the plug out of his ear again and studied Dekker's judgmental face. "You think I stay here just so I can drink up my pension without anybody interfering, is that it?" He waited politely for a response before going on, but Dekker was mute. "What I mean by 'friends,' " his father said then, "is people who can help us. Both of us, Dekker. I do drink, that's true. But drinking buddies are better than no friends at all when you don't have any future."

"You *could* have a future!"

His father shook his head. "I'm afraid not, Dek. You'll have to have it for both of us."

16.

THE TALL, SKINNY Martian physique works fine on Mars, but a lot less well on Earth. What makes the difference is gravity. The Martian who comes to Earth suddenly discovers that he has an extra forty or so kilograms to carry around with him—all the time—and his body's musculature isn't up to it.

So the muscles are built up with polysteroids. That's easy enough. But then the muscles can exert more force than the bones they are attached to can withstand, so to keep the skeleton intact the bones have to be built up with more calcium. That works, too, but more slowly; so while the skeleton is becoming denser and more rigid the long bones of the legs, particularly, need to be scaffolded from outside: thus the leg braces. But then there are other problems. Those new muscles demand more oxygen, so while the bone marrow is making more red corpuscles an extra couple of liters of whole blood are pumped in to tide them over. Then there's the heart itself. It has to work harder in order to move all this extra blood around. A whole array of beta blockers and stimulants are needed to help the heart do its new job.

And then, when all this has been done, the result is a body that has been beefed up, but still remembers its birthplace conditions. It tires. It slows down. What they say is true: It's easy enough to take the boy out of Mars, but you can never, ever, take Mars out of the boy.

17.

WHAT DEKKER WAS good at wasn't worrying. It was working, and he worked. He worked at the courses that made no sense to him, even English history and "political science," whatever that was. He put the shocking thought of the possible cancellation of the Oort project out of his mind, and when his first grades came in on the text screen in his father's apartment he was pleased, and slightly astonished, to discover that he had placed third in the class.

His father, on the other hand, only nodded. "You've been working hard and studying hard," he pronounced. "What did you expect? Only bear down a little harder on the math, because it has to look good."

"What has to look good?" Dekker asked, but his father already had the earplugs in and was turning on the Nairobi-Jo'burg soccer game. Dekker went back to his studies.

The only thing he really worried about was how his class-mates would react to this new Martian kid, this new *white* Martian kid, placing above twenty-nine of the thirty-two of them. As it turned out, they didn't seem hostile at all. Afira Kantado, the young woman who was fourth in the class—that is, the one who would have been third if Dekker hadn't preempted her place—did give him one short, surly look when the grades were posted. But the others congratulated him, joked with him, or didn't talk about it at all, which he liked best.

The jokes they made were about his accent, but Dekker had that long since squared away. He wasn't the one who talked funny. *They* talked funny, because—Mr. Cummings had told him, when they chatted for a moment before class one day— that was the perfectly natural way one spoke when one came of parents who had attended good schools. "Good schools," Dek-ker discovered, were limited to two: a pair of universities named "Oxford" and "Cambridge." The reason these young people were in this prep school was that as soon as they graduated most of them, too, would be off to complete their educations in this "England" where the "good schools" were.

Learning these things made Dekker feel better. When he also discovered that these students were about the brightest Nairobi had, he didn't feel quite so worried about comparisons with Martian students.

The other thing Dekker began to learn was that not all black was the *same* black. In his original, parochial view, all Earthies had been just Earthies; from his father he had learned that these particular Earthies were identified as Kenyans; now he found that even Kenyans thought of themselves more fractionatedly still. About half the boys, and almost all the girls, considered themselves what they called "Kikuyu," while the handful of tall, weedy, almost Martian-looking ones were called "Masai." Even that wasn't all, because there were a handful who came from other "tribes."

Dekker had to have that word explained to him. A tribe was not at all, Dekker discovered, the same thing as a deme. Tribes were a matter of genes, not location. Surprisingly, you con-tinued to be part of your tribe even if you moved to some other tribe's deme.

All that astonished Dekker greatly. What did it matter what your relatives were?

But it seemed that it did matter, although except for the fact that the Masai were of pleasingly stretched-out proportions compared to the Kikuyu, Dekker could not distinguish between one tribe and another. The Kenyans all could, though. Infallibly. A fair proportion of the "citizenship" classes, as the shove-and-grunt sessions were properly called, were devoted to the subject, Mr. Cummings invariably beginning by reminding all the students that it didn't matter what tribe their ancestors had come from, they were all not only equal but, really, the *same*.

He got challenged on it, too. Afira Kantado raised her hand and pointed to Dekker. "He's not the same," she said.

"Of course he is, Kantado," Mr. Cummings said patiently, "or at least you should act as though he were." She looked unconvinced, so the teacher explained. "You know what the basis of good citizenship is. You don't have to like any other person. If you have bad feelings, that's all right. It's perfectly natural for you to dislike another person. The important thing is that you must always *keep your resentments to yourself*— except in these sessions, of course. If you let the hostilities and angers out in the outside world, that's when conflicts start— and violence—and, in the long run, it could even lead to wars. We don't want that, do we? So we must— DeWoe? Did you want to say something?"

Dekker had his hand up. "That isn't the way we do it on Mars," he pointed out.

There was a faint sound from the class, almost a titter. Mr. Cummings gave them a warning look. "No, of course it isn't, DeWoe," he agreed. "Different places have different customs. I understand on Mars the thrust is to make you *like* each other, isn't it?"

Dekker frowned. "Not 'like,' exactly. There are plenty of people I don't particularly like. But we have to trust each other, and care for each other—we have to make sure everybody's being treated fairly. Like—" He had been going to say, "like the Law of the Raft," but changed his mind in the middle of the sentence."—like we're all *family*."

Mr. Cummings nodded tolerantly. "I suppose that's quite important on Mars, where the conditions are so much more— severe. And of course it would be even more so under even harsher conditions, would it not? For example, DeWoe, you're planning to go out into the Oort cloud to work. Why don't you tell the class what it's like out there?"

"I've never been there," he objected.

"But your father has. He must have told you stories about it."

The fact was, he hadn't. But Dekker was not prepared to admit that in public, so he did his best. "Out in the Oort," he said, "it's like Mars, only tougher. You can't throw your weight around. You can't afford to be jealous of somebody else, or try to get an advantage over him. You have to try to understand how the other person feels."

"It sounds good to me," Walter Ngemba put in, not bothering to raise his hand.

"It sounds *stupid*," Afira Kantado commented. "What about sex?"

"Sex?" Dekker repeated, trying to imagine what sex had to do with docility—or "citizenship."

"You keep saying 'him.' What about men and women? Don't they ever have two men loving the same woman?"

"Oh," said Dekker, relieved, "that. That's no problem. A man takes a duty wife—or a woman takes a duty husband—and they live together as long as they both want to. Then they stop."

One of the Masai had a hand up, snickering. "When your old man was in the Oort, did he have a duty wife?"

Dekker answered hotly, "My father *has* a wife. She's my mother. What would he want another wife for?"

Half a dozen hands went up then, over grinning faces. Mr. Cummings shook his head. "This is a very interesting discussion," he pronounced, "but the period's over. We'll resume it at our next session if you like—but now, good afternoon to you all."

As they clumped together at the door, Walter Ngemba touched Dekker's arm and said consolingly, "I'm sorry about that chap Merad. It's just that he's Masai, you know."

Dekker looked at him in surprise. "I thought everybody was supposed to be the same."

"Oh, everybody is. Even Masai. It's just that they are so, well, *uncivilized*, sometimes. But, look, I've had a thought. Have you got anything planned for the weekend? Because my father said he'd be delighted to have you come have a look at our farm."

"Farm?"

"Our family place. It's out in the Rift Valley. Can you come?"

It was a surprise, but a very pleasing one. "Why, sure. Thanks," Dekker began. Then second thoughts occurred to him. "I do have a lot of studying to do—"

"We can study together; we've got a lot of the same subjects, you know. Do you need to ask your father?"

Need to? "Not exactly," Dekker said.

"Well, talk to him about it. I expect he'll be out there waiting for you, won't he?"

But, as it turned out, that particular afternoon Boldon DeWoe wasn't. There was no sign of the little trike. As Dekker stood uncertainly on the sidewalk, looking up and down at the traffic, the Peacekeeper woman hurried over to him, putting her phone into its pouch and looking concerned.

"You're Dekker DeWoe, aren't you? Well, I've got a message for you. You have to go pick up your father at the Sunshine Shabeen."

"The what?"

"It's a bar," she explained. "Do you know where it is? It doesn't matter; you'll have to take a taxi anyway and the driver will know. All the drivers know the Sunshine Shabeen."

She turned to blow a peremptory blast on her whistle and, before Dekker could ask any questions, a cab swooped over out of the traffic screen. Yes, the driver certainly did know where the Sunshine Shabeen was. Then all Dekker had to worry about was whether the few cues on his amulet were going to be enough to pay the bill.

They weren't. Dekker had to rummage in his father's pockets to find the money to pay the driver, and then enough to pay him again to take the two of them back home. His father was no help. His father was snoringly drunk and impossible to rouse. He was almost impossible to move, too, and Dekker certainly couldn't have managed the task by himself.

Fortunately there were two bulky Peacekeepers waiting outside the shabeen, and when they'd had a look at tall, skinny Dekker they did the job for him.

What surprised Dekker was that that was all they did. Once they had shifted Boldon DeWoe into the waiting cab the larger of the Peacekeepers wished Dekker a good night. They turned away, although they certainly would have been within their rights to do things far more severe. When Dekker saw the caked blood and snot around his father's nose he had no doubt that the old man's behavior had been *very* antisocial.

Yet the Peacekeepers hadn't arrested him.

That was a puzzle, but Dekker had other things on his mind. Unfortunately there were no handy Peacekeepers at the apartment building, nor did the sulking cab driver show any interest in helping. Even more unfortunately, a light sprinkling of rain had driven the stoop loungers indoors, and Boldon DeWoe, shriveled though he was, was more than Dekker could manage up the front steps.

Then he heard a voice from above: "Hi there, down below!" When he looked up it was their next-door neighbor, Mrs. Garun, leaning out the window. "Just hang on there a sec, please. I'll get Jeffrey and Maheen to give you a hand with your dad."

Jeffrey and Maheen showed up in a matter of seconds, huge, good-natured, quick to lug Boldon DeWoe up to the apartment and even lay him down on his bed. "He'll be right enough if you just cover him over and let him sleep it off, chum," one of them advised as they left.

Dekker did as instructed. Jeffrey and Maheen clearly had more experience in these matters than himself, and anyway there didn't seem any need to do anything else. After he had thought that out, Dekker looked considerably at the refrigerator, then abandoned the thought of making a meal. Instead, he pulled out his lesson cartridges and began to study.

He was doing calculus exercises—though he didn't know what he would ever need to know calculus for, when pocket math machines were always available—when he heard a knock on the door.

It was Mrs. Garun again, this time bearing a covered pot of soup.

"I thought you might like a bit of something to eat," she said apologetically. "Your dad, too, when he wakes up. The lads said he was probably gone for the night, but whenever it is you can just heat a dish up for him."

"Thank you," Dekker said, lifting the lid and sniffing. It was some sort of killed-animal and vegetables, and actually it smelled very good.

Mrs. Garun tarried for a minute. "He's a good man, your

father," she said, wiping her hands on her apron. "It's a shame he got hurt that way in the Oort."

"Thank you," Dekker said again, for lack of a more appropriate response, but the woman hadn't finished.

She hesitated, then said in the tone of a confidence, "You know, Dekker, I thought once I might go out there myself."

That startled Dekker, and the expression on his face made her laugh. "Oh," she said good-naturedly, "I didn't always work in the billing department for the electric company. When I was young I had bigger ideas, you know. I studied engineering at Newcastle-on-Tyne, and I thought terraforming Mars from the Oort was the biggest, most wonderful idea anybody ever had—only, of course, then I married Mr. Garun, and he didn't want me to go off without him. So I did the next best thing."

She looked expectantly at Dekker, who said, guessing, "You went to work for the electric company?"

"Oh, no, not that. I mean about the Oort. I decided to help the project my own way. So when Mr. Garun died I put the insurance money into Oort bonds." She untied and retied her apron meditatively before she added, "Only the things have been going down a bit lately, haven't they?"

"I really don't know much about financial things," Dekker apologized. "We don't have that sort of thing on Mars."

"Well, I know you don't. Only—it's a bit of a worry, isn't it? I hate to sell and take a loss. On the other hand, what's the future going to be? I wouldn't care to wake up one morning and find I was penniless." Then she smiled at him. "What keeps my spirits up is young people like you, Dekker, giving up everything to go out there and make it work. God bless you. And, please, if there's anything you need, just knock on my door!"

When Mrs. Garun was back in her own apartment, Dekker ate the soup thoughtfully. It was in fact very good, though he couldn't recognize exactly what species of killed-animal had gone into it, but he was conscious of a faint bad taste in the back of his mouth. The taste wasn't the soup. It was something quite different, and worse.

He looked in to make sure his father was still sound asleep. Then he rinsed the dish and took out the latest communication from his mother to track down something she had said.

Gerti DeWoe hadn't missed a week, expensive as keeping in touch from Mars was; she was there on his screen every Thursday, always looking tired but alert, always with little bits of news: Tinker Gorshak was sick, Tinker was better; they've started the new windmills on the slope over Sagdayev, and that was good because the dust storms had been fierce lately and the photovoltaic farms were always getting covered over; she'd been asked to represent Sagdayev again at the all-deme parliament in Sunpoint City—Dekker shook his head in continuing surprise at that; his mother a *politician*? Tsumi Gorshak had been cautioned for cutting his docility classes. And the import budgets were cut again.

That was the part he was looking for. He played it over twice. The reason cues were short, his mother said, was that they'd had to postpone the new issue of the Bonds, because the Earthie financiers had informed them that the market was temporarily too "soft."

Dekker scowled at that. Why were these Earthies always making trouble about the Bonds? A deal was a deal, wasn't it? Everybody had known from the very beginning that the Bonds would not pay off until the Oort project was complete—or complete enough, anyway, for Mars to start growing the crops that would produce the cues to meet the payments. So why did the price keep going up and down—or, actually, mostly just down?

It made no sense to him. And it wasn't just Mars that was hurt by these financial tricks; decent Earthies like Mrs. Garun were feeling the pinch, too.

Dekker yawned and tried to put these impossible questions out of his mind. He turned off the screen and crawled into bed, dropping his clothes to the floor. His father's snoring was less raucous now, though Dekker was perplexed to hear an occasional low rumbling sound that mixed with it sometimes, and definitely did not come from Boldon DeWoe. Dekker lay on his back with his eyes open, thinking about Mrs. Garun, thinking about his mother—then, almost drifting off to sleep, thinking about his parents, trying to recapture the memory of when all three of them lived together, before his father went off to the Oort. Dekker was nearly sure his parents had been happy. The question had never seemed to come up, but they *acted* happy enough, and his mother had definitely cried when Boldon DeWoe left. So what had gone wrong?

A huge boom from outside interrupted his thoughts. Startled, Dekker limped naked to a window to look out.

The gentle rain had become a storm, violent and electrical. Great flashes of violet-white light sliced through the black sky, making the city's buildings stand out in black silhouette. The distant rumbles had become sharp cracks of thunder that rolled and crashed, and the rain pelted down violently. It wasn't just rain, either. Some of the droplets bounced away as they struck his windowsill, and Dekker realized with astonishment that he was looking at the thing they called "hail."

And everything he saw was oddly shimmering—the streets, the two-hundred-meter towers downtown, the creeping car lights along the road—because it was wet.

There was a marvel! Everything *wet*. Wet with profligately wasted water, falling from the sky. Unplanned and unforced, perhaps even sometimes undesired. Torrents of it. Making the streets and building roofs shine as they reflected the lightning.

This, Dekker thought wonderingly, was what it was all about. This was what Mars would be some day, when the last Oort comet had dropped its final blessing of water and gases onto the old planet and made it young again. It would all be worth it, then. Dekker promised himself it would: all the sacrifices, like Mrs. Garun's; all the pain, like his father's; all the work—like his own . . .

Then an especially loud crash made him jump, and a moment later he saw a reflection in the window and turned.

His father was there, leaning on the back of a chair, holding a sheet over his broken body.

"Are you all right?" Dekker asked.

His father was silent for a moment, as though researching the answer. Then he said, "Sure. Are you the one who brought me home?" Dekker nodded.

"That's all right, then," his father said. It wasn't an expression of regret for having needed to be carried home, and it certainly wasn't any kind of an apology. But it was all Boldon DeWoe had to say on the subject. He went on gazing silently at the rain.

Dekker remembered Mrs. Garun's advice. "Do you want some soup?"

"Christ, no. Old lady Garun's been around? Nice of her, but no."

It was as good a chance to talk to him as Dekker was going to get, and there were things Dekker had been wanting to talk to him about. He cleared his throat. "Dad," he said, beginning

with the less important thing, "Walter Ngemba invited me to
come to his father's farm this weekend."

His father turned painfully to look at him. "Ngemba," he
repeated thoughtfully. "His father's the plantation owner, out
in the Mara?"

"I told him I'd come."

Boldon DeWoe gave a small acquiescent shrug. "You might
as well, Dek. You've been looking pretty tired; you could use
the rest. Anyway, the Ngembas are the kind of people it might
be useful to know."

Dekker took a breath and got to the more important one.
"They were asking about you in school today."

His father looked wary. "You were talking about me?"

"Well, more or less. They were talking about living in the
Oort, and duty wives—and things like that—and, well, it made
me wonder something," Dekker said. "About you and Ma.
You never came back home after your accident, Dad. Don't
you ever miss your wife?"

His father looked at him without expression. "Do you know
how badly I got hurt?"

"Well . . . not exactly. Pretty badly, I guess."

"Badly enough." His father stared out at the rain for a
moment. "I guess your mother didn't want to talk about it," he
said at last. "It was dope, Dek. You can't dock a spotter ship
when you've been doing drugs, so there was a crash. You know
what it's like in a spotter ship? You're practically part of the
ship; your suit fits right in to fill all the space there is, and you
don't get out of the suit until you get back. So when the bow
of the ship crumpled it got my legs and the lower part of my
body, and I pretty nearly died. Well, I did die. My heart was
stopped by the time they got me out, and they had a hell of a
time bringing me back. It didn't help the lock much, either—
they gave me a hard time about that. It could have cost me my
pension, but I guess they figured I was paying enough anyway,
the way I am. Oh," he said, noticing Dekker's appalled look,
"yes, Dek, it was me that did it. I was the pilot that was doing
drugs."

"But we don't *do* that!"

His father looked very weary. "No, we don't," he agreed.
"Not at home. I never did before, but it's different out in the
Oort. You're out there spotting, weeks at a time, all by yourself.

And other people do it. They do it a lot here on Earth, and some of them take the stuff with them wherever they go."

"But—"

Dekker swallowed the rest of that particular "but." He shook his head—not in reproach, or not just in reproach, but principally in sorrow and shock. It took him a moment to remember what it was that he wanted to know.

"But you could have come home," he said.

"I didn't think so, Dek."

"Because you were, well, embarrassed, yes, I understand that. But didn't you miss your—" The word would have been "family," but pride got in Dekker's way. "—your wife, anyway?"

His father looked at him for a moment before he said, "What would I do with a wife now?"

By Friday the storm was long gone, the sky was cloudless, and the African sun hotter than ever. If Dekker DeWoe had thought Nairobi was sweltering hot, as indeed he had, when he reached the Masai Mara he discovered a whole new order of heat.

It didn't hit him right away. Walter Ngemba had a private plane waiting on the outskirts of the city. They drove out to it in the long, blue limousine, the pilot touched her cap as they strapped themselves in, and the plane took off for a private landing strip at the foot of a mountain. The strip didn't look like much of an airport, and it wasn't. It was nothing but a thousand meters of hardtop scratched out of the sparse brush, a wind sock that hung listlessly from its pole, and nothing else at all. There wasn't even a shed to protect a waiting passenger from the sun's rays. There weren't any waiting passengers, either. There was nothing but scrub and bare, dry soil. After the bustling streets of Nairobi, with their crowds of human beings, the place looked almost homelike to Dekker DeWoe. Even almost Martian.

"Look over there," Walter Ngemba said. He leaned over Dekker's shoulder—he had politely let Dekker take the copilot's seat, since there wasn't any need for a copilot in the tiny plane—and pointed to something like a large bug that was sliding across the scrub toward them. The thing was trailing a cloud of dust. "That's our ride coming. And, see, there's our compound, up there on the hill past the watering hole."

Dekker couldn't see anything that could be called a compound. He couldn't see much of anything at all, the way the plane was banking and twisting, not unless the quick glimpse of scarlet rectangles among the blotchy dun of the landscape was the roofs of buildings. Dekker wasn't really spending much effort on looking, either. He was busy clinging to his seat, because this aircraft was no ponderous Martian dirigible. The thing swerved and darted. The pilot had already buzzed the strip once—apparently to scare away something that moved in the brush beside the strip—and then spun around in a tight curve to make her landing.

By the time the plane had slowed at the end of the runway the buglike vehicle had reached the strip. It turned out to be a hovervan, with a tall, skinny Masai woman jumping out of the driver's seat to open the door for them.

That was when the heat really hit.

This wasn't Nairobi's dank air, it was parched and toasting. It was Dekker's opinion that if he had to stay out in this bake-oven for more than minutes, his brains would coagulate, like a cooked egg. He didn't have to, though. The interior of the van was air-conditioned, and as soon as the woman had closed the door on them she hurried over to help the pilot carry their bags to the van's luggage compartment.

Walter paid her no attention. He rummaged in the van's little chiller for a moment and produced a couple of beers. "Welcome to Ngemba country," he said, lifting the can in a toast. "I hope you don't mind if we take the hover; I'm afraid it makes the dust a good deal worse, and lord knows the dust's bad enough anyway, but we won't bounce our kidneys around so much on the game trails. Did you see the lions?"

Lions. Dekker thoughtfully sipped the beer, trying to remember just what strange creatures he had seen. Along the way up from Nairobi Walter had been nudging him every few minutes, pointing out the window at elephants, giraffes, and grazing animals of a dozen kinds, all previously known to Dekker only from pictures. But lions? "I don't think so," he said. "When was that?"

"Now, of course," said Walter, pointing. "They're right over there. Don't you see them?" And not more than ten meters away, in the shade of a clump of thorny bushes, half a dozen large, tawny cats were peering incuriously out at them.

The hairs on Dekker's forearms sprang to attention. "Jesus," he said.

And said it many times again, though mostly under his breath, over the next twenty-four hours or so. First appearances had been all wrong. The Ngemba "farm" was a *very* un-Martian place.

Simply physically, being on the Ngemba farm was an ordeal for Dekker. The heat was blinding out in the open air, and the air-conditioning next to freezing inside. What was more, the main house was dismayingly full of stairways that had to be climbed and descended. Psychologically the strain of being there was even greater. Dekker's ideas of spaciousness, already revised upward from his Martian standards, expanded again as he began to grasp the size of the Ngemba household. There was a dining room and a breakfast room, there was a "morning" room and a "sun" room, and there was a library. Dekker couldn't help looking startled when they came to the library. It was full of books. Not the kind of book cartridges Dekker was used to dealing with. *Real* books, printed on paper and bound in cloth or leather, great heavy things that lined all four walls of this very large room. "Yes, the old gent's a great reader," Walter said indulgently. "A touch old-fashioned, too, wouldn't you say? Of course, he doesn't just spend his time reading; this is where he manages his investments, too."

Dekker looked around wonderingly. "How?"

Walter grinned and touched a keypad. One whole row of what had seemed to be the spines of books slid away and revealed a bank of screens. "Direct channels to all his brokers," he said proudly. "I won't turn them on, though; he'd go through the roof if he caught me playing at them. He buys and sells securities." Then, when he saw Dekker's expression, "You do know what securities are?"

"Like the Bonds?"

"You mean the Oortcorp bonds? Well, yes, those are securities, but there are all different kinds. Common stocks, preferred stocks, double-dips, self-liquidating debentures—good lord, *I* don't know what they all are. Father's most active in futures right now, I think." Walter sighed. "Oh, you don't know what futures are. Well, you sign a contract. It says that maybe six months from now you'll sell some securities at a certain price, and some other chap signs the contract with you to buy them then."

"How do you know what the price will be in six months?"

"Well, that's the tricky part, isn't it? Maybe you don't. Maybe you guess wrong, and then you're stuck. The good guessers make money—like the old man."

"It sounds—" Dekker had been about to say "stupid" but revised his intention. "—complicated," he finished.

Walter laughed. "No offense, Dekker," he said, "but Martians just don't understand the market, do they? But come, I haven't shown you the game room yet."

All in all, there had to be at least thirty rooms in the rambling main house, to be shared only by Walter; his younger sister, Doris; and his parents—his parent and stepparent, actually, the slim and youthful Gloria Ngemba being his classmate's father's second wife. And, of course, their *many* servants, all in one curious uniform or another. Dekker did not succeed in counting the servants. However many of them there were, their number wasn't relevant to the space-to-occupant ratio, anyway, since Dekker discovered that the servants had their own fairly spacious quarters—at least by Martian standards—down past the vehicle shed and the repair shop.

It was a close decision for Dekker as to which of these new categories of living beings was the more grotesquely strange: the wild animals roaming around loose out in the Mara, or the servants that populated the Ngemba compound. Nothing on Mars, or even in Nairobi, had prepared him for either. Nor had he been prepared for the problems of "dressing for dinner"— why would anyone put on special clothes just to *eat?*—or for Mr. Theodore Ngemba.

He didn't meet Mr. Theodore Ngemba at once. Mr. Ngemba was unavoidably detained by business matters, and so Dekker was welcomed to the estate by the two female members of the family, the beautiful Gloria and the teenage Doris, both in riding habits and smelling faintly of the horses from which they had just dismounted. He was escorted to his rooms—rooms!— by a servant, and then immediately taken for a walk around the grounds by Walter.

Dekker appreciated the courtesy. He didn't appreciate the exercise. Most of the walking was up and down steps, because the compound was at the top of a small hill. "To keep the animals out," Walter explained. "Not that most of them would come near us anyway, but some of the buffalo are pretty stupid."

Not all the animals were kept out, though. In the rose garden three gardeners were repairing damage done by some of the invaders—"Baboons," Walter explained—and leaping through all the shrubbery were little, long-armed furry things that Walter said were called colibri monkeys. By the swimming pool a tall Masai wearing a thing like a white nightgown patrolled the area with a slingshot; his job was to keep the monkeys away from the water. "Oh, damn," Walter said as they approached the pool. "The infant's there, curse the luck."

The infant was his sister, tying up her hair by the side of the pool. She studied Dekker, looking up from under her hair. "Do you like to swim?" she asked.

Dekker considered the question. There was certainly a possibility that there might, somewhere, once have been a Martian who had possessed the skill to keep himself afloat in a body of water, but Dekker had never encountered such a person. He didn't say that. He only said, "I don't know how."

"I'll teach you, if you like," she said. "It's easy. Watch me."

He did, and discovered that the kid sister, Doris Ngemba, wasn't really all that much of a kid. When she threw off the robe to dive into the pool she was wearing nothing over her breasts and only the tiniest of patches over her pubic area. Dekker's eyes attentively followed every movement. Not just Dekker's eyes, either. The Masai with the slingshot was watching her closely, too, until he saw Walter watching him; then the man grinned in embarrassment, turned, and sent a random shot with his slingshot into the shrubs before he stalked away.

Doris had swum the width of the pool and returned; now she was clinging to the side of it, wet and smiling up at Dekker. "How about it, then?" she asked.

"How about your not showing your breasts off in front of the Masai?" her brother said angrily.

"Oh, the Masai," she said, dismissing the whole tribe at once. "I wasn't talking to you anyway, Wally dear. I was talking to Dekker. Are you game for a swimming lesson?"

"Maybe tomorrow," Walter told her, answering for his guest. "Dekker's got to bathe and dress for dinner now. And you'd better get on with it, too, because Father doesn't like to be kept waiting."

* * *

Mr. Theodore Ngemba wasn't kept waiting for dinner. It was a close thing, though, because when Walter discovered that his guest didn't have a dinner jacket he had to scour the servants' quarters for clothes from some former Masai butler to fit him. At least fit him closely enough to get through a dinner, though the long-gone Masai butler had been a much fatter man and the jacket hung loose on Dekker's Martian frame.

They were six for dinner: the Ngembas, Dekker, and an elderly woman who wore pearls—six diners and, Dekker saw, eight servants to see that they had the food to dine on. One servant behind each person at table, and a couple of others to carry dishes in and out. It wasn't only the elderly woman who wore expensive baubles, because both Doris and her stepmother had bright mineral stones in their hair and around their necks, and even Mr. Theodore Ngemba had a thick chain of gold supporting a gold medallion of some sort around his neck. Dekker had seen no such display of wealth since that long-ago dinner party with Annetta Cauchy's family on the night of the first comet strike.

Uncomfortable in his scratchy jacket, Dekker found himself seated between Mrs. Ngemba and the elderly woman, who turned out to be a business associate of Mr. Theodore Ngemba. She was named Mrs. Kurai. She ate quietly, listening to the others talk—a welcome bit of luck for Dekker, he thought, since he had no idea what a proper dinner-table conversation should be.

Walter filled all the conversational gaps. He leaned forward to address his father. "Dekker was very interested in the library, sir."

Mr. Theodore Ngemba looked indulgently at his son's guest. "Are you a reader then, Mr. DeWoe?"

"Yes . . . sir," Dekker said, glancing at Walter to make sure he was saying it right.

"Indeed. What have you read recently?"

With everyone looking at him, Dekker thought back. Damn little, actually, if you didn't count school texts. Then he remembered a good subject. "There was this book I read once by a man named Mark Twain. It's called *Huckleberry Finn*. Huck Finn is floating down the Mississippi River with a man named Jim, an escaped slave, and they talked about what they call the Law of the—"

Tardily he saw that Mr. Ngemba was frowning and trailed off. "That," his host said heavily, "is an offensive book. I do not permit it in my library. It contains words which are not tolerated in decent conversation."

"Sorry, sir," Dekker said, wishing he were somewhere else.

Mrs. Kurai saved him. When her personal servitor had put the soup course before her she said, friendlily enough, "I understand you're going to work in the Oort cloud."

"I hope so," Dekker said politely, watching to see which spoon she took. "Do you own some of the Bonds?"

The woman looked amused. "A few. I used to have more, of course; I suppose we all did, in the beginning."

Dekker looked at her curiously. "But it still is the beginning," he told her. "It'll be another twenty-five years before the project's finished."

"Forty," called Doris Ngemba, and her brother straightened her out.

"He's counting in Mars years, twit," he said.

"So you think the project will continue," Mr. Theodore Ngemba said from the head of the table, waving away the servant with the platter of killed-animal. "It's turning out rather expensive, isn't it?"

Dekker frowned. "My mother's on the all-deme planning board," he said, "and she hasn't said anything about extra costs."

"Perhaps not, perhaps not. But of course it isn't just the physical cost, is it? There's the cost of the money—amortization and interest. And there do seem to be other alternatives to repairing that planet of yours, Mr. DeWoe. It's true that our own farms do not provide enough for the world's population, especially here, with those confounded beasts continually breaking into the crop areas—"

"The government pays us for all the damage they do," his daughter pointed out.

"Point granted, Doris. We do get reimbursed, so the people in Nairobi can keep their precious animals alive to show the tourists. Not reimbursed as well as we properly should, perhaps, but that's not the point. The point is that the food we grow then goes into the mouths of elephants and hippos, and not of people. Oh," he said, gazing expansively around his table, "we do ourselves well enough here, I suppose.

What we don't eat the servants do, and what they can't swill down themselves they steal for their families. I imagine four or five hundred people have a taste from our kitchens now and then. Still, the population grows faster than the food resources, doesn't it? And so we have to provide for the future. I suppose, Mr. DeWoe," he said kindly to Dekker, "that the notion of growing crops on Mars must have seemed very attractive at first. My father believed so, I'm afraid. That was why he put so much of our capital into the Bonds. But now . . ." He shrugged and smiled.

And then Doris was demanding that Dekker tell them all what life on Mars was like, *really*, and he never did get a chance to hear more of what the "but now" could possibly refer to.

By the next afternoon Dekker had learned many things, though not that one. He had learned what the word was that Mr. Ngemba thought so offensive. "It's a bad word," Walter told him at breakfast, glancing around. "I don't like to say it when the servants might hear, so I'll spell it out. N-I-G-G-E-R. Don't ever use it, please."

"I never have," Dekker said. "I didn't think anyone did, either, not even in those citizenship classes. After all, that story's about a time long ago. People had different standards then."

"Well, we don't have those standards here, Dekker. Please."

"Sure," Dekker said, inspecting his meal. That was one of the other things he had learned, what a proper English breakfast was like. It included covered dishes containing killed-animal things like "kippers" and "kidneys" as well as large quantities of toasted bread and tea. Under Doris's attentive tutelage he had learned, almost, to swim, though not to swim well, of course, since there was not enough fat on his lean Martian frame for buoyancy. Simply staying afloat took vigorous effort. He had had a taste, all too brief a taste, of the "game room," where Walter had displayed, among other things, what wealthy Earthies owned in the way of virtuals. He had learned what "tennis" was, though he was excused from actually playing the game on the grounds of fragility, while Mrs. Ngemba and her two step-children took turns on the court. He wasn't excused from croquet, though. That turned out to be the kind of game a Martian could play—it was skill and precision that counted, no brute strength involved—and he managed to beat both Doris Ngemba and her brother through the final wicket.

Lunch was on the terrace, with the adults all pleasingly absent. When it was over Walter said, "I promised you we'd study, Dekker. Shall we do it?"

Surprisingly, Walter was serious about it, and Dekker found that studying with a friend was a big improvement over sitting all alone before the screen in his father's apartment. Dekker was better at math than Walter Ngemba, but the Kikuyu boy came into his own when they turned to planetary astronomy. Dekker was surprised at how much Walter Ngemba knew about the moons of the gas giants, the orbital patterns of asteroids, and especially about the dimensions and characteristics of the planets themselves. It was not a subject that Dekker had spent much time on. It didn't seem useful. Dekker could see that it was possibly interesting as a matter of scientific curiosity, but he had no personal intention of venturing anywhere near any of the less benign planets.

Walter had no such reservations. He knew as much about the gas giants as about the Earthlike ones. He rattled off radii, masses, orbital periods, and chemical compositions of everything from Saturn through Pluto as handily as though they related to stock on his father's farm.

The studying went so well they kept it up right through dinner, which, at Walter's suggestion, they had brought to them in Walter's study. It had never occurred to Dekker that that might be an option, and he was delighted to be spared the company of the elders.

"You seem to be really fond of astronomy," Dekker said, finishing the last bites of his omelet.

He hadn't meant anything by it, but Walter flushed. "Aren't you?" he asked.

"Well, sure. Sort of. When I was a kid I used to spend a lot of time out on the plains at night, looking up at the stars."

"So did I. Hell, Dekker, I still do. Listen, it's dark; finish your coffee—or take it with you—and we'll go out on the terrace."

It wasn't quite full dark; a hint of a dull purplish glow still hung over the western escarpment. But the stars were out and so were the comets, more of them than ever, and Dekker regarded every one of them with proprietary pleasure.

"Great sky. It's almost as clear here as it is at Sagdayev," he commented.

"I'd like to see Sagdayev sometime," Walter said wistfully. Dekker didn't respond to that; of course, a rich Earthie could take a tourist trip to Mars anytime he liked— maybe even get the hard-pressed Martian economy to pick up the bill for it, if he wanted to and if Mr. Theodore Ngemba still owned any of the Bonds. But it didn't seem polite to say that to his friend.

He leaned over the rail, peering out onto the dark plain. Nothing was moving there, though he could picture in his mind a vision of that hunting lion he had seen by the airstrip slipping noiselessly through the brush. There was a warm breeze coming up from the plains, but the night was silent. Dekker could hear only a faint sound of conversation from the card room inside, where Doris was playing canasta with her stepmother, and the distant *zzzt, zzzt* of insects being incinerated in the bug zappers scattered around the grounds.

"There's Mars," Walter said, pointing at the sky.

Dekker was startled. "Where?" And when he'd located it—bright enough, but pale yellow rather than red, he thought, hanging close below the far-brighter white dot that was Jupiter—he gazed wonderingly. So tiny and so distant, but still his own whole world.

"Tell me about Mars," Walter ordered.

So Dekker tried to describe Sagdayev for his friend, and then Walter Ngemba talked about his own life. Dekker was surprised to find that the people he had met were not Walter's whole family. He had two younger sisters. Both of them were living with their mother, Theodore Ngemba's first wife, in a villa at one of the fashionable resorts in the Seychelles. During the school week he stayed with an aunt in Nairobi—she was the one who supplied the pale blue limousine. He had a privileged life, he admitted. And yet he wanted more.

He did not say what "more" was, and Dekker did not ask, either. After they had been silent for a while, Dekker turned to him, thinking to mention that it was about time for bed.

Walter was staring raptly at the comets. Dekker had been about to say something to him, but the yearning expression on the Kenyan boy's face stopped him. But what in the world did a rich Earthie have to yearn for?

The Sunday morning breakfast was a leisurely affair, with the adults drinking champagne and Mr. Theodore Ngemba holding forth. He had been watching the early news as he dressed and was not satisfied. "Citizenship training," he announced, "is not doing its job. Have you seen the stories? It's just one kind of violence cropping up after another, all over the world. Right now there's a major strike going on in a place called Khalistan, whatever that is."

"It's in India," his daughter informed him. "They're striking because they want independence—like Mara."

"Mara," Mr. Ngemba said, contempt in his voice. "What foolishness."

Walter saw Dekker's confusion and explained. "Mara is something the Masai say they want, Dekker. This is Mara. The Masai want to have their own country, independent of Kenya, and they call it Mara."

"Yes," his father said, "and what would they do with this Mara if they had it? The Masai have no industry, no universities, no real culture. They can't even run a farm properly themselves."

"The ones in our school seem bright enough," Dekker offered.

"Perhaps the very few elite, yes," Mr. Ngemba conceded generously, and clearly conscious of his generosity. "But how many are there of those?"

Mrs. Kurai chuckled. "Enough to throw you out if they all got together, Theodore," she said. "Just like your great-great-grandfather threw out the English."

He smiled back at her. "But, you see, my dear Dolores, they can't. The Masai don't have any Mau Mau to do the trick for them, and if any of them tried to start one we'd just put the rascals in for rehabilitation until they got the notion out of their heads."

There were more questions there than Dekker wanted to ask in this group. He bode his time until he and Walter were alone before asking for explanations. Walter looked slightly

embarrassed. "Oh, the Mau Mau. Yes, several of our ancestors were Mau Mau—had to be, didn't they, or our family
wouldn't have amounted to much afterward. It was a political thing. You see, Kenya used to be an English colony,
until a man named Jomo Kenyatta organized the Kikuyu
into the organization they called the Mau Mau, to drive the
English out."

"By calling a strike, like these people in Khalistan?"

Walter looked at him in astonishment. "Hell, no, Dekker.
By killing enough English to make them decide it cost too
much to stay. I thought you'd know that. The Mau Mau
would just gather around some English farmhouse one quiet
night and butcher everybody inside, and then they'd be gone
before the troops could get there. Bloody business, yes, but
it worked. A few years of trying to catch those chaps and the
English took the hint and packed it in."

Dekker was speechless. When Walter saw the look on his
face he added quickly, "That was a long time ago, of course.
Things are different now."

"I hope so," Dekker said.

"Well, they are. Listen," Walter said, forcefully changing
the subject, "I think we've done enough studying for one
weekend, and I don't want to subject you to more of my
father than is strictly necessary. What say we take a safari
van and take a tour around the game trails?"

They did, and, with Walter driving, it was an experience.
Bumping over the potholed game trails Dekker wondered if
he could keep the breakfast down, but the bizarre things he
saw made him forget his discomfort. Dekker spotted the
corpse of a little antelope kind of animal in a tree, and when
he asked about it Walter called, "That's a leopard kill. They
put the animals they catch up there for safekeeping, but
we're not likely to see an actual leopard today, though."
They didn't. However, they did see elephants, thirty or forty
of them at a time, wandering slowly across the brush and
munching vegetation as they went. They saw hippos in the
bend of a river, with a loglike creature, as still as though
stuffed, patiently watching from the bank. "It's a croc,"
Walter said. "It's hoping to catch a baby hippo off by itself." They saw antelopes of many kinds, and buffalo, and

giraffes—infinitely taller, when seen from the ground, than they had appeared from the plane on the way up.

If you left out the animals and the heat—and, of course, the air—Dekker thought, you could almost imagine you were on Mars. The plains looked quite a lot like the rose-rust slopes around Sagdayev, if it hadn't been for the scraggly vegetation that cropped up all around. It almost made him homesick. And then Walter stopped the van and glanced at his watch. "I've been thinking," he said, and stopped there.

Dekker took his opportunity. "So have I," he said. "Walter? What did your father and Mrs. Kurai mean about the Oort project?"

Walter looked embarrassed. "I wondered if you'd ask about that. They've been selling off their interests in the project, I think. Well, no. I mean, they really have. They're not satisfied about the financial prospects. It has something to do with those new habitat things."

Dekker stared at him. He had heard of the habitats, of course, everyone had: tin-can things in space, orbiting Earth sometimes or perhaps not orbiting anything much at all, completely self-sufficient. "They're talking about growing crops on the habitats," Walter explained. "Father's invested in them rather heavily, I think. Supposed to be more economical than growing on Mars, with all that shipping—and, of course, the habitat farms would be a lot quicker to pay off."

"But that's not the point," Dekker said sensibly. "Mars is a whole *planet.* I know we're supposed to pay off the Bonds with crops—and we will, with interest, too, don't forget that—but that's not all of it. We'll have a whole new *world*!"

"Of course," Walter said. "I'm just telling you what Father says." He hesitated and changed the subject. "You'll be leaving the school soon, won't you?" he asked.

"I will?"

"Well, that's what Mr. Cummings said. To take your Oort training, I mean."

"I suppose I will," Dekker said slowly, wondering how it happened that this boy knew as much of his plans as he did.

Walter nodded. "You know," he said, "I wasn't going to say anything—and, for God's sake, please don't breathe a word about it at home—but there's just a chance I might see you there. Fact is, I've been hoping to take a shot at Oort training myself."

"What does your father think of that?"

Walter looked glum. "He doesn't know yet. He'll hate the idea. But I'll be of age this fall, and then I'm going to apply."

Dekker studied him. "Good luck," he said. "Is that what you were thinking of?"

"What?"

"You said, 'I've been thinking.'"

"Oh." Walter grinned, and glanced at his watch again. "No, what I was thinking about was something else. Look, Dekker, I saw the way you've been looking at Doris. She's a terrible flirt, but of course she's much too young for, well, anything—not even to mention how Father would feel. But there are other possibilities."

Dekker was baffled—a little resentful, too, because he certainly had had no particular intention of ever going any farther with Doris Ngemba than looking. "What kind of possibilities?" he demanded.

"I'll show you," Walter said, looking happily guilty, and started the van up. And in ten minutes they were in a village of thatched-roof huts set in a circle around a plaza of trampled earth, with idle Masai men drowsing in the afternoon sun and Masai women bustling around. There were flies all over, and a pervasive stink. "Cow dung," Walter said, grinning. "They use it to plaster their huts." Walter stopped the van and got out, Dekker following.

Walter looked around, and then pointed at one hut. "They'll take care of you in there," he said. The man outside it had climbed to his feet and was nodding to Walter. "That's Sheila's place. You'll like her; there's another one in the next hut over I'll take."

"Take?" said Dekker, beginning to understand but unwilling to commit himself until he was sure.

"That's how they make their living," Walter said impatiently. "What else do they have to sell but sex? If it's the money you're thinking of, don't give it another thought; it's my shout, of course. You're my guest. But, I say, you've had your hi-vac, haven't you?"

"Hi-vac?"

"HIV vaccine. Oh, hell. You haven't, have you? Well, hang on a minute." He stepped over to the hut, whispered for a moment with the man at the door, and came back with a pack of condoms. "Wear one of these, Dekker. Just don't kiss her, you'll be all right." He stopped to think. "Oh, listen—you're a Martian—these things only come in one size, but they stretch. They'll fit you all right, won't they?"

So when Dekker got back to his father's flat that night he had learned an additional new skill: not only croquet, swimming, and the art of selecting the right fork at a formal dinner, but how to patronize a prostitute. It had been a very educational weekend.

His education, though, was not quite complete. He had questions for his father, and was pleased to see that, though there was a bottle on the table beside him, and an empty glass, Boldon DeWoe was very nearly sober.

The first question was mostly rhetorical: "Is it true that they're actually going to go ahead with that idea of growing crops for Earth in space habitats?"

His father looked surprised, then depressed. "They say so. The Japanese are supposed to be starting to do it already, but it looks to me like it's still mostly talk. You saw the program on the screen. Anyway, I still think they've got too much invested in Mars now; they won't be able to stop it."

"And did you tell the school I'm leaving?"

His father's expression changed—a little guilty, a little resentful. "Somebody's been telling stories, hey? No. I didn't tell the school. I did tell Brian Cummings about it, because I needed his cooperation."

"What kind of cooperation?" Dekker demanded.

His father shrugged. "Just cooperation. Anyway, it's true. You've gone about as far as you can go here. We're going to Denver."

"Denver?"

"It's in Colorado," his father snapped. "In America. Where the Oort headquarters are."

"I know where the Oort headquarters are," Dekker said stiffly.

"I hope to God so," his father said. "That's where you have to go to take your psych test and your entrance examination, and you'd better pass them both, Dek, because getting us set up there is going to cost a pisspot."

"Can you afford it?"

"It's about the only thing I can afford," his father said sourly; he looked thirstily at his bottle, but didn't drink.

18.

SUPPOSE YOU WERE put in charge of a vast corporation that proposed to tweak comets out of the Oort cloud and carry them a few billion kilometers away to bring air and water to the planet Mars. It's a huge project. Take all its widespread parts together and it barely fits within the extreme boundaries of the entire solar system, but it needs a particular place it can call a home. It needs a headquarters.

If you had to choose where that headquarters should go, where, in all that vast space, would you put it?

Several competing choices might occur to you at once, all of them good. First, you might put the headquarters out in the Oort cloud itself, where the miners tagged the likeliest comets and the snake handlers threaded them with instruments and Augenstein drives and sent them down toward their destiny on Mars. A somewhat inconvenient location to get to, true, but that would be where the raw materials were located.

Or you might put the headquarters somewhere near one of the two Co-Mars satellites, the pair of control stations that sit in Mars's own orbit at its Trojan points, a hundred and twenty degrees away from each other, and each sixty degrees from Mars. That's where the incomings are nursed all the way from the Oort and around the Sun and back up toward Mars itself.

Or, finally, you might even put your headquarters in orbit around the planet Mars itself, where the final fine-tuning and demolition took place before each impact.

All good spots . . . but none of them was the spot the Oort Corporation finally chose. They chose a mountaintop outside of Denver, Colorado, U.S.A., Earth. Right at the bottom of Earth's gravity well. Right on the surface of the revolving Earth itself, so that for half of each day the planet they were sitting on obscured their line-of-sight communications to half the solar system, and so they could communicate with their satellites only by relay.

Oh, that site had defects, to be sure. But it had one great advantage not shared by any possible orbital alternative:

The headquarters of Oortcorp sat firmly on their own planet, where they alone could control it, and where no one could ever question who owned it.

19.

DENVER WAS A whole other thing from Nairobi—colder, damper, the people conspicuously whiter—but Dekker DeWoe didn't have much time for sightseeing. He and his father didn't have that much money left, either, so they took the blimp instead of a supersonic fixed-wing airliner and got there just about in time to locate a furnished room and get ready for the first hurdle Dekker had to pass.

That was the psychological test, and "ready" was an exaggeration of his condition. To take the test Dekker had to drag himself out of bed on four hours' sleep and ride a bus halfway up the mountain, and then the Earthie woman administering the test—who said her name was *Doctor* Rosa McCune—started by ordering him to take his clothes off. "That's right," she said, "all of them. Get naked, DeWoe. What's the matter, are you ashamed of your body?"

Of course, that had never occurred to Dekker, who had only been thinking that this examining room was cold even by Martian standards. He could think of no good reason to say that, and good probable reasons for not, so he simply followed her orders. While he was stripping down the woman studied him and made a little speech. "Dekker DeWoe," she said, "assum-

ing you get into the program, and assuming you stay in it—and
the chances are you won't do either of these things, so don't get
your hopes up—you'll have these psychological tests often.
Not regularly. I didn't say that; there won't be anything regular
about them. But often. The reason for that, of course, is that
the career you're applying for is very demanding. Weak people
can't cut it, and when we find weakies we kick them out. Do
you understand that?"

"Sure," Dekker said, grinning.

She made a note on her keypad—about, he supposed, the
fact that he was smiling, so he stopped. Then she went on.
"However, I should point out that this particular test is different from any other. Would you like to know why?"

"I suppose I would," Dekker agreed. He tried again to sup-
press his grin, although it was certainly amusing that the
woman not only had made him take all his clothes off—even
the leg braces—but had not even allowed him to sit down.

"The difference is," she said precisely, "that this time you
knew in advance you would be tested, so you had a chance to
prepare yourself for it. You won't have forewarning again.
Now do you see that wall screen? Take the controller in your
hand. When I tell you to start, press the switch and then keep
the cursor within the target circle until I tell you to stop."

Dekker looked at the blank screen. "What cursor—?" he
began, but she was already saying:

"Start."

The screen flashed into light at once and Dekker blinked at
it. Most of the screen was filled with a multihued dazzle pattern
of shifting shapes and intensities, but he made out the moving
pale green circle—the only circle on the screen—and the bright
golden point that had to be the cursor. The hand controller was
an unfamiliar design, but Dekker solved it quickly enough and
brought it within the circle . . . and kept it there, pretty well,
though not easily. What made it hard wasn't only that the circle
moved unpredictably, but that the psychologist was paying no
attention to him. Indeed, she yawned and moved toward the
window and then began to change her clothes before him. A
loud bang behind him distracted him for a second; when he had
decided that was a deliberate attempt to break his concentration the screen itself flickered, went out for a second, then
reappeared in a whole new configuration. Then the door
opened and a man appeared, pushed his way between Dekker

and the screen and began a loud conversation with the psychologist, now down to her underwear. . . .

It went on like that. Interminably. And when it was over *Doctor* Rosa McCune, without pause, began administering the written test, which was even longer and more boring—and he had to stay naked and standing on his weary legs through all of that, too.

"Of course," Dekker told his father when he was back in the little furnished room they had taken, "they were trying to shake me up, I know that. Being naked and all. And making me stand up without the braces."

"They're tough on Martians," his father said. "You have to get used to that."

"I will. Well, I am, pretty much. Anyway, I think I can get along without the braces a lot of the time now. It was all pretty funny, too. Like the questions on the test: 'When did you last talk to God?' And, 'Are your stools black and tarry?' They must have a sense of humor, anyway."

"All psychological tests are funny. Psychology's a funny subject," his father said, and paused to cough for a moment. He cleared his throat, refilled his glass, and said, "The important thing is that you passed."

"I don't know that for sure. She didn't say anything."

"She didn't say you failed, so you passed. Anyway, you're a Martian. Naturally you can handle stress." Boldon DeWoe got up and limped over to the tiny refrigerator for more ice cubes. He was looking frailer and sicker than ever, Dekker saw. This climate wasn't good for him.

"How long are you going to stay here?" Dekker asked.

"Until you get into the academy. Now, listen. I've hired a tutor for you, his name is Marcus Hagland; he got through the course himself, but before he got assigned they threw him out on some charge or other. You're going to have to keep on studying, Dek."

"I know."

"I know you know," his father said, sitting down again with a sigh. "Did you ever hear what the Martians here call this place?"

"I didn't know there were any Martians here."

"The smart ones aren't, they left Denver long ago. But the ones that are left call it 'Danktown.' That's what it is, cold and dank and miserable. I hated it while I was training, and I hate it worse now. At least thank God it isn't snowing."

"I wouldn't mind seeing snow," Dekker said.

His father nodded. "I felt the same way once," he said. "When I first came here." He paused, looking at his son, then he smiled. "Dek, do you remember I gave you a present when I left? A little stuffed animal?"

"I called it Brave Bear," Dekker said, suddenly uncomfortable; he was not used to sentimental reminiscences from this long-lost father.

"I don't suppose you still have it," his father said, almost wistfully.

"Well, I do, though. I mean, not here. But I never gave it away."

His father nodded. Dekker couldn't tell whether or not he was pleased. His father sipped his drink, then said, "About those Martians in Denver. They can't do us any good, Dek, and we don't have time to be social. Marcus will be around in the morning, and then all you're going to be able to do between now and the examination is study."

That was true enough, it turned out. The tutor arrived and stayed all day, and the whole day was spent on studying. Dekker wasn't sure he liked the tutor. Marcus Hagland was Martian, but uncharacteristically glum, almost even hostile. He had a cough almost as bad as Boldon DeWoe's, and when Dekker took advantage of a break to ask him why he stayed in Denver he would only say, "Things are going to change."

"Change how?" Dekker asked, but Marcus only shook his head.

"The only way they *can* change," he said. "Now let's get back to your trajectory curves. For a first approximation you can ignore everything but the major planets within a hundred million kilometers or so of your trajectory and the Sun itself, but then, when you need to pin down the deltas for your correction burns—"

And so on, and on. After the first few days Dekker began to wonder if there really was a city outside the furnished room. The room itself wasn't much smaller than the flat in Nairobi had been, but it smelled worse and it was colder.

The colder part was a plus; Dekker had never adjusted to Kenyan heat. The other big plus was that if Dekker crawled out onto the fire escape and leaned as far as he could over the rusted rail he could see the distant mountain that was capped by the Oort headquarters. He couldn't really see the headquarters, of course, just an occasional glint of reflected light from a window when the sun was just right. But it was there. It was where he had taken the psych test, and it was where he was going—if he passed the entrance examination.

At which point, each time he came to it, he dragged himself back to his screen for more study. Busy as he was, Dekker was not too busy to observe that his father was not only coughing more than ever but drinking heavily. That observation was not made in person, because Boldon DeWoe did very little drinking in the furnished room they shared. What he did was to go out by himself—"So I won't interrupt you while you're working, Dek"—and come home coughing and staggering.

The only good part of that was that his father had become a touch more mellow, mellow enough that sometimes, when he came home smelling of whatever cheap liquor he had been drinking, he was even willing to be sociable with his son.

Dekker liked that part. He liked hearing his father talk about his time in the Oort—not about the accident and the drugs, but about the companionship, the sense of purpose, the excitement.

"I guess you wish you were back there, sometimes," Dekker offered, and his father glared at him.

"Hell, boy! What's the use of wishing?" But then he softened. "If I were going to wish for something, I'd wish you were in the academy already so I could get out of here and go back to Kenya. Maybe get to know your fancy Mau Mau friends and get invited out to their farm."

It was the first time Dekker had heard his father use the term "Mau Mau." "I didn't know you knew about the Mau Mau," he said.

"How can you live in Nairobi and not know? Most of them don't talk about the Mau Mau much anymore. They don't like to remind anybody that their ancestors went around raping little girls and butchering babies. But you can't blame them too much for that. It was a long time ago. The whole planet was different. Everybody was still fighting wars here then, and some of them were a lot worse than anything the Mau Mau did."

Dekker shook his head. "The way they feel about each other, I don't see how they ever stopped having wars."

"Well, they didn't have any choice, Dek," his father said,

pausing to blow his nose. "Fighting wars got to be bad for business. It didn't used to be. Wars used to be *good* for business, or they thought so, but then they got too big and there was just too much disruption. So they started the Peacekeepers. People get too unruly, they just throw them into rehabilitation until they calm down."

"But—" Dekker began, and then had to wait while his father got through a fit of coughing.

"But what?" Boldon DeWoe wheezed finally, his face red and eyes streaming.

If Dekker had had a question, he had forgotten it in concern for this father. "Are you all right?"

"Christ, no. How can I be all right in this goddam climate?" his father demanded. "Dek, listen. I think I'm going to have to lie down for a while, but first I've got something for you." Painfully he limped over to the closet, pulled out his pack, fumbled at the lock. He was sweating and clumsy. It took him three tries to get the combination right, but then he pulled out a cartridge in its sealed envelope.

"This is what you're going to study," he ordered. "Tell Marcus to work out all the exercises with you tomorrow. He can explain anything you don't understand."

Dekker fitted the cartridge into his machine and looked doubtfully at the screen. "What is it?"

"What does it look like?" What it looked very much like, Dekker thought, was a copy of an entry test for the Oort program. There was a list of fifty questions scrolling up the screen, and they weren't simple multiple-guess choices. Most of them called for complicated calculations or essay answers and all of them were hard.

Dekker gave his father a suspicious look. "Where did you get this?"

The old man was breathing hard now, but he managed a cocky grin. "I'd say that's nothing you have to bother about, Dek. It came from a friend. A lady friend." He started to turn away, then looked back at his son. "But you know something? The lady isn't a bad looker. You might've missed a pretty good chance there, boy."

"Who? What chance?" Dekker demanded, but his father was coughing again.

"Never mind," Boldon gasped. "Dek, I can't talk now. Just get on with it, will you? I'm going to bed."

And Dekker did get on with it, wonderingly, while his father was wheezing and coughing on the far side of the room, with his face turned away. He made up his mind that he was going to have a showdown on this as soon as his father was in shape to answer. Meanwhile he worked at the questions until he was too tired to think anymore.

His father seemed sound asleep. Dekker pulled the blanket over him, then lay down in his own bed, closed his eyes, was asleep in a moment . . . and woke up in the middle of the night, thinking he had heard something.

The room was very quiet. Alarmed, Dekker got up and peered at his father's cot.

It was empty.

While he was sleeping his father had got up and gone out again, and, in the morning, was still gone . . . and did not show up all that day.

When Marcus Hagland turned up for the day's cramming he knew nothing about Boldon DeWoe's whereabouts. "What are you asking me for, DeWoe? Your old man and I aren't close friends. It's just a business relationship. Did you report him missing?"

"Who would I report it to?"

"The Peacekeepers, for Christ's sake. Who else? Still," Hagland added comfortably, "I wouldn't be in any hurry to bother about that if I were you anyway. He probably passed out on some barroom floor and he'll show up when he feels like it." That was all he had to say on the subject of Boldon DeWoe, and he turned to the cartridge Boldon had given his son. He began to grin. "Looks like he does have some friends, anyway," he said. "What'd he pay for this?"

"I don't know." That was the simple truth, Dekker thought, though he also thought that the truth would be unpleasantly far from simple if he ever learned it.

Hagland nodded, with the faint half smile of a tolerant accomplice. "Maybe you just don't ask questions like that? Or," he said, looking thoughtful as his tone changed, "maybe I've misjudged you and your old man both. It looks to me like the two of you are willing to bend a few rules for a good purpose. Do you take after him, DeWoe?"

"My father wouldn't break any laws!"

"No? Whatever you say, but how about yourself, then?"

"I don't know what you're trying to say."

Marcus took his time about responding to that, studying Dekker. Then he said, "It's simple. You might be able to do some good if you wanted to. You know the Earthies are screwing around with the project. Suppose you could do something to straighten that situation out—say, maybe something that might be pretty much against the law. Would you be willing to take a chance?"

"On breaking the law? No. And," Dekker added, disliking this man, "if anyone seriously asked me to break a law I think that's when I would start thinking about talking to the Peacekeepers."

The tutor looked at him with sour contempt, then shrugged. "Okay," he said. "Forget I asked. Let's get to work." He scrolled the screen to the first question. "Here we are. 'Spectral analysis shows the following concentrations in a target comet. Evaluate for suitability.' Show me how you'd start your evaluation."

And so they began the session, and as the day wore on Dekker's dislike of his tutor receded, replaced by growing worry about his father. It wasn't until Marcus had gone, and Dekker was fixing himself something to eat late that night, that it occurred to him that perhaps he should take the man's half-hearted advice after all and report his father's absence to the Peacekeepers.

Who knew all about it, it turned out.

The night clerk at their local precinct had the records right there. Boldon DeWoe had managed to go farther than even the usual tolerance for drunks allowed. He had been arrested for starting a fistfight in a barroom—a *fistfight*! The trial was already over; Boldon DeWoe had been convicted and sentenced to rehabilitation, and he was already beginning to serve his time in the Colorado Rehabilitation Facility, in a place called Pueblo.

Pueblo wasn't that far from Denver, but the price of the train ride knocked a big hole in Dekker's few remaining credits. He couldn't help that. He didn't hesitate; he knew at once what he had to do, and at the crack of dawn the next morning he was on his way. It was his father.

Dekker DeWoe had never been in a maglev train before. The ride took him through tunnels and on bridges across deep,

wooded valleys, and—he observed, without feeling much pleasure in it—the scenery was magnificent. The ride could have
been a joyous new experience for Dekker DeWoe . . . if only
there had been enough collateral joy anywhere else in his life to
let him appreciate it.

There wasn't. Wherever Dekker looked his life was troubled,
and the worry about his father was only the newest and most
urgent of his problems. Conscience made him try to study on
his pocket screen as he rode, but his mind wouldn't stay concentrated. He gave up, put the reader back in his pocket, and
closed his eyes.

He dozed for the last fifty kilometers of the trip, and got out,
stiff and aching, in Pueblo's noisy terminal. The city of Pueblo
turned out to be only a smaller, slightly less dingy Denver, and
it took him half an hour to find out just where the rehabilitation
facility was and to locate the cheapest way of getting to it. The
Pueblo people weren't that helpful, either. Clearly none of them
had ever heard of the Pledge of Assistance, and when he did
manage to get one of them to talk to him long enough to
discover that there was a bus that went to the door of the
facility he arrived at the terminal just in time to see one pull out.

It was an hour before the next one, and he nearly missed that
one, too, because he fell asleep in the hot, crowded waiting
room. Then it was half an hour more, after many stops, before
the hot and crowded bus reached the gate of the facility.

Dekker was the only person to get off there. A Peacekeeper
was standing before the barred gate, gazing at him without
pleasure. When Dekker limped up to him, his braces heavier
than ever, the man didn't respond to his greeting; he just nodded and tugged at the amulet around Dekker's neck before
Dekker had a chance to remove it and hand it to him. The
Peacekeeper thrust it into a hand-reader and studied the results.
"Dekker DeWoe," the man read from his screen. "You're a
Martian, aren't you? We don't get many Martians here."

"I hope not," Dekker said.

The man wasn't listening. He released the amulet and said,
"You can go on in. Go straight to the main door and don't
leave the walk. There are alarms, and you don't want to set
them off."

Then there was the long walk along a gravel path to the main
building, creamy-white and featureless. Evidently there were a
lot of people in need of rehabilitation in Colorado, for the

building was huge. Six stories at least, Dekker thought, though
it was hard to be sure since the facility didn't have any windows
that Dekker could see. And when he was admitted he was kept
waiting for nearly an hour before a clerk consented to see him.
"Yes," the woman said, nodding, "he's here. Boldon DeWoe.
You're his son?"

"Yes."

"Well, let's hope you can do better than your father. He got
picked up because he committed an act of violence at a place
called Rosie's Bar and Grill in Denver. Convicted, Fifth Munic-
ipal Court, Justice Harmon; got the usual indeterminate sentence."

Dekker blinked. "Indeterminate sentence? What does that
mean?"

She shrugged. "It means he stays here until he's rehabilitated.
Whenever that is. Let's see, it's his third conviction"—Dekker
blinked again; his father had said nothing about previous con-
victions—"so he isn't likely to get out very fast. I'd say he'll be
with us for at least three months, probably, maybe six or more
if he gives any trouble. But maybe he won't. He can't get
anything to drink in here, and it looks like he generally keeps
his nose clean when he's sober. I suppose you want to see him."

"That's what I came here for, yes."

The clerk cocked an eyebrow at him, but only said, "You can
have a ten-minute meeting in the interview room. You can't
have it now, though. Rehabilitees aren't permitted to leave their
units during cycle hours, so you have to wait until the cycle
ends. That'll be at half past six."

"Half past *six*?"

"You do want to see him, don't you?" Then, almost kindly,
she added, "His shift's at meal now. You can look in on them
if you want. Up two flights, where it says 'Mess'; don't go
anywhere else, because there are alarms. There's a viewing
window there."

There was. There was a whole viewing gallery, in fact, with
a one-way mirror that allowed them to look in on the vast
dining hall, and about twenty people there to look through it.
Most of the people watching were visitors like Dekker himself,
but four were guards, laughing among themselves, but their
eyes were roaming over the prisoners, alert for infractions.

There were at least five hundred prisoners at meal, seated
stiffly erect on backless benches at bare wooden trestle tables.

If Boldon DeWoe was among them, Dekker could not pick him out. The rehabilitees were of all kinds—old and young, male and female, skins of all the colors human beings came in—but they all looked alike from behind the one-way window: silent, quick in their movements, eyes fixed on their plates, almost like machines. At a harsh beep they all rose quickly and filed out of the room.

That was when Dekker recognized his father at last—when he stood up to leave, though he was limping and bowed, he was enough taller than those around him to stand out—though there were, surprisingly, three or four other Martians in the room. Boldon DeWoe looked old and sick, Dekker thought worriedly.

Then the Peacekeepers stood up. "Show's over," one of them called. "On your way, people. We need to get this place cleaned up."

Everyone else seemed to know what to do. They turned and headed for the exit, but Dekker tarried. "Excuse me," he said to the Peacekeeper. "I'm waiting to see my father."

The man stared at him. "Rehabilitees aren't permitted to leave their groups until the cycle's over," he said.

"I know that."

The Peacekeeper shrugged. "There's a visitors' lounge. One flight down, and don't try to go anywhere else; there are alarms. But he won't be able to see you until six or so."

"I know that, too," Dekker said. Most of the visitors were already gone, but as Dekker attached himself to the tail of the group he saw another door open. Six men and women in inmates' uniforms were waiting there, mops and brooms in their hands, their heads cast down. None of them was his father.

"Step it up," the Peacekeeper called. "They can't come in until you're all out, and they've got work to do."

The visitors' lounge was large enough for several dozen people, but the only other person in it was an elderly woman who was eating her lunch. She looked up at Dekker three or four times before she said, "Didn't you bring anything to eat?"

"I didn't think I was going to be here this long."

"They never tell you anything ahead of time, do they?" She considered for a minute, and then offered him half of a sweet roll. The price for that was conversation, but Dekker was glad enough to pay it. The woman knew the ropes. All those other people watching the rehabilitees eat? They just came in for that, to have a look at whoever it was dear to them now undergoing rehabilitation; each inmate was limited to one outside contact a month, but still you did want to see them now and then, didn't you? The one she was going to see today was her daughter, and, yes, she knew all about the place—had been there twice herself in her younger days. It wasn't so bad. It wasn't *good*, either, because the guards were always trying to get you to start a fight, or at least talk back—when they weren't spilling things on the floor or pushing over a pile of laundry just to make you have to do everything over. But you could stand it, mostly. And hardly anybody ever had to stay there more than a year.

When she had finished her lunch she gathered up the crumbs—"They'll just have to clean them up if I don't, you know"—and pulled two chairs together to make a place to go to sleep.

Leaving Dekker to his own thoughts. But he didn't like them, and so doggedly he pulled out his screen and immersed himself in trajectory planning and impact analysis, while slowly the room filled around him . . . and his time was being eroded away.

When the Peacekeeper finally bawled his name he was admitted to a tiny visiting room, and his father was sitting there already—as far as Dekker could see, older and sicker still. They were given two facing wooden chairs, a meter and a half apart, and they weren't allowed to touch. There was no guard present to enforce the rule, but one of those windows was set into the wall, and Dekker had no doubt there was someone behind it. "Hello, Dad," he said. "How are you?"

It was a rhetorical question. Boldon DeWoe's eyes were bloodshot and he looked ten years older than he had forty-eight hours before. He was still wheezing, but all he said was, "Well enough," and stopped there, leaving Dekker to try to think of something to say.

Ten minutes was not very much time, but even so there was not enough conversation available between them to fill it all up. After all, what was there to say? His father acknowledged that he had been guilty of the infractions charged—that took ten seconds, at most—and Dekker said he was keeping up his studies, and then there wasn't much left. Only at parting Dekker was galvanized into speech.

"Look," he said desperately, "things aren't so bad. You'll be out of here in a couple of months, with any luck at all, and then you can start taking care of yourself. I'll be in the program by then, so you won't have to worry about me."

"Sure, Dek," his father said.

"I'll pass the test. I promise."

His father nodded.

"So then you can go back to Nairobi, get out of this cold, wet climate—"

"Right."

Dekker shook his head. "Dad," he said, "I *care* about you."

His father was silent for a moment. Then he said, "I know you do," and looked around, and then quickly stepped up to his son, flung his arms around him, and kissed him on the cheek.

When he stepped back he was grinning. "That'll put at least an extra ten days on my time, I guess," he said, "but it was worth it."

20.

THE NEXT MORNING, back in the furnished room in Dank-town, Dekker awoke to a hammering on the door. When he got his braces on and had limped over to open it Marcus Hagland was there, looking accusing. "What are you doing, sleeping late?" he demanded. "Where were you yesterday?" And when Dekker had explained, Hagland looked angrily amused. "Sure they locked him up," he said. "He's a Martian, isn't he? I bet the guy he was fighting was Jap or Yankee or some other kind of Earthie, and I bet they didn't arrest *him*. You really ought to open your eyes and see what's going on, DeWoe."

Dekker didn't answer that. He shuffled over to the hot plate and asked, "Do you want some coffee?"

"Why not?" But Hagland was watching him closely, and before Dekker had poured it he said, "We'd better talk money first. You owe me for yesterday even if you weren't here; I did my part, I showed up. So let's get this account up to date before we start today."

That took Dekker by surprise. "Oh," he said, "right. I see what you mean. But I can't do anything about that. I don't have enough cues left on my amulet."

"You *what*?"

Dekker said, embarrassed, "Well, my father was the one who paid you, wasn't he? I just had enough for incidentals—and most of that went yesterday."

"Jesus!" Marcus snarled. "How dumb can you be? You saw him; didn't you think of getting him to transfer funds to your account?"

"I'll take care of it right away," Dekker promised.

"Damn right you will. Forget the coffee; you need it more than I do. And I'll be back tomorrow to collect."

It wasn't just a matter of paying Marcus Hagland for tutoring, Dekker realized; he was also going to need money for food. So as soon as he was dressed he went in search of his father's bank.

When he finally found out where it was, the assistant manager was polite but unhelpful. "You see, our problem is that your father's not here to authorize transferring his credit balance," he explained. "From what you say, he's a rehabilitee."

"He *is* a rehabilitee. He's in Pueblo. That's the whole problem."

"Well, rehabilitees' rights are safeguarded by law," the man said primly. "Maybe you are this Boldon DeWoe's son, maybe you aren't. Probably you are—no, Mr. DeWoe, don't bother trying to prove it. That's not the point. What difference does it make if you are? We have to keep in mind that your father may not want you to receive his credit balance."

"But I don't have any other money!"

The assistant manager shrugged in mild sympathy. "If there's nothing else—?" he suggested.

"I don't even have enough to eat on."

"If you could get a notarized statement from your father—"

"He's not allowed to do anything like that! I visited him, and he can't have any other outside contact for the rest of the month."

"A court order, then?"

"How do I get a court order?"

"You retain a lawyer, of course. It's quite simple," the assist-

ant manager told him, looking surprised. But could not tell him
how to "retain" a "lawyer" when he didn't have the money to
"retain" him with.

Back in the empty-feeling room, Dekker was sure that there
had to be a way, if he had the time, and the luck, to find out
what it was—some sort of retrainees'-aid society, or free legal
services for the indigent—*something*.

On the other hand, he didn't want to do any of that. That was
tantamount to accepting Earthie charity, and he was a Martian.
Martians took care of their own problems, and the very idea of
begging for aid made him feel unclean.

In any case, he reminded himself, it was only a matter of four
days until the entrance examination would come up.

Dekker took stock of his resources. The apartment rent was
paid until the end of the month. There was some food in the
little chiller—not enough for four days, but since there was
only himself to eat it perhaps there was enough, maybe, for the
first couple. And, although the trip to Pueblo had mortally
wounded his credit balance, there were a few cues left on his
amulet—if he ate lightly.

If he ate lightly, that was, and if he didn't spend anything at
all on everything *but* food, and if he was careful to save out the
fare to get up to the mountain for the entrance test, and especially if he gave up Marcus's services. That was a given, anyway. A single day's pay to Marcus would have bankrupted him;
the one day of cramming he already owed remained as a considerable grievance in Marcus's eyes, and the tutor flatly refused
to provide any more of his time for any mere promise of even-
tual repayment whenever Boldon DeWoe got out of the correc-
tional facility.

So Dekker did the only thing possible. He closeted himself in
the little room, and he studied. When he was hungry he tried to
put the thought of food out of his mind. Sometimes he succeeded.

Unfortunately, he discovered that he had another growing
appetite, as well. It had been a long time since the Masai village
and Sheila.

The Peacekeeper secretary who had admitted him to the
Pueblo center had not struck him as particularly attractive
when he was there, but for some reason images of her crossed
knees floated before his eyes when they should have been firmly
focused on his screen—of her knees, and of Doris Ngemba's

bare breasts and warm chocolate-colored rump. Even of some of Sheila's more useful parts, though his memories of Sheila were not visual, because it had been dark in the hut.

There were so *many* women in the world, he reflected. Even this harder, nastier world. Surely there was one woman somewhere—perhaps even one right here in Denver, if only he knew where to look for her—who would not object to a little bed time with a fairly healthy and passably good-looking young Martian?

But not for a Martian without any money at all. It was a long four days.

When the test was over and they informed him he had passed and would be able to enter the dormitories the next day, Dekker thanked the proctors and went away. Other candidates were there, rioting and jubilant or slinking away in depression. Dekker didn't talk to any of them.

He hadn't needed to be told that he had passed. He had known it as soon as he looked at the test questions, and confirmed his belief that they were identical to the ones his father had given him to study.

21.

IT COSTS A lot to make a dead planet live again. It takes a tremendous mobilization of talent and treasure.

The treasure is the physical assets, and they are very considerable: the space stations, the spotter ships, the transports, the Augensteins that pull the comets out of their Oort orbits and deliver them as atmospheric replenishment to the surface of Mars, and all the associated tools and instruments and control mechanisms.

The talent is even more costly, because there's a lot of it and it constantly needs to be replenished. To start, there are the crews out in the Oort itself: six hundred miners and snake handlers, plus the mechanics and supervisors and cooks and doctors and all the others that support the miners; there are two hundred and fifty of them to be added in. In each of the co-Mars stations there are another two hundred controllers, plus fifty support personnel, and the same in each of the Mars orbiters. Total personnel in space at any one time thus comes to just about 1,850.

Of course, that doesn't complete Oortcorp's payroll. There are the administrators and the instructors and all their helpers at Denver base, five hundred and more of those. There are the pilots and crews of the resupply ships that feed the stations in space, not to mention the tens of thousands employed by the corporation's suppliers, the people who make the Augensteins and the drill snakes and all the other bits and pieces of equipment that keep the operational teams working; Oortcorp is certainly a major employer.

But it is in space that the academy graduates are employed. If you subtract the support teams, that leaves 1,400 who are operational crews on duty, plus another five or six hundred operational who are on leave, or in transit; and all of these men and women, nearly two thousand of them, have to be trained at Denver base.

As do their replacements. The operational crews don't last forever. Ultimately they retire, or they are invalided out, or they die. The average working life of an operator is less than ten years, and so the academy keeps busy grinding out replacements. They produce only fifteen or twenty a month—no more than they need.

No more than they need, and every one of them is paid for through the Bonds, and thus is a running charge on the future export earnings of the planet Mars . . . whenever those earnings may start.

22.

THE ACADEMY FOR Oort training was tough and demanding, but it was only a school, and by Dekker DeWoe's third week in it he was beginning to feel confident about his prospects. It wasn't that he didn't have worries. The Earthies were having another flurry in their "securities" exchanges, and the news screens were filled with the usual mix of scandals, strikes, bitter lawsuits, and political name-calling. Now and then there was an occasional—actually, quite a lot more than occasional—very unpleasant feeling about the admissions test. And always there was the thought of his father, immured in the Colorado Rehabilitation Facility.

Yet, with all of that, Dekker was very nearly *happy*.

The objective facts justified reasonable pleasure with his lot. He was where he wanted to be, learning what he needed to know to serve his planet. He had a fine place to live, decent meals to eat, even a fifty-cue-a-week stipend from Oortcorp for any little luxuries he might desire, and every hour's training brought him one hour closer to getting out in space to help make Mars green.

Of course, that day of triumph might never arrive for Dekker DeWoe. It surely would not for a fair number of his classmates. Dekker was well aware of the probabilities. It was common knowledge that an average of 10 percent of the students flunked out in each of the six phases of the course, and what he had learned in all those math courses had made it easy for him to estimate what that meant. It meant that it was a statistical probability that nearly half his class would be kicked out before they finished.

Dekker DeWoe simply determined that he was not going to be one of those recurring 10 percents.

Actually, he wasn't in any immediate danger. Dekker was breezing through Phase One, since that was nothing but basic

science review and indoctrination. The review of basic theory
was a snap for Dekker; all those hours of study were paying
off—with the help of Boldon DeWoe's useful tips from God-
knew-where. The indoctrination was a snap for everybody,
because it was just a matter of sitting there while their instructor, a slim, sallow man named Sahad ben Yasif, explained, as
though anyone in the class needed explanation, just what kind
of disastrous hell a comet could raise if it fell on the wrong place
on Mars—or if it, God forbid, hit a spaceship, or a habitat, or
even, though certainly nothing of that sort could ever really
happen, the wrong *planet*.

Taken all in all, Phase One was not much more demanding
than a paid vacation for Dekker DeWoe. His quarters were,
well, *lavish*. He had never in his life had so much space to live
in. He not only had a bedroom that was all his own, but he had
to share the common study room and bath with only a single
other person.

That person was an Earthie, of course; there were only three
other Martians among the thirty-four trainees in his class. But
Dekker's new roommate didn't seem to be a bad fellow. He was
that particular breed of Earthie called "Japanese," a slim, well-
dressed, profane, and indolent man, with a weakness for late
rising and single-malt Scotch, and when they first met he stuck
out his hand and said, "Hi. I'm Toro Tanabe, and I don't snore.
And you're . . . ?"

And then his voice trailed off as he got a good look at the
stainless-steel credit amulet that hung around Dekker's neck.
Tanabe blinked in surprise. Fingering his own gold one, he said,
in some embarrassment, "Well, shit, money isn't everything, is
it? We'll get along, I guess."

As a matter of fact they did. Tanabe's obvious wealth didn't
bother Dekker, and Dekker DeWoe was Martianly decent
enough to do nothing to bother Tanabe. For roommates, they
saw surprisingly little of each other, because Dekker kept to his
room when he wasn't studying in the sitting room they shared,
and Tanabe was seldom in the way. The man didn't seem to
bother to study, ever, and on weekends, when students were
allowed to leave the base for the excitements of Denver, Tanabe
simply was not around.

Actually in Dekker's first-impression judgments, all thirty-
three of his fellows seemed a decent enough lot, not the least of
their assets being that among them there were no fewer than

fourteen presumably unattached but quite possibly attachable *women*.

Dekker definitely marked their presence, particularly the one named Cresti Amman, since she not only had interesting red hair and a pretty face but happened to be Martian herself. Still, he didn't spend a great deal of his time trying to attach even Cresti to himself, at least at first. They exchanged home-towns—she was from a little deme called Schiaparelli, up on the flank of Alba Petera—and sought vainly a time or two for friends in common. That was all. Dekker hadn't forgotten the sexual hunger that had filled his thoughts on his last few days in Danktown. But Cresti seemed thoroughly preoccupied with her studies. Anyway, the hunger just wasn't as obsessive as it had been when there seemed no clear way of finding a part-ner—not gone away, no, but submerged to a bearable level in the great adventure of finding himself with a real place in the world at last.

Oh, Dekker's world wasn't perfect. Tanabe didn't fail to tell him when his father in Osaka wrote that the Bonds were drop-ping on the market again. And there were still those other little worries that never quite went away. But his life was pretty good just as it was, and Dekker had no doubt at all that it was destined to keep getting better.

There was a "final" test on the last day of Phase One. Dekker breezed through it. So, surprisingly, did everybody else in the class, and Sahad ben Yasif shook his head ruefully. "That's one for the books," he declared. "I must be a hell of a teacher, because we usually wash three or four of you out at this point. Tell you what. You're a good class, so let's give you a prize. Come back after lunch and I'll take you all on a class trip."

The man next to Dekker looked suspicious. "What kind of class trip?" he demanded. His name was Jay-John Belster and he was a Martian, too, but an Earthified and not a very friendly one.

"Come back and find out," ben Yasif said, and walked away. In the dining hall speculation was wild. "He's going to give us an extra shove-and-grunt session," one guessed. And another offered, "Maybe a tour of the top ten whorehouses in Dank-town?"

Jay-John Belster shook his head. "Whatever it is, he can keep it. I've got my own plans for this weekend. I've seen enough of this place for one week."

But in any event Belster did show up in the classroom after lunch, and so did Toro Tanabe, though he was sulky about missing the chance to get an early start on his weekend. When they had all straggled back to the classroom ben Yasif appeared and looked them over.

"All right," he said, "let's see how smart you are. How do the controllers in the orbital stations keep track of their incomings?"

Two hands went up, and the instructor pointed to the small Oriental woman nearest him, Shiaopin Ye. "They have virtuals of the solar system to track the comets. Every twelve hours they check each one, and order correction burns as needed."

"That's right—as you'll all find out in Phase Four, if you get there. But here in the academy you won't use virtual helmets. What will you use?"

A voice from the back: "There's a big tank up the hill."

"There is. We use that for training purposes, so everybody can see what everybody does when it's their turn in the basket. That's where we're going. I've got permission to take you all up for a tour of the operational control training section."

That made a stir; even Toro Tanabe looked pleased. As they trooped toward the great elevator that would take them up to the top of the hill, ben Yasif added, "There's one rule you have to remember. That is, *don't touch anything.* The second rule is don't talk to any of the student operators unless they talk to you first. The third rule is don't get in anybody's way. The comet data is taken right from the control-station reports, and it's *real.* What you'll see in the tank is exactly the way the comets are at this moment deployed in their orbits, and we don't want anything messed up by visitors. So, I'll say it again, don't *touch.* If any of you fuck up here, you're out of the program, that minute. Only," he said seriously, "I'll be having something to say to you first."

What that sounded like to Dekker DeWoe was a threat of actual physical violence, bizarre though the thought was. But Sahad ben Yasif was a physical sort of person. Some of the students said ben Yasif had been busted out of the Oort itself because he failed his psych tests for quarrelsomeness, so it was, maybe, possible. . . .

Then Dekker forgot the instructor's past history, because the elevator had stopped at the control level, and all thirty-odd members of his class piled out, staring around.

The control chamber wasn't on just one level, like any other classroom or lab in the complex. The control chamber was two levels high, and at the center of it all was a huge interior space surrounded by balconies. Around the balconies were at least fifty workstations, each with the instruments and controls a controller needed to do his job. Fewer than twenty of the workstations were occupied, and what filled the entire interior space was . . . space.

It was the solar system that lay spread out before them.

It wasn't to scale. The proportions were distorted, because if the planets—or especially if such tiny bodies as the comets—had been plotted to their proper relative size they would have been invisible in the vast emptiness of the solar system. But everything that mattered was there. A glowing orange ball the size of a grapefruit hung in the center of the space; that was the Sun. Smaller red globes represented the planets, as far out as Neptune. Pluto wasn't in the tank, of course. There wasn't room for it, and if Pluto ever presented a problem, which was hardly likely, it would be dealt with by the launchers out in the cloud itself. Each planet flickered faintly in its own pulse-code, and so did every planet's moons; Dekker couldn't read the codes, but he certainly could tell which planet was which—after all, there only were eight of them in the tank. Five bright white stars, two large and three smaller and close together, marked the location of the control stations. The big ones needed no recognition code—they were the stations that shared Mars's own orbit around the Sun, and even a beginner could identify them by their positions. The three in arecentric Martian orbits were coded, but the codes weren't important. There was no particular need to distinguish among them, since the tightest communication beam aimed at any of them would be received at all three. Finally—or almost finally—were the hundred or more winking blue lights that represented the ships currently traveling in space, some in inner-planet orbits and one or two, obviously supply ships, looping up toward the Oort.

Then there were the objects that really mattered: the comets.

The comets were what Oortcorp was all about. The comet dots came in two colors, purple and yellow. There were hundreds of them in the tank, and they flowed in two great streams. Dekker didn't have to be told which was which. The purple stream was made up of the comets principally controlled by Co-Mars Station One; they were still dropping down from the Oort toward their rounding of the Sun. The yellow belonged to Co-Mars Two, as it trailed sixty degrees behind Mars; those comets had completed their critical perihelion-passing maneuver and—God willing!—were now on their proper trajectory for their rendezvous with Mars, the operators on Co-Mars Two fine-tuning them all the way.

Of course, the comets didn't really need to be color-coded for identification. As with the major planets, they identified themselves simply by their positions in the tank. Every object that was *not* a comet lay close to the plane of the ecliptic, that great disk of sky in which all the Sun's planets and asteroids and moons revolved. Everything that was out of the ecliptic was certainly a comet. The natural comets that human beings had wondered at for thousands of years could come from any direction in the sky, since the Oort cloud was a spherical shell around the entire solar system. The ones that were ripped untimely from the Oort to replenish Mars were a different case. They all came from the same general point, somewhere around the constellation Cetus; that was the particular region of the immense cloud where the Oort miners were busy selecting them and preparing them and launching them down.

As Dekker's class filed in, ben Yasif waved them around the lower gallery, muttering to each as they passed: "Spread out. Pick a control station and stand behind it, but if there's anybody in it don't talk to him. And don't touch anything." Dekker found himself grinning; he had a quick flash of recollection of a long-ago school trip to the copper smelters at Sagdayev.

He found himself standing with a classmate named Fez Mehdevi behind a fifth-phase student who was nervously studying the control board. Nothing seemed to be happening. All the fifth-phasers were sitting idle, most of them turning around to glance at the new arrivals. They were all on the lower tier, though Dekker caught a glimpse of someone moving about on the upper one.

When they were all in place, ben Yasif called: "Remember, you're only here on sufferance, so *no fooling around.* I'm going to keep my eye on you all, and I won't be the only one."

He nodded to the fifth-phase instructor, who spoke into his microphone. "You're on, Torres," he said. "Your shift is starting; begin your checks."

* * *

They were there only half an hour before the fifth-phase instructor muttered to ben Yasif, and ben Yasif cleared them out.

It wasn't enough, but, Dekker DeWoe thought, it was *wonderful.* Every one of those things was headed straight for his home world, and every one would bring Mars just a trifle nearer to the promised paradise.

Most of the class was as thrilled as he, and they dawdled on the way back to the dorms. Cresti Amman was chattering about the pair of comets, 65-A4 and 65-BK, that had been entering perihelion—"That's the part that scares me; that's where you can really screw up"—and Jay-John Belster was shaking his head.

"That's what Co-Mars Two is for," he said. "If it comes out anywhere near trajectory, Two will get it in its envelope."

Somebody else was complaining about the Oort miners. "Did you see that little one, 67-JY? It's less than a kilometer across; why would they waste a snake on something like that?"

"And they're going to have trouble with that one at perihelion," Cresti Amman predicted. "Thank God it'll pass before I get out there!"

It was all good talk, shoptalk, and for almost the first time Dekker felt as though he were part of a group that could have been nearly Martian. When he finally got back to his dorm room he was not surprised to find that Toro Tanabe was there before him, just coming out of the shower and beginning to dress. "Well, DeWoe," his roommate said, pulling on pants, "how did you like it?"

"It was *great,*" Dekker declared enthusiastically, and would have gone on if Tanabe hadn't held up a hand to stop him.

"I'll tell you what I didn't like," he said. "I didn't like the psychologist taking notes on us. Did you see her?"

Dekker frowned at him. "The psychologist? Oh, hell," he said, remembering. "Rosa McCune, right? In the upper gallery?"

"That's the one. She was watching everybody, and making little notes on her screen."

"I guess I didn't recognize her," Dekker admitted. "With

her clothes on, I mean. Anyway, she was probably checking on the fifth-phase people, don't you think?"

"They always check on *everybody*," Tanabe said sourly. "Just hope you didn't do anything stupid, DeWoe, because she can boot you out of here anytime she wants to."

Then he finished buttoning his shirt, looking pensive. "Too late to worry about it now, I guess. Well, what about it, DeWoe? Are you coming into town this weekend?"

"I don't think so."

"Ah," said Tanabe, understandingly, fingering his credit amulet. "Well, another time, maybe. I can't wait to get out of this place for a couple of days."

"Aren't you going to eat first?"

"That slop?" Tanabe shuddered, though Dekker couldn't have said why; as far as he was concerned, the food was both edible and plentiful. "No, thanks."

"What about tonight's shove-and-grunt?"

"I'll have to skip it this one time if I'm going to get an early start tonight," Tanabe said, glancing at his dressed self in the mirror. He ran a comb through his stiff, short, un-combable hair and turned to go.

Then he paused. He looked around at Dekker. "DeWoe? Do you want to know what I think about that little comet?"

"The, what was it, 67-JY? What about it?"

"I have a hunch," Tanabe said wisely. "My father told me that the farm habitats want some comets of their own—you know, so they can mine them for water and gases and save importing them from Earth. I'll bet a dinner in Denver that Oortcorp's sneaking through a few comets that are reserved for them."

Even shove-and-grunt seemed tolerable tonight, with the uplift from the visit to the control-training center. Dekker was in a good mood as he hurried over to it.

It was not the kind of thing that any Martian was likely to need, but Martians were no more exempt from attending the sessions than the surliest and most tightly repressed Earthie. Still, Tanabe's gossip about the farm habitats had left Dekker DeWoe with the barest suggestion of an atavis-tic urge to do something violent. How *could* they? Those comets were meant for *Mars*. They were *paid* for by Mars— or at least would be, when enough of the terraforming was complete for crops to be grown there and the interminable cue-slavery of paying back the loans had begun.

His usual shove-and-grunt partner was the rather large Martian, Belster, but when Dekker was suited up and headed toward where Belster was waiting the proctor stopped him. "New partner today, DeWoe," he said. "Amman's complaining that Ven Kupferfeld's too strong for her, so we're giving her a different partner. You."

That was good enough news to restore Dekker's cheer, because he was reaching the point where he did want to get a little closer to Cresti Amman. So far it had been nothing but sitting with her at breakfast once or twice and comparing notes, because Cresti was floundering in the course and willing to spare no time for dates.

Still, there was a certain amount of consideration due another student. Dekker asked, "What does Belster say about it?"

"What has he got to say? Anyway, Belster's a lot, ah, rougher than you, so he can take on one of the others. After all, he's been on Earth for a long time, hasn't he? Get over there. Amman's waiting for you."

And she was. And she looked good in her exercise suit, properly tall and slim the way a person ought to be, and with that red hair falling all over her face. When they were locked in the first struggle exercise, each trying to force the other to move a planted foot, she felt even better than she looked. There was a sweet, female smell about her, and a soft, slick, promising feel to her sweaty skin; all the young-male yearnings that the stresses of the last few weeks had kept submerged began to flood through Dekker DeWoe's body.

And then, when they had dressed and the whole class was strolling back to their quarters, it was perfectly natural that the two of them should walk together. When Dekker suggested a beer later that night, Cresti Amman pursed her lips, hesitated, and then said, "Why not?"

It would have happened, too.

What kept it from happening was a last-minute impulse. On his way out of the rooms Dekker paused to check his messages.

The message signal wasn't flashing, but sometimes Toro

Tanabe took his own messages and forgot to turn the system back on for his roommate.

This was one of the times.

There was only one message waiting for Dekker DeWoe, but it was a nasty one. The face on the screen was a woman in the uniform of a Peacekeeper of the Colorado Rehabilitation Facility, and what she said, as though reading a stock report, was:

"Dekker DeWoe, the Colorado Rehabilitation Facility regrets to inform you that your father, Rehabilitee Boldon DeWoe, died of respiratory and cardiovascular complications at ten twenty-two this morning."

Because it was after hours it took Dekker two hours and twenty minutes to get through to someone capable of answering questions at the Colorado Rehabilitation Facility, and that person wasn't enthusiastic about the idea. "The administration office is closed for the weekend," he said. "If you'll call back at nine on Monday morning, someone will consider your request."

"I don't have any fucking *request*," Dekker said, gritting his teeth. "I have a fucking *demand*. I want to know what happened to my father. *Now*."

That didn't do it, quite, but another five minutes of profanity made his point. "Oh, very well," the man said, hostile but surrendering. "Let me check the data base. The name was Boldon DeWoe, you said? Hold on for one moment."

Dekker held. Not just for one moment, either. He held for what seemed like an eternity—not long enough for his anger to pass off, but long enough for him to quarantine his feelings in one isolated section of his mind so he could think concretely about what he would have to do. The first problem he would have to deal with was time. He would need time off. That was likely to cause trouble for him, since the Oort faculty wouldn't take kindly to having him go that far from the mountain. Yet surely there must be some sort of arrangement possible for emergency leave. And what did Earthies do about funeral arrangements? The Martian customs would not apply here. And what would it all cost? And what about the apartment in Denver? And what—

The man's face reappeared. "Yes," he said, studying an invisible screen, "Boldon DeWoe. He died of respiratory and cardiac complications at ten twenty-two yesterday morning. If there's nothing else—"

"Hold on! What do I do about having the body taken care of?"

The man looked puzzled. "Body?"

"My *father*'s body," Dekker exploded. "I need to make funeral arrangements."

"But you don't, you know," the man said reasonably. "There aren't any arrangements to make. Standard procedures were followed; cremation was at twelve-thirty in the afternoon and the ashes were disposed of. There *is* no body."

And, after Dekker had hung up, it was nearly an hour before he remembered Cresti Amman, waiting—but surely not waiting any longer—for him to show up for their date.

23.

OORT TRAINING DIDN'T cover everything. Before a candidate could even take the entrance test for Oort training, he—or, approximately 47 percent of the time, she—had to have completed the prerequisites. These included three years of college-level courses in mathematics; two of gas chemistry and chromatography; three years of physics, at least one of which was nuclear physics with particular emphasis on antimatter reaction processes and products; and whatever other courses were necessary to secure a bachelor of science degree or equivalent. And that was not the end of it. It was also necessary to have a pilot's license of some sort, preferably, though not necessarily, for spacecraft.

The course itself ran twenty-four weeks, divided into six four-week segments: Phase One, Orientation and Review; Phase Two, Antimatter Propulsion and Instrumentation; Phase Three, Comet Capture and Preparation; Phase Four, Orbit

Planning; Phase Five, Orbit Control; and Phase Six, Review and Specialization—including, for those destined for the Mars orbiters, Demolition and Impact Control.

But that was not the end of the training. That was just as far as anyone could go in the school, and the course got harder as it went along.

Phase Two was where the hard part started. Oort workers didn't usually have to be Augenstein mechanics. It was just that when they did have to—when something went wrong and there was nobody else around to fix it—they had to be very good ones indeed.

24.

PHASE TWO WAS hardware. It started out by covering emergency repairs to the Augenstein drive, the thing that drove the little spotter ships out in the Oort, and Dekker saw immediately that the easy times were over. He wasn't sorry. The harder the work was, the less time he had to think about the death of the father he had lost for so long, and regained for so little.

By the third day of Phase Two, when they had the shell of their Augenstein off, Dekker's partner stuck his head inside and pulled it out with an expression of despair. "All these parts are so *heavy*, DeWoe," he complained. "I do not see why we must do this dirty work when it is enough to understand the theory."

"The corporation doesn't think so," Dekker told him. "Move over. Let me have a look."

But when his own head was inside he was startled at the sheer bulk of the components, too. Of course, Dekker knew the theory of the Augenstein. What he knew was nothing but theory, though. He had never seen a real one, and hadn't been prepared for the labyrinth of piping and the vast shell of the magnetic containment that kept the whole thing from blowing up in their faces.

It couldn't really do that there, of course, because they certainly didn't have a real, powered-up Augenstein in the shop. There was no fuel inside the containment shell. Nobody ever had real antimatter anywhere on Earth, or on Mars, either, except maybe in the tiniest amounts in some research laboratory. Nobody was ever that reckless, because antimatter didn't stay antimatter when there was any normal matter anywhere around for it to react with, and you didn't want to be there when that reaction occurred. What they had were dummies of the drives, a dozen of them to share around the class, and each one the size of a hydrocar.

Since they contained no fuel, they could never be made to work, but they were structurally complete, great heavy things you could walk right into once you'd pulled the interior plumbing out. On Earth that was a sufficiently tough job by itself, because in gravity you needed hoists and jacks to lift the five-hundred-kilogram parts and ease them out of the way.

What the trainees had to do was to strip their Augensteins and put them together again. In space you wouldn't need the hoists. On the other hand, no one ever would do that sort of thing in practice, in space or anywhere else. Anyone who ever tried to take a live Augenstein apart would die of radiation sickness very soon thereafter. The idea, though, was that they had to know how all the parts worked just in case some minor part *should* fail—which was unlikely to happen in practice, fortunately—and happen to be repairable—which was pure fantasy.

It was hard, dirty work, and nothing in Dekker's studies had prepared him for this kind of labor in a 1-g environment. At that, he was better prepared than the partner the Phase Two teacher had paired him with. At least Dekker *had* done hard physical labor in his life—naturally; he was a Martian. Fez Mehdevi clearly had not. As far as Dekker could see, the man had never before lifted a finger for any task more arduous than pushing the button to start a machine, and not much of that. "For this sort of thing," Mehdevi groaned, sucking a knuckle he had just skinned on a pipe end, "we hire mechanics in Tehran."

"Can your mechanics handle a magnetic containment system?"

"Can anyone?" Mehdevi looked sorrowfully around at the clutter of parts. "This must be dangerous," he complained. "Look, it is unstable. Without the magnetic containment the antimatter will surely touch the walls of the vessel and explode. Yet when the Augenstein is not operating there is no power to run the magnets.''

"That's why they ship them with external power," Dekker said, peering into the cluster of cooling elements.

"But what if it fails?" He gave the thing a look of loathing and pleaded, "You uncouple that tubing, DeWoe, please. I am injured."

So it was Dekker DeWoe, the limitations of his Martian physique notwithstanding, who did most of the grunt work of tearing the damn, dirty thing down and putting it together again, and when he got back to his room at night he was too tired to worry about anything else.

Which did not, actually, keep him from worrying.

Night after night, Dekker DeWoe lay in his bed, listening to the faint snores and occasional grunts and moans from Toro Tanabe's room across the hall, and thinking. Dekker had never experienced insomnia before. Insomnia simply wasn't a Martian kind of problem. He didn't like it. He didn't like the black depression that came over him when he thought of his father's last days, caught in the dehumanizing tedium of the Colorado Rehabilitation Facility, or, for that matter, of his father's last years, the pain-filled and futureless wreck of the former daring Oort flyer.

Fez Mehdevi, at least, had formally offered condolences when he heard of Dekker's loss—that was the main reason Dekker hadn't pleaded for a change of partners—but no one else in the class had seemed to care. Of course, he'd passed the news of Boldon DeWoe's death on to his mother at once, but all Gerti DeWoe had to say about it in her return message— voicemail only, no picture—was, "It's a pity, Dek. I guess the important thing to remember is that he did his best."

It was a shorter and less personal response than Dekker had expected; it did not occur to him that she might not have wanted her son to see her, perhaps, crying. He agreed that it was a pity. But there didn't seem to be any supply of pity anywhere in this world to spare for the tragedies of Boldon DeWoe.

There was one complication in his life he didn't have to worry about any more, though. That was Cresti Amman. Cresti no longer figured in Dekker's future prospects. She hadn't been angry about being stood up, at least not after Dekker explained

what had happened. On the other hand, Cresti's forgiveness no
longer mattered much. The psychologist's note-taking in the
control center had had its consequences. Cresti had been caught
at something, no one knew what. The next morning an advisory
had appeared on every screen in the dorms to say that three of
Dekker's classmates, Cresti included, had been summarily
dropped for "insufficient diligence." The class size was down to
thirty-one, and Cresti Amman was history.

Amazingly, Toro Tanabe was still around.

In spite of the fact that Dekker had never seen him study,
Dekker was astonished to learn that the man had actually come
in second in the class, half a dozen names above Dekker's own
respectable, but not startling, eighth place in the standings.

"How the hell do you manage it?" Dekker demanded one
night, rubbing the muscles that ached from trying to heave
hundred-kilogram masses of metal around in the shop all day.

Tanabe looked startled. "What do you mean? My grades?
Oh, perhaps that first phase was just the natural result of a good
education. I notice that you did quite well yourself, DeWoe."

"That was theory. What I'm talking about is what we're
doing now. The Augenstein. Your team got through the containment check twice as fast as mine did today."

Tanabe spread his hands. "But that is also only training and
practice, DeWoe. This whole segment of the course is foolishness, of course. If anything went wrong with the containment
while we were out in spotter ships, ten or twenty million kilometers from the base, we would not be repairing it. We would
simply die. But as we were aware this segment would be required for the course, my father and I arranged for special
instruction."

"How did you know?" Dekker asked, and then stopped himself. Tanabe's expression had clouded over, and Dekker had
remembered the interesting fact that his own father had, somehow, known in advance just what would be on the entrance test.
"I mean," he amended himself, "what do you mean, 'arranged'? You didn't have an Augenstein to practice on, did
you?"

"But I did have one." Tanabe smiled. "My father's business
interests include space ventures. Because of that good fortune
he was able to provide me with a dummy quite like the ones in
the shop, as well as a technician to help me learn. It is true," he

said, looking regretful, "that my father did not approve of my decision to come here. My father is unfortunately no longer of the opinion that the Oort project is economically sound. Still, once I had convinced him that the training was what I wanted, and he had given his permission, he helped me in every way he could." He finished lacing his cowboy boots and stood up. "Of course," he added, "I imagine your team would have performed better if your partner had not been Fez Mehdevi."

Dekker didn't answer that. It wasn't that he didn't agree, but there was some sort of cloudy loyalty to his partner involved. Tanabe didn't press the point. He glanced at himself in the wall mirror. "Well," he said sunnily, "it's about time to 'knock back' a few beers, as you say. Would you care to join me?"

Dekker, who never said anything like "knock back" about anything, shook his head. "There's a test tomorrow," he reminded his roommate.

"Of course there is," Tanabe agreed. "Study diligently, then, DeWoe. I'll see you later."

All that physical exercise was reshaping Dekker DeWoe's body—that and the shots. He no longer needed the polysteroids; his muscles had responded to Earth-normal gravity by thickening and strengthening themselves until he no longer felt he was carrying another person on his back. The calcium intake had increased the density of his bones—pretty well, anyway. He couldn't compete with the bigger and stronger Earthie males in shove-and-grunt, but he did abandon the leg braces.

After he reached that plateau, walking just for the sake of walking around became a lot more pleasant. More interesting, too. When the weather was good Dekker allowed himself the recreation of walking around on the mountainside, among the many buildings of the Oort center.

It was a pretty place, more like a college campus than he had realized—though he had never seen an Earthie college campus before. Buildings of various ages, originally intended for an assortment of various purposes, had been assimilated by the Oort authorities and bent to their own needs as the project grew, while new special-purpose ones had been constructed. His own dormitory, he learned, had been built originally as a "sanitarium" for people with lung ailments, long ago. The headquarters building had at one time been a deluxe resort hotel, and still possessed the swimming pools and tennis courts it had started with. The central auditorium had begun life as a "movie" theater, whatever that was. Down lower on the mountain, below the classrooms and workshops and offices, there was still a scattering of private homes and other, smaller hotels, though none of them were "private" anymore; now they housed the administrative employees of the corporation and the faculty of the training center. So damn *many* employees, Jay-John Belster once pointed out bitterly—and the salaries of every last one of them paid for out of the money raised by the Bonds, which would sooner or later have to be paid off by Mars.

At the top of the mountain, though out of sight, was the actual working headquarters of Oortcorp itself.

Of course, you couldn't see that from outside. All of that was not only new but firmly underground—because, Jay-John Belster sneered, of the rich Earthie fear of crowds and demonstrations. All you could observe to prove it was there was the overhead array of communications dishes, the vast fixed one that always pointed south and east to the main geostationary satellite at the end of the Skyhook that hung over the west coast of South America, and the smaller—but still meters-across—geared antennae that tracked Oortcorp's dozens of special-purpose satellites.

And all around, in every direction, were the lovely peaks of the Rocky Mountains. They were a balm to the vision. Mountains in themselves were nothing special to a man who had lived on the slope of Olympus Mons, but these were beautifully green and sometimes spectacularly ice-capped, and Dekker DeWoe was delighted at their sight.

When the results of the test on Augenstein and antimatter theory were posted Dekker had managed to improve his standing to fifth. But number one was still the same Earthie woman, someone named Ven Kupferfeld, and right below her name was Toro Tanabe's, still firmly in place with the second highest grade in the class.

It was possible, Dekker thought glumly, turning off the screen, that that particular Earthie was simply smarter than he was.

He didn't like that thought. He didn't have much time to brood over the question, though. The class had already moved on to the subjects of maintenance on the spotter ships themselves and the care of the suit insert that an Oort miner had to live in for twenty or thirty days at a time.

When the survivors moved into the suit-insert shop they found six actual spotter-ship suits propped up around the room, waiting for them and looking like half a dozen headless store-window dummies from a fat-men's shop. The suits came in six different sizes, all of them too short for any full-grown Martian, and so the old partnerships were dissolved as the class arranged itself by size.

"Fucking Earthies," Jay-John Belster grumbled in Dekker's ear as they sorted themselves out into teams—both the surviving Martians in the team with the longest and skinniest suit, of course, along with three of the tallest and leanest Earthies. "They could have got us one decent suit, but they just don't give a damn for Martians here."

Dekker didn't answer, because the suit-insert instructor had climbed on a chair to address them. She was a new face to Dekker, a "European" Earthie named Liselotte Durch, and a good deal older than anyone else in the room. Her hair was white, her face was lined, and her voice was strident. "Don't touch the suits until I tell you," she ordered. "Don't complain if they don't fit when you try them on, either. I already know they aren't going to fit. If you ever actually make it out into the Oort, which I also know damn few of you will, you'll get one that's custom made to your own body. That's not because they want it to look nice. It's because you have to live in your suit for weeks at a time. When you're out in your spotter ship you'll piss in your suit and crap in it, and some of you guys will probably want to try to jerk off in it, but I warn you now that that isn't going to work. You'll be catheterized before you leave the base ship, and if you let your glands run away with you and get an erection while you're in the suit, it's going to hurt."

The sole function of the suit, she went on, telling them what they already knew, was to act as an interface between the tiny, stripped-down, one-man spotter ship and the human body within it. The suit would keep them alive. It would feed them, give them air, and remove their wastes; and the auxiliaries would evaporate the water out of those wastes and give it back to them to drink. *Just* to drink.

"Drinking is all you'll need water for," she said, "because you aren't going to be able to wash or anything like that.

Naturally by the time you get back to base you're going to stink, but, hey, that's what you're signing up for." She gave them a challenging look, as though seeking protests. There weren't any, so she moved on. "Now, one of you in each group, strip down and climb into the suit. The controls are all depowered, but don't touch them anyway, and don't put the helmets on. DeWoe? Which one of you is DeWoe? All right, DeWoe, leave your team and come over here a minute."

Surprised, Dekker did as he was told. Durch didn't look at him at first; she was watching the teams as they wrangled among themselves to see who would go first. When one member of each team had finally begun to undress she took time to look down at Dekker. "Your name's DeWoe. Are you any relation to Boldon DeWoe?" she asked.

"My father," he said. "He just died."

She nodded as though the news didn't surprise her. "I heard something about that. Too bad. You know he really messed himself up," she said, as though Dekker could possibly have been unaware of his father's condition. "I knew him in the Oort. Smart man; I liked him. Good pilot, too, but he couldn't leave the dope alone. I hope you don't take after him."

When you were spotting comets out in the Oort, Liselotte Durch had told them, you would be put into your suit by trained professionals, and they would take care of threading the tubes into your personal parts, and checking for wrinkles in the fabric and adjusting the fit to your body before each mission.

That was what it would be like out in the Oort. In training it was different. In training you just stripped down to your skivvies and stood still while your teammates pulled the suit up around you and did their best to get it all zipped up. "Actually," the instructor said, "you want to remember that when you put this on you're not just wearing the liner suit. You're wearing the whole ship."

It felt like wearing a whole ship, as a matter of fact. When Dekker was sealed inside, trying to hunch his tall frame down to fit into a space at least half a dozen centimeters too short, he felt like a mummy. Nothing moved easily, but then, in a real spotter ship, hardly any parts of his body would be moving at all. The spiky invigilation tubes that would be inside him in actual use were now pressing painfully against sensitive parts of his body. The whole thing seemed to weigh a ton—did weigh a hundred kilograms or more, and Dekker had to strain to stand up in it.

If others could handle it, Dekker could. There was a personal challenge involved for Dekker DeWoe, too. As the instructor had reminded him, his father had worn a suit just like this, a long time ago and those billions of kilometers away.

So Dekker pushed the hands of his teammates away and stood erect. "Ready," he said, and when Liselotte Durch gave the order, Jay-John Belster picked the helmet up and set it on over his head. His whole team pitched in to settle it in place and snap the connections in.

For a moment Dekker was in total blackness. This wasn't like putting on a hotsuit to roam the slopes around Sagdayev; it was heavier and more constricting, and there wasn't enough air. For a moment he almost panicked. Then the external air supply kicked in and he felt a soft, refreshing movement of air around his face.

A moment later the taped virtuals came on.

He was blind no longer. He was still surrounded by blackness, but the blackness, wherever he looked, was punctuated by a universe of stars—bright ones and faint, diamond white or hued in blue and yellow and pale red. It was only a partial virtual, with no sound and certainly no touch or smell—but then, in the emptiness of the Oort, there would be no external sounds to hear. It didn't matter. The vision was enough. Dekker was seeing what his ship's eyes saw—at least, what a real spotter ship would see, out in the Oort. The stars that surrounded him whichever way he turned his head weren't real, of course. They were only the spectacle that some ship had once observed, taped, and reproduced for this training session. But they were wonderful. He was *there*.

Liselotte Durch's voice startled him when she whispered in his ear. "Are you all right? Are you getting your feeds?"

"I'm fine," he said.

"Then start your drill," she ordered, and he began the list of procedures. His fingers found the keypads that controlled the ship movements and instrument readings sprang up before his eyes: state of consumables, rate of acceleration, function checks on all the parts of his imaginary "ship." Another touch, and the radars reported distances to the nearest orbiting comets—a few million kilometers at the least, because the Oort was a very thin cloud; another touch, and the one he had selected popped closer to his eyes, a dull, lumpy potato of a thing that showed no sign of the great luminous tail it might develop if he chose to tag it and thread it with its instruments and drives and send it down to enrich the air of Mars.

He only had ten minutes in the suit. It wasn't enough; but when Dekker got out he was grinning. The next one up was the woman in their team, that very bright—and also, in an Earthie way, very good-looking—pale-haired one named Ven Kupferfeld. She gave Dekker a curious look, then a smile as she began to disrobe. "You look pleased," she said.

He didn't answer; the grin stayed on his face, and it was answer enough. Jay-John Belster and another man helped Dekker pull his legs out of the suit and readied it for the woman, now down to her brightly patterned and quite minimal underwear.

"This is the best part," Belster muttered to Dekker as they watched her get ready to enter the suit. "I wouldn't mind taking a little piece of that."

Dekker grunted without a specific reply, though he shared the notion. Ven Kupferfeld's underthings were not only minute, they were just about transparent besides. She was very tall and thin for an Earthie, which made her all the better looking for Dekker DeWoe. When she was into the suit and the show was, for the moment, over, Dekker and Belster together picked up the helmet, with all its lines and cables for air supply and external feeds, and waited for their other teammates to do the tedious work of tugging and twisting and zipping the suit into some sort of fit.

Dekker glanced to the front of the room. Liselotte Durch was at her teacher's lectern by the door, talking to another woman who looked vaguely familiar to Dekker. He couldn't pin the vagrant memory down. "Belster?" he said to the Martian. "Do you know who that woman is?"

Belster looked, but the woman was already turning away to leave. "Can't tell," he said. "Probably she's another instructor. But, listen, DeWoe, I was meaning to ask you. Did old lady Durch just say she knew your father in the Oort?" Dekker nodded. "Well, that's a damn good break for you. I guess you might get a little help now and then."

Dekker said, "My father gave me all the help he ever can, Belster. He got hurt in the Oort years ago, and a couple of weeks ago he died of it."

Surprisingly, the Martian didn't look surprised. He just said. "Well, I didn't actually mean help from your father, but now that you mention it, I guess I did hear something about it. Fucking Earthies let him just rot, didn't they?"

Dekker shrugged, and Belster nodded sagaciously. "Fucking Earthies," he repeated. "They don't give a shit about Mars. This whole thing's just so they can bleed us dry, and now they're talking about folding the whole operation."

"They can't do that," Dekker said with conviction.

"They can if we let them get away with it."

Dekker looked at him curiously. "They don't have any right," he said with conviction.

Belster seemed to approve. "Good man," he said. "Look, Kupferfeld's ready for the helmet. Let's give her a hand—and don't mess her pretty hair."

Dekker gave Ven Kupferfeld more than a hand, actually, at that evening's shove-and-grunt. In fact, he got the chance to give her a fairly complete massage. As he came into the room the short, sallow Fez Mehdevi came over to him. "Please," he said, "would you care to be my partner for this evening, too?" He sounded aggrieved.

"I already have a stress-reduction partner, Mehdevi."

"So did I, but she has decided I am not enough of a challenge for her, so she has arranged to make some changes. She—But here she is, she can tell you for herself."

The "she" was Ven Kupferfeld. She was grinning. "Forget this one, Mehdevi," she said. "I'll try him out myself. You go find somebody else."

Dekker never enjoyed a stress-reduction session more, though the stresses it relieved were surely overbalanced by the new stresses it brought about. Kupferfeld's exercise briefs were less transparent than her underwear had been, but they still exposed a lot of skin, and as they wrestled Dekker got the chance to touch a lot of it.

It was a pleasure, but not without its drawbacks. It was a foregone conclusion that a Martian like Dekker, however well he had responded to shots and exercise, wasn't ever going to be strong enough to do shove-and-grunt with a male Earthie student, except perhaps a short and marshmallow-soft one like Fez Mehdevi. He began to wonder if he was strong enough to do it with Ven Kupferfeld, either. It wasn't that his polysteroided muscles were seriously less powerful than hers. The problem was skeletal. As he tried to flip her forcefully resisting frame over on the mat, he wondered if he was going to snap some flimsy Martian bone.

But they got through it without disaster, and as they were headed for the showers she grinned at him, panting. "Good workout, DeWoe," she said. "Hey. I hear you were in Kenya before you came here."

Dekker had given up wondering how everybody in the class seemed to know so much more about him than he knew about them. "That's right, Ven."

"A grand place," she pronounced. "I was there myself, years ago. Did you see the game herds?"

"Some. I had a friend who had a farm in the Mara."

"Tanzania's better—hell, Tanzania's *wonderful*. My grandfather took me when I was fifteen and we saw all those giraffes and wildebeests and lions—all running free, even killing right before your eyes."

It had not occurred to Dekker that killing was a spectator sport. He said so, and she grinned at him. "That depends a lot on who's doing the killing and who gets killed, doesn't it? Anyway, we ought to get together and talk about it sometime."

Something inside Dekker crowed in triumph and joy, but he kept his expression cool. "I'd like that," he said. "When?"

"Oh," she said, "some time soon. Listen, DeWoe, I heard about your father. I'm really sorry."

"Thank you."

She studied him for a moment. "A lot of you Martians blame us—what's that thing you call us? 'Dirtsuckers'?—blame us dirtsuckers for things like that. Like what happened to your father, I mean, and I'm glad you don't feel that way."

Since Dekker was not in fact sure that he didn't blame the dirtsuckers, he felt a sudden tightness in his throat. Could that be anger? he wondered. Was he spending so much time with Earthies that he was beginning to react like them?

He knew that the feeling was wrong, but he couldn't help saying sharply, "What makes you think I don't?"

She didn't take offense. She just nodded as though the response was not only natural but, in some way, even right. As she turned away toward the women's shower stalls she said, "Don't forget, we want to talk sometime."

Dekker's heat cooled swiftly. He called after her, "There's a weekend coming up—maybe Saturday?"

She paused long enough to smile at him over her shoulder. "Not this Saturday, no—I'm going away for the weekend. But soon, Dekker. We have a lot to talk about."

25.

WEEKENDS WERE QUIET for Dekker DeWoe. Half the students would be gone, mostly to the fleshpots of Denver, and the rest studying frantically to try to keep up. Dekker was one of the studying ones, but not particularly frantic: the next part of Phase Two was communications hardware, the sort of thing they would be using in a spotter ship, or for that matter anywhere in the Oort project's control system. Dekker did not need a great deal of study for that—after all, he'd been using very similar commsets on the Martian airships.

So he allowed himself to take time off—not to do anything in particular; actually to do nothing at all, or as close to nothing as a healthy and active young Martian ever could. He watched newscasts until they got too repulsive: The Khalistan secessionists had given up, but now there was some other trouble in a place called Brazil. And the markets were unstable again. He roamed around the campus, strengthening his new legs and breathing the sweet mountain air: wonderful grass growing, wonderful flowers. Wonderful insects, even, buzzing from plant to plant; this place was so *full* of life. He chatted with his classmates still on campus at their leisurely weekend meals. He recorded a long, affectionate letter to his mother. He drowsed, and slept late, and listened to music, and was well content.

For Dekker DeWoe on that weekend his worries seemed far away. Ven Kupferfeld offered the possibility of future pleasures, maybe—Dekker did not allow himself to count on anything with Earthies, especially Earthie women. The questionable way Dekker had got into the training course dwindled in his memory; surely it could not matter anymore as long as he continued to do well in the class work . . . and even his father's death became just another slowly mellowing pain.

He went peacefully to bed on Sunday night without any hint of insomnia. He woke only partially to hear Toro Tanabe stumbling in—of course at the last possible moment after his long weekend in town—drowsed quickly back into a pleasant dream that involved someone who looked a lot like Ven Kupferfeld—

And was suddenly jolted fully awake, startled and angry, an hour later.

It was the middle of the night. His room lights were on. A man he had never seen before was standing over him. "Up," the man snapped, jerking the covers off Dekker's body. "No, don't try to get dressed. You've got no time for that. Get your ass out here! You've got work to do, and you have to do it *now.*"

It was an unforgivable intrusion on his personal time. He wasn't the only one who thought so, either, because furious shouting from Toro Tanabe's room told him that the Japanese was being awakened in just the same way, with even more resistance. But when Tanabe came stumbling out into the common room, wearing a silk gown of the kind he called "kimono," Dekker saw that the person with him was the psychologist woman, Rosa McCune.

Then it all became clear.

Tardily Dekker understood what was happening. The almost-forgotten warnings had come to pass. It was a surprise psychological check. On their study table was a tool kit and a model of the refrigeration unit that was part of an Augenstein. "Get busy," the woman commanded. "Strip it. Check the parts. Put it back together, and do it *fast.* You've got twelve minutes, and the clock's running."

At that hour of the night, without warning, that was a nasty task—especially for Toro Tanabe, who was clearly still half-drunk and wholly incompetent. Dekker had never before worked with his roommate as partners, and as he grimly began twisting at the latches with the unlocking device he hoped they never would again. His biggest problem was keeping Tanabe's fumbling fingers out of the way. He almost wished for Fez Mehdevi instead. He did wish that, at least, the two psych people would shut up, but of course they didn't. They kept a running stream of distracting chatter, with uncomplimentary references to Dekker's straining efforts to wrench apart the resisting coils and Tanabe's frequent need to clutch the side of the table for support. "At least," Tanabe moaned, "let me for Christ's sake *piss* first."

"You wouldn't have time to piss in the Oort, stupid," Dr. McCune snapped. "Move it! You've got seven minutes left!"

The seven minutes went faster than Dekker would have believed possible, but somehow, with minimal help from Tanabe, he got the job done. Then the woman demanded his arm for a moment while she took some blood—for what, Dekker could not guess—and then it was over. When the psych team had taken their hardware to plague some other students, Dekker and Tanabe rubbed the pinpricks where the blood had been taken from their arms and looked at each other.

"Shit," Tanabe said. It was all he needed to say. It included everything, from the indignity of being dragged out of bed in the middle of the night, through the misery of his half-drunken state, to the fear that they had failed.

"What did they want the blood for?" Dekker asked.

"What the hell do you think? Drugs," Tanabe moaned. "If they find dope in your blood you're gone. Thank God all I had this weekend was booze; they don't count that. But *shit.*"

"I think we probably passed," Dekker offered consolingly.

"How do you know that?" Tanabe demanded, anxious to believe but afraid.

"Because they didn't tell us we failed," Dekker said. "That's the way my father told me to look at it, and he's been right so far."

The whole class had had the same treatment. "Yes," Fez Mehdevi said sadly as they began to plumb the solid-state mysteries of their communications set, "they did it to me, too. It is not pleasant, this course."

"Well," Dekker said judiciously, the light of the morning illuminating the confusion of the night, "I guess it's not such a bad idea. Testing us like that, I mean. If we ever really had to do some kind of emergency repairs out in the field there'd be worse stresses than they gave us."

"I hope to my God I never have to," Mehdevi said prayerfully. "Now, what is one to do with this transponder?"

The week went well enough for Dekker, mostly. The only failing was Ven Kupferfeld. Dekker had no doubt that there had definitely been an invitation from the woman, in fact a promise. Yet every time he found a chance to come near her she seemed reasonably friendly though entirely busy with more important concerns.

It was probably, Dekker thought, just the way Earthie women were. It had no doubt been a mistake to think that she really had any interest in him. Because he was a Martian, perhaps? No, he decided, it wasn't that, at least not this time, anyway. Ven Kupferfeld didn't appear to have any prejudice against Martians. Whenever she did seem to have a private conversation with anyone else it was as likely as not to be that other Martian (though not *very* Martian, anymore), Jay-John Belster. The two of them spent what Dekker considered to be an excessive amount of time talking together, away from the rest of the class.

He took consolation in the fact that he was doing well otherwise. The communications sessions were as easy for him as he had expected, and, most important, he had survived Rosa McCune's pop psych test. Two members of the class had not. Whether it was drugs or simple failure to meet standards, they were gone.

Toro Tanabe did not seem consoled. He stayed in the dorm that Friday night, looking resentful and unhappy. He didn't spend his time studying, of course. That would have been too much of a change; but he retired to his room early. He stayed on campus all that day, too, but that night he approached Dekker gloomily. "I must ask a favor. I do not think I did well for myself this week," he announced.

"You didn't get washed out," Dekker pointed out.

"Yes, but there is a problem. I do not want to spend all of my weekend in this boring place, and I cannot afford to risk another—situation. I almost did not get back last Sunday, you know."

"I didn't know."

"Well, it is true. I had been drinking, and the taxi driver was not helpful in returning me to the dorm."

Dekker waited, aware that more was coming. It took Tanabe a moment to get to it. "What I would like," he said, sounding uncharacteristically apologetic, "is for you to accompany me to Danktown tomorrow. Just for the day. I did not think I should allow myself the entire weekend. Oh, do not worry about the money; I will pay the fare. I will even see that you get something to eat, even some drinks, if you wish. But I wish you to make certain that I am back by midnight at the latest. I may not wish to go, but you must insist. I think that what happened last Sunday night was a warning."

"What are you worried about? I thought with your grades you were in solid."

"Nothing," said Tanabe mournfully, "is 'solid' here. I sometimes wish I had listened to my father. Anyway, will you make sure I am on the last bus, if possible, or a taxi at least? Then let us get some sleep and make an early start."

Right after breakfast they took the bus down to the city, Tanabe paying both fares as promised, and Dekker discovered that Denver when you had money to spend—even someone else's money—was a whole other place than Denver when you didn't. Tanabe hailed a taxi, flashed his gold amulet, and gave the driver an address.

It was a church. Dekker stared up at the huge marble edifice as their taxi drew up before it. "I didn't know you were, well, a Christian," he said while Tanabe was paying the driver.

"Christian? Of course I am not a Christian," Tanabe said indignantly. "A church is an excellent place to meet women, and I have been told there are many attractive ones here." He checked his watch, then nodded in satisfaction. "The morning service will be ending now, and we will simply drink coffee and mingle."

Dekker had never been in a church before. He looked around curiously as they entered an anteroom banked with flowers. When he peered through the open double doors into the church itself he was fascinated to see nearly a hundred male and female Earthies, in their best clothes, standing around to drink coffee and chat with each other.

"Wait," Tanabe said. "Before we go in, we must conform to the mores of the community." He paused at a table in the hall and picked out plastic name badges. He handed one to Dekker. "Put 'Mars' after your name," he ordered, carefully lettering out his own.

"Why? They can see I'm a Martian, can't they?"

"Remind them," Tanabe advised. "I am told that people in churches like foreigners. If we are lucky we may have to beat the women off with a stick."

But it didn't happen that way. There were plenty of Earthie

women in the church, but not many of them very young and none who seemed interested in anything beyond a comment on the weather. After his second polite rebuff, Tanabe had an idea. "Watch what I do," he ordered, and went up to a man in flowing robes. "I would like to make a contribution to your church," he said, Dekker interestedly close behind.

"That's very kind of you, Mr.—Tanabe," the minister said, peering at Toro's badge.

"Quite a large one, perhaps," Tanabe added, glancing around to be sure he was observed. Indeed, a good-looking woman standing near the minister was nodding approvingly.

"Wonderful," the minister said. "Elsie? Will you show Mr. Tanabe to the collections register?" And the woman came smiling forward to lead Tanabe—who gave Dekker a complacent wink as he departed—to donate his money. But he was back in five minutes, looking ruffled.

"That cost me twenty cues, and the woman is married to the priest!" he complained to Dekker. "That is scandalous, isn't it? I thought priests did not marry."

"Some do, I guess," Dekker said consolingly.

Tanabe scowled. "This is not a success. I think it may be because you are with me. Perhaps they do not like all foreigners equally, after all. Come, let us get out of this place. At least we can get something to eat."

So, sulkily, Tanabe took Dekker to a downtown hotel for what he called "brunch." That was a whole new experience for Dekker, too. The hotel lobby was more like a cathedral than the church they had just left, and the restaurant almost as ornate. And the food!—Dekker had never seen anything like the counters loaded with hot pots and trays of fruits, crisp salads, pastries, breads of all descriptions. The closest he had ever come was at breakfast on the Ngemba farm or in that dim childhood memory of Annetta Cauchy's party in Sunpoint City, when the first comet struck—but this was a hundred times more opulent than either.

Not, however, more successful for Toro Tanabe. Here, too, all the potentially interesting women seemed to be with men they found interesting. The few who were breakfasting alone or with other women did not respond to Tanabe's overtures.

He was scowling again when he returned to where Dekker was experimentally trying out his first eggs Benedict. "Tell me,

DeWoe," he said, "have you had success with women here on Earth?"

"Some," Dekker said, thinking of Sheila in the Masai hut.

"No, that Cresti Amman does not count," Tanabe said, obviously having misread that situation. "After all, she was a Martian, too, wasn't she?" He peered at Dekker's plate, and added, "That looks good. Get me some."

If there was anything Dekker DeWoe had learned on Earth, it was that the person who paid out the cues was the person who gave the orders. He didn't particularly mind, but by the time he got back to the table with Tanabe's own order of eggs Benedict his were cold and Tanabe was staring at his pocket screen angrily.

"What's the matter?" Dekker asked.

Tanabe, with his mouth full of poached eggs and sauce, said, "I have lost on the lottery again. It is nothing."

Dekker laughed. "That's the point of a lottery, isn't it? So practically everybody loses?"

"Don't you gamble on Mars?"

"No. Not much, anyway, and not lotteries. Some of the old people play cards."

"No, no. *Really* gamble. So that if you hit a winner you get really rich."

Dekker tried not to laugh anymore. "If a Martian got rich," he explained, "what would he spend the money on?"

"Why—luxuries! Things from Earth!"

Dekker shook his head. It was too much trouble to explain that no Martian lottery was likely to pay off in Earth cues, and if it did no Martian really wanted to give Earth any more money than was essential to survival. "How do you do it?" he asked, more out of politeness than interest, and then regretted it. Because Toro Tanabe explained in great detail. There was a lottery every week, he informed Dekker; you picked ten numbers from zero to ninety-nine, and then there would be a drawing and if you got all ten right you would win *billions*.

"You mean really billions?" Dekker asked, impressed.

"Well—if you don't have to share it, anyway," the Japanese conceded. "Sometimes a lot of people get the same winning numbers, and then you have to divide the profits with them. But I have a system. See, all numbers have the same chance of winning, but the payoff is bigger on some than it is on others."

Dekker frowned. "Why?"

"Because," Tanabe explained, happy to show his superior insights, "a lot of people bet *particular* numbers. Their birthday. Or their girlfriend's birthday, or their anniversary. But very often the numbers they pick will be from dates, and so there's a heavy play on one through twelve for the months, and one through thirty-one, for the days. Then a lot of people like to bet on numbers with a seven in them—they think seven is a lucky number—and a lot who like double numbers, especially seventy-seven, and then you always get a big play on the sexy numbers, like sixty-nine." He paused to wipe some sauce off his pocketscreen and began chewing again.

"What's sexy about the number sixty-nine?" Dekker asked, curious.

The Japanese looked at him. Then he shook his head. "Never mind, DeWoe. But that's part of my system: I stay off the heavily played numbers. So my chances of winning are just as good with my numbers as anybody else's—you can sum up the chances—"

He hit keys, and the screen displayed a series of fractions:

$$\frac{1}{10} \times \frac{1}{11} \times \frac{4}{49} \times \frac{7}{97} \times \frac{1}{16} \times \frac{1}{19} \times \frac{2}{47} \times \frac{1}{31} \times \frac{1}{46} \times \frac{1}{91} = .000,000,000,000,057,142$$

"That's the chance of any random ten numbers winning—about six in a hundred trillion or so. But if you play the same numbers as other people do you have to split the prize too many ways." He fixed Dekker with a look. "I don't like to split," he said.

Dekker tried not to pass judgment. He only said, "I thought you were rich already, Tanabe."

"But I am, of course."

"Then why—?"

Tanabe was laughing at him now. "Oh, DeWoe," he wheezed, "you Martians are so *quaint*. There is no such thing as *enough* money, don't you know that?" And then, sobering, "In any case, nothing is sure. The market is fickle, DeWoe. Many people who were as rich as we are are now as poor as—as a Martian, even. Almost. It is true that my father has rid himself of most of his Oort securities, but who knows if even the farm habitats will succeed?"

"Unless they get a comet," Dekker suggested.

"Or even if they do get a comet. They are an untried technology, and who knows what might go wrong? But, Dekker, please, remember that what I said to you was indiscreet. It is a confidence."

"Who would I tell?"

"No one, I hope." Tanabe gazed sadly at the empty plates before him, then around the room. He brightened. "Ah, some new women have arrived. Let me see if luck is in."

But it wasn't, and when he came back he said, "This place is not useful, either, and if I am going to have female company I do not want to waste any more time. I am leaving."

"All right," Dekker said. "Where are we going next?"

Tanabe shook his head. "*We* aren't going anywhere. I am going alone. I do not have time to play these games with these annoying American women this weekend, so I guess I'll have to pay for it," he said sulkily, "and I'm not paying for you."

"Pay for what?" Dekker asked, who had never imagined that prostitution existed outside of a Masai village. He stared incredulously as Tanabe explained.

"So you find something to do for a few hours," Tanabe finished. "Go to a museum or something, if you like. Then meet me where I will be having dinner—it is called Turly's, down on the Strip; that's where some of the people from the base will be. It's a salaryman sort of place," he said, with a faint lip curl, "but the Americans like that kind of thing. And we'll have a few drinks, and then you can take me back."

So there was Dekker, alone again in Danktown.

He was under no obligations to follow Tanabe's orders, of course. Also of course, he had no more attractive ideas. He knew no one in Denver—not counting Marcus, that was. For a moment he thought of trying to find the tutor, if only to talk to the only other person anywhere near who had ever known his father. But there was nothing appealing about seeing Marcus.

There was also the question of money.

Dekker's slim savings from his stipend would not carry him very far in the big city. When, for lack of a better idea, he did as Tanabe had ordered, he found that even museums weren't free. Just to enter the art museum and the planetarium cost more than he wanted to spend from his slender credit line. Still, he comforted himself, he need not worry about buying meals.

He still had a full stomach from the lavish brunch. And promised himself dinner would be even more lavish.

And tried not to think of the sexual adventures Tanabe would be having while he himself was gazing at centuries-old paintings.

The planetarium was nice, though the exhibits of Mars were sadly out of date, and the modern-art museums, if not attractive, were certainly curious. After the last display of interactive holo art Dekker had a severe case of museum feet. Or legs—or, actually, museum body, all of it, because everything from the midriff to his toes was complaining about the extra work he had given it.

He sat in a square, puzzling over a map of the city of Denver. He squinted at the sky, trying to decide which way was north, but there was not much there to help him. The sun was out of sight behind clouds. Under the clouds there was a steady procession of cargo-carrying heliblimps, sliding down toward the port of Denver, dodging among the thickening clouds; that was some help, because he found the port on the map.

So to get to the place where he was to join Tanabe he would have to go north from here, he concluded; and, yes, there seemed to be a bus line that went in the right direction to find the "salaryman" place—whatever a salaryman place was—where he would meet Toro Tanabe.

It was early, of course. But it wasn't a lot of fun to be sitting there. He tried to interest himself in the nonhuman fauna of Earth, like the insects—there weren't any insects flying around on Mars, and who knew which ones were likely to bite?—and the pigeons. He tossed the pigeons some crumbs from the roll he had filched at the brunch, and then regretted it. He was definitely getting hungry.

Dekker stared at the traffic around the square. It was a weekend, wasn't it? So why were all these people driving these hydrocars around, with a plume of steam coming out of each exhaust? Didn't Earthies ever walk? Or stay *home*? The exhausts were saturating the air, he thought. . . .

And then perceived that—oh, God yes, of *course*—the moisture that was dampening his clothing was no longer just the vehicle exhausts that justified Danktown's name. It had begun to rain again.

*   *   *

Earthie buses didn't ever seem to go just where they were pledged to go. It took a change, and a long ride in a second bus, and then the stop was blocks from Turly's, the rain still coming down. By the time Dekker finally reached the restaurant he was both drenched and late.

"Why couldn't you get here on time?" Tanabe grumbled, looking around irritably when Dekker touched his shoulder. "We've already eaten almost everything we ordered. I don't know if anything's left, but you can see what you can find." He started to turn back to the dark-skinned Earthie man he was talking to, then thought of another complaint to make to Dekker. He said accusingly, "Why are you so wet? You should have bought yourself a raincoat, or at least an umbrella."

"Sorry," Dekker said flatly, meaning to say that he had not really got used to a planet where sometimes it was blisteringly hot enough to make a Martian sweat, and often freezingly cold enough to make you wish for furred boots and gloves, and all too often wet. Whoever thought of supplying himself with so many different kinds of clothing?

Tanabe blinked at his tone, then shrugged. "Sit down somewhere," he said testily. "I suppose you know everybody here."

"No, I don't," Dekker said, but Tanabe had already returned his attention to the dark-skinned man. The man was from the class ahead of their own, and Dekker vaguely recalled that he came from somewhere in Africa—not Kenya, which at least would have given Dekker something to talk to him about, but from some other African place called something like Upper Volta. Anyway, it appeared that the two of them were busy comparing notes on their sexual adventures of the afternoon, in which Dekker could not compete.

He found an empty space farther down the table and sat down. The vision of a lavish dinner evaporated from his mind; whatever food the people from the training center had ordered, its remnants were sparse and unattractive. Still, it was possible to drink, at least. Dekker located a glass that seemed to be clean, and poured himself beer from a pitcher in the middle of the table. He sipped it, looking with distaste at the remains of one of the things they called "pizza" on the table, cold and gluey.

"Are you hungry?" a woman's voice asked him.

He turned to see Ven Kupferfeld looking down at him.

"Yes," he said simply.

"You looked that way. There's a free lunch over there—" she waved to the end of the room, almost obscured in smoke and fug. "You're cold, too, aren't you?" He nodded, discovering it was true.

"Well, you'd better borrow my sweater," she told him, untying the sleeves she had wrapped around her waist. She herself couldn't have felt cold at all, Dekker thought. She certainly wasn't dressed for warmth, because all she was wearing was a skimpy halter top and a skirt that scarcely covered her hips. "You people get sick pretty easily, you know," she went on.

"We people don't," he corrected her, "if we've had all our immunizations, and I have." Still, the baggy sweater felt agreeably warm on his chilled body—it must have been immense on her—not to mention that as he pulled it over his head he caught a charming, compelling scent of Ven Kupferfeld.

Unfortunately, that train of thought led nowhere. As soon as her errand of mercy was done she had left him to resume an intense, low-voiced discussion with some male student Dekker didn't know. Dekker regarded the table without pleasure. It smelled of spilled beer and tobacco smoke, which made him feel queasy without diminishing his hunger. He got up and walked over to explore the "free lunch." It turned out to be little more attractive than the revolting cold pizza; there was nothing on the counter but sandwich materials and strange-looking killed-animal pastes spread on crackers. Dekker studied it dispiritedly, mourning for the lavish displays at the brunch; this was no substitute.

It occurred to him to wonder what he was doing in this place. Tanabe showed no interest in him. It appeared that the only reason for being there was to get drunk, and Dekker had good family reasons for not wanting to do that. It would have been more interesting if he had had Ven Kupferfeld to talk to, but she hadn't been encouraging. Most of the people in the bar were unfamiliar, or busy talking to somebody else. He saw Jay-John Belster at the bar, talking to another Martian. Then Dekker looked again to make sure, for, surprisingly, the other man wasn't a trainee. It was unmistakably Dekker's former tutor, Marcus Hagland. Belster looked his way, but Dekker turned away.

As Dekker was making a sandwich out of fatty slices of killed-animal and soggy bread Belster came over. "Hi," he said, picking up a piece of the stuff, folding it and jamming it into his mouth.

"Hi," Dekker said in return. "I didn't know you knew Marcus Hagland."

"Marcus? That his name? I don't really know him; he just hangs around here. I think he used to be a trainee, but they say the corporation threw him out for cheating." He munched thoughtfully, then added, "Your buddy Tanabe's getting really sloshed."

"It's his business," Dekker said shortly, though what Belster said was true enough. The Japanese was flushed and sweating, and Dekker observed that he had switched from beer to Scotch.

Belster chewed and swallowed. "Doesn't that make it yours? I thought you were going to be his nursemaid, getting him back to base?"

Dekker didn't answer. Belster was a great disappointment to him—considering how few fellow Martians there were in the training group, they should have been friends. But the man couldn't help being offensive, it seemed. "Is there anything to drink here but alcohol?" he demanded.

"Soft drinks, probably," Belster said, "but you'll have to pay for them. Listen. I hear your mother's a big shot back home."

"She's a representative to the Commons, if that's what you mean."

Belster gave a short, sharp laugh. "Fucking Commons. They've really screwed things up, trying to save a few cues to please the Earthies."

"My mother works real hard for Mars," Dekker said stiffly.

"Oh, sure she does. Only she's on the Bonds commission, isn't she? And they're the ones who got me fired, you know."

"Fired from what?" Dekker asked in surprise.

"I was working for the trade delegation here—not a bad job, you know? Then they started that damn parliamentary commission, and they started firing people left and right—cutting expenses."

"But they had to cut back! The debt was simply getting out of hand—"

"I know all about the damn debt," Belster growled. "All I'm saying is, I'd still be working in San Francisco right now if your mother's commission hadn't come along." He looked sulkily at Dekker, then conceded, "Not your fault, I guess." He jerked a thumb at Tanabe. "He's the bad guy here, not you or me. His father's got big money in the farm habitats. Why do you hang around with him?"

"I didn't pick him. They gave him to me for a roommate," Dekker said, then added more honestly, "Anyway, today he invited me to come down to Denver with him. I couldn't afford it on my own."

"Sure he invited you," the Martian agreed. "Why wouldn't he? The Japs've got all the money, them and the Russians and all. And it doesn't look to me as though he's being really generous with his invitation." He glared at Tanabe with undisguised loathing. Without taking his eyes off the Japanese he said to Dekker, "Wouldn't you like to take it all away from them?"

"I suppose so, I guess," Dekker said, not understanding, but also not—quite—willing to break off the conversation with this unpleasant person who seemed at least to be trying to be less so. "But that's just what we're going to do anyway, Belster, isn't it? When the project begins to show results, and Mars has its own atmosphere and we can start developing the planet—"

"I don't mean fifty years from now, for God's sake. I mean now."

Dekker shrugged. It seemed as though Belster was trying to get at something, but Dekker could not see the point. "Supposing you're right, how would we go about doing that?"

Belster blinked at him with a curious expression. "Maybe there's ways," he said. "See you later." And he left Dekker alone again.

The trouble with being a guest was that you couldn't leave until your host wanted to go. Dekker was not enjoying himself. Everyone else at the table seemed to be settled there for life, wrangling and arguing in ways that struck him as perilously close to outright affront. It didn't surprise Dekker that the voices were getting more quarrelsome. There had been a lot of alcohol already, and more coming all the time. Although Dekker had figured out that drunkenness was the tolerated Earthie escape from the imposed regime of at least keeping your hostilities to yourself, if you couldn't avoid feeling them, he wondered how much farther some of these people could go before the Peacekeepers came in.

Now that he had dried off, the place was unpleasantly warm, too. He pulled the sweater off and tied it around his waist, looking around the room. It was more crowded than ever, though he could not see Marcus Hagland anywhere. That was just as well, he thought, and thought resentfully again that there was no good reason for him to be here. There was no one he particularly wanted to talk to in the room but, maybe, Ven Kupferfeld, and she was busily head to head with another man again.

Maybe, Dekker thought, there wasn't any good reason for him to be on Earth at all. To help his planet, sure. But if the whole Oort project was as shaky as everybody seemed to think, then it might easily happen that he'd get through the course just in time to find that there were no jobs. Then what about his career?

Then, for that matter, what about Mars?

He didn't like that thought. Lacking anything better to do, he headed for the free lunch again.

There wasn't much left of it. As he was trying to pick out enough scraps to make another sandwich, someone bumped into him.

"Sorry," she said, and as he turned he saw it was the female instructor he had seen talking with Liselotte Durch.

"That's all right," he said, and began to turn back to his sandwich when she put out her hand to touch his arm.

"Wait a minute," she said. "I know you."

"You've probably seen me around. I'm a trainee. My name's Dekker DeWoe."

"I know you're a trainee," she said impatiently. "I don't mean that. I mean you look a little bit like—oh, my God," she said, "you're the Martian kid, aren't you?"

He stared at her, then memory flooded back. "From Sun-point City, yes," he said. "And you're—you're the one who had the party, just before the first impact," he said to the grown-up Annetta Cauchy.

She hadn't changed much. Oh, she had certainly filled out: The budding breasts were now fully adult, and she was wearing more makeup than she had ventured at her parents' party. But not enough, Dekker saw critically, to hide the spiderweb of broken blood vessels around the eyes. Annetta Cauchy had been through an explosive decompression at some time.

There was one significant change: Her name wasn't Cauchy anymore. It had become Bancroft. "That was my ex-husband," she explained. "I dumped him long ago—no, that's not true. He was the one who dumped me, when he found out I wasn't going to inherit a few million cues. I suppose I kept his name to spite him."

He was astonished to find out how short she was, at least twenty centimeters less than himself. When she was standing with Liselotte Durch she had been at instructor height on the teacher's platform, elevated above the students. At close range he could look right down at the top of her head. She wore an oddly placed barrette, high on the left side, pulling her hair forward to fall over her left shoulder. But the barrette had slipped a little, taking some of the hair with it, and under it he caught a glimpse of a ragged white scar, six or seven centimeters long.

She saw what he was looking at and reached up to touch the barrette. "Souvenir of Station Two," she told him.

"Ah," he said, nodding. "One of the co-Mars orbitals. I'm hoping to go out to the Oort itself, actually."

"Sure you are. All you recruits think that's the only place to be, but without the co-Mars controls how would you ever get the comets onto the planet?" She smiled and shook her head. "Anyway, we had a docking problem and my head got in the way, so that's where I got these little mementos. Station Two was okay, though. I was out there for a year, until they sent me back. Not for the accident. Medical problem," she added, though he hadn't asked. "*Physical* medical, none of that psychological crap."

"I didn't say anything," Dekker said.

"Well," she said, almost apologetically, "I know you didn't, but I get a little sensitive because there's all that talk around about people cracking up in the stations. I wasn't one of them. Anyway, it's nice to see you again. How do you like the Earth?''

"It's fine," he said flatly, poking around the remnants of his sandwich.

She studied him quizzically, but all she did was ask, "What are you eating that crap for? Oh, wait a minute. Are you hungry?"

"Do you think I'd be eating this if I weren't?"

She grinned suddenly. "I could stand something, too. Come on over here; do you like steak?"

He held back. "I can't afford steak," he said.

"Hell, neither can I, but we're not going to pay for it." She tugged him over to the bar. "Two cheese steaks and a couple of bottles of decent beer," she ordered, "and put them on the tab for that guy over there." She was pointing at Tanabe. Then she turned to Dekker. "So you're going to help straighten out your planet?"

He wasn't prepared to joke about it, even for a free meal. He just shrugged. "Oh," she said, "I shouldn't kid you. I know what it means to you."

"And to you?"

"You mean you want to know what I'm doing in the program?" She thought for a moment. "Partly I signed up because the damn Oort thing just about wiped Daddy out when it went sour—he's still holding on to those bonds, but that's just because he can't afford to take the loss if he sells them. Partly because, I guess, I did get affected by your people when I was there as a kid. You Martians are all crazy, sure. Mars isn't worth all this trouble. But I have to admire you, a little." Their orders arrived and she looked at them coldly. "When I think of the way we used to eat then—Oh, well, Dekker, we live and we learn, don't we? Tell me, are you any relation to this Martian senator that's getting in the news all the time?"

He hadn't realized that Gerti DeWoe was getting so famous, but he nodded. "My mother."

She stared at him, then nodded. "Oh, sure. I remember her. She was the one who called my parents after that party and bawled them out for getting her kid drunk. . . . But that was a neat time, Dekker, wasn't it? I mean that whole night, not just the party but the fireworks and all, watching that first comet splash down? I never forgot it. And then what did you do after I came back to Earth?"

"Grew up," he said, smiling. But she wanted to hear details; and so, as a matter of fact, did he.

And actually, Dekker found as they exchanged life stories, he was beginning to enjoy himself. The food was a help. So was the bottled beer, imported from Japan, he saw, and an order of magnitude better than the slop in the pitchers. When Annetta finished hers she pushed the plate away, drank the last of the beer, and stood up. "I've got to get back to the base. Nice to see you. But remember, when you get into my class I'm still Teach, no familiarity."

"Sure. Thanks for the steak, too."

"I told you, I'm not paying. It goes on your Jap friend's bill."

"Tanabe? But why would he pay for it?"

"Don't worry about it, he owes me." She glanced over at the long table, where voices were rising. "It looks like it's about time to get him back, too, before he gets himself in trouble."

She was right. Dekker sighed and walked over to where Tanabe was sitting with Ven Kupferfeld and several others. He unwrapped the sweater from his waist and handed it back to her. "Thanks," he said. She glanced at him incuriously but accepted it and returned to her discussion. It was a three-way argument now, Ven as deeply engaged as either of the others. "You Western people," Tanabe was telling them, slurring his words, "you're history." He smiled affably at her, but his eyes were narrowed and hot. "You were important for a while, maybe, but never as important as you thought you were."

"Really?" she snapped. "But you Japanese must have thought we were pretty important. Considering how you copied us."

"Oh, my dear Kupferfeld," he giggled, "is that what you think? But you were such devoted *missionaries*, Kupferfeld. You wanted so *much* that everybody in the world would learn to be like you in all your little ways—it was only good manners for us to do it." He poured himself another drink. "Especially the Russians. Do you remember how that went? You were so desperate to have the Russians copy you. Yes, and the Chinese, too. You wanted them to adopt American ways—American elections and American churches and American traffic jams and, most of all, American free-enterprise business. Didn't it ever occur to you what was going to happen when the Russians and the Chinese, with all their people and all their resources, began to copy your economy? Why, they almost put *Japan* out of business, let alone America!"

One of the other trainees said nastily, "We were doing all right until you bastards sneaked out of the Mars deal."

"Sneaked out?" Tanabe giggled. "But we merely changed our investment portfolio a bit. Obviously the habitats were a better prospect."

"You left us holding the bag!" the man brayed.

"What a pity you did not see the situation clearly," Tanabe commiserated.

"Now we're stuck with the goddamn Martians!" the other man cried.

And from behind Dekker, Jay-John Belster rumbled, "Hey, watch what you say about Martians!"

Tanabe glared drunkenly at him. He seemed to try to struggle to his feet—almost, Dekker thought in shock, as though they were going to *fight*—but then he looked around the table. There weren't any friendly faces. The other trainee was as hostile as Belster, and almost as big.

Tanabe collapsed back in his chair and grinned sloppily up at Dekker DeWoe. "I think," he said, hiccuping, "that now is a good time for you to take me home."

And yet, to Dekker's surprise, when they were out in the open Tanabe straightened up. "I dislike these people very much," he muttered, no word slurred. "Here! Taxi!"

And when they were inside he pillowed his head on the corner of the seat and closed his eyes. "Wake me when we get to the base," he ordered, and was at once asleep.

26.

PHASE THREE OF the Oort project's training course was what they called "snake-handling." It was an important one, for the most skilled workers on the Oort program weren't the comet controllers or the pilots who went out and found the comets in the first place. The hardest job there belonged to the snake handlers, who were the people faced with the task of tagging and priming a comet for capture.

To capture the desired comet and send it on its way, it first needed to be threaded with a long, loose chain of instruments, Augensteins, and machines. That was not easy. It was like sculpting dust. That's what comets are, dust and snow; the snow is frozen gases and it has no more structural strength than a Popsicle. Driving the chain through it by remote control from thousands or even millions of kilometers away took skill, not to mention the fact that somehow the whole fragile mass of the comet had to be reinforced enough to stand the thrust of an Augenstein drive. The chain of instrumentation was called a snake, and the people who stitch those chains into the comets' crumbly cores were the ones called snake handlers.

The snakes they handled were probably the hardest in the universe to deal with. Handling cobras would have been a good deal less trouble.

27.

WHEN THEY HAD finished Phase Two, three more class-mates had been washed out, including Dekker's former teammate, Fez Mehdevi, but Dekker's own class standing had risen to number three. Ven Kupferfeld still led all the rest, as always. On the other hand, Toro Tanabe had slipped to fourth. What he had gained on the Augensteins he had lost on the communications systems and the sensors, because his father had unfortunately not been able to buy him duplicates of those.

"Fourth place. That is not good enough," Tanabe said, staring at the screen. "My father would say I should apply myself more, so I will perhaps stay home entirely this weekend. I may even study."

"Then," Dekker told him, "you might as well come along to the mess hall with me for dinner."

"No," said Tanabe, sighing, "that far I do not need to go yet. I have some ramen noodles my mother was kind enough to send me. They need only boiling water, and I will heat some water here."

Dekker shrugged and turned to go. Then he paused. "Tanabe," he said, "I've been meaning to ask you. What have you heard about people being sent down from the control stations on psych tests?"

Tanabe looked surprised. "You did not know? But that is where Dr. McCune went, to Co-Mars Two. And of course as soon as she got there she began washing people out."

"I didn't even know she was gone," Dekker said ruefully.

"It is not something to be sad about, I agree, although the one who replaced her is probably no kinder. Now let me start my dinner." He hesitated, then said with embarrassment, "I think I will also pray."

On the way out Dekker saw Fez Mehdevi sitting in the lobby

with his bags. "Oh, hell," Dekker said, taking in the situation. "Bad luck, Mehdevi."

"Very bad," Mehdevi said bitterly. "My father will be quite furious, DeWoe. It is not a happy thing to be a youngest son."

Dekker had no comment for that, since he was too new to this apparently universal concern about fathers to have pinned down his own feelings about them. Instead, he asked, "What are you going to do now?"

Mehdevi looked up at the ceiling for an answer, as though the question had never occurred to him before. "Why," he said, "I suppose I will go back to my wife in Basra. Whatever my father and brothers may have to say to me, I expect that she will be pleased to have me back. Or actually," he corrected himself, "I don't imagine she will be pleased at all, but at least I will have my physical needs properly taken care of again."

Dekker, who was beginning to understand the urgency of physical needs all over again, was curious, if not exactly sympathetic. He said, "I thought I heard you were signing up for a dating service."

Mehdevi glowered at him. "There is no privacy here, none," he declared. "However, that is true. I did sign up. No one responded. It is because I am Moslem, of course. How all these Americans and Japanese and Europeans stick together! They treat us like dogs."

Dekker made an effort to be consoling. "They treat me pretty much the same, Mehdevi," he offered.

"Oh, but you're a Martian," Mehdevi said, surprised. "No offense, DeWoe, but it is not the same thing at all."

So for Phase Three the class strength was down to twenty-nine and Dekker had a new partner, a woman named Shiaopin Ye with black hair and skin the color of beach sand. She was quick, smart, efficient—but she was also a good deal older than Dekker and, she had already made clear to all the unfettered males in the class, married. Those considerations removed her from any more personal connection in Dekker's eyes, but all the same he liked the woman. She was a great improvement over the fumble-fingered Mehdevi. She had stood a consistent and respectable sixth to ninth in the class ratings, and there were times when she was able to help Dekker DeWoe through a tricky simulation.

He needed all the help he could get, too.

The first week of Phase Three wasn't bad. The instructor was a woman named Eva—she pronounced it "Ay-va"—Manuela Martina, and what she was teaching in the first week was spectrographic identification of cometary constituents. What that took was book learning. Dekker had plenty of that. He had no trouble matching the computer readouts produced when an imaginary "laser" zapped the surface of a make-believe "comet" and produced a rainbow of lines and colors. The computers marked the spikes and valleys, and Dekker was quite able to diagnose the value of the simulated body involved—this one marginal, too much carbon monoxide and silicates; this one a real treasure, because it was heavily laced with ammonia, which was to say scarce and precious nitrogen.

Then they came to the snake-handling.

Operating the snake-handling controls took more than knowledge. It took practice and skill. Even in the first few days, when all they did was familiarize themselves with the boards and screens in each two-person workstation, it was tricky. It took a steady hand and a sharp eye to operate the controls that would send a snake of instrumentation as much as sixty million kilometers away into the heart of a comet, and have every last commset and diagnostic sensor and Augenstein nozzle wind up in its exact right place.

Working at such long distance was the hardest part. To be sure, the "distance" wasn't any more real than the "comet" or the "instrument snake"; they were all simply bits of programming from inside the school's data bases. But they were good programs, and their effects were convincing. The readings from the instruments took precisely the two hundred or so seconds that were required for electromagnetic impulses to travel the sixty million imaginary kilometers, and the return instructions as long to get back to the snake. You couldn't respond to what just happened, out there in the comet itself; you were too far away. What you had to do was to *anticipate* what was going to happen next, and Shiaopin Ye was better by far than Dekker DeWoe in sensing the troubles that hadn't quite got around to occurring yet in the distant heart of the target.

He did, sometimes, wish that she were freer, and maybe just a little bit better looking. She was certainly not his first choice in the more intimate hopes he continued to nurture. Ven Kupferfeld remained his most promising target of opportunity, but she also remained merely friendly. Sometimes she was quite friendly, in a warm, sisterly way, as when she happened to sit next to him at a meal and told him how much she admired Martians, but the only actual touching of her flesh allowed to him came in the weekly sessions of shove-and-grunt . . . and more than half the time, now, he found himself stuck with some other partner there.

Dekker had some hope that when the class moved from target-zapping to snake-handling he might wind up with Ven as a work partner. Another of those pop psych ordeals had washed out two more trainees. That meant some reshuffling of partners, and working together could lead to studying together, and studying together could lead to more. That didn't happen. Ven Kupferfeld got a new partner, all right, but the partner was Jay-John Belster.

So it was Shiaopin Ye who sat beside Dekker as they prepared to do their first "actual"—if in fact simulated—comet preparation. "You two will go first," the teacher decreed, pointing at Dekker and Ye, "and everyone else will gather around and watch. Will this make you nervous? Yes, but think how nervous you will be when you are dealing with a real snake and a real comet, and the stakes are higher than simply performing an exercise. In any case, since this is your first penetration, I have set the range for half a million kilometers, so it will be easier than anything you will normally experience in the Oort. Do you both understand?"

Ye and Dekker nodded, and she said, "Very well, then. Do it! I will activate your display."

And she leaned forward to press the activation stud, and there on the screen was the image of a comet body.

It had no tail, naturally—out in the Oort, where comets were tagged and prepared, there was not enough solar-thermal radiation to boil the frozen gases out of the gray-white, lumpy object on the screen. Hovering near it was the "snake"—not very snakelike now, because it was still compacted into the untidy package of its travel mode.

"Ready," Dekker said, preparing for the first step.

Beside him Shiaopin Ye took a deep breath. Then, "Deploy the snake," she ordered, and obediently Dekker keyed the instructions for releasing the package into penetration mode. Seconds later the untidy package released itself, and Dekker watched it uncoil as his partner began to set up the program for the insertion bite. Dekker was not involved in that. His job at the moment was to make sure that the snake untangled itself and that each element in the string could move freely. The snake's components were all "smart" on their own—had to be, of course, for the times when the distance involved was more than a mere five hundred thousand kilometers, and any correction from the snake handler was likely to arrive too late to save a broken string and perhaps even a lost comet. But sometimes, he knew, the autonomous parts of the string might malfunction.

"Bite completed," Ye reported. On the screen the head of the snake had seated itself firmly on the comet's crust, and the readouts showed that it was secure.

"Beginning penetration," Dekker said, as he activated the program that would guide the snake's antimatter thruster as it melted its way through the snowy, flaky, crusty, lumpy body of the comet. And, seconds later, he saw it begin to pull its long train of instruments and strain gauges and polymer-mix tanks behind.

"Not too fast," Ye cautioned, and Dekker gave her a quick glance. It was the first time she had showed any signs of nervousness. Dekker gave her an encouraging wink, and she smiled back, embarrassed.

The warning was unnecessary; Dekker was not being careless. You couldn't afford to be careless when you were guiding a thermal thruster as it melted its way through the layers and pockets of frozen gases, towing the snake behind it.

As soon as the head was well embedded Dekker activated the snake's polymerizers. They were what made it possible to apply an Augenstein's powerful thrust to anything as crumbly as a comet. The polymerizers fed seeds of long-chain organic molecules into the melted ice as it moved along. When the thrusters had passed and the line of slop they had created refroze, it wouldn't be simple ice anymore. Then it would be a strong cable of polymers that would hold the comet together when its Augenstein thrusters began to fire.

All that was just the preliminary work that had to be done to push a comet around. The comet's structural integrity couldn't be trusted. As a sort of sherbet of frozen gases, comets didn't have any. Each one of them had to be laced with not just a single thread of polymers but a spidery webbing of braces to hold it together under the Augenstein's quarter-g thrust, because otherwise the thing would simply break apart. Moving a comet was not unlike trying to bulldoze a three-kilometer-high mountain of Jell-O.

Dekker took another quick look at Shiaopin Ye. She had settled down, the nervousness gone, and she was setting up the programs for drive emplacement. That was good, for what she was doing now was actually the most demanding part of snake-handling. She had to study all the data pouring in from those sounders and strain gauges, to find the best possible sites for mounting the Augenstein drives in that fragile mass. She made her choice and quickly marked a blue-green circular overlay where they were to go.

"Check, please," she said, sitting back, and Dekker studied the readouts.

It looked good. "Confirm," he said, and Ye began the task of threading the simulated snake into position.

Just as Dekker became aware of a sweet hint of perfume from behind him its owner spoke. "Good work, Ye," Ven Kupferfeld said amiably. Dekker frowned and put his finger to his lips; it was not a good time to break Ye's concentration. Kupferfeld said, lowering her voice, "I wish I had her steady hand."

"It's gentleness that does it," Dekker whispered back. "You can't jerk it. Just slide it in easy, where it fits—think of threading a needle with very weak thread, you know?"

She gave him a quick, veiled look. "I wouldn't know," she said. "I've never threaded a needle."

After the snake was in place Dekker and Ye accepted the congratulations of their classmates, and even the teacher said it had been a satisfactory exercise.

On the way back to the dorms both Ye and Dekker were surrounded with little knots of their classmates. What particularly pleased Dekker was that Ven Kupferfeld was one of the people who attached themselves to him. What pleased him less was that Jay-John Belster was tagging along, but, pleasingly, that didn't last. Most of the others turned off toward the gym; Belster hesitated, looked at Ven Kupferfeld, and then waved and followed.

Leaving Dekker and Ven Kupferfeld alone. "Well," Dekker said. "Here we are."

"And about time," Ven said warmly. "We've taken a while to get around to that talk we were going to have. It's been a tough couple of months, hasn't it?"

"I wouldn't think it was tough for somebody who keeps coming up number one in the standings."

She grinned at him. "I'm just lucky, mostly, I guess," she said modestly. "But anyway it looks like I'm still going to be here for the next module. You, too, DeWoe. You were fantastic on the practical." He made a deprecating gesture, but that was not entirely sincere; he knew how well he had done. Then she looked at him speculatively. "Tell me something. Are you married?"

Startled, he gave her an honest answer. "No. Never got around to it."

"I see," Ven said. "So then why don't we go have that beer or something?"

It was certainly a something, but it definitely wasn't a beer.

It wasn't in the student canteen, either. Ven had a car—a private *car*!—parked outside the school, which explained a small question that had lingered in Dekker's mind: the reason he saw so little of Ven Kupferfeld around the dormitories at night was that she didn't live there. She drove the two of them halfway down the mountain, flashing a card at the perimeter guard. Who simply waved her on.

They pulled up in a parking lot among a group of buildings Dekker had never seen before. "What is this?" he demanded, looking around.

"They tell me it used to be a ski lodge once, until the project took the whole hill over. You can still see the towers of the lift." She waved at a line of metal structures that marched up the mountain, still there though their cables and seats were long gone. "This is where I live."

Where she lived was an apartment that looked down the mountain toward distant Denver. It was a spectacular view. "Make yourself comfortable," she ordered, and disappeared in another room.

Her apartment was twice the size of DeWoe's family home— not the little cubbyhole his widowed mother had taken when her son went off to the Oort, but the spacious two-room suite Dekker DeWoe had grown up in. "It's what they used to call a condo. My grandfather gave it to me," she explained, opening a bar. She had changed into a blouse and skirt, and looked even prettier than before. She gestured. "That's him on the mantel."

The mantel was more interesting than the grandfather, because it was over a real *fireplace*, a place where combustible materials could be *burned* inside the house! But when DeWoe looked at the picture he was startled. "Why is he wearing that odd suit?" he asked.

The girl paused in handing him a drink, as though considering whether he really belonged in her room. Then she relented. "My grandfather was a general," she explained. "That was his uniform."

" 'Uniform,' " DeWoe repeated, tasting his drink, half of his mind wondering why a "uniform" had to be so ornate, the other half testing the strangeness of the liquor—it was full of flavors, smoky and deep and sweet.

"All people in armies wear uniforms, Dekker. It's how they show that they're soldiers. Of course, they don't do it any more. Granddad was out of work for the last thirty years of his life when they did away with all the armies. He was a fine man, though. He had time on his hands, and he took me a lot of places."

"Is he the one who took you to Africa?" Dekker asked curiously.

She hesitated. "Well, one of the ones. The first one, anyway. My father was a wimp, but Grandy Jim made up for it. He took me to a lot of places." She straightened the picture fondly. "Africa was the best," she said.

She seemed to want him to ask why, so he did. She gave him a secret sort of smile. "I don't think I know you well enough to tell you that yet. Are you hungry?" When Dekker admitted he was she said, "Then give me a hand."

The woman not only had living space enough for two families, she had food enough for six in her chiller, and she set out enough for almost that many on her table. "I usually eat here," she said, as though Dekker hadn't guessed that already. "Is that all right?"

Dekker grinned and nodded, munching his sandwich—it was guinea pig, with peppers and oil, and a berry wine to wash it down.

"It's Martian food, isn't it? I thought you'd like it."

Dekker's grin came back, this time at the thought that she'd planned all along to invite him here—why else would she have stocked the kind of thing they ate in the demes? Of course, second thoughts told him, he wasn't the only Martian in the class. He didn't like those second thoughts, though.

She was eating as heartily as he. Between mouthfuls she was saying, "If it hadn't been for Grandy Jim, I wouldn't have any of this; my idiot of a father lost all his money. I'm as poor as you are, Dekker."

"That's too bad," he offered, not meaning to be taken seriously.

He wasn't. She grinned back at him. "Oh, it hasn't been all that bad, and the traveling was fine. Grandy didn't just take me to the tourist places. We went to Gettysburg, and Volgograd, and the Normandy coast, and all kinds of other places. He loved old battlegrounds, Granddad did, and I guess I got to love them a little bit myself. As a little girl I wanted to be a general, too, when I grew up, but—"

She stopped there, looking at him thoughtfully. "Do you think that's strange?" she asked.

He shrugged uncomfortably, since he did.

"It's old-fashioned, anyway," she admitted. "But you're a little old-fashioned yourself, aren't you, Dekker?"

He thought about how to answer that, and picked the simplest way. "I'm a Martian," he said.

She nodded. "And Jay-John Belster says you're a good one. You want your planet to have everything that's coming to it, don't you? That's nothing to be ashamed of, Dekker."

Dekker, who had never once thought of being ashamed of anything connected with being a Martian, and was not pleased at having been rated by Jay-John Belster, said only, "No, it isn't."

"The other thing Belster says about you is that your mother's a big shot on Mars."

Her tone had changed, and it made him uncomfortable. "She's a senator, yes. I suppose that's about as big as you get on Mars, but of course Mars isn't that big a place—yet."

"But you'd like it to be big, wouldn't you?"

"Well, hell, Ven! Of course I would! Why do you think I'm here?"

She didn't answer that. "I guess," she said, "it's tough being a Martian—I mean, when you're so poor, and most people here are so rich. I mean—" She gestured around her condo. "—I'm a pauper, the way people like your buddy Tanabe think of it, and yet I've got a lot more than you do. Do you ever resent all that?"

The woman asked odd questions, he thought. He tried to find

an answer that wouldn't hurt her feelings and settled on "It doesn't seem fair, I guess. Martians work a lot harder than you people do, and we don't have as much to show for it."

That seemed to satisfy her. She changed the subject. "Why does your ear look that way?"

"It's a transplant. My original one got frostbitten."

She reached out dreamily to touch it. Her touch felt good. "But you do have all your other parts?" she asked. When he nodded, she lifted her glass in salute. And a moment later, to Dekker DeWoe's astonishment, she stood up, lifted her skirt and pulled it off over her head.

What she wore underneath was a different version of what he had seen when they tried on skinsuits, skimpy and almost transparent and prettily ornamented with hearts and flowers. "Well?" she asked, gazing at him in a businesslike way. "Are you going to show me how your parts work?"

"Well, sure," DeWoe said, because that was obviously the answer she expected, and not at all unlike what he had been thinking of himself. It took him by surprise, that was all. And then very quickly both of them were naked and in each other's arms in Ven Kupferfeld's soft, springy bed, the warm strength of her solid little body astonishing him all over again, before they got around to kissing each other for the first time.

The copulation was like all other copulations, infinitely different and always the same. As far as DeWoe's experience could let him judge, their intercourse was successful. Certainly it lasted adequately long, by any reasonable standard. Certainly it relieved all those tensions and cured all those aches for him, and the sleepy way she hugged him when they had spent all they had to spend indicated satisfaction on her part, too.

They didn't talk much afterward. She was actually asleep when, not much later, DeWoe got up, dressed, and quietly let himself out.

In the parking lot he looked wistfully at her little hydrocar, but of course he would have to get back without it. No matter. The exercise would probably be good for him. He paused before beginning the long climb to look up at the sky. It was a clear night on the slope of the mountain, with Earth's few stars almost washed out by the quarter moon, but it was bright with streaks of light from the comets on their way to rejuvenate Mars. They were a pleasing sight to Dekker DeWoe, who was well pleased with the world in general just then. One huge comet spread like a splash of liquid silver across half the sky, and there were a dozen more distant ones, but mostly fully tailed, plainly visible.

"And that," said Dekker to himself, "is what it's all about." And hardly minded the long, uphill climb back to the dormitories.

By the time he had reached the cluster of dormitory buildings his Martian muscles and Martian bones had seriously begun to mind, though.

Not that it wasn't worth it. Satisfaction long delayed was satisfaction enhanced; the copulation had only confirmed, not dulled, the notion that had been growing in Dekker's mind that copulating with Ven Kupferfeld was perhaps something that would be worth doing over and over again.

Perhaps even for the rest of his life.

What Dekker was beginning to wonder was whether he could possibly be "in love." It was an interesting question. It—almost—made the long walk home go quickly.

He wasn't entirely sure what the diagnostic signs of that condition were supposed to be. He was pretty sure he didn't have *all* of them, anyway. For instance, it wasn't that he thought Ven Kupferfeld was the only possible woman in all the worlds for him. It wasn't even that he thought she was perfect. Or, really, anywhere near it; for the woman certainly had some freakish attitudes toward life—generals! battlegrounds!—and Dekker had no doubt that there was a whole lot of the interior person of Ven Kupferfeld that she had not exposed to him, however entirely she had offered him her physical body.

All the same, as he limped into the lobby of his dormitory he was joyous. Not overjoyed. Not carried away; not ready to slay dragons for the woman, or pine if she lost him, but at least joyed.

He was surprised to find that the lobby wasn't as quiet as it usually was on a weekend night. A new class was coming in. A couple of the first-phase trainees were still shouldering their bags to their new dormitory rooms, looking around wide-eyed and curious. Dekker, as a third-phase old hand, beamed tolerantly at them and opened the door to his room.

It was dark. Toro Tanabe was gone for his weekend in Danktown, and before Dekker was far enough into the room for the lights to come on he stumbled over a package just inside the door.

The package was for him.

It was from the Colorado Rehabilitation Center. A note was sealed to its outer wrappings, with his name and address on it, and what it said was that the Colorado Rehabilitation Center was pleased to forward to him, as next of kin, the effects of his late father, Boldon DeWoe. The package contained some clothing, some toilet articles, and a letter.

There was not much imaginable else that could have driven the thought of Ven Kupferfeld out of Dekker's mind.

He sat on the edge of the little couch in the common room for a long time, with the letter in his hand, though he wasn't really thinking about his father's letter—he was thinking about his father. He was thinking about the sad, ruined man who had chosen to live the wreck of his life where no one he cared about could see, and about the way the world could have been if Boldon DeWoe had not had his accident out in the Oort.

Dekker didn't cry. He might have. He would not have been ashamed. He simply was feeling something deeper than he had often felt before, and, although there was sorrow, there was also peace.

He read his father's letter one more time. It said:

My very dear son Dekker:
  Since it looks as though I'm dying they are letting me write this. What I want to tell you is that I'm sorry I didn't come back. I wanted to. I wanted to watch you grow up, and I wanted to be with your mother. I just wasn't man enough to face pity.
  I don't have any right to give you fatherly advice, but I'm going to give you some anyway. Do your best to take care of your mother. Stay away from Marcus and all the other people like Marcus, because they are sick. Or maybe they're just evil; I can't tell the difference. And the most important thing: Please don't envy the Earthies; above all, don't try to be like them.
  I wish I'd been a better father to you, Dek. You deserved better.

                                                    Your father

And there was a PS that said: "Take care of Brave Bear. I'm glad you kept him. I would have given you more if I could."

28.

IT WAS THE Oort miners—the spotters, the snake handlers, the launchers—who considered themselves the most important part of the project, because they were the ones who started each comet on its long drop from the cloud to impact. That was as far as they went, though. Their original course programming merely aimed the thing in the general direction of the Sun.

That was close enough, for the first three or four years. Then each incoming needed to be caught and corrected, and that was even harder . . . or, at least, hard in a quite different way.

The comets came in from the Oort on a thousand different headings, and all of them were wrong. The right heading was the one that would take it close to the Sun at perihelion—close enough to get maximum deltas from the Sun's gravity, but not so close that the Sun's heat boiled too much of its mass away—and on just the right heading so that it would come away from the Sun on a trajectory that led to Mars. That was the tricky part.

That was the part that was taken over by the control satellites in the co-Martian orbits. They analyzed the trajectories for each incoming comet, and they commanded the burns that would correct those trajectories. It wasn't a onetime deal. At every point along the comet's long fall it needed to be tended, and nursed ever closer to the optimal Sun-swing insertion. As many as five hundred course corrections were necessary to fine-tune that important moment when the Sun's pull would wrench the comet out of its original course and put it squarely in the plane of the ecliptic, at the same time slowing it through the right burns at the right fraction of a second so that it would creep up on Mars at just the right point in Mars's orbit.

That was what the students learned in Phase Four. Some said it was the most important phase in the course. Others—notably the ones in the stations orbiting Mars, as well as the ones in the Oort itself—said it wasn't, but, really, they were all right. There were no parts of the hard, long job of guiding a comet from Oort to Martian impact that were not important.

29.

BEING POSSIBLY "IN love" or at least "in like"—or, Dekker corrected himself, perhaps simply "in heat"—was certainly giving him a lot to think about, but not so much that he neglected his studies. Ven didn't, either. The two of them actually studied together, on those evenings she was willing to spend with him—part of the time, anyway.

It helped his concentration that Phase Four was interesting. It wasn't just the subject matter, though that certainly did interest Dekker DeWoe. The other interesting thing about it, in more or less a personal way, was that the instructor was his old party friend from long-ago Sunpoint City, Annetta Bancroft.

Dekker respected the woman's position of authority and did not address her by her first name, or attempt any kind of intimacy with his teacher. It wasn't hard to avoid familiarity, anyway. They were kept busy. After the first few days of lectures and testing, they went back to the simulated control chamber they had visited briefly weeks earlier.

Dekker was pleased to find that he had a natural gift for comet handling. Ven was admiring—maybe even a little jealous, too—and Annetta Bancroft patted him on the back. "You ought to put in for one of the Co-Mars stations," she said, and when he said his real intention was the Oort itself, only looked thoughtful. But he knew she was right. He was as good as any in the class at the vital tasks of keeping the comets on course, solving orbital problems, and commanding burns. Was it because of his piloting experience? Dekker didn't think so. The general problems were the same—guidance and thinking ahead—but, of course, here most of the course planning was done by computer. It was the computers that plotted positions and trajectories for each incoming, interrogating every one of them and making a new plot every ten seconds of all the seconds in all the years each comet took to get to its destination. Still, a human being always had to verify the computer's solutions before each burn. That was gospel: computers rarely made small errors, but it took human beings to catch the big ones in time.

And time after time in the control training center, when Dekker punched in his proposed trajectory and watched the golden prediction line extend itself from the comet to the point on the grid where it would reach perihelion, then keyed "normative" to check it against the actual controller's solution, from far out in the Mars orbit, the two lines matched perfectly. Once the rest of the class even broke into spontaneous applause as they watched. Of course, Annetta Bancroft hushed them immediately, but it occurred to Dekker that his father would have been pleased.

He didn't think about his father all that often, though. He hadn't forgotten Boldon DeWoe; there was a sore place in his heart that contained his father's memory. But Dekker had many nearer concerns, and one that, in fact, was present with him in person much of the time, and in his thoughts most of his remaining hours: Ven Kupferfeld.

Spending that much time thinking about Ven Kupferfeld, or indeed about any other woman, was something brand new in Dekker's experience. She wasn't the only woman he had ever bedded, not by more than a dozen. But he had never mooned so over another human being before. When they were together he was fully conscious of the differences between them: Earthie/Martian, rich/poor, sophisticated/naive—most of all, perhaps, simply female/male, because on Earth, Dekker had come to believe, the fundamental differences between men and women were considerably more marked than he had ever observed them to be on Mars.

But when they were apart, the differences didn't seem much to matter. The thought that dominated his mind was just a wish that they were together.

They were in practice together a lot less than Dekker would have wished. Having granted Dekker entry to her bed once, he assumed there would be repeat performances ad lib. There were, to some degree, but not as often as he would have preferred. From time to time, as he approached her at the end of a day's session, she would give him that warm but opaque smile that told him she was going to say she had something else she simply had to do that night.

There were still plenty of evenings together, and after a while even Toro Tanabe noticed. It took the very self-centered Tanabe more than a week to observe that they had switched roles; now it was Dekker who was coming back to their quarters very late and very pleased with himself. Then it took Tanabe less than a second to puzzle out why. He flicked off his screen and gaped up at his roommate as Dekker entered. "For Christ's sake, it's Ven Kupferfeld, isn't it?" Tanabe said, amazed.

"We study together sometimes, yes."

"Oh, of course, yes, I know exactly what you study. I am sure you learn a great deal from all this studying. But that woman is out of your class entirely, DeWoe."

Because Dekker had thought along those lines himself, his response was hotter than it might otherwise have been. "She doesn't think so. If you must know, she's almost as poor as I am."

Tanabe shook his head. "Class is not simply a matter of money," he announced. "At least, once in a great while it may not be. Kupferfeld comes of a very important *family*, while you're a—"

He recollected himself in time to keep from saying "Martian." He didn't say anything at all for a moment. Then, moved by some momentary impulse toward kindness, he changed the subject. He gestured at his lightless screen. "I am going insane with these integrals," he moaned. "I can work them out so easily here on the screen, but when we are actually trying to guide a comet it is so much more difficult."

"Is that what you were doing?" Dekker asked, curious, because the glimpse he had caught before Tanabe turned it off had not looked like schoolwork.

Tanabe looked sulky. "Not at this precise moment, no," he admitted. "One needs some relaxation—it was a Marsie, as a matter of fact."

"Oh, hell," Dekker said, laughing.

"I simply wished to understand what your world was like," Tanabe declared.

"You won't get that from the Marsies." Dekker had seen few

of those popular shows, because they offended him—highly adventurous blood-letters on Mars, impossibly evil Martian settlers kidnapping Earth women, living like animals in their crude underground shelters, fighting. *Fighting!*

"I know," Tanabe said humbly. "They are of course highly exaggerated, but still . . . And the news is so bad, so I turned it off. The Tokyo indices were down a hundred and fifty last night."

"I don't know what that means," Dekker said, polite but incurious.

"What it means is that my father is about half a million cues poorer than he was yesterday," Tanabe said bitterly. "Oh, there's plenty left—so far. But where will it end?"

Dekker covered a yawn. "It's only money, Tanabe. Is that why you're studying so hard now?"

"While you are studying quite other things with that woman?" Tanabe hesitated, then said, "I know this is not my concern, DeWoe, but listen to what I say. Ven Kupferfeld is not only well connected, she is far stronger than you are. She will eat you alive, man."

"Yes, I'd like that," Dekker agreed, to make the annoying man shut up. Tanabe did. Without another word Tanabe retired to his own room, and when they both got up the next morning he was polite but did not refer to the dangerousness of Ven Kupferfeld again.

Dekker did, though.

The next time he was at Ven's condo, finishing the micro-cooked meal that they had prepared out of her larder "to save time for studying," he could not help telling her the amusing story of how Tanabe had warned him against her.

Ven didn't seem surprised. She wasn't even offended. She simply handed Dekker her dirty plate and silverware thoughtfully. She watched him carrying them to the cleaner before she said, "What do you think, Dekker? Am I doing you any harm?"

"Of course not," he said, meaning to reassure. "I don't even think Tanabe thought you'd actually *hurt* me in any way. He was just trying to say that you were very different from me."

"Am I?"

Dekker started to say a positive "No," then thought for a second. "Well, of course you're different. There's nothing wrong with that, though. I like you like that."

"Different how, Dekker?" she insisted.

He spread his hands, grinning. "Where do you want me to start?"

"Anywhere you like. Start with the first thing that comes to your mind."

"Well—" He thought for a moment. After rejecting the first two or three "first" things, he settled on one. "Well, just experience. You've been so many places I've just heard about. With your grandfather, I mean."

"Which places?"

"I suppose *all* of them. All those old battlegrounds, for instance. And Africa. Why did you go there, anyway? There aren't any battlegrounds in Africa."

"The hell there aren't," she said. "Africa's about as bloody as any continent in the world, and that's saying a lot. But that's not why I liked it best."

Remembering, Dekker said, "But you wouldn't tell me why because you said you didn't know me well enough yet. Do you now?"

"Probably not," she said, kissing his cheek, but when they were sitting side by side on her couch she began to tell him anyway. "The African game was all protected—you know that." He nodded. "Well, we managed to make a kill anyway."

He sat up to look at her. "How?"

"How? Grandy Jim bribed the rangers, what do you think?"

As she told the story Dekker looked at her almost unbelievingly. But it seemed to be true. Her grandfather had "contacts." His contacts took his money, smuggled him and his then teenage granddaughter onto the reserve, suborned the park rangers, even gave them weapons, two of them, .38-caliber magnetics. The guns were nothing you could kill an elephant with—but even the bribed rangers wouldn't dare anything as immense and conspicuous as an elephant—but they were plenty to kill anything smaller, if you caught it right.

Even a lion.

"That's what Grandy wanted me to have," she said, sounding half fierce, half sentimental. "A lion. An old, mean one, with a black mane. A man-killer. So when the ranger found the right track and spoor—that's shit, Dekker, lion shit—and we knew there was a lion around, the ranger sloped off. My grandfather shot a Grant's gazelle for bait—not to kill, just in the shoulder so it couldn't get away very fast—and we tracked that damn thing limping away until the lion came. Oh, Dekker," she said, her breath coming fast, "I was *scared.* I had just that little popgun, you know! But I let the lion make its kill, and then I killed the lion. One shot. Right through the eye and into the brain. Grandy picked me up and gave me a big kiss, right there."

She stopped, studying Dekker's face. Then she laughed—not a sneering kind of laugh, just a fondly amused one. "Oh, Dek," she said, "it's a good thing you Martians fuck better than you fight. So what do you say? Why don't we get back to what you're good at?"

It all went as well as ever, but while Dekker was still breathing hard, Ven Kupferfeld was already sitting up. "I don't think we finished the wine, did we? Let's not let it go to waste."

He followed, still naked—but then, so was she. She was looking at him contemplatively. "That kind of thing shocks you, doesn't it, Dek? I mean, shooting a lion illegally? I'm sorry. Maybe Tanabe was right—"

"The hell he was," Dekker said, all the more forcefully because he wasn't sure it was true.

"I admit it's not what you'd call socially sound. I can't help it. My grandfather was a fine man, and they destroyed his career."

Dekker came back to stand over her, trying to find grounds for consensus between them.

"I guess," he said, not sure whether it was true, "that there were some good people hurt when they abolished wars."

"They didn't abolish wars, Dekker. They only abolished armies, and they'll be missed when the next war comes."

He looked at her in astonishment. "How can there be a next war? What would they fight it with?"

She shook her head. "Never underestimate the ability of human beings to find ways to fight. Maybe it's atavistic, but I do miss the old days. Dekker? Don't you Martians hate anybody?"

"Hate? I don't think so," he said, searching his memory. "There are plenty of people I don't like much, though."

"No, I mean *hate.* My grandfather hated the Japs."

"But Toro Tanabe—" he began, but she interrupted him impatiently.

"I'm not talking about your fucking roommate, I'm talking

about all of them. Grandy said they were the ones that got wars abolished, them and their Peacekeepers. And now they're king of the heap." She stopped and looked at him as though she expected him to say something, but Dekker had nothing to say. This kind of thing was un-Martian, and therefore out of his experience—well, unless you counted the Ngemba family and the Masai. But none of the Ngembas had ever said "hate."

"What about us?" she asked. "Earthies, I mean. Don't all you Martians hate the dirtsuckers?"

He said stiffly, "There's a certain amount of fear, I guess, and resentment over the cost of the Bonds, and—"

"Not fear. *Hate.* Wouldn't you feel pretty good if something bad happened to the Earthies? I don't mean killing them, maybe."

"No." He thought for a moment, and then said it more forcefully. *"No."*

"Well, I would, if something bad happened to the Japs. We whipped their asses once, and I just wish we could do it again."

She sat thoughtful for a moment, then she reached up to caress his cheek.

The simple touch to his face altered the tone of the discussion for Dekker. "I see what you mean," he said vaguely—and really quite untruthfully—preparing for a rerun of their usual entertainment by sitting down next to her and putting his hand on her. But apparently he had mistaken her intentions. She didn't move toward him, as he had expected. She didn't move away, either. She just sat there, leaning back against a corner of the couch and studying him. Then she said abruptly:

"Why are you so frightened of wars?"

That made him sit up. "I'm not *frightened* of wars, Ven. I just think they're barbaric. We're better off without them."

She persisted. "Are you sure you know what you're talking about? Have you ever seen a war?"

"Of course I haven't. How could I? Nobody has."

"Oh, I don't mean a real one," she said impatiently. "I mean a war virt."

He was honestly surprised at that. "I didn't think people had virtuals of *wars.*"

"People who can afford them have all kinds of things, Dekker. Even people who can't afford them do, if they used to have rich grandfathers." She looked at him speculatively for a moment. "Of course," she said, "they're better if you get in the mood first—"

He puzzled over that, then his brow cleared. "Oh. You mean if we drank some more wine?"

"Not exactly. Well, wine will do, I guess. Question is, are you brave enough to experience a war?"

If she hadn't used the word "brave" Dekker might well have refused. That was undoubtedly why she had used it; and a few minutes later they were in her bedroom. She pulled virtual-reality helmets out of her cupboard and was helping him slide the headset over his shoulders.

The virtual-reality headset wasn't at all like a Martian hotsuit, he discovered. It was a lot worse. As with the spotter-ship suits it had no visor. Although here, too, fresh air flowed to his nostrils, he had the same sensation of choking in the dark. When Ven spoke to him her voice was muffled. "Are you ready?" she asked.

"As ready as I'll ever be."

"Then let's do it. What we're going to see is from the American Civil War, what they called the Battle of the Seven Days. Here we go—"

And there it was.

There was no click, no warning flicker. Simply Dekker was suddenly looking out on the banks of a stream, ten meters wide, with swampy, wooded lands lining its margins. He had full surround—not only sight and hearing were involved but other senses, too. The air that came to his nostrils was damp and wet, and tinged with the smell of burning wood—from camp fires, perhaps?—as well as some other burning smell, a chemical, unpleasant one that he couldn't identify. He heard the sounds of distant explosions over occasional birdsong and the constant buzzing of insects.

He heard something behind him and turned his body. Though the whole scene, he knew, was only computer-drawn images electronically painted inside his helmet, his view moved as his body did. Around a bend of the river he saw that some men in blue uniforms were urging a team of horses to pull a cannon up out of the river on the far side.

A *cannon*. It was a real *war*.

"That's the Chickahominy River," Ven Kupferfeld's voice

said in his ear. "What we're watching is the beginning of the Battle of Seven Pines."

Dekker frowned to himself. "I thought you said the name of it was Seven Days."

"Don't be dense, Dekker. Seven Pines is one of battles that made up the Seven Days, for God's sake. Let's take a look at some of the generals."

The scene swooped and shifted. Now he was looking at two gray-uniformed men who stood by themselves, poring over a map they held between them. One was tall and unkempt, the other dapper though his jacket was stained with sweat. Beyond the generals white-skinned men on horseback were riding by in a loose formation, rifles held loosely at their sides. Forty or fifty black-skinned men in assorted clothing—mostly shirts, cotton pants, bare feet—were panting and grunting to themselves as they dug up a lawn to make earthwork walls while three black-skinned women in long skirts and kerchiefs carried buckets of water to them.

"Those two men are the Confederate commanders," Ven was saying. "The big one's General Thomas Jackson. He got famous later on, when they called him 'Stonewall,' but right now he's just a corps commander under General Robert E. Lee. That's Lee next to him. He's going to turn out to be the greatest general of the war, and he's just been given command of the Army of Northern Virginia. Hold on."

Another quick scene shift. Dekker found himself looking at another group, this one by the side of a dirt track. Loaded wagons were rumbling along the track toward a river—the same Chickahominy? Dekker supposed so; and these men, too, were studying maps. "This is the other side, Dekker. The good-looking young fellow in blue is George McClellan. He commands the Union armies, and they're invading the South. See, Dekker, right now he's brought his armies within about a hundred kilometers from Richmond—that's the capital of the Confederacy—and if McClellan can push on through and take Richmond, the war will be over."

"Will he?"

"No," she said, scorn in her voice. "He could have, but he won't. The asshole had everything he needed to do the job, but he's going to back off because Lee fooled him. If you want to know the way it went, it was a disgrace. The North didn't take Richmond for three more years, and then it wasn't McClellan who did it. That's why this is an interesting battle, Dekker, because McClellan had all the advantages and Lee kicked his silly ass anyway."

She was silent for a moment. There were, Dekker noticed, singing birds and buzzing insects here, too, and the air was as warm and sodden as on the other side. It wasn't as bad as he had expected. The woods were pretty. These ancient men did not seem particularly monstrous. No one appeared to be getting hurt, and if this was a fair sample of what wars were like, Dekker could not see that they were so awful.

But then Ven Kupferfeld said, "Now watch. This whole series of battles took seven days, remember, so naturally we can't watch all of it. All we can do is hit some of the high spots—"

Then Dekker DeWoe got his first taste of war.

The high spots he saw on Ven Kupferfeld's virt were not at all high for him; they plumbed depths he had never experienced before.

War was not a matter of courtly men tranquilly poring over maps. War was bloody violence and brutal death. War was filled with the stink of blood and excrement and burning flesh. War was men screaming, and horses trying to stand up with guts cascading out of their bellies; it was wounded soldiers trampled behind their breastworks as the enemy leapt over with bayonets, and cavalrymen sabering gunners trapped against their cannon. War was *murder*; repetitive, multiple, and without end.

Ven was switching the virt almost at random from one scene of carnage to another, careless of time or sequence. At one moment Dekker saw a sun fiercely high in the sky, at another they were in a tangle of swamp and scrub with a violent thunderstorm raging in dawn light as drenched men crept through thickets, firing as they moved; at still another they were in midnight darkness lit with thunder of a different sort, orange tongues of flame that licked out from batteries of cannon massed on a hillside, pouring shot into screaming masses of men on the dark slopes below.

Dekker had seen all he ever wanted to see of war in the first few seconds, but he made himself watch for ten long minutes more. He needed to be sure that he understood everything there was to understand about this ancient and forgotten—but apparently not entirely forgotten—record of frightfulness from the human race's barbarous past.

Then he had had enough. There might be more to learn, but Dekker DeWoe was unwilling to learn it. He pulled the helmet off his head and set it on the bed beside him, careful not to tangle the leads to the control panel.

Next to him Ven Kupferfeld was sitting tautly erect, her hands clasped in her lap and her head hidden by the massive virt helmet. The Virginia killing ground was gone from Dekker's sight. What he saw around him was again only Ven's warm, comfortable bedroom. Incongruously, he could still hear the sounds of combat continuing inside the helmet, faint and remote, but he didn't know how to shut the thing off. He didn't bother. He just sat there.

Dekker was not physically sick, he was simply sickened. He waited patiently, without speaking or moving, until at last Ven Kupferfeld removed her own helmet and the tiny sounds of carnage stopped.

She stared at him angrily. "Well?" she said. "What do you think?"

He considered his answer. "I think I'm ashamed of the human race," he said.

She got up and carefully stowed the helmets away before she responded. Then she gave him a pitying look. "Oh, you're a real Martian, all right, aren't you?" she said. "You don't want to face up to what human beings are really like."

"I don't like people getting *killed.*"

"Why does that bother you so much, Dekker?" she asked, becoming reasonable. "Dying isn't an aberration. People die all the time. Everybody dies, sooner or later, and sometimes the way they die is a lot nastier than getting a bullet through your head in a battle. What's wrong with people dying for a purpose—because they believe in something enough to put their lives on the line for it?"

"What were these men dying for? You told me this war kept on going for *years.* As far as I could see," he said, "they died for nothing."

"It wasn't for nothing," she said, "because the South won those battles. It doesn't matter what happened later, that time they *won.* Naturally there were casualties. In those seven days the South lost twenty thousand men, and McClellan maybe a little more."

He stared at her. "Forty thousand dead men," he said wonderingly.

"Oh, hell, no, not all of them dead. Maybe half of the casualties actually were killed, or died of their wounds, but, Jesus, Dek, what of it? That was a long time ago. What difference does it make if they got killed? They'd all be dead by now anyway, wouldn't they? Anyway, that's not the point."

"Then what is the point?"

"Winning, Dekker! Winning's the point. Winning is what matters, because when you win you can take everything that you're entitled to have, no matter who tells you you can't." She looked at him, and then her expression softened. "Well, we won't talk about it anymore now. Trust me, you'll change your mind, Dekker, when you grow up a little. Now do you want to come to bed?"

He studied the woman he had, perhaps, been almost in love with. She was very pretty, lying back on her elbows on the bed they had shared. She wasn't smiling, but her face was flushed and her breathing was rapid.

He shook his head and stood up. "Not this time, I think," he said, sober and polite. "Thank you for dinner—and for the virt—but I think I'll just go on back to the dorm."

30.

DEKKER DIDN'T SEE Ven Kupferfeld again for a while—that is, he *saw* her, and he even spoke to her in class when he had to, and she responded, amiably enough, in the same way. That was all. Ven seemed content to wait Dekker's mood out. Neither of them referred to the Civil War virt they had watched together, and neither made any moves toward spending an evening together again. It was as though it had never happened.

It had happened, though. It had left Dekker DeWoe in a turmoil, and it was not without effect. It even interfered with his work, so that Annetta Bancroft reprimanded him for daydreaming in front of the whole class. When it was over she stopped him on his way out. "What's your trouble, DeWoe?" she asked, not unkindly.

He shrugged. "I've had a lot on my mind," he said.

She watched him for a moment. "I know about your father," she said, and paused invitingly. He didn't respond. She waited a moment, then became businesslike. "Whatever it is, we'd better deal with it. According to your chart you're about due for a psych interview anyway, so I made an appointment for you tonight. Report to Dr. Kalem. If something's bothering you, let her try to help you straighten it out. You've done well so far. Don't blow it now."

He considered for a moment, then said, "Thanks." He almost meant it; he could see that the woman was trying to help him, and it was not her fault that she couldn't.

Dekker didn't expect much from the interview with Dr. Merced Kalem, either, and didn't get any more than he had expected. It was routine. He wasn't asked to strip, this time, and he was prepared for the usual tests and harassment while he was being tested. When Kalem sat him down afterward and began questioning him about any problems he might be having, Dekker was prepared. Taking his cue from what Annetta Bancroft had said, he was ready with the story of his father's death and his worries about the possible effects of competition with the farm habitats, and the name of Ven Kupferfeld never once came up.

Neither did the subject of war; and when the doctor released Dekker he was fairly sure that the woman was not going to make any irremediable entries on his record. He was even, he saw, through in time to get the scraps of a late dinner at the dining hall.

He ate quickly and alone, and when he was finished he felt better. There was nothing *real* to worry about, he told himself. All right, Ven Kupferfeld had some repulsive aspects to her character; what of it? Most people did—if they were not Martians, anyway—and none of those hidden, aberrant, animal lusts and yearnings really mattered, because they were what all the socializing training and hostility-reduction sessions were supposed to deal with. The sessions obviously worked, too. They weren't as good as docility training on Mars, granted, but what on Earth was? And the results were clear: Even Earthies didn't fight wars anymore.

He was so convinced that he had worked all his problems out that he was surprised when, back in his quarters, he found Toro Tanabe looking at him with barely hidden concern. "How did it go?" Tanabe asked.

Dekker shrugged. "The usual stuff. Kalem's not as much of a bitch as McCune, anyway."

"Few are," Tanabe agreed, but even the self-centered Toro Tanabe was not willing to let it go at that. He studied Dekker for a moment, then confronted his roommate. "It is obvious to me that something is really troubling you. What is it?" he asked.

"Nothing," Dekker said. Then he changed his mind. "Well, there was something I saw the other night," he admitted. "Tanabe, have you ever heard of virtuals of *wars*? I mean the kind that have scenes of really bloody stuff, with people getting their guts blown out and all, right before your eyes?"

Tanabe looked surprised, then amused. "But of course, DeWoe. I sometimes almost forget that you are a Martian and do not know what everyone knows. These are what they call 'snuff virts.' They come in many varieties. Not just wars, but stories that are filled with all kinds of torture and death, and mob violence and murders and rapes and—listen, DeWoe, I don't want you to get the wrong idea. I do not myself care for them, but unfortunately it seems that there are many who do. There is no city on Earth where they cannot be bought."

"That's shocking! They *kill* people in those things!"

Tanabe laughed out loud at that. He raised his hand to cover his mouth, and said, "Oh, DeWoe, you are priceless. Do you think all those people are actually killed? But you underestimate the virt technicians. Most of the most violent parts are merely computer simulations, of course. It is remarkable how real they can be made to seem."

"*Most* of them?"

Tanabe looked uneasy. "Well, it is of course against the law to really kill people for the sake of making a virt. Still—remember, I am only repeating gossip—they do say that sometimes some of the killings are—what should I say?—unedited. That is, perhaps some of the deaths are real—though of course I suppose the actors do not know this when they are hired for the jobs. I do not know if this is true." He hesitated. Then, delicately, "You have seen such a virt yourself?"

Dekker nodded, and Tanabe sighed.

"I told you that woman would eat you, DeWoe," he said.

The trouble was that Dekker had *enjoyed* being with Ven
Kupferfeld. He missed her. It wasn't just that he missed their
very rewarding lovemaking, either, though he did miss that a
lot and increasingly; he missed touching her, and talking to her,
and knowing that they would meet and make love and talk
again. He missed the very differences that divided them: how
often did he get the chance to talk intimately with someone as
unlike himself as Ven Kupferfeld? Not that she wasn't *wrong*.
She was. But it was fascinating to see how deeply her sense of
rightness had led her into wrong channels.

And, then, she was always there. In class he could see her at
her assigned workstation, halfway around the tank from his
own. The top of her fair head was always visible as she bent
over her board; from his viewpoint she was out past the tank's
glowing image of the planet Saturn, with eight or nine bright
purple comets clustered near her. She never looked up at him—
not when he saw, anyway. She was all business. Whatever else
Ven Kupferfeld was, Dekker reminded himself, she was a dili-
gent student and a hard worker. She deserved to get what she
wanted—

Though not, he thought, *everything* she seemed to want.

Over his head, Annetta Bancroft's voice came from his
speaker. "Your turn, DeWoe. On the mark, your board goes
live. *Mark.*"

The keypad before him blinked at a dozen places, in different
colors of light, then was still. Out in the tank the great virtual
orrery that represented the solar system and all its parts was his
to control. He knew that it was moving, each object in its own
individual orbit, though of course he could not see any motion
of the planets themselves. Even Mercury, which revolved
around the Sun in only eighty-eight days, crept imperceptibly in
the display. In all the huge tank there were only a few signs of
movement. Dekker could see Mars's two natural moons, and
its three close-orbital stations, crawling around the planet, and
two of the comets close to perihelion were actually visibly in
motion.

Those comets were the first objects Dekker checked on his
board. Both trajectories were optimal.

That was a reprieve, because it was at perihelion that the

control had to be most exact and unforgiving. If the comet did not come up from its close solar pass with the right vector and velocity, it could lead to serious trouble. Then the Co-Mars Two controllers would have all they could do to correct the last leg of its flight to rendezvous with Mars. Sometimes they couldn't, and a whole expensive comet, with all its investment of time and equipment, was irretrievably lost—well, not absolutely irretrievably, maybe, because at some later time it would reach aphelion and begin to fall back again.

But that time might not be for a century.

When they broke for lunch, Dekker had ordered four burns, two of them on a single comet—3P-T38's damned orbital elements had still been wrong after the first burn—and confirmed, with the aid of the computers, that the other eighteen comets in his charge needed no immediate corrections. He nodded to Annetta Bancroft as he passed her at the door. "Sorry about the extra burn," he said. She shrugged.

"You had an unstable comet," she said. "I checked against the Co-Mars controller. She had problems with 3P-T38, too."

That was a relief. Dekker knew that sometimes the placement by the snake handlers was not exact, or the comet itself had pockets of loosely compacted material that the sensors had missed; he would have to watch that particular comet carefully in the next session.

She held out a hand to delay him. "Dr. Kalem passed you," she told him. He nodded; of course, he had assumed that, since he was still in her class. She didn't let it go at that, though. She said, "You don't want to let your balls get in the way of your studies, DeWoe. I don't have to tell you that, do I?"

"No."

"But I'm telling you anyway, right?" she said. "Ven Kupferfeld's good, too. I'd like to see you both pass, because you're the kind of people we need out there. I'll be going back myself soon, they tell me, and I'd be happy to have either of you to work with. But," she said, "maybe not both of you in the same place."

That was the end of the conversation. When Bancroft dismissed him, Dekker replayed it in his mind all the way to the dining hall, trying to figure out what hidden message the instructor had been trying to give him. And what an Earthie trick that was! On Mars people came right out and said what they had on their minds—if it wasn't offensive, anyway. Why couldn't Earthies do the same?

By the time he got to the mess hall his classmates had filled three tables and there were no seats left at any of them. Shiao-pin Ye gave him an apologetic grin, but that was more than compensated by the look of acute hostility he got from Jay-John Belster.

He sat down by himself . . . and was surprised, a few minutes later, when someone put a tray on the table across from his own. And when he looked at the person he saw that it was Ven Kupferfeld.

"Hi," she said brightly.

He grunted a response. She smiled. "You're still mad at me. You really didn't like my virt, right? I guess it was pretty bloody, for a first experience. Did you think it was real?"

He shrugged, and she went on persuasively. "But, Dek, it couldn't be, could it? They didn't have virtual-recording equipment in the 1860s. It's just a reenactment, you know? The kind they make for collectors."

Dekker put down his fork and stared at her. "But people buy these things?"

"Of course people buy these things! Not everybody is a weakling who can't stand—" She stopped herself. "Sorry. I didn't mean to hurt your feelings. I just meant people have different tastes."

Dekker began to eat again, thinking it over. Then he swallowed his mouthful of potatoes and killed-animal gravy and said, "Well, what we saw was real once, wasn't it? The virt people didn't make all that up. If people are sick enough to want to watch make-believe murder that's sad; but when this actually happened it was *real*."

"That's just *history*, Dekker!"

"That's the kind of history we're supposed to have outgrown," he corrected.

She shook her head. "Dekker, you just don't understand. War isn't just *killing*. Sure, there were a lot of casualties in the Seven Days—that's why it's a famous battle—but not every battle was that way. Some of the biggest victories in history have been won without firing a shot. Look at the way Adolf Hitler conquered Austria and Czechoslovakia. He rolled his tanks right in. Nobody got killed; there wasn't any resistance at all, because everybody knew it wouldn't do any good. Look at how the United States licked the Russians. Didn't fire a shot. Just the fact that they *could* do it won for them."

Dekker considered that for a moment, then shook his head. "It doesn't make any difference. I don't know much about wars, but, statistically, how many wars would you say were won without killing people? One out of ten maybe?"

Ven admitted, "Not that many. No. Usually both sides take casualties. But wars *can* be."

"Supposing that's so, even then, the only reason they win is because they *can* kill people. Whether they actually do it doesn't matter much. Murder is wrong, Ven. Force is wrong."

"Even to do something *right*?"

It seemed to Dekker, looking across the table at her, that she was prettier than ever as she argued her case. Fairness made him give her the chance to say what was on her mind—fairness, yes, and perhaps also, to a tiny extent, the way the faint hint of her perfume crossed the table to him.

"Who is to judge what's 'right'?" he asked.

"Everyone has to judge that for himself, of course. Even if it's just you, and most of the world thinks you're crazy—maybe even *especially* if that's so. Dek, do you know what a terrorist is?"

He looked at her with wry amusement; how the woman did switch around in arguments! "Of course I know what a terrorist is. You used to have them here. I know what a dinosaur is, too, and they're both extinct."

She put her elbows on the table, surrounding her cooling lunch, and leaned forward to look into his face. "Maybe that doesn't appeal to me as much as it does to you. Would it be so bad to have a Tyrannosaurus rex around now and then? Can't you imagine one of those great big things crashing through a jungle somewhere?"

Dekker laughed. "So you could shoot it, like the lion."

She looked startled, then almost angry. "Damn it, Dekker! Watch what you say where people might be listening; that's an extraditable offense."

"Sorry. It's just that killing seems to get into a lot of what you want to talk about."

"Why shouldn't it? Killing's natural. We do it ourselves, or we pay butchers to do it for us—or else we wouldn't have any meat to eat. Terrorists are natural, too."

"Oh, hell, no," he protested. "I've read enough of your history for that. Terrorists set bombs and hijacked planes and killed innocent people."

"True," she said, "but it's your history, too, isn't it? Where do Martians come from?"

He shifted uncomfortably. "You've got a point to make, I suppose. What is it?"

"The point is that terrorism is what you do when the odds against you are so overwhelming that you don't have any choice. Do you know where Israel is?"

"Next to Egypt somewhere?" he guessed.

"Close enough. It's a great little country, Dekker; Grandy Jim took me there, too, because he wanted to see what terrorists looked like after they won. The terrorists were running that country, Dek, or at least their descendants were. They didn't call them politicians anymore. They called them statesmen. But it was the terrorists—the Stern Gang, the Irgun Zvai Leumi, and so on—that set the bombs and killed the innocent people and gave them the country in the first place. You were in Kenya! So you know about the Mau Mau and Jomo Kenyatta—the father of his country, they called him later on. After they'd finished calling him a vicious murderer."

He finished his mashed potatoes before he spoke. She waited him out. Finally he said, "I don't care what you call killers. Killers is what they still are. I'm sorry, Ven. We just don't agree."

After a moment she said, "What a pity," and got up, leaving her meal untouched.

31.

PHASE FIVE WAS where it all paid off. By the time a comet had completed its long drop to the Sun, made its perihelion run, and been vectored to its final Mars approach, its course was set and its relative velocity down to a few kilometers per second. It was almost home . . . but that last step could be a killer.

That was where the stations in Mars orbit came in.

For the last few days of the comet's life they had it under their control. The control got easier as the comet caught up with the planet, because the distances diminished and the response time became shorter and shorter; burn corrections were actuated almost as soon as commanded. But at the same time the fine-tuning became more urgent. The comet couldn't splash down just anywhere on Mars's old crust. It couldn't come within five hundred kilometers of a deme or an industrial outpost. It couldn't strike the Valles Marineris or Olympus Mons or any other of a hundred Martian surface features, because they were, it had been decreed, sites of significant value. In short, the comet had to land where it was meant to land, with a circular error probability of no more than two hundred kilometers—and that included 99 percent of its fragments.

So the last hours of a comet's life were by far its busiest. Its final impact had to be set. Its Augensteins had to be blasted loose and sent into safe orbits for retrieval—certainly no antimatter could enter the Martian atmosphere, however thin that still might be. The comet's demolition charges had to go off in just the right sequence, with just the right strength, to convert the impact into a violent shower of pieces, not one single destroyer. And there was no room at all for error.

32.

BY PHASE FIVE there were only twenty-one left in Dekker DeWoe's class. That was no worse than was to be expected from normal attrition, but the other new fact was a lot more unpleasant. Dekker himself had dropped to number eleven in the class standings.

That he had not expected at all. It was Ven Kupferfeld's fault, he told himself grimly. If he hadn't wasted so much time playing lovesick Romeo to Ven's bloodthirsty Juliet, he would have been right up at the top, where he belonged. But, thank

God, that was over, and now he could get back to what really mattered. . . .

It was annoying, though, to see that Ven herself was still proudly number one.

It was even more annoying to have to face the fact that he didn't stop thinking about her. He missed Ven Kupferfeld. He missed all of her; her talk, her touch, her pretty hair, her sweet, wet interiors, her perfume, her warmth beside him as they drowsed in her comfortable bed—yes, he even missed her startlingly rough-edged way of looking at the world, which was certainly improper and wrongheaded and even by any reasonable standard actually repulsive; but still her own. They had disagreed irreconcilably on some of the most fundamental questions of human values, of course. Yet even their disagreements had been interesting.

Dekker felt obscurely cheated by the way the woman kept creeping into his thoughts. It didn't seem fair. It seemed to him that the fact that they weren't lovers anymore should be easy enough to take under the circumstances. After all, he was the one who had made the decision to break it off. But it wasn't.

The good part was that Phase Five was only four weeks from Phase Six, and Phase Six would end with Dekker actually going off to tame comets for Mars—assuming he got his grades back up where they belonged, that was. He devoted himself to doing so.

What made doing that easier was that in Phase Five he was actually seeing the greening of Mars *happening*. Each workstation in the training room had its own simulations, two sets of them. If the student controller selected one of them he was looking at a display of the surface of the planet Mars. If he selected the other he saw a tank, like the one for the Co-Mars stations, but much smaller in scope; it showed nothing but the region around the trailing segment of Mars's orbit. The rest of the solar system didn't matter. Apart from the odd ship in nearby space, the orbiter controllers only cared about Mars, its moons, the three Mars orbiters . . . and the string of trailing dots that were comets—all yellow now—that had been handed over to the orbiting stations for their final creeping approach toward impact.

The instructor for Phase Five was a Martian named Merike Chophard. "Chop-hard," Dekker said the first time he talked to him, but the teacher corrected him amiably enough. "It's 'choe-fard,'" he said; but, however he pronounced his name, Dekker was pleased to have him there. Chophard was the first Martian Dekker had seen to occupy a position of authority in this enterprise devoted to Mars's regeneration. Well, of *some* authority—as much as a teacher ever had—at least it proved that Martians weren't always restricted to the very bottom of the totem pole in this Earthie-dominated place.

At the first session Chophard started by sending all the class to workstations—"Any ones you like. Just sit down, and familiarize yourself with the controls." There wasn't much competition for seats. With the class now attrited down to the mere twenty-one survivors, they filled hardly half the available spaces.

The most demanding part of the job was the part shown in the orbit simulation; that was where the final approach trajectory was shaped, and where the last-minute work of fracturing the huge comet body into manageable bits took place.

It wasn't the part that most fascinated Dekker DeWoe, though. When time permitted he delighted in switching the view from the incomings to the Martian surface itself. The view was marvelous. The Mars-orbit stations were in five-hour orbits, circling even closer to the planet than the nearer of its two little moons, and in the simulation Dekker could see the Martian landscape sliding slowly by beneath him. He could identify the familiar geography easily enough, regardless of whether it was day or night below; the station's sensors were not limited to visible light. He was even able to pick out the sites of individual demes, though the buildings themselves were too tiny to be visible in the simulation's coarse resolution; he caught his breath when he first saw the mountain on whose slope Sagdayev rested come up over the horizon toward him.

And he saw comet strikes actually happening. Well, not actually "actual." Like everything else in the training displays they were either simulated or recorded from the real events that had already taken place, but no less thrilling for that. He saw two of them close together in one session, one just inside the dawn line, the other coming down eight hundred kilometers away and half an hour later. He saw the gases boil up from each of the fifty or sixty impact points that came from the fragments of each strike.

The gases formed instant mushroom clouds, towering into

the sky . . . and, Dekker realized with a thrill, the clouds were lingering. He didn't have Ven Kupferfeld anymore, but he had something that was far more important: Mars was beginning to come to life.

When he got back to his quarters that night there were two messages waiting for him. He played the picmail message first. Surprisingly, it was from his old Nairobi classmate, Walter Ngemba.

It was odd, Dekker thought, that Ngemba had sent him a recorded visual message instead of just calling him up. Because of the time difference? Surely not simply to save the extra cost of a two-way. When the Kenyan's image flashed on the screen Walter didn't look any different—same smart, well-pressed shirt and shorts, same carefully coiffed hair, same friendly smile—but the smile faded as he began to speak: "Dekker, my friend, I am sorry to say that I won't be coming to join you in Denver after all. On my birthday I told my father of my plan to apply for Oort training. He asked me to wait until he could make some inquiries, and I did. When his replies came he invited me into his study and let me read the screen.

"Dekker, I'm afraid that there would be no point in my applying for the course. I am not permitted to say what intelligence agency my father consulted, but I am convinced their report is quite reliable. It stated that there is definitely a decreasing need for the terraforming of Mars, because the farm products that would justify it can be produced more quickly and cheaply in other ways—I suppose, because of the new farm habitats that the Japanese are building—and it said that the entire project was going to be under review within the next few months. I'm afraid that means cancellation. Under the circumstances, my father said, it made no sense for me to apply. I was forced to agree. So, sadly, I will not see you there. But, Dekker, please remember that if the training center closes you are always welcome at our farm."

When the message was over Dekker stared at the blank screen. At least, he thought, that explained Walter's using picmail; he hadn't wanted Dekker to be asking questions about these "intelligence" sources. But how reliable were they?

Dekker glanced up as he caught a flicker of motion at the door to Toro Tanabe's room. The Japanese was standing there, looking guilty. He coughed apologetically when he saw Dek-

ker's accusing look. "Please excuse me, DeWoe. I didn't intend
to eavesdrop."

"But you did."

"I *heard*, yes." He hesitated, then added quickly, "I think it
is unfair of this African person to blame the Japanese; we are
not alone in this, you know."

"But your own father put up the money for the habitats,
didn't he?"

"He invested heavily in them, yes," Tanabe admitted.
"Please remember that my father is a businessman. In business
it is necessary to be practical. The habitats can be producing
crops in large quantity in less than ten years—and how long
would it be for Mars? Another thirty or forty years at best. So
I fear there may be some truth to these reports, though I would
not say it is definite that the project will necessarily be canceled.
. . . But, Dekker," he added pleadingly, "we Japanese are not
all unwilling to help your planet. I don't want it canceled,
either. After all, I'm here."

He didn't wait for an answer, but retreated into his room and
closed the door. A moment later he came out again, his coat
over his arm, and left the apartment without speaking again to
Dekker.

Dekker sighed. Well, he thought, he had heard plenty of
rumors already about the project being in danger. Assuming
they were true, what could he do about it? No more than he was
doing already: Keep on plugging away, and hope the rumors
turned out to be wrong. . . . Then he remembered the other
message. This one was voicemail and—he saw with a quick
uplift—from his mother.

He wished he could see her face, for Gerti DeWoe sounded
tired as she spoke. "I've got good news and bad news. The good
news is that maybe I'll see you soon, Dek, because I have to go
to Earth for a meeting about the Bonds. The bad news is that
I have to. The Commons appointed me. The Earthies are being
bitchy about the next issue. They want to renegotiate the terms,
and they're getting really tough about it. As long as I'm coming, though, I'm going to try to steal a little time for myself and
make it to your graduation—so there's a silver lining, anyway."

That was all.

After a moment Dekker turned off the screen, stood up,
washed his face, and left for the mess hall. He went alone. The

fact that Toro Tanabe had left without waiting for him was all right with Dekker. He didn't much want to talk to Tanabe just then. He wanted to sort out his thoughts on his own.

The thoughts were not joyous. It was certainly a real pleasure to think that Gerti DeWoe might be there soon—maybe even to watch him graduate?—but the rest of the thoughts that crowded through his mind were a lot less pleasing. Renegotiate the terms! But there was simply nothing more to give; the Earthies had the next six generations of Martians mortgaged already! He wished his mother were there already so he could talk them over with her. Or with his father. Or even—running through the list of people he would have liked to talk to—with Ven Kupferfeld. She probably would know no more fact than he did, but at least she might have been able to help him understand what was behind all this, even if only to tell him what the Earthies really wanted. They already had everything. Couldn't they spare a little assistance for their fellow humans on Mars?

Just asking the question gave Dekker the answer. He knew exactly what Ven would have said, and that she would have been laughing at him as she said it. What the Earthies wanted was undoubtedly what Earthies always seemed to want. They wanted *more*.

He had no appetite, but he collected a tray of food at the mess hall counter. When he sat down in the corner of the room where his class usually assembled, he wondered if he should talk to any of them about his questions.

The opportunity for that wasn't there, though. The whole class was busy chattering to each other about something else, a new story that was flashing around. The word was that the class that had just graduated already had received their posting orders. Every one of them was going to Co-Mars Two, no matter what they had put in for.

"It's from psych testing," Tanabe was saying emphatically, waving a fork as Dekker approached. "DeWoe, have you heard? They must have their own Rosa McCune there; Co-Mars Two has sent down half their complement for 'instability,' and so they're running shorthanded."

"So we will go out at once," Shiaopin Ye said, looking up from her bowl of soup. "That's good."

"But that's not what I was aiming for. I wanted to go right

out to the Oort itself," another grumbled. So had Dekker DeWoe. So had most of them, because the Oort cloud was where the pay was best and the glamour most appealing.

Then, thinking it over, Dekker decided to make the best of it. "I think," he said, "that I will request a Mars orbiter." The more he thought of it, the better he liked the idea. "Yes, definitely I will," he said. The Mars orbiters had one conspicuous advantage. If he were only some hundreds of kilometers away from Mars, rather than many light-days, he could even hope to get home now and then. Mars-orbiter personnel did get time off. It wouldn't take much; a week's pass would get him five days in Sagdayev.

He saw that, across the table, Jay-John Belster was looking at him with an amused, faintly contemptuous expression. But it was Tanabe who spoke. "You weren't listening, DeWoe. I didn't say anything about the Mars orbiters. What I said was *Co-Mars*. That's where they have the problem so that's where everybody's going. I guess the people in Mars orbit don't crack up as fast because they aren't under as much strain."

"But that," Ye said meditatively, "is strange, isn't it? I don't mean the crews in Mars orbit, I mean the others. Nothing like that has happened with the crews out in the cloud, has it? I have heard nothing of large numbers of them being sent down for psychological problems. And yet the miners must be even more stressed; one would think that it is there that they would crack up."

From across the table Jay-John Belster put in, "They will. Count on it, because it's tough out there in the Oort. Strong people can handle it, but weak ones turn into drunks and dopers. Remember DeWoe's father."

When Dekker left the hall, Shiaopin Ye walked with him for a bit. "Forgive me, Dekker," she offered after a moment. "You're troubled."

"It's nothing."

She shook her head. "That man," she said. "Belster is a dishonest person, Dekker. He isn't your kind."

"He's a Martian, isn't he?"

"No," she said, "I don't think so. He was a Martian once, but now he's just a greedy grabber like any other. He wants more than he's entitled to, and nothing will satisfy him."

Dekker stopped to look at the woman. Had she been reading

his mind? "But that's wrong," he said, fumbling in his memory for the long-ago thing that would explain why it was wrong. Finding it. "It's the Law of the Raft," he said triumphantly.

"What is the Law of the Raft?"

"It just says that people shouldn't take unfair advantage of each other. Everybody has to be satisfied, or everybody will be miserable."

"It is a reasonable law," she said. "It's a pity that Jay-John Belster doesn't understand it. Good night."

She left him standing there, discontented, unwilling to go back to his dorm room and Toro Tanabe. He didn't particularly want to study, anyway. He had been doing enough of that since Ven Kupferfeld stopped being a distraction in his life.

It was full dark now, and chilly. He thought for a moment, looking around. He was surprised to see Jay-John Belster standing in the door of the mess hall, looking at him; but Belster made no attempt to come over to him, and Dekker certainly didn't want to talk to Belster. On impulse, he turned around and went up the hill to the training center. If he wasn't going to study, at least he could do something useful, and the training center's library study virtuals were usually left open until late at night. It could do no harm for him to get a head start on Phase Six—particularly since checking things out in the virtuals would very likely give him pleasure.

So half an hour later Dekker DeWoe was sitting with a virtual helmet on his head, in the otherwise empty library room. Since he might well be going to Co-Mars Two, the first virtual he ordered up was a kind of travelogue of the station. There was a voice-over to keep him company as he roamed through the station's parts. "The Co-Mars stations," the deep, rich voice in his ear was telling him, "provide a nearly zero-g environment, and the first thing for any new crew member to learn is the art of getting around without gravity to hold him down." Quick shots of obvious newcomers floundering wildly about in wide corridors, trying to grasp one of the holdtights in the brilliant red walls. "Since there is no 'up' or 'down,' all the passages are rectilinear and marked in different colors: red, green, yellow. This is a control station." Scene of a board and tank, very like the ones in the training room, with an operator running trajectory checks on a pulse of four comets. "The control station is where the real work of the Co-Mars stations is done, but there are only four of them, and usually only two of those are in operation at any time. All the rest of the Co-Mars stations, fifteen thousand tons' mass, are just support systems for the controllers on duty. But the support systems are vitally important, too, because without them the controllers couldn't function. Let's look at the crew quarters, where you will learn to sleep in microgravity when you are off shift—''

Dekker's "virtual" self had paused in front of a sealed door—like every entranceway in the station, capable of being instantly locked airtight in the event of catastrophic loss of pressure. Willy-nilly he entered and looked around him. A young woman was asleep in a kind of infant's car seat, her knees partly drawn up, her arms folded across her waist.

Dekker studied the room critically. It was small, certainly, but not damagingly so. It was not nearly as small as the ship's stateroom he had occupied on the way to Earth—and not, really, much smaller than the room he had shared with his mother back in Sagdayev. A Martian could be quite comfortable in a room like that, he thought—until the tour took him to another room, minutely more spacious, where there were two of the "beds" strapped side by side to a wall, and the voice explained that these were "conjugal" quarters.

How nice it would be, Dekker thought, if he had someone to be conjugal with on the station. Not Ven Kupferfeld, of course; that was out of the question. But there surely were other women there.

The rest of the tour was less entertaining—perhaps because the woman was hovering on the edge of his thoughts again. It was instructive, of course. He got his first real understanding of just what it took to keep a handful of controllers functioning several hundred million kilometers from the nearest other human being. What it took was everything a human being might need for survival: alarm systems, automatic safety features, communications networks to tie everything together, kitchens, toilets, "relaxation" rooms with virts and game boards and places just to sit and talk—and, of course, the juice to make it all grow: the power plant, which consisted of a pair of constantly working Augensteins that were devoted to producing heat, rather than thrust, and so generated magnetohydrodynamic electricity to run the station's systems.

Even that wasn't everything. There was the mushroom farm of antennae that sprouted from the outer skin of the station; there were the "fixbots," the little spotter-ship-like repair vessels that circumnavigate the external shell when one of those indispensable dishes developed a glitch; and there was the sick bay—almost a small-scale hospital, because some kinds of medical emergencies couldn't wait for the two-week trip to the nearest planet. Co-Mars One and Two weren't just space stations. They were miniature cities that simply happened to be nowhere near any kind of solid ground.

They were also too complicated to take in in a single dose, and Dekker cut the feed long before the tour was finished. He didn't take the helmet off. He thought for a moment, then took a look at the base station out in the Oort—not very like the Co-Mars stations, but not very different, either, except in the fact that half the crews were going out on comet-tagging missions into the cloud itself. He sampled a Mars orbiter—almost identical to the Co-Mars stations, he thought—and then, out of nostalgia and longing, peered at a revolving virtual globe of Mars itself.

It would be a long time before he got there again, he thought.

He took a quick look at the repeat from the Co-Mars training tank, just to make sure nothing had changed. Nothing had, of course. Even that pesky little 67-JY was plainly in sight, now well out from its perihelion and climbing back up toward Mars. Or at least he hoped it was Mars. Could it be possible that it was going to be hijacked to the farm satellites?

He turned the set off and removed the helmet, not much more at ease than when he had started . . . and was astonished to find that he had a visitor.

Annetta Bancroft was watching him from her perch on the low divider that separated this workstation from the next.

"I wondered who was in here," she said. "I had an idea it might be you, but I didn't know if you were ever going to come out of that."

He didn't have a response for that. "Sorry if I worried you, Bancroft."

"Oh, come on, Dekker. I'm not your instructor anymore. We've known each other a long time, haven't we? Besides, we may well be working together in another month. Try again. What's my name?"

"Annetta. Well, Annetta, it's nice to see you," he said politely, as a prologue to saying good night.

She stopped him as he was about to rise. "What've you got to rush off to? You know, you don't look as though you're

having much fun these days, Dekker. Is it because Ven Kupferfeld has her hooks into you?"

"Of course not!"

"Meaning it's none of my business? Well, maybe it isn't. Only
I wonder what it's going to be like if the two of you get sent to
Co-Mars Two together." He shrugged. "Because I expect to be
there, too," she added, "and if there's trouble for anybody it
makes trouble for everybody."

That reminded him of his conversation with Shiaopin Ye.
"Right. The Law of the Raft."

Surprisingly, she nodded. "That's a Martian thing. You said
something about it at that party, when we were kids."

"I did?"

She laughed. "I didn't say you were *coherent*, Dekker. That
little rat Evan got you pretty wasted, didn't he? Serves him
right; he married that stupid bitch he was showing off with, and
they can't stand each other. But I looked it up afterward; it
comes from a book by Mark Twain." She slipped off the low
wall and took his arm, walking him toward the door. "So tell
me," she said, craning her neck to look up into his face, "how
do you think you'll like Co-Mars Two?"

"Is it definite I'll be going there?"

She grimaced. "As definite as anything gets until it happens,
I guess. Is that what you wanted to do?"

"No. I wanted the cloud."

"Well, I don't blame you—the pay's better, for one thing. If
you can stand the loneliness. So will you try to get out of the
Co-Mars?"

"No," Dekker said, realizing that he had just made a decision, then impelled to supply reasons for it. "Co-Mars is the
most important place. Somebody has to make sure the comets
get to Mars on a trajectory that the orbiters can handle, and I'll
be glad to be one of those people."

"Spoken like a true Martian. Only," she added seriously, "it
could be a mistake, you know. Martians don't usually make it
in the Co-Mars stations."

He stopped short and glared down at her. "What are you
talking about?"

"Don't jump on me, Dekker, it's a statistical fact. Do you
know that two out of three of the Martians that were on Co-
Mars Two were in the batch that just got sent down? Don't ask
me why. For Earthies it was only about one in ten. Maybe

that's just coincidence, but that's bad odds and it's a fact. I didn't make it up. You can look the records up yourself."

"You're no Martian," he pointed out, "and you got sent down."

"That was a whole other thing! I was in an accident," she said harshly. "Don't get nasty with me, Dekker. I've got my own troubles."

"Yes, I know, Annetta. Rich people always think they've got troubles, even if they don't really know what trouble is."

She frowned at the tone of bitterness in his voice, then relented and almost laughed. "I'm not rich, love. You're living in the past."

"But back in Sunpoint City—"

"Back in Sunpoint City," she said patiently, "my father was CEO of a major bank and trust, but that was then. He didn't shift the investments fast enough, and the bank fired him. That was years ago." She wrapped her arms around her breasts, shivering; they were standing in the open, and the breeze coming down from the mountaintop was cold.

"Was it the Bonds?"

"You bet your ass it was the Bonds. He should've got the bank out of them before anybody else; then it was getting too late. So now you know why I've been working for Oortcorp the last four or five years. You Martians cost me my happy little rich-girl life, so it's only fair you should pay me back." She shivered again. "Dekker?" she said. "I kind of like talking to you this way, but it's goddam cold here. Can't we go somewhere else?"

He considered the question. "Where?"

"My rooms're just up the hill," she offered. "I've even got some beer."

Dekker had never been in the permanent staff headquarters before. He wasn't sure why he was there now, either. If a Martian woman had invited him to drink a glass of beer with her in her room back in Sagdayev because it was cold outside—assuming there had been a cold, windswept place to stand anywhere around Sagdayev—he would have understood that the invitation was to be taken at face value. Here, maybe not. After all, Ven Kupferfeld's very similar invitation had turned out to be for considerably more.

So he kept his mouth shut and his options open. Anyway, it

was an interesting experience. The building they quartered teachers and staff in had once been another of those resort hotels that Oortcorp had taken over. It was still more ornate, in an old-fashioned kind of opulence, than anything else in Dekker's personal experience. When he walked in with Annetta Bancroft, he half expected someone to ask for his ID. Surprisingly, no one did, not even a remote voice behind a surveillance camera. There didn't even seem to be a surveillance camera. Two or three people were sitting in a corner of the lobby, drinking coffee and chatting; they didn't even look up at Dekker and Annetta as they came in.

As Annetta led him toward elevators he saw another couple of instructors wearing helmets and bodysuits in a little room off the main lobby, off no doubt on some full-body virtual-reality trip, and a woman bent over an origami model by the side of a fountain. None of them looked up, either.

Annetta spoke to no one, not even to Dekker. She led the way down a corridor on the fifth floor and pressed the palm-pad at her door. When it opened she motioned Dekker inside and closed it behind them.

He looked around. Larger than the quarters in the co-Mars stations, but smaller than the rooms he shared with Toro Tanabe. A lot less neat, too. There was a bed, and it was only sketchily made, a spread pulled lumpily up over pillows, and it was covered with skirts and jeans. "I was going to spend the evening sewing my clothes," she said.

He didn't sit. He walked over to the window and glanced out at the mountainside, falling away below them toward the distant lights of Denver. Even above the city skyglow the half-dozen nearest comets were already brightening the sky. As she waved him to a chair and opened the refrigerator he said, "Don't they give instructors better rooms than this?"

She looked at him narrowly, then laughed. "I keep forgetting that Martians say what they think," she said. "I could've had better, if I'd wanted to pay for it. But this is just until they pass me to go back to Co-Mars Two." She handed him a beer and sat down at the end of a little couch. "I hear you don't get along with Jay-John Belster," she said conversationally.

"Should I?" he asked, annoyed by the fact that everybody on this world seemed to know a great deal about what he had considered his private life and therefore sparring with her.

"Come on, Dekker, this is your old pal Annetta talking to

you. To answer your question, yes. You should get along with Belster, and with Ven Kupferfeld, even if you don't want to boff her anymore, and in fact you really ought to try to get along with everybody, because that's your Law of the Raft, isn't it?"

That stung a little. "I don't think Belster cares about getting along with everybody. I don't think he cares about anything that doesn't do some good for himself."

"Do you think I do?"

He considered the question. "I don't know you well enough to have an opinion," he said.

She didn't dispute it. She picked up the blouse and held it to the light, then began to repair a seam. "I hate this," she said. "I hate being poor. Tell me what you don't like about Jay-John."

"Why?"

She shrugged, and bit off a thread. "He and I are friends. He's poor, too."

He couldn't help laughing. "So you're friends with everybody who's poor?"

"No," she said, not smiling, "just with the ones who are willing to do something about it."

"Do what? Belster's a violent man, Annetta. I can't help thinking—"

She waited, and when he didn't finish the sentence she nodded. "I think I get it. You don't like dishonest and violent people."

"That," Dekker said, "is an accurate statement."

"And you've got the idea that Jay-John is up to something criminal. Probably you think Ven is, too. Do you also think I'm part of it, Dekker?"

"How the hell do I know?"

She studied him for a moment, then sighed. "Oh, shit, Dekker," she said, "I know what's bothering you. You think Jay-John should be a Boy Scout because he's Martian. You don't want to believe that a Martian could be doing anything crooked."

"Not just crooked! I don't like the way he talks, or Ven, either, a lot of the time."

She sighed. "I guess they had more hopes for you than I did, Dekker."

He scowled at her. "What kind of hopes are you talking about?"

"Well, hopes that—never mind. Just hopes. Look, Dekker. Suppose you're right. Suppose there's some sort of criminal activity going on. What would you do about it?"

"Why—why, I don't know. It depends on what it is."

"But if it was violent, you'd feel obliged to stop it, wouldn't you?"

"Of course," he said, surprised.

She was grinning now. "I'm sorry, Dekker," she said. "It's just that you're so *Martian*. Anyway, you're partly right. There is something, and it's against the law, only you won't do anything about it. When you're poor, and you don't want to stay poor, you have to take some shortcuts. That's what we do. Do you want to hear what the shortcuts are?"

He considered that for a moment. Then, honestly, "I don't know if I do."

"Well, I know, so I'm going to tell you. What we do is sell information to people who want it—information, for instance, about what the tests are going to cover. Do you think that's wicked of us, Dekker? I don't. I think we're just trying to get even with the system that screwed us up."

He set his beer down in indignation. "Hell, Annetta! It's not just some prep-school course here! If you're letting people pass who don't really know what they're doing, you're endangering the whole project—not to mention actual human lives!"

She shook her head. "Wrong. I've been there," she reminded him. "Once you start work on a control station you've got the old hands standing over you for the first month, watching you like hawks. Anything you don't know when you got there, you're going to learn before they let you handle anything yourself. So there's your conspiracy, Dekker," she finished. "And now why don't you just go back to your dorm and get a good night's sleep? Because you can't blow the whistle on us, you know."

"The hell I can't!"

"But you can't," she said seriously, "because you'd be out on your ass if you did. Remember the entrance test you took? The one your father gave you the answers for before you took it? Well, hell, Dekker! Where do you think he got them?"

33.

SOME OF THE students at the Oortcorp training school called Phase Six the "garbage course." When those students graduated and shipped out to work for the project they might change their minds, because Phase Six was important.

The reason it was important had to do with the places where they would go to work. Those places were spread out over many billions of kilometers of space and they performed quite different functions, but they all had one vital feature in common. Each one was no more than a metal shell that was afloat in the most hostile environment human beings have ever tried to survive in: space.

Space is lethal to a degree that nothing on Earth can match. Stripped naked of resources anywhere on Earth, a human being could still survive, at least for a time. He could go weeks without food, days without even water. Without air to breathe, though, he would die at once. If that same human being were cast unprotected into space his lungs would burst, his blood would boil, and he would be dead in minutes.

The only thing that keeps all spacefarers from suffering that quick and brutal death is their complex of pumps and water purifiers and air regenerators and power-plant and life-support systems, and those systems were practically identical in every station of the Oortcorp project.

If anything went wrong—as, sooner or later, something always does—it had to be fixed at once. If it wasn't, people would die. There would be no outside experts to save them. There wasn't any plumber to call up or ambulance to summon across the million-kilometer stretches of empty space. The people who worked there had no one to rely on but themselves. It was they alone who had to learn every last one of the skills that were needed to keep that complex and fallible system running; and that was what Phase Six was all about.

34.

DEKKER'S CLASS HAD started out with a full complement of thirty-four chosen men and women, every one of them carefully selected for education, ability, and intelligence. It dwindled fast.

By the end of Phase Five nearly half of the original thirty-four were gone. Dekker DeWoe was still there. So were Ven Kupferfeld, and Toro Tanabe, and Shiaopin Ye, and Jay-John Belster, and a dozen or so others from the original roster, but that was all. Sixteen of those bright and able students had turned out to be not quite bright and able enough—or, Dekker could not help reminding himself, dishonest enough—to keep their grades and psychological fitness high enough to survive the ordeal, and so the class number was down to eighteen . . . for one night.

When that night came Dekker didn't know it was coming. He was getting ready for bed, staring into the mirror as he brushed his teeth, not liking what he saw. It wasn't the physical reflection that bothered him; physically Dekker was in about the best shape of his life. The polysteroid and calcium shots were down to bare maintenance levels, and the braces had lain untouched under his bed for months now. It was almost possible for Dekker to forget that he was a Martian suffering from the environment of a more dire planet than his own . . . except when, now and then, he was reminded by such bizarre happenings as the sudden, surprising first autumn fall of snow. Snow! And his progress at the school was—well—optimal. It deserved congratulation . . . provided you didn't know how it had been made possible.

After all, simply getting as far as Phase Six was a victory of sorts in itself. What spoiled it for Dekker DeWoe was the knowledge that the victory was riddled with fraud. Not just his own, either. Dekker hadn't talked much with Toro Tanabe

after the conversation with Annetta Bancroft, because after
that he had understood at last how the Japanese had breezed
through so easily. When he looked at the rest of his classmates
it was with suspicion: how many of them were fakes, too? And
when he looked in the mirror what he saw was that very un-
Martian creature, a cheat.

It was terrible to know that Annetta, and probably Ven, and
perhaps any number of other people knew the truth about him;
but the worst part of all was simply knowing it of himself.

Even the little bits of recent good news had suddenly turned
into bad. It was good that his mother would be there for his
graduation . . . but, when he saw her, what was he going to tell
Gerti DeWoe?

When, that night, he heard a commotion in the hall outside
his quarters, he peered out of the bathroom, toothbrush in his
hand, to see what might be going on. Toro Tanabe was already
at the hall door, talking excitedly to someone outside. When
Tanabe turned and saw Dekker, he called, "Come and see,
DeWoe! We have some new blood for Phase Six." And when
Dekker hesitated, he added irritably, "It doesn't matter that
you are getting ready for bed, come anyway. Hurry."

Dekker did hurry, after his fashion. That is to say that when
he washed his face and pulled on a robe he did it rapidly, but
by the time he got to the door the last of the new people was
already disappearing into a doorway down the hall. Dekker
looked after him in puzzlement. "Did you say they're coming
into Phase Six with us?"

"Yes, exactly, DeWoe. But that is not all. They are not
ordinary students. These people are all veterans—eight of
them—and from the Oort cloud itself, actually! They have been
on Earth on R-and-R between tours of duty, only instead of
going back to the Oort they have been ordered to join us for a
refresher course and then to go to Co-Mars Two."

Dekker looked at his roommate in perplexity. "I never heard
of such a thing," he said.

"There has never been such a thing! It is quite irregular. Do
you see, DeWoe, it must mean that Co-Mars Two needs people
very badly!"

"My name," the Phase Six instructor said the next morning,
"is Marty Gillespie, and I used to be head of services at the
Nairobi Skyhook plenum until I retired." He looked retired; he

was an elderly man with no hair at the top of his head but a scraggly white pigtail tied over the back of his neck. He was short and plump, and there were lines in his face, but he looked amiable enough as he studied his new class. "What you're going to learn here is what you need to know about housekeeping on a space station, but before we get into that I want you all to stand up and tell me your names."

Dekker, up close to the instructor, turned around to see which were the new ones. They weren't hard to pick out. There were eight people who had been in the Oort, six men and two women, and they were conspicuous among the familiar faces. They carried themselves with an air of assurance that most of the others lacked, and they had clumped themselves together in a tight group. Dekker noted that one of the women, though apparently a little older than himself, was quite tall and not at all unpleasant to look at. He filed her name away in his mind: Rima Consalvo.

Gillespie had also noted the grouping and shook his head. "You're going to have to pair off to share terminals, and I don't want you new people all sticking together; so if you're one of the ones that're in from the cloud, I want you working with a buddy that isn't. You can tell him what things are like out in the field, and he can tell you what he's just learned here and you've probably forgotten. So, let's see, you and you, you go with her, you two together—"

Dekker recognized a chance when he saw it. All it took then was a little inconspicuous sidling through the crowd, and when Gillespie came to Rima Consalvo, Dekker was right beside her. She gave him a quizzical look, then, when Gillespie obligingly paired them, a grin.

"Nice to meet you," Dekker whispered, and she nodded.

"Remember who you're with," the instructor ordered. "Now, you probably want to know what I mean by housekeeping. I don't just mean tidying up your quarters, though you'll have to do that, too. Mostly I mean staying alive, you yourself and everybody in the station with you. That means knowing how to deal with power loss, or accident, or fire. Second, I mean making sure the station does its job: that's instrument and communications maintenance. Last there's keeping the crew fed and healthy and reasonably happy in their work, which means food preparation, laundry, cleanup, and general repair—anything from fixing a squeaking door to tackling a stopped toilet. Any questions about any of that?"

He was looking around at the expressions on the faces of the class. None of them were looking pleased, but it was Toro Tanabe who put his hand up first. "I did not enter this course to fix toilets!" he said.

"Nobody ever does," Gillespie said pleasantly, "but sometimes the toilets have to be fixed. You crap in them, you fix them if you have to. Any other questions?" He looked around briefly, then said, "You probably don't know what to ask yet, do you? Well, let's get into it. You teams take your places—pick any screens you want, they're all the same—and let's start with a look at how we go about maintaining pressure integrity."

When they had their seats, Rima looked at Dekker inquiringly, Dekker nodded, and so she was the one who started the display.

It was, like all the school's training programs, clear and complete—though not, to Dekker, very interesting. Maintaining pressure integrity was not a challenging subject for someone who had grown up in an airtight Martian deme. It wasn't for someone who had spent four years in the Oort cloud, either. All the same, side by side they watched the 3D schematics of a station's air system, along with the automatic programs for sealing every door and bulkhead in the event of pressure drop; Dekker noticed approvingly that Rima Consalvo paid attention, in spite of the fact that she, too, must have known all this long before. He considered that her attitude was very nearly Martian. They had an interactive screen, of course, but for this first tutorial there was nothing for them to do but watch, and they both kept their hands off the keypad. Dekker had plenty of chances to notice that Rima Consalvo had a nice profile and that, although her perfume wasn't Ven Kupferfeld's, it was still quite pleasant.

When the program had run and the instructor asked if anyone hadn't understood anything, it was a while before one of the students raised her hand. "Maybe we just haven't come to that part of the course yet," she said tentatively, "but what happens if there's a massive collision and the power for the automatic systems goes out at the same time as the hull is breached?"

Gillespie gave her an approving look. "Good question,

Clarkson. You're on your toes, but you're right, we just haven't come to that yet. In a minute we'll set up some problem simulations for you to deal with, and that'll be one of them. Any other questions? Then go to step two on your screens, and let's see what some of the problems might be."

On the way to lunch they walked together, naturally enough, and Dekker had plenty of time to tell Rima Consalvo all about himself. He did it with smiles and animated gestures, not entirely because he was aware of the fact that Ven Kupferfeld was only a few steps behind them. Consalvo responded, too. She showed definite signs of being interested in him, he thought, as well as being quite interesting herself. She had evidently had a privileged childhood—well, didn't every Earthie child?—but then she had signed up for the Oort. She described her four-year hitch out in the cloud, where she specialized in snake-handling by choice, now and then taking her turn in one of the spotter ships.

"But that really wears you down, DeWoe, out there all by yourself for weeks at a time. Snake-handling's better. You don't have to wear those damn bodysuits, and you're on the base ship with your friends so when you're off shift you have somebody to talk to. I was really afraid I'd be missing all those guys," she added, as they joined the counter line, "but it looks to me like there are some good people here, too."

That was a remark that pleased Dekker, since naturally he concluded that he was one of them. Unfortunately they got separated in the line, because Consalvo had had to go back for a clean tray, and their conversation was interrupted just when it was going well. Dekker was careful to save a seat for her on the assumption that they would have the whole lunch hour to get to know each other better. Maybe even to get her to answer a few questions more explicitly. Like why she had made the jump from a life of ease to the Oort. Like her age, for that matter. He guessed, as well as he could, that Consalvo was in her early thirties, Earth years, but she seemed to have that strange reluctance of Earthie women about revealing their ages—as though ten years or so one way or another could make much difference. Anyway, she certainly did seem to like him, and Dekker considered that that promised well for the future on Co-Mars Two.

But when Consalvo came off the line with her tray she passed right by him with a nod and a friendly, but not inviting, smile, to sit down two or three tables away.

That was a disappointment. It was a surprise, too, when he saw that the person she sat with was, of all people, Ven Kupferfeld. A moment later another man joined them—Dekker recognized him as one of the new group from the Oort, somebody named Berl Korman.

Then there was a second surprise and maybe an even more unwelcome one, as Jay-John Belster put his tray down at the same table.

Dekker concentrated his attention on his killed-animal cutlet. He wasn't really being snubbed, he explained to himself. It was only natural that Rima Consalvo would want to get to know as many of her new classmates as possible—but why those particular two new classmates? At least, he thought, her choice of companions seemed to prove that she wasn't avoiding him because of some prejudice against Martians—supposing that anyone could still think of Jay-John Belster as a real Martian.

When they got back to the training center after lunch, Consalvo seemed as friendly as ever when she took her place right beside him again. The rest of the class was still drifting in, which gave him a chance for a little conversation. Dekker debated mentioning that he had been looking forward to having her company at lunch. It was certainly true, but he guessed that it probably wasn't a good idea to say it, since it might sound to her as though he were trying to be, well, possessive, and without much excuse considering the shortness of their acquaintance.

Still, he couldn't see any reason not to say, quite casually, "I didn't know you knew Jay-John Belster."

"Belster? Oh, yes. Met him last night," she said. "Kupferfeld, too. Were your ears burning? She was saying some very nice things about you, DeWoe."

That was another surprise. It was unexpected enough to keep him from saying anything else just then, and a minute later they were deep into the afternoon's lesson and any further personal remarks had to be postponed. "The key to all the safety systems," Marty Gillespie announced, picking up where he had left off, "is communications. The sensors won't do you any good if their data doesn't get to the safety relays, and so the intrastation communications links are vital. They're all triply redundant, of course, but that doesn't mean they can't all go out at once. That's what we call 'common vulnerability,' meaning that sometimes what makes one of them fail will do the same thing to the others as soon as they come on. So we're going to work on the communications net now; fire up and start with the next step."

So Dekker and Rima Consalvo spent the afternoon tracing communications links on a model space station. There were plenty of them that had to be learned: the emergency net that dealt with such potential disasters as fires, pressure drops, or solar flares; the relays that kept the controllers' displays continuously updated; the forwarding circuits that passed on communications from outside the station; the intrastation voice links and all the others.

The final task of the day was to check the links between the station's comet-watching instrument, and the display, on the controllers' boards. As Dekker already knew, of course, Co-Mars Two's sensors continually interrogated every one of the comets and received status reports, which were passed on to the displays at each station; then, after the computers had produced their analyses and solutions, the controllers' burn instructions retraced the same steps back to the receivers on the comets themselves.

"The worst problem here," Marty Gillespie told them, "is when there's a fault in the downlink on the comet body. There's an example right here. Look at that little one on the up leg there, 67-JY. It's been giving erratic responses for months now; the controllers have had a lot of trouble with it. Tomorrow we're going to see what kind of commands you can use to conduct two-way parity checks and system search scans to try to straighten one out when there's what looks like a hardware fault out on the comet and you can't send a team to fix it in person; but that's all for today. Get a good night's sleep, and I'll see you in the morning."

Rima Consalvo stood up, stretched, and yawned, while she watched Dekker turning off their screen. He smiled at her. "Is it all beginning to come back to you?"

She gave him a puzzled look, then understood. "Oh, you mean comet handling. Yes, I guess so, but I'm glad we're getting this refresher. I think I need it. DeWoe? If I get stuck on anything, would you put in a little study time with me one of these days?"

"Well, sure," he said, feeling a glow. "How about tonight?"

She shook her head. "Not tonight," she said regretfully, "because I've made plans—matter of fact, I see my date's waiting for me. But thanks, DeWoe, and I'll see you in the morning."

"Good night," he said, watching her go—watching, especially, to see which of his lucky male classmates was going to be the one waiting for her.

But it wasn't any of them, and that was another big surprise from this surprising woman; because the person standing in the doorway, greeting Rima Consalvo, wasn't a student at all. It was Annetta Bancroft. And what very bad luck it was, Dekker thought, that the people Consalvo seemed most interested in spending time with included so many of the people he was most anxious to avoid.

One of the other people he had been avoiding was his roommate, but when Dekker got to his quarters he found Toro Tanabe gazing despondently at their study screen.

All those childhood repetitions of the Pledge of Assistance had left their indelible imprint on Dekker DeWoe. He could not help a feeling of sympathy for his roommate; Tanabe might be a cheat, but he was also a friend, more or less. Anyway, what right did Dekker have to criticize another cheat? He said, cordially enough, "Cheer up, Tanabe. It's been a tough time, but we're on the homestretch."

The Japanese gave him a sulky look. "I suppose so," he said, "but what of it? When we graduate, what have we to look forward to?"

"You're really worried about having to fix toilets," Dekker guessed, but Tanabe shook his head. Dekker tried again. "Then you missed out on another lottery?"

"Actually," Tanabe said with dignity, "I had five numbers on one card last time; if it had only been six I would at least have had eight or nine hundred cues for a consolation prize." He hesitated, then confided, "It isn't the course. It's the market again, DeWoe. It has dropped nearly five hundred points over the last two months, you know."

"I haven't been following it," Dekker admitted.

"No, of course not. Martians don't care for such things, do they? Still, it is a worry. It is going to get serious for my father if it goes down much more. He has a good many futures buying contracts coming due."

"Well," Dekker said cheerfully, not at all tempted to try to have a futures buying contract explained to him again, "at least you'll have a regular job on Co-Mars Two, so you can support him in his old age if he goes broke. Personally, I'm off to dinner."

"I'll come with you," Tanabe said, getting up. On the way to the dining hall Dekker puzzled over something about Tanabe's behavior, and realized just as they were coming off the line what it was. Tanabe's money worries must be real; it had been weeks since he had allowed himself a weekend in Denver, and he was actually eating almost all his meals with everyone else in the school cafeteria.

Out of charity Dekker made a point of being upbeat all through the meal, and by the time they were back at their study screens Tanabe seemed to have recovered. "I think," he said judiciously, taking a break to make them some of that nearly flavorless Japanese tea that Dekker hated, but drank out of politeness, "I think you are right, DeWoe, or almost. My father is not after all likely to go entirely 'broke'—a bit less rich, perhaps, but by no means a pauper—and even if I did have to repair toilets I suppose I could do it. For a while. But it is more likely that I would draw something like power-plant mainte- nance. That is a decent job, and if you remember I did well in that part of the course—and anyway," he added, actually smil- ing, "it is a known fact that nothing ever goes wrong with the Augensteins. It can't; if they break down seriously, everyone dies."

"What a cheerful creature you are," Dekker said. "All right, let's take another look at the debugging programs."

By the third week of Phase Six, Dekker calculated, his mother was only days away from docking at one of Earth's Skyhook orbital terminals, which was a pleasing thought. He was doing well in the course, too, though no more than break- ing even with Rima Consalvo. They did study together a time or two, but she was friendly but impersonal, and most of the time invisible after school hours. Her behavior, in fact, was not unlike what he had observed in Ven Kupferfeld for the first weeks of their acquaintance.

It was quite possible, Dekker told himself, that this was simply the normal conduct of unattached Earthie women with an interested male. He could not be sure of that. It certainly wasn't Martian. Still, he reminded himself, if that were the case it might bode well, for in the long run things had developed very rapidly with Ven Kupferfeld. So perhaps all he needed was patience.

Meanwhile he was learning more than he had thought possible about the things that could go wrong with a complex mechanism like Co-Mars Two. Doris Clarkson's question had been long answered: if a large-scale collision caused a pressure drop and a failure of the main power supply at once, the station would simply switch over to standby power. All the doors would seal themselves; air to the parts of the station that still had pressure would continue to come from the reserve tanks; the crew would survive locked in wherever they had happened to be caught—not comfortably, but not dead, either—until they either managed to make repairs or a service ship from Earth or Mars could get there to rescue them.

Anyway, that sort of collision was unlikely. A service ship or one of the fixbots that performed out-of-station repairs and surveys might crash on docking, but surely never at high speed. A wandering natural comet or errant asteroid might do a great deal more harm, of course, if it hit the station. But it wouldn't. The chances of such a thing were tiny to begin with. And if, miraculously, one such did turn out to be on a collision course with the station, the sensors would pick it up in plenty of time and the station would simply use its position-keeping thrusters to move out of the way.

A more real threat was a solar flare. They weren't improbable. They happened all the time, and the particle rain from the Sun was deadly. But the station's Sun-spotters would detect the optical flare long before the particles arrived, and everyone would simply retreat to the shielded core chamber—which every man-made object in space had as a basic necessity of design—and wait it out.

No, the real dangers were all internal. An explosion of the Augensteins would be instantly fatal—though, as Toro Tanabe had pointed out, very unlikely. The greatest concern of all was fire.

That surprised Dekker at first, for what was there on a space station to burn? But the answer was that there was plenty. Not the structure itself; the station was designed to contain almost nothing flammable in its parts. The people who manned the station were another story. Inevitably crews would bring their choicest possessions along and, given the right chance, many of those would burn. The fires that might occur would not be huge—no one would be likely to roast from a bonfire of sports shoes and shirts—but they didn't have to be. Where there was fire there was smoke, and in the enclosed space of the station the smoke was where the real danger lay. The smoke could kill.

There was a cure for that, a simple but drastic one: the emergency evacuation systems. Those could drain the air almost instantly from any part of the station—even from the whole station, except for sealed compartments, if that should be necessary. Every compartment and passage door would lock. Then the fire would starve for lack of air. When it was out the station could be sealed again by closing the blowout vents, and the air would be replaced from stores.

Shiaopin Ye raised her hand after they had gone through a simulated air drain. "That seems dangerous to me. What if someone decided to blow off all the air when there wasn't a fire?"

Gillespie said, "Let me answer you this way, Ye. Do you cook?"

"Sometimes, of course."

"And do you have sharp knives to fix the food with?"

"Naturally."

"Do you ever cut your throat with one of them? No, don't answer. I know you don't. Dangerous accidents do not occur if no one makes them happen. There are dangerous things around all of us, all the time. The next hydrocar driver you see could turn the wheel and run you down, but he doesn't do that. We just have to learn how to live with things that could kill us."

That night, as a group of them were waiting to begin their hostility-release session, Ye brought the subject up again. She said to Dekker, "I'm not satisfied, DeWoe. I still think it's dangerous."

"Gillespie says it doesn't happen," Dekker offered, noticing that Rima Consalvo was listening.

"Gillespie could be wrong. What if someone wanted to commit suicide and take the whole station with him? He could blow out the air, or override the safety controls on the Augensteins, or crash one of those fixbot ships into the hull. What would stop him?"

Dekker didn't have an answer for that, only a generalized feeling that the instructor had been right. Rima Consalvo answered instead. "That's a nonexistent problem, Ye. He would stop himself. What do you think all those psych tests are for? Suicidal people don't get onto a station. They're weeded out in advance."

"Every time?" Ye asked doubtfully.

"Every time so far, anyway," Consalvo assured her. "You'd better work out hard tonight, Ye, so you can get rid of some of those negative feelings." Then, dismissing Shiaopin Ye's fears, she turned smiling to Dekker. "DeWoe, I feel as though I could use a really good workout, too. Do you want to try partnering me tonight?"

Of course he did. When they were stripped down to exercise clothes he discovered what he had expected all along: however aged Rima Consalvo might be, she still had a first-class figure. They did push-away, and squeeze, and then they did flopover wrestling.

In his heart of hearts Dekker still regarded this shove-and-grunt thing as a foolish Earthie waste of time. No Martian would ever need that kind of therapeutic struggle, since every Martian learned from childhood the necessity of tolerating one another rather than simply masking intolerance. But when you were doing these very physical things with an attractive woman whom you would like to know a lot better than you did, it wasn't a bad way to spend an evening at all.

He had always been wary of working out with an Earthie, even a female Earthie. To his surprise he had little difficulty with Rima Consalvo. She did not succeed in pushing him off the square, and when she tried to resist his turning her over onto her back as they struggled on the floor, she suddenly yelped in pain and stopped resisting. "Hey, DeWoe! You're pulling my arm right out of its socket. Take it a little easier, please," she gasped.

Startled, he released her. He hunkered down next to her supine form to make sure she was all right. She was gazing up at him ruefully, rubbing her collarbone. "I know you're a Martian, but, remember, I just came back from being out in the Oort for four years. I had to take shots for Earthside leave, too, just like you—so, please, not so much muscle in the clinches."

"I'm sorry," he offered.

"Nothing to be sorry about." She got up slowly, still breathing hard. "You got me all sweaty, too," she complained. "I must stink like a pig."

"You smell pretty good to me," Dekker offered, and she gave him an ambiguous look, then grinned.

"Anyway, thank God the session's over. Oh, look, the cavalry's coming over the hill."

Dekker looked around to see that everybody was getting ready to leave and Consalvo's former colleague from the Oort, Berl Korman, was hustling toward them. He was scowling at Dekker. "Are you all right?" he asked Consalvo, though his eyes remained on Dekker.

"Of course I'm all right. He's just a mass of muscle, this fellow, but there's no permanent damage. Do you two know each other, by the way? Berl was our ace spotter out in the cloud, Dekker. I always liked fitting out his comets, because they were all solid and easy to handle."

Dekker shook the man's hand. "Were you the one who tagged that runty little 67-JY?" he asked, meaning to put the conversation on a civilized basis by poking some good-natured fun.

Korman didn't take it that way. His scowl returned. "Why do you want to know?"

"Easy, Berl. DeWoe's just being friendly," Consalvo said quickly.

"He is? Why'd he mention that particular comet?"

Dekker answered for himself. "No special reason. Just that it's little, and they seem to be having trouble getting it vectored properly." He might have said more, but Consalvo interrupted.

"Forget it, Berl," she ordered. "You go on ahead and I'll catch you later." And when the man had rather sulkily left she said to Dekker, "You see, that embarrassed him. Actually he really was the one who tagged 67-JY. He's a little sensitive about it."

"Oh," Dekker said, no longer very interested. What had caught his attention was that she was going to see the other man later—the other man, and not, for instance, himself.

"Actually, if you want to blame someone, I was the one who threaded it, for that matter, so we're both kind of sensitive. Still," she added, smiling, "they're better too small than too big, aren't they? You wouldn't want us to be sending down any plutons?"

The remark startled Dekker. "Christ, no!" Everyone knew what plutons were—immense comet bodies, the size of the Pluto that gave them their name. One of those could pretty near fill Mars's airspace by itself, but only at the cost of destroying Mars. Then he realized she, too, was probably joking.

He changed the subject back to the one that interested him. "You like Korman, don't you?"

"Well, of course I do. He's a good man." Then, studying him, she added, "I like you, too, Dekker. I hope you know that by now."

"You do?"

She laughed at the skeptical tone. "Come on, Dekker. I know I've been sort of, well, hard to get to know. It isn't that I don't like you. It's mostly that I do." While he was puzzling that out, she added earnestly, "Look, you don't know what it's like on a station, even Co-Mars Two. Once you're there you spend a lot of time with the same people. That means you don't want to get too close with anybody too fast, because maybe you'll regret it. Then you have some kind of break, and that usually means some kind of hard feelings go along with breaking up— and that's trouble. You don't want that kind of trouble coming up when you're stuck with a small group of people."

"The Law of the Raft," Dekker said, nodding.

"Well, I don't know what the Law of the Raft is, but that's the idea. Unless they change their minds again upstairs, we'll both be going to Co-Mars Two. That means we're going to be together for a long time, Dekker. I want to be sure of what I want before I get in too deep. Do you understand what I'm saying?"

Dekker beamed at her. "Of course I do," he said, and, casting caution to the winds, took her by the shoulders and gave her a quick, impulsive kiss, and then turned away and headed for the showers, more sunnily than he had felt in some time.

The thing people didn't realize about the Oort project stations was that, of the two hundred or more people on a station like Co-Mars Two, only about twenty worked regularly as controllers. The rest worked as cooks, cleaners, systems maintenance, and all the other support tasks that kept the controllers in business.

That was what Marty Gillespie pointed out to them in their last week. He added, "You'll be getting your extra-duty assignments soon. That's what they call them, as though you were just going to do them when you had a few minutes off from jockeying comets around. Don't take that word 'extra' too seriously.

The fact is that they'll be your main work. You'll be spending more time on them than on controlling, at least until the next batch of new blood comes up and relieves some of you of the scut work."

Toro Tanabe's hand shot up. "I have not taken all this dreary technical training simply to become a houseboy," he complained.

"Haven't you? What a pity, because it'll be a while before you get to use that glamorous technical training. Oh, they'll put you on shift now and then, to keep your skills up—or, really, to learn them, because you'll always be teamed with a real pro, and he'll be watching every move you make. Then if you're good enough sooner or later you'll get to be a certified operator. Meanwhile, you'll do what you're ordered to do, Tanabe. Including repairing toilets, if that's still worrying you."

He smiled politely at the Japanese, who looked rebellious but was quiet. "Okay then," Gillespie went on to the class at large. "You're not actually going to learn how to fix sanitary facilities here, though. What you're going to learn now is how to use the tutorials in the station data base; they'll do the teaching, not me. Starting now." He paused to move his fingers over his keypad, then looked up at the class. "I've just simulated a broken toilet. Now you people go ahead and start your diagnostics, and let's see which team can get it fixed first."

The class bent to it. The first team finished wasn't Dekker's, although both he and Rima Consalvo knew the technique—people who had lived on Mars or in the Oort had practice in those matters. What slowed them down was Dekker, because testosterone was enlivening his senses every time they brushed arms or their hands touched on the keypad—and, wonderfully, Consalvo seemed as conscious of his presence as he was of hers.

That was about all the touching they did. There wasn't any more kissing, either, though once or twice Rima Consalvo gave him an affectionate clasp of the arm or touch on the cheek before she went off to whatever other social matter engaged her evenings. On the rare occasions when Dekker happened to see her talking with anyone else, the group usually included Ven Kupferfeld or Annetta, sometimes Jay-John Belster or the other Oort cloud alumnus, Berl Korman. When Dekker overcame the restrictions of manners and common sense enough to ask her just what they did together, Consalvo simply shrugged.

Dekker didn't press the question. He didn't want to find out

that perhaps Consalvo was interviewing other candidates for a
more meaningful relationship once they got out in the field, and
that maybe one of the others was, for instance, Jay-John Belster.

On the night before graduation some of the more eager members of the class proposed a celebration. They had reason to
celebrate. Amazingly, no one had failed Phase Six and the
rumor had become fact: they were all going in a body to Co-
Mars Two.

It sounded to Dekker as though it were going to be one of
those Earthie drinking matches, probably with singing and a lot
of loud talk—not really the kind of thing he liked. Still, no
doubt Rima Consalvo would be there. He decided to go, but
took his time about it. He stopped by way of his quarters to see
if his formal orders, as well as his extra-duty assignment posting, had arrived.

They hadn't, but there was a voicemail message waiting for
him, and it was from his mother.

"Hello, Dekker. I'm in a blimp somewhere near Panama, I
think, although all I can see out the window is water. That
means I landed safely and I'm on my way. I'll be arriving in
Denver early tomorrow morning. Don't meet me at the airport;
they're providing me with a car and driver. They're putting me
up at the Oortcorp VIP quarters, too, which all sounds nice
except that I have the feeling they're trying to fatten me up for
the kill. Anyway, I'll give you a call in the morning—and I'll
get to see you graduate after all!"

So Dekker got to the celebration late, though it didn't seem
to matter. It turned out to be a leaden kind of a party, and a
sparsely populated one, too. Only about half the class was
there, quietly seated at tables in the recreation hall and sipping
an occasional beer as they talked desultorily. Of the people
Dekker was most interested in there were almost none—well,
none at all, if you counted properly, because the only one he
was really looking forward to seeing was Rima Consalvo, and
she, Shiaopin Ye informed him, had left early with Ven Kupferfeld. Toro Tanabe was gone, too, and some of the others had
never showed up at all.

In a way—though not the most important way—that was a
relief. Dekker had not looked forward to noise and drunkenness. For manners' sake he said a few words to some of his

classmates and then sat down with Ye and drank half a glass of beer. Without Rima Consalvo to brighten up the room it seemed a waste of time; and when Ye said that she thought she'd better go back to her quarters and pack, Dekker left, too.

He expected to find Toro Tanabe in their rooms, no doubt also packing up and agonizing over what treasures to leave behind to make the mass limit. It wasn't quite the way he expected. Tanabe was there, and packing, but he was randomly flinging everything he owned into bags, swearing to himself and looking furious at the world. Dekker stopped and regarded him. "Won't you have to leave some of that out?" he asked mildly.

"I will leave it *all* out," Tanabe said angrily. "I will take nothing at all, not even me, for I am not going to Co-Mars Two! Do you know what they have assigned me to for 'extra duty'? It isn't even fixing toilets! They expect Toro Tanabe, the son of Waishi Tanabe, to work as a *cook*."

"Hell," Dekker said. He knew that, in spite of everything Marty Gillespie had said, Tanabe had still expected that the one in a million chance would work out for him and he would go directly into comet control. Once a lottery player always a lottery player, Dekker thought.

He said generously, "That's a damn shame, Tanabe, considering that your grades have been good all along—better than mine."

Tanabe shook his head. "Of course they were, and of course they should have given me some more dignified work instead of the sort of thing we give to Hainan *peasants*. But it isn't just grades. These people never forget," he said dolefully. "You do recall that I had some disciplinary problems—?"

"Coming in late and drunk, you mean?" Dekker said, trying to be helpful.

Tanabe glared, then shrugged. "That sort of thing, yes. They still have all those early demerits on the record, so they pay no attention to my other grades."

"Yes," Dekker said, nodding. "The grades you got from the test answers you bought from Annetta Bancroft."

Tanabe looked surprised and embarrassed at the same time. "Bancroft? Was it she who provided the answers? I didn't know; I got them from your dear friend, Kupferfeld, and she never said where they came from. That is a surprise to me. I had thought of Bancroft as a quite honorable person."

Dekker was also surprised, but it all made sense. Tanabe went on, his voice lowering. "I am sorry you know that of me, DeWoe." Dekker shrugged uncomfortably. "Still, what difference does it make who knows it now? They can't expel me anymore. I will attend the graduation, but then I will inform them I resign, and fly home to Tokyo to tell my father I have finally come to my senses."

"It's still too bad," Dekker offered.

"Thank you. But perhaps not; I think my father may need me now. In his last mail he said there were rumors of some developments that will surely affect the market, one way or another. He says that there is supposed to be a high-level Martian delegation coming. Is that by any chance—?"

"Yes," Dekker said, nodding. "It's my mother. She's part of it, anyway."

"So," Tanabe said softly, and left it at that. "Well, I must pack. And by the way, DeWoe, aren't you curious? Your own orders were on the machine, too. I took the liberty of reading them. It is not a bad assignment, I think. It is damage control specialist."

35.

IT HAD SNOWED overnight, and Dekker was shivering as he climbed the hill to where his mother was staying. When he got there, he thought at first he was in the wrong place. He knew he had never been in the VIP quarters before, but the funny thing was that as he walked into the lobby of the building, leaving clumps of snow from his feet to mark his trail, it all looked familiar. It *was* familiar, and when he heard someone call his name and turned to see Annetta Bancroft coming toward him out of the breakfast room, carrying a cup of coffee and looking startled, he realized why. He was in the former resort hotel where she had her tiny room.

She gave him a hostile look. "What are you doing here, DeWoe? Are you looking for me?" she demanded.

"No. My mother's supposed to be here somewhere, if this is the VIP quarters."

"Oh, right," she said, thawing slightly. "They're up in the tower. You have to take those other elevators, down the hall." As he nodded and started to turn away she stopped him. "Listen. Let's talk. I'm shipping out with you, you know. We may not be friends, but we might as well act friendly."

He shrugged, impatient to get on but accepting the logic of the statement. "All right."

"Good, then. Did you get your extra-duty assignment yet?"

It seemed that the acting-friendly directive was to take immediate effect, so Dekker followed her example. "I drew damage control," he said, just like any two colleagues comparing notes. "I guess it could've been worse."

"Yes, it could," she said, approving. "That's about as good as you can get—outside of actual controller, I mean. You'll be working all over the station, so you'll get a chance to meet everybody and learn everything."

"It isn't what I trained for, though."

"Hell, DeWoe, whoever gets what he trained for right away? Your time will come, probably. Listen, do you know who Pelly Marine is? No, you wouldn't, yet, but Pelly's the station chief of Co-Mars Two, and he started out in damage control, too. I served with him two years. He's a good man." She gave Dekker an appraising look. "He's a lot like you, in fact," she added, leaving him to ponder that as he rode the elevator to the VIP floors.

He didn't ponder it long. Gerti DeWoe was waiting for her son, and at his first tap on her door she opened it, beaming at him. "Hey, Dek," she said fondly. "Come on in and let me get a look at what they've been doing to you."

When they kissed she didn't put her arms around him, the way she used to. She couldn't. She was holding onto a walker for support against the harsh Earth-gravity weight, but her lips were warm against his cheek.

"Do you want some breakfast?" she asked at once.

"I ate while I was waiting for you to phone," he said, shaking his head. They studied each other for a moment. She was, Dekker saw with discontent, looking tired and frail and—well, *old.* It was only her voice that hadn't aged at all. It was still the soft, clear contralto that had sung him to sleep as a child, now complaining that he was *fat*.

"That's the polysteroids," he said. "You get used to it."

She shook her head and hobbled over to a straight-backed chair by the window. "I won't be here that long," she said. "A week or two at the most, I hope; I have to be in Tokyo tomorrow morning."

"How does it look?" he asked.

She made a face. With an effort she leaned forward to the low table before her chair and took a flask out of her bag. When she poured something out of it into a glass, Dekker was startled to realize it was whiskey.

He tried to keep the disapproval off his face, but Gerti DeWoe wasn't fooled. She laughed. "Come on, Dek, honey," she said, chiding him. "It's not as bad as you think. I need a drink because I *hurt*. Anyway, it may be morning for you here but for me it's maybe midnight. So it's all right to have a drink, and don't worry; I'll be sober for your graduation." She took a quick sip, and then leaned back against the chair.

"To answer your question," she said, "the Earthies want to renegotiate the terms of the loan, and I'm here to try to persuade them to keep the terms the way they are." She thought for a minute, then said, "No, that's not quite true. What I'm really here for isn't to negotiate. It's to *beg*."

He blinked at her. "Oh, Dekker," Gerti DeWoe said sorrowfully, "don't you pay attention to what's going on? Just this morning on the blimp I heard a news story; now the Russians are talking about putting up farm satellites of their own, along with the Japanese. I think they'll do it, too, because when they figure out their spread sheets, the satellites come up as a better investment. One way or another, somebody's satellites are going to be shipping farm crops to Earth in five years. Ten at the most. We can't match that, so some of the underwriters are backing off."

"But they can't call the project off, can they? They've got so much invested already—"

"No, they can't—I hope. At least, they can't kill the project outright. What they can do, though, is hold us up for higher interest, and we can't afford that." She took another pull at her drink. "I guess the future isn't even as bright as we thought it would be, Dek. Not that we were that well off anyway."

Dekker gave his mother the kind of shocked look an American politician might have given a colleague who intimated that George Washington hadn't been a particularly good president. "What are you talking about? Mars is going to be self-supporting and free!"

"Mars is going to be their plantation and we're going to be their slaves," Gerti DeWoe corrected her son. "We're going to hoe their cotton and plant their corn, and sell them their raw materials and buy back their manufactured goods—like the old British Empire, the people at home getting rich on the poverty of their colonies. Oh," she said, looking remorseful, "I'm sorry to be talking this way today, Dek—on your big day, when you're just about to go out there and do your job for us. But that's the way it's going to be if I can't get them to leave the terms alone. See, they don't just want higher interest. They want guarantees."

"They already have guarantees!"

"Not like the ones they want. They want their loan treaty to be the basic law for Mars, superseding even the constitution. They want the treaty to give them the right of repossession of Martian land, using Earth police, in case we don't make the payments."

"*Police*? With *guns*?"

"Oh, no, nobody said anything about guns. Why would they need guns with us? They probably wouldn't even need those Peacekeepers of theirs, because Martians always keep their promises. All they want is to own us."

"You can't let them do that," he said positively.

"I'm afraid we can't *not* let them do it, if they insist. They're the ones with the money." Then she shook her head in annoyance at herself. "Anyway, that's what I'm here for, to try to get them to act decently; maybe I'll succeed. God knows I'll give it a good try. Earthies are human beings, too, and they're not all wicked exploiters. If I can just get them to remember that we're all part of the same human race—" She shook her head. "Change the subject; how are you doing?"

Dekker couldn't make the transition quite that fast—apart from the fact that he didn't really want to answer that question, or at least not all of it. "Fine," he said, getting up and wandering over to the window

His mother turned painfully to look with him. "I was sitting here looking at the snow before you came," she said wistfully. "It's pretty."

"It is," he agreed, glancing at his watch. His mother didn't miss it.

"Should you be getting ready for your graduation?"

"Pretty soon. Not right this minute. It won't be much of a ceremony, you know," he added. "They don't make a big deal of graduating here. We just sign the articles of employment, and one of the instructors makes a little speech to congratulate us and wish us well, and that's it."

"It'll be a big deal for me, Dek," his mother said. She hesitated, then said, "You know, I was going to bring Tsumi with me as my assistant."

"Tsumi?"

"Well, I would rather have had you, but what you're doing is more important. Tsumi wanted desperately to go. I wish I did have somebody to help out. Somebody with younger legs than mine."

"But *Tsumi*!" Dekker said, unable to keep himself from remembering that it had been so very difficult to scrape up the fare to Earth for him—and so evidently easy to do it for Tsumi Gorshak.

"I know you don't like him, Dek. All the same, I felt I owed it to Tinker. But it didn't work out. Tsumi was going for a piloting license, and he failed the test, and—and he tried to bribe the instructor, Dekker. I didn't have any choice. I fired him."

"I see," Dekker said, seeing much more than she had said. She was looking at him curiously.

"Is something on your mind, Dek?" she asked.

He hesitated. But what was there to tell her? That he was a cheat, and covering up for other cheats, and, really, not that much better than Tsumi Gorshak?

He shook his head and looked again at his watch. "It's just that I'd better get on down there. We have to read the articles and get a blood test before the ceremony."

"A blood test? For *narcotics*?" And when he nodded she said sorrowfully, "Maybe I was wrong about the Earthies. Maybe we're not part of the same race after all."

And ten hours later they were on their way: Dekker's graduating class, the bunch from the Oort, and Annetta Bancroft.

There was only one surprise, and it was Toro Tanabe.

At the last moment, shamefaced and not looking at Dekker,

Tanabe had stepped forward and signed the articles of employment with everybody else. It was only when they had broken ranks and were getting ready to leave that Tanabe saw Dekker's eyes on him. The Japanese grinned in embarrassment. "After all," he said, "it would be a pity to come this far and not go the rest of the way, would it not? And at least if I am to do the cooking, I may even be able to enjoy the food."

36.

Co-Mars Two was in the same orbit as the planet Mars—that was why it was called Co-Mars—but it trailed Mars by a sixth of a Martian year, in what is called a "Trojan" point. There was another control station just like it at the orbit's other Trojan point, the same sixty degrees away but in the other direction. These two Co-Mars stations commanded the entire sky. The stations in orbit around Mars itself could help if necessary, but that seldom happened. Actually any of the stations could, in a pinch, handle all the comets at once, at least all the ones not blocked by the Sun. The reason they divided the work was for safety's sake. Co-Mars Two was the one that vectored the incoming comets on the final legs of their approach to Mars and thus it was the most important of all . . . or at least its personnel liked to think so.

Co-Mars Two wasn't small. It was about the size of a seagoing cargo vessel of Earth, and it would weigh around fifteen thousand tons if it weighed anything at all. Being in orbit, it didn't. Nothing inside it weighed anything, either, because there was no spin on Co-Mars Two. Therefore there was no centrifugal pseudogravity to hold the objects inside to the shells as there was in, say, the stations in the Oort cloud itself. Co-Mars Two couldn't afford the luxury of spin. Its myriad antennae were all aimed with great precision at particular points in the sky, and they couldn't be allowed to wander.

Nor did the people who manned it experience even the tiny

microgravity that was found in the transfer stations at the top of a Skyhook. They didn't experience any gravity at all, which caused a lot of queasy stomachs. Co-Mars Two's corridors went in all three of the directions of three-dimensional space, and there was no such thing in it as a stairway. For the convenience of its crew the corridors were colored red, green, and yellow, corresponding, but in no particular order, to left-right, front-back, and up-down.

Once they got used to its little eccentricities, the crews of Co-Mars Two found that it wasn't a bad place to be. There was plenty of power from their Augenstein-powered MHD electricity generators for civilized comforts. They needed a lot of power. The station's sensors, after all, had to reach out past the orbit of Neptune to keep in touch with their quarry. Those sensors were powerful, and before the supply ship came within ten thousand kilometers of Co-Mars Two whole banks of them had to be turned off, because otherwise the radio energy the sensors emitted would quickly fry everybody aboard.

37.

THEY WERE DOCKED, they were actually on the station; Dekker DeWoe was now a part of Co-Mars Two and thus of the whole Oort project! He could not repress that wonderful glow of Being There. He couldn't really take time to enjoy it, either, because first things had to come first, and before Dekker DeWoe or any of his shipmates had the chance to look around their wonderful new surroundings, the supply ship they had come in had first to be unloaded.

That was hard work. Awkward work, too; there Dekker was, sweating like a pig, weightless, unskilled at being weightless, doing his best. "Coming through," Jay-John Belster would yell from inside the hatch, and Dekker, or somebody else, would have to dive and scramble for the carton or sack or machine part as it came floating through the ship's hatch and try to slow

·it and guide it to the handiest wall. That was their whole job.
Once there, it would stay there, because there were stick-to-me
patches on every piece of the cargo and the walls of the hold
were covered with the stuff. The flow of cargo kept coming,
though. By the time you got one thing firmly secured, another
was already floating through right at you, and you had to try
to flounder back into position in time to catch it.

It was dumb, difficult grunt work. Dekker bashed himself a
dozen times against ungiving wall or sharp-cornered machine
part, but he didn't care, not as long as he could feel that glow
building up inside him anyway. Dekker DeWoe was *home*. He
was well aware that he was a tiny cog in a machine as big as the
solar system itself. Yet, as he flung himself at a bale of something as big as himself and scrabbled for a handhold to help him
slow it down, he felt fully satisfied. He was *there*. He was at last
taking a real part in the rebirth of his planet. When, weeks or
months later, the shattered fragments of some arriving comet
crashed down onto the Martian plains and left their increment
of life-promising gases, it would be because Dekker DeWoe
was part of the team that had made it fly there straight and true.

It was a pity that his stomach didn't enjoy it as much as he
did. His first experience of weightlessness was taking its predict-
able toll. The saliva glands under his tongue were fountaining,
and Dekker was not at all sure that his unease would stop there.
Already two of his classmates had surrendered to motion sickness and gone off for shots, but he wasn't ready to give up.

He envied the easy maneuvering of the station personnel who
had drifted by to share the work. He watched them when he
could take a second off his own efforts, because they were the
ones who knew what they were doing. They swam nonchalantly
into the room, one hand on a holdtight and the other for work;
sometimes, he saw, they could even use two hands to work,
because they would brace themselves with no more than the toe
of a foot while they tugged some item from the wall where it
had just been put. They didn't bother with the toss-and-catch
of the actual unloading. Their job was to tow the things to
wherever they belonged in the recesses of the station itself.

One thing puzzled Dekker. For some reason, before any of
them left the entrance hold, each one had to stop at the exit.
There a woman went over each item with an instrument that
looked like a funnel stabbed into a metal box.

Dekker couldn't identify the instrument, but he recognized

the woman easily enough. She was Rosa McCune, the psychologist who had given him his entrance examination. He swallowed a mouthful of saliva and nudged Shiaopin Ye, by the chance of the moment next to him, though upside down. "What's she doing?" Dekker panted.

"I think she's checking for drugs with that sniffer," Ye said, pressing something round and soft against the wall.

"Drugs," Dekker said scornfully, and then had to pause as the muscles of his abdomen began to heave ominously. He grabbed a wall bracket and closed his eyes, to see if that would help, but it didn't. He felt as though he was falling, corkscrewing, tumbling; his inner ear squawked complaints about the signals it was getting, and the saliva glands under his tongue pumped faster.

"Are you all right, DeWoe?" Ye asked worriedly. "Look, Dr. McCune is watching you."

Dekker opened his eyes, and the psycher definitely was. She was hanging by one foot, the sniffer in her hand, staring at him. "You there," she called. "What's the matter?"

"I'm fine," Dekker called back, stretching the truth.

"You don't look it. You're DeWoe, aren't you? All right, lay off while we get that taken care of. Garalek! Take this man in and get him a shot; we don't want him puking all over our supplies."

Dekker might not have made it to the aid room by himself, though it was only twenty meters away. He didn't have to. The man McCune had told to take him there tugged him by the collar, at high speed, and as soon as he had slapped a onetime shot into Dekker's arm Dekker began to feel better.

The man was grinning at him. "It passes," he said. "Your name's DeWoe? I'm Lloyd Garalek, health services."

Dekker shook the man's hand. "I guess I'd better get back," he said.

"No big hurry," Garalek told him. "You won't want to miss Parker's big welcome-aboard speech, but he won't even show up in the hold until all the cargo's off the ship."

Dekker was feeling enough better to be curious. "Who's Parker? The station chief?"

"Station chief? No. That's Pelly Marine. Simantony Parker's just the deputy; he's one of you lot, you know. Anyway, after His Lordship gives his little speech he'll probably pull a practice flare alert just to get you new guys started off right—or," he said, thinking about it, "probably not right away, I guess, because Pelly Marine's off shift now and Parker's got too much sense to wake him up."

He stretched and yawned. Then he kicked himself gently across the room and caught himself at the door to look back at Dekker. "Give yourself another five or ten minutes, anyway," he advised. "I wish I could, but I have to get back to work, because Rosie McCune'll have her eye out for me. Can you find your way?"

"Well, sure," Dekker said, feeling slightly insulted. "I just turn left when I come out of the door."

The man laughed. "Turn left, huh? Which way is left when you're standing on your head? Watch the numbers, DeWoe; you want to go toward the down numbers. See you later."

Dekker didn't take ten minutes, but he did take three or four, mostly to practice kicking against a wall to cross a room the way Lloyd Garalek had. It took a little more skill than he would have thought, but by the time he risked the green-patterned corridor that took him back to the hold he was feeling reasonably confident of making his way around without skull fractures. He didn't really need to look for the numbers on the doors, either; the hold was instantly identifiable by the noise coming out of it.

The unloading was almost complete, and the old-timers had already hustled about half the cargo out. And Simantony Parker had arrived, identifiable by the orders he was shouting to everyone in sight.

Dekker understood immediately what Garalek had meant by "you lot." He meant Martian, because Simantony Parker was definitely that. He was also that strange and unusual thing, a *fat* Martian. "You cargo stores, hold it down," he commanded. "All you new people, grab a hold over here so I can talk to you for a minute." He waved to a reasonably bare section of the storage wall, and Dekker managed to loft himself over there with his classmates. In the awkward groping for places Dekker found himself holding to the same wall loop as Ven Kupferfeld, who gave him a friendly smile.

Dekker smiled back. It wasn't an instinctive reaction; it was the result of a conscious decision. They were going to be close together for a long time, he reminded himself, and the Law of the Raft told him what he had to do.

They didn't speak, because the deputy chief was getting ready to speak. "I said quiet down, all of you," he ordered. That didn't stop the crew members from continuing to shift cargo out or Rosa McCune from searching for contraband with her sniffer probe, but the new controllers did, after a fashion, quiet down.

"My name's Simantony Parker," the deputy chief said. "I'm sorry Pelly Marine isn't here to talk to you. Pelly's our chief of station, but he's off shift now, so it's up to me as his deputy to welcome you aboard."

He paused to survey his audience, then granted them a smile. "We're glad you're here, because we've been pretty short-handed. We still are; with you people we're just a little less shorthanded is all. The good part of that is that we have more living space open than usual, so you've all got single room assignments. That's just temporary. If any of you want to double up with someone else you can be accommodated. You don't have to do it now; you can change over whenever you like." He looked at his hand screen for reminders. "Oh, yes. You all have your extra-duty assignments? Good. When you get to your quarters query your screen for your department head—I assume you all know how to use a station comm system?—and contact him; he'll let you know when to report for work." He looked at the screen again, then at the audience. "Are there any questions?"

Toro Tanabe's hand was the first up. "When will we start working at our primary jobs?"

Parker grinned. "You mean when do you get off your extra-duty? I can't promise anything about that; you'll have to work up to it. However, we know how you feel, so we're working out a rotation. We're going to put one of you new people on a shift team every day, so each one of you will get at least one tour at a control workstation over the next—what is it?—the next twenty-six days. After that we'll see. Anybody else?—oh, wait a minute. Have you got something for us, McCune?"

"Damn right, I do," Rosa McCune snapped from the door. She was standing by a carton, holding a probe that was beeping plaintively. "It's definitely narcotics, Parker," she said. "I've got a positive read."

"Jesus," the deputy chief snarled. "What son of a bitch is bringing dope onto the station? If any of you new bastards—"

But McCune was shaking her head. "It isn't any of theirs, I'm afraid. Come over here and take a look at the consignment tag."

Parker pulled himself over to the door, squinted quickly at the suspect package, then looked up with a face of thunder. "All right," he said. "Get on with your work, all of you. Leave everything here. I'll sort this out myself."

Dekker's room assignment was Yellow B3-43, and once he found out which of the corridors was Yellow B3 he had no trouble locating it. Several of his classmates were in the same area; he saw Doris Clarkson coming out of her door as he laboriously tugged his backpack to his own, and she told him that Shiaopin Ye was right across the hall.

The room itself was exactly as he had seen it on the virtuals: larger than a closet, without chairs or beds—because what would you use them for when you never sat or lay down?—but altogether bearable. The storage space in the walls was adequate for his few personal possessions. He didn't have a private bathroom, of course, but that wasn't serious; a Martian would not even have noticed such a lack if he hadn't been spending time amid the luxuries of the Earthies. He pulled out the sleep harness, fingering it curiously, and decided that he could get into it easily enough. Whether he could then sleep comfortably in it was another matter. Still, if the two hundred others on Co-Mars Two had learned to do that, Dekker DeWoe would certainly learn, too. Sooner or later.

The screen was easy enough to operate, and when he scrolled the menu to "emergency control" it supplied him with the call code for the head of the department, Jared Clyne.

Clyne was a surprise, not because he was black—although he was, as deeply purple-black as Walter Ngemba had been—but because Dekker had somehow not expected him to be a Martian, too. "Oh, hi," he said, peering out from the screen. "You're Dekker DeWoe? Good. Sorry I wasn't there when your ship came in, but I didn't want to get involved in one of Parker's all-hands-to loading bees. Anyway, I'm glad to meet you. Let's see." Clyne glanced up over the camera lens—at a clock, Dekker surmised. "We ought to get together pretty soon. How are you fixed for sleep?"

"Fine, I guess," Dekker said. With the adrenaline flow of arriving on the station the question hadn't occurred to him.

"Well, then. Come by when you get a chance. Not right away; better wait till the surprise flare drill is over, otherwise we'll just get interrupted. Red 2-11, do you know where that is?"

"No, but I'll find it."

Clyne laughed. "You're right about that. That's one of the many things you can't get on the station: lost."

His picture disappeared as he disconnected, and the screen went to its "ready" menu. Dekker hung thoughtfully before it for a moment, thinking about what to do next. Was he hungry? Not really, he thought, but still he would be, sooner or later. So he selected "food services," and was just learning that the dining halls were open twenty-four hours a day and that there were three of them scattered around the station when he heard a familiar polite cough from behind him.

It was Toro Tanabe, peering in the open door to Dekker's room. If he hadn't heard the cough, Dekker might not have recognized him at once, because he had never seen Tanabe's face at about a hundred-and-fifty-degree angle from his own vertical before. "Come in," Dekker said, waving Tanabe to a loop on the wall. "Well. How do you like Co-Mars Two so far?"

Tanabe took the question seriously. "It is not so bad, I suppose, if one does not expect comfort. But I do not care for this business of narcotics. I do not have strong moral feelings about dope, DeWoe, but it is foolish to have it on a station, when you must know you will be caught."

"Evidently somebody didn't think so. Do they know whose it was?"

"Not as far as I know. McCune would say nothing, and neither would this Parker person. Do you know him, DeWoe? No, I suppose not—I suppose it is only Earth people who think all Martians must know each other, just as Americans think of Japanese. Anyway," he said, beginning to look more cheerful, "in some ways this place is quite civilized. Voicemail to Earth is available; I have already called my broker to buy my lottery tickets for this week."

"Good luck with them."

"Yes, thank you." Tanabe cleared his throat. He seemed slightly embarrassed. "I am just down the hall from you, DeWoe. I—ah—I think I should apologize for not asking if you would like to share quarters with me here, as we did at the academy."

"Oh, that's fine," Dekker said, having never for a moment considered that option. If he were going to share quarters with anyone, the roommate he would have wanted wouldn't have been Toro Tanabe. It would have been Rima Consalvo. Or Ven. Or even Annetta.

Tanabe appeared to be thinking along the same lines. "It is just that, if I have any luck, I think I may follow the local custom of 'duty wives' here. It has much to recommend it, I think."

Dekker tried not to grin. "Do you have anyone in particular in mind?"

"Not yet, no. I would not be surprised if you did, though. Although I do not think the choices are as large as one might have hoped; there are more men than women on the station, and I am told that most of the women are already taken."

Dekker digested that before asking, "Do you happen to know if any of our people have taken, ah, duty wives?" Or become duty wives, which was what he really wanted to know.

"I don't think so. I don't think they've had time. Still, if you have any particular plans I think it would be a good idea to start making your—holy God!" he interrupted himself, startled, as a harsh hooting sound blared all over the station. "What the hell is that?"

"I think," Dekker said, "that it's the solar flare alarm. I'm pretty sure it's only a test, Tanabe. But maybe it isn't, so I guess we'd better get on down to the flare shelter."

Dekker wouldn't have had to know where Co-Mars Two's flare shelter was—all he and Tanabe had to do was to follow the casually moving traffic, all in the same direction—but of course he did know; all those hours studying the virtuals had taught him the layout of the station. The shelter was not in the center of the structure, as it was on spaceships and on the terminals of the Skyhooks; on those things the safest places were central, because they rotated from time to time. Co-Mars Two didn't. The center of the station was filled with the reserve water tanks and the heavy machinery that pumped water and air around the station. The shelter lay just past those solidly radiation-opaque masses, on the side away from the Sun, and when there was no flare or drill in progress it was used as the station's gym.

For two people just up from the training school on Earth, the hard part wasn't finding it, it was getting there. Neither Dekker nor Tanabe had yet mastered the art of getting around in zero-g and so they floundered and bumped into each other and the walls of the passages. Tanabe panted, "Thank God this is only a drill. I would hate to have to do this in a real emergency!"

"It's never a real emergency," Dekker told him, with the wisdom of someone who had grown up on a planet where solar flares were sometimes a problem. He thought of explaining to Tanabe that the radiation from the Sun always came in two installments: first the visible-light sighting of the flare itself, then, hours later, the shower of particles. He would have done it, too, if he had been able to spare the breath. The two of them piled up at an intersection, and while they were collecting themselves to change direction from yellow to green Dekker caught sight of Annetta Bancroft and Dr. Rosa McCune, some way down the green corridor. They weren't moving toward the shelter. They were simply hanging there, and they were in the middle of an argument. It looked like a hot one, too; Dekker was astonished to see that Annetta was in furious tears, while the psychologist was stonily shaking her head.

Tanabe was staring at them curiously, but Dekker tugged at his arm and the Japanese followed reluctantly. "What was that all about?" he panted.

"Not our business, anyway," Dekker said, as a proper Martian. "They'll come along when they're ready. There's the shelter."

It took a while to get into it, because there was a knot of people waiting at the heavy air-seal door, and a loud babble of talk from inside. When they had got through, Dekker looked around curiously. The room was bigger than he had expected, all six of its walls lined with the spring-loaded exercise machines everyone on the station had to use regularly to try to keep their bones hard and muscles from weakening. People hung about the room in clusters, at all angles.

By the time Dekker had found something to anchor himself to he saw that Shiaopin Ye was swimming toward them. She was upside-down to Dekker, but he saw the expression of worry on her face. "What's the matter?" he asked.

She shook her head, twisting around so that they were closer to a normal conversational position. "I don't know what kind of place we've come to, DeWoe. Were you there when they found narcotics in the cargo?"

"Yes."

"Did you know who it belonged to? It was in personal effects for the chief of station, Marine. And they woke him up and gave him a test, and he had drugs in his bloodstream. Rosa McCune is sending him down with the ship; now this man Parker is the chief."

"Jesus," Tanabe said. "The *chief*? And he is being *fired* from his own station?"

Dekker shook his head. "If he's doing drugs, he has to go. Of course. *Especially* the chief of station."

"But if the chief of station is an addict," Ye persisted, "what does that say about Co-Mars Two?"

Dekker had no answer for that. He squirmed around to look toward the doorway. The last few stragglers were coming in; he saw Annetta Bancroft hauling herself along the wall, no longer weeping but the expression on her face still furious. Close behind her were Rosa McCune and the deputy chief—no, now the *chief*. Parker gave an order, and the door closed, sealing them inside.

He picked up a microphone. "Quiet down," he ordered. "I have an announcement. Narcotics have been found on the ship, and therefore Dr. McCune has ordered a blood test for all personnel. There is no actual flare. This is only a drill. But each of you will give a blood sample before you leave. The drill is over, but you can start lining up for your tests now." And added, as a late afterthought, "Please."

Dekker realized very quickly that testing two hundred people was going to take time. That was an annoyance, but he became aware of a greater annoyance still. There was one simple biological task he had neglected ever since getting on the ship. Before very long he would have to relieve his bladder.

There had to be provisions for that in the flare shelter, he realized. There were; there were a dozen of them, along one stretch of wall.

He was, however, now in zero gravity.

He was grinning when he came out, proud of himself for having managed the unavoidably complicated machinery of a zero-g toilet, and he discovered his boss, Jared Clyne, hanging nearby. Clyne was grinning, too. "I saw you go in, so I thought I'd better stay around in case you needed help, your first time," he said. "How'd you do?"

"I don't think I'll ever *like* it. But all right."

"Good," Clyne said. "Listen, we're going to be here for a while yet, so we can talk now instead of your coming to the office. You've trained on the emergency systems? Then I won't have to teach you anything. All you need, probably, is to walk around the station with me or one of the others in the section, so you can get the feel of the place. The virtuals are good, but, I don't know about you, personally I don't feel as if I know a thing until I get my hands on it. Wang's on shift now. He'll be off in about an hour; if you're up to it, why don't the three of us get something to eat and you can meet him?"

"I'm up to it," Dekker said. "After that, maybe I should get some sleep."

"No problem." Clyne turned himself around to look toward the exit. Half the crew were still clustered around there, waiting their turns to give blood samples.

"Clyne?" Dekker ventured, puzzling over something. "Did you say this other person was on shift? You mean working as a controller?"

"Right. Part-time. Everybody on the station gets a shot once a month or so."

"Yes, but what if this had been a real flare? Don't the controllers have to take shelter, too?"

"Ah, no, DeWoe. All the boards are in the flare shadow—they're put there on purpose, because the shelter here is between them and the Sun. They're pretty safe there. In a bad flare the controllers might take a little secondary radiation—you know, reemitted from the structure of the station itself. But the doses should be light. Of course, you have to keep track of light doses, too, because you have to watch your total lifetime exposure, so next time there was a flare a different team of operators would be manning the boards."

He cast another look at the door, and shrugged ruefully. "We'll be a while yet. Where are you from, DeWoe?"

"Sagdayev. It's a little deme on Mount—"

"Oh, hell, DeWoe, I know where Sagdayev is. I'm from Kennedy—you know, on Elysium? But it's been a long time since I saw it." He looked at Dekker thoughtfully. "If you're from Sagdayev, you're probably related to Gerti DeWoe?"

"My mother," Dekker said, waiting for the complaint about her he had learned to expect.

He didn't get it. "She's a great woman, DeWoe," Clyne said sincerely. "My uncle served with her in the Commons. I'm glad to have you here."

"Well, thanks," Dekker said, warming to the man. Anybody who admired Gerti DeWoe was automatically a friend of her son's; and, actually, the more he learned about Jared Clyne, as they talked, the better he liked the man. Clyne, he discovered, had been upped to full-time controller after Rosa McCune's purge of the "unstable," but he was pulling double duty as head of the damage-control unit—"It's not that I don't trust the other guys, DeWoe; it's just that I wanted to hang on until the station got back to strength."

"Is it now?"

"Well—not really. But closer, at least." He hesitated, then said, "Anyway, I don't have as much interest in time off as I used to. My wife was one of the ones who got sent down."

"Oh, hell. Too bad."

Clyne nodded. "I thought so—still, she was acting sort of jumpy, the last couple of weeks. What I'm hoping is that whatever it was that bothered her they'll fix in the clinics, and then she'll be back here—well, if I'm lucky, anyway." He cleared his throat and turned away, gazing at the diminishing crowd at the door. "Maybe we should start lining up," he offered.

"All right." Dekker watched carefully as Clyne gracefully pushed himself from one wall to the other, neatly missing collision with any of the other people still in the shelter. He tried to copy him. He very nearly succeeded; with only one small bump he brought up just behind his boss, and looked around.

There were only about thirty people left in the gym. Three people were taking the blood samples, Rosa McCune and, Clyne informed him, the station's two medical doctors. It wasn't a complicated procedure; a jab, a pause, a name scribbled on the little ampul of blood, a Band-Aid on the arm, and the subject was allowed to exit.

Annetta Bancroft was just going through. When Jared Clyne saw Dekker was looking at her, he said, "Tough break for her."

"Annetta? Why? I mean, she was obviously upset about something, because I saw her arguing with McCune just before they came in here. But I don't know what it was about."

"I think I do," Clyne said. "I'd give big odds it was about

Pelly Marine. McCune sent him down, you know? Found narcotics in his shipment from Earth?"

"I heard."

"Well, naturally Annetta was upset. She used to be his duty wife."

38.

I F YOU WANTED to give Mars an atmosphere as dense as Earth's, you would have to find a lot of gas somewhere. How much is "a lot"? Call it about 4,000,000,000,000,000—that's four *quadrillion*—tons of gas.

That's a lot in human terms, all right, but rather little in the larger numbers used by astronomers. Fortunately it doesn't all have to come from the Oort. There's a fairish supply on Mars itself.

The principal things you need to make a planet capable of sustaining life are what scientists call "volatiles," principally water and air.

If you look at the composition of the planets of the solar system, you can see that these volatiles are distributed in a fairly orderly way. Mercury, the planet nearest the Sun, has practically none; whatever it may originally have had of them has long since been volatilized by the Sun's heat and—because the hotter volatiles get the more rapidly their molecules move, thus attaining enough speed to overcome the pull of the planet—they have been lost into space.

Venus and Earth, being farther from the Sun and also a lot bigger than Mercury, are luckier; they have retained much of their volatiles. Then, when you get farther out, past the asteroid belt, you find that practically all of the volatiles have been retained; in fact, the gas-giant planets, from Jupiter through Neptune, are essentially nothing *but* volatiles . . . but, partly because they are so large and their gravitational grip is therefore so firm, and also because these planets are so far from the

Sun, and therefore so cold, the volatiles haven't been able to escape.

All of that is quite orderly and sensible, and fits the pattern of how the solar system was supposed to develop—with one exception.

There's the unusual case of the planet Mars.

Mars seems to have been shortchanged on volatiles. It ought to have more than it does. It did have, once. There are clear indications of river valleys on Mars, which means that there must have been liquid water at some time. Indeed some of these features, like the Valles Marineris, are huger than anything on Earth. They look like a magnified Grand Canyon, and if, like the Grand Canyon, they were carved out by the erosion of liquid water flowing, that amount of water must have been very great. In fact it must have been enough, once, to have given Mars great oceans. How great? Enough, if the water involved had been spread evenly over the surface, to cover the planet half a kilometer deep. It wouldn't have been spread evenly, of course; it would have collected, like Earth's oceans, at low points. But it would have been a lot.

So where did those volatiles go?

Most of them must have been lost to space, simply because Mars's weak gravity could not hold them forever. They weren't all lost, though. Visibly, there is still enough of them left to make the Martian polar ice caps. Invisibly, bound into the minerals of the Martian surface, there is a great deal more.

That's where the Oort program gets its biggest bonus. Once enough comets are dumped on the surface to raise the surface pressure and the surface temperature a little, all those locked and frozen invisible volatiles can begin to become visible again.

39.

O<small>N</small> CO-MARS Two an exercise session was mandatory, every day, for everybody. It was also hard work. Worse than that, Dekker believed it was, for a Martian who never intended to go back to Earth if he could help it, largely unnecessary work: he didn't need the polysteroided muscles that had kept him alive through the training school, and if a little calcium migrated out of his bones, so what? "For your heart, then," Jared Clyne advised. "As one Martian to another, that's what I tell myself. It doesn't matter *why* you do it, anyway. The best reason for doing it is that you don't have a choice, because if you skip more than two or three days a month Rosie McCune will have you out of here on the next ship."

So Dekker spent his hour a day in the gym, like everyone else, working his arms and legs against the springs that provided the only real resistance his muscles would ever get to fight against on the station. The machine he hated most was the one they called "the rack." You buckled your feet onto one set of springs and stretched up as far as you could to grip the handles of another set, and then you did your best to pull your left leg up and your right arm down, and then the other way around, for a prescribed minimum of ten nasty minutes.

When he finished with the rack he was always aching. As he unstrapped himself he saw that the person who had begun working out next to him was Annetta Bancroft.

She gave him a cheerful, but noncommittal, nod. "Hi," she said. "How are you getting along?"

"Outside of aches and pains, you mean?" he asked, rubbing his thighs. "Just fine. And you?"

She said she was doing just fine, too. The conversation might have stopped there if Dekker hadn't added, "I'm sorry about what happened. With Pelly Marine, I mean."

She looked at him with the suspicion of a smile. "There aren't any secrets in a place like this, are there? It's true enough; Pelly and I were together for more than a year. I admit the whole thing took me by surprise, because he never did any drugs while I was with him. But people change, don't they? I guess Sime Parker just did what he had to do. They tell me Pelly was acting sort of suspicious and jumpy the last few weeks before we got here."

"You're very forgiving," Dekker told her, meaning it—even liking her for it; how many Earthies could be so objective in a case like that? "That's funny, though. That's pretty much what Jared Clyne said about his duty wife. The one that Rosa McCune sent down for instability."

Annetta gave him a sharp look, then bent to check the fit of her foot grips. She finished strapping herself in before she responded. "Maybe there's some kind of instability epidemic going around the station. Take care you don't catch it, too, DeWoe."

For a while Dekker thought that maybe there really was something contagious going around Co-Mars Two, because everyone seemed a little jumpy—or abstracted—or merely mysterious. Some of his former classmates, Ven Kupferfeld and Jay-John Belster for two, appeared almost to have disappeared from sight. They spent no time at all with the group they had come up with, somehow having integrated themselves instantly into the permanent party of Co-Mars Two. Nor, apart from that one brief contact in the gym, had he seen anything of Annetta Bancroft or, more importantly, of Rima Consalvo, except when he called Rima on the interstation a time or two. When he did get her what he got was a friendly brush-off. Friendly it was; she said very sweetly that they really had to get together sometime soon. But a brush-off nonetheless.

It astonished Dekker that in a community of only about two hundred people five or six could so effectively vanish from his sight.

Dekker didn't have a lot of time to brood about it, though, because the other thing that was going all around the station was Dekker DeWoe himself. He became a part of the damage-control survey team at once. He never went out on the team's inspections by himself; if it wasn't Jared Clyne who was with him it was one of the other team members, like Dzhowen Wang—"Joe," for short—or Wang's duty wife as well as teammate, the dark little woman named Hattie Horan. Centimeter by centimeter Dekker and his partner of the moment traveled all the station's corridors, from air locks to water pumps. From time to time he came across old classmates at work: Shiaopin Ye in the communications plenum, supervising the routing of incoming messages to the person or department they were meant for; Doris Clarkson glumly a gym attendant; Toro Tanabe—surprisingly not glum, for a change—hard at work in the station's "kitchens." When Tanabe saw Dekker come in he shoved the casserole he was holding into an oven, pulled off his gloves, set the timer, and pushed himself over to greet him. "This is Joe Wang," Dekker said. "My former roommate, Toro Tanabe. You look like you're enjoying your work, Tanabe."

Tanabe hooked one foot into a wall loop so he could wipe his hands on his apron before shaking hands with Wang. "To be truthful, DeWoe," he said judiciously, "I mostly am enjoying it, yes. The work is quite easy, as you see. For most dishes it is only a matter of taking things out of the freezer and putting them in the microwave. But the food could be better, don't you think?"

Dekker thought for a moment. "Seems all right to me," he said.

"Yes," Tanabe said kindly, "but you're a Martian, aren't you? Still, it is not as bad as the slop the school served us, I know. I think the worst part is that we can't fry anything, not even tempura. It produces too much fat for the air recirculators to handle. But the noodles are good. Come sometime when I'm on duty and I'll fix a special sukiyaki for you; I had my mother's cook send me the recipe. You, too," he added to Dekker's teammate.

"Don't try to bribe the inspectors," Wang said, and then took the sting out of it by smiling. "Anyway, we have to check for spilled food, and how you're handling your wastes, and for the seals around the cooking units—I smell something baking."

"Only when we open the ovens," a tall Martian said, coming over; he turned out to be the head cook, and while Dekker and Wang were looking for possible fire hazards he and Dekker managed to exchange hometowns and schools.

On the way out, Dekker commented, "They seemed all right. You know what surprises me, Wang? I didn't expect there would be so many Martians here."

"Why not?"

"Somebody told me Martians just didn't seem to fit in well," Dekker said.

"Bullshit. Martians do as well as anybody else. Anyway," Wang said earnestly, "I *like* Martians. Matter of fact, Hattie and I are thinking of settling on Mars when our time runs out here."

"You'd certainly be welcome," Dekker said, touched—it was the first time he'd ever heard that from an Earthie. But of course, he reminded himself, he was on an Oort station. These were not ordinary Earthies. These were men and women who had volunteered to leave their homes on Earth and venture out into space, for years at a time, to help Mars come into its rich and rightful heritage. It couldn't have been just money that brought them here. There had to be an idealism, too.

He counted himself lucky to be with these decent human beings. Only when he and Hattie Horan were checking the emergency systems in one of the exit air locks, where great spacesuits stood like headless scarecrows for the occasional extravehicular maintenance, he caught a glimpse of the comet-control workstation next door. He didn't know either of the women working there, but he felt a sudden heat in his chest. *He* should be there, too, he thought. . . .

And, within the next few minutes, convinced himself that it was only fair that he was not; after all, the new station chief was a fair man—undoubtedly he was; he was a Martian, after all—and he had promised that everyone would get a turn.

An hour later, back in his quarters, the new rotation orders came out on Dekker's screen, and suddenly he was less sure of Simantony Parker's fairness.

Parker had promised one of the new shipment would have a turn each day. He had kept the promise. The rotation was for the next five days, and there were five names from the shipment on it.

They were Ven Kupferfeld, Jay-John Belster, Berl Korman, Rima Consalvo, and Annetta Bancroft.

Three cheats and two last-minute substitutions from the Oort. Only those, and no others. It was, Dekker thought, really quite a strange coincidence.

When he reported to Jared Clyne the next morning he couldn't help bringing the subject up. Partway up, anyway.

Dekker couldn't make himself mention the subject of cheating, but what he did say was: "How do you suppose the chief picked the new people to go on the control boards?"

Clyne gave him a quick and not particularly friendly look. "How do you mean?"

"Well—there's Consalvo and Korman, for instance. Why those two and not any of the others who came from the cloud?"

Clyne seemed to relax. "He has to start somewhere, doesn't he? And there's Annetta Bancroft. She's on the list, too, but the reason for that is that she's had the experience here already."

"Yes, but—"

"Yes, but," Clyne said patiently, "you still don't like it. Well, you're not the only one. I don't like it, either, because Parker's reshuffled everything. He's put me back on shift every day—I'll have to be on in a couple of hours, in fact. That'll be ten days straight for me, DeWoe. We never do that."

"Then why did he do it?" Dekker asked, surprised to hear the plaintive sound in his boss's voice.

Clyne shrugged. "He's the station chief; he makes those decisions. Now can we do a little work? Dzhowen Wang thinks we ought to have one of the air pumps pulled down for maintenance, so, before he gets here, let's take a look at its service record. See if you can get it on the screen for me."

Of course Dekker could get it on the screen, but while they were poring over the schematics a window opened in the corner of the picture. Shiaopin Ye's face looked out at them. "Clyne? This is the communications center. We're having some trouble with the solar optics, and I thought you ought to take a look."

Clyne frowned at the screen. "Let me talk to your boss," he ordered.

"I'm sorry. Toby Mory isn't here, just Carlton and me. Am I reporting to the wrong department? Because Carlton wasn't sure, only I thought since the optics were part of the emergency system for solar flares—"

"No," Clyne said, "you've got the right people. We'll take a look and call you right back." As he reprogrammed the screen for the solar-optics circuitry, he glanced up at DeWoe. "She's one of your people, isn't she?"

"Yes. Shiaopin Ye. She was in my class. A good student."

"Well, then we'd better check it out."

They did, Dekker and Clyne, and then, when Dzhowen Wang came in a few minutes later, all three of them ran test signals through the complex fiber-optic net. "I didn't know this was really our job," Dekker commented.

"The communications, no. The alarm systems, yes. But I don't see anything; do you, Joe?"

Wang shook his head. "If it's intermittent we might not, though."

"Right." Clyne pressed the numbers for the comm center again, and this time he got the head of the department, Toby Mory, who looked annoyed.

"Sorry, Jared," Mory said. "I was only out for half an hour. Ye should've waited for me to come back instead of bothering you."

"No harm done, Toby. Listen, we can't find any discrepancies in the net, either, so I'm going to ask Wang and DeWoe to take a look at the hardware outside—I'd do it myself, but I have to get ready for my shift. Could be the solar scope is shifting alignment. I'll have them let you know if they find anything."

When he was off the screen he turned to his assistants. "Well, guys," he said. "What do you say? Feel like taking a little ride in a fixbot?"

Since inspections had taken him just about everywhere on the station, Dekker had been in the worklock before. A fixbot, though, was something else. Through a port he could see the fixbot moored just outside, and the idea of getting into it, even in a spacesuit, made his nose tingle.

While Dzhowen Wang was checking them in on the screen, Dekker looked around. The spacesuits, the lock hatch, the emergency vent controls, the little window that looked out on the controllers' workstation next door—that was an irresistible temptation, and when he peered through the window, for a yearning look at the lucky pair of controllers who were actually on shift, it took him a moment to realize that he knew one of them.

It was Annetta Bancroft. She and another woman had their heads down over the board, checking trajectories—probably getting ready for a burn, Dekker thought jealously. That was one of the things about Co-Mars Two's comets; they came up from the Sun with a lot of excess velocity, and every one of them needed repeated burns to kill off enough of it to make their Mars approach within tolerable limits.

He was staring longingly at her—not resenting her good fortune, just wishing he had shared it—when Wang finished his report and pushed himself away from the screen. As he caught Dekker's shoulder to stop himself he said, "It's okay. They're going to turn off the transmitters between here and Sunside so we won't get fried." He peered past Dekker into the workstation. "Hey, that's Bancroft in there, isn't it? Wonder how she feels about it?"

Dekker turned his head to look at him. "About what?"

"Why, about being here. Right next to the lock where she had her accident. Look, you can still see scratch marks on the lock where she hit. Didn't you know about it?"

"I heard something," Dekker admitted.

"Well, it was a damn close call. She was in her suit, getting ready to go out, only she didn't have a firm grip on anything when she blew the air out. So the suction threw her against the edge of the lock. Almost ripped her suit; she nearly got killed. Not from the accident, you know. There were complications from her condition."

"What condition was that?" Dekker demanded.

Wang hesitated, then said, "I guess it isn't a secret. She was pregnant. She lost the baby. This place has to be bad memories for her."

He pushed himself away, floating toward the rack of suits. "Anyway, let's get on with it, DeWoe. They don't want us to be out for more than fifteen minutes, so let's be on our way."

Thoughtfully Dekker helped Wang into his suit, then let Wang help him into his own. He paid full attention—he knew what it meant to check your suit before going extra-v—but a part of his mind kept repeating wonderingly, the *baby*? Annetta had never said a word about a *baby*.

Actually the spacesuits were not much unlike the suits he had worn to walk the surface of Mars—no reason they should have been, since the difference between Mars's thin air and the vacuum of space hardly mattered. It was fortunate that a couple of the suits were built in sizes for Martian physiques, though the fit was only approximate.

When they were suited up, Wang leaned his helmet over to touch Dekker's. "Stand clear while I evacuate the lock," he said. "Have you got your key?"

Dekker remembered to take his out and offer it, but Wang only nodded. "Just checking. I'll use my own." He pulled the emergency key out of the suit pocket and inserted it in the board. There were ten separate controls there, each of them lighting up in turn: one to evacuate each of the station's ten worklocks. There was a flashing red light under each to show that the locks were not sealed; Wang touched the keypad, and behind Dekker the seals to the interior of the station slid closed.

Then he turned the key. The outer lock opened; Dekker felt the quick tug as the air in their little space rushed out into space. The two of them crawled into the fixbot—a tiny, fragile-looking skeleton of a ship, no more than a framework with drives and handling tools to repair anything that went wrong with the station's externals, entirely open to space—and then Wang cut it loose.

Dekker caught his breath. All thoughts of Annetta's baby and everything else vanished from his mind in the wonder of where they were.

They were floating in space. Station Co-Mars Two was a huge presence beside them—or below; or above; it sat there next to them in some dimension, but Dekker could not have said which—and there was nothing else anywhere around, in any direction, for millions of vacant kilometers. And, everywhere Dekker looked, there were points and splashes of lights: stars, planets, above all the host of bright comets that were bringing life to Mars—so many scores of them, large and near or distant and dim, their torches of bright gas lit as, for the first time in their billion-year lives, they began to be warmed by the Sun. From the surface of Mars the comets had been bright, even seen through the sludgy air of Earth they had been almost overpowering, but here—here they illuminated the heavens.

There was no time to stare at them, because Wang was getting impatient. He waved to Dekker to warn him to get braced for acceleration, and started a thruster. The fixbot was too tiny a vessel to have any use for anything as violent as an Augenstein. It had to have drives, but they were only scaled-down versions of the same hydrogen peroxide thrusters that the station itself used when it needed to correct orbit. The fixbot's were much smaller, just enough to nudge the tiny thing gently out of the lock. Wang dexterously brought it to relative rest, and then gave it the little thrust it needed to move toward the Sunward side of the station.

Dekker could see that the warning lights were out on all the beam sensors on their side—otherwise they would have been fried. They floated over the disks and rectennae of communications transceivers, sensors, and scopes, and as they rounded the shape of the station their faceplates clouded at the first impact of the blinding Sunlight. A moment later the barrels of the Sun-facing telescope appeared.

Wang stopped the handler above them and raised a magnifier before his helmet, signing Dekker to do the same.

After a moment he leaned over and touched helmets. "What do you think, DeWoe? See any damage?"

Dekker took his time to be sure. If there was anything physically wrong with the station's external eyes it should have been visible—a shattered mirror from a micrometeorite strike, perhaps, or a component that had somehow come loose. "They all look okay to me," he said.

"Me, too. The connections look tight. I can't see a thing wrong. Let's go back."

"Do we have to?" Dekker asked, enthralled by the sights around him, yearning to stay. But he waited to ask until the helmets were no longer touching, and by then, of course, he knew that Dzhowen Wang couldn't hear.

The spell didn't vanish simply because they were back in the station. Dekker couldn't help grinning with remembered pleasure as they came out of the lock, grinning at nothing, grinning at Annetta Bancroft and her partner as they appeared at the control station door, just coming off shift.

Annetta gave him a startled look, then smiled back. "Nice to see you happy, Dekker," she said.

Wang looked at her, then, in a more curious way, at Dekker, then gave them a flip of a wave and left. As he and the other woman disappeared down the passage, Annetta added, "By the way, thanks for letting us have our display back."

"Display?" Dekker repeated. He was caught off balance, halfway between the rapture of being out in space and the returning recollection of the baby. Then he realized what she was talking about. Of course. All the controllers' displays would have been cut off with the shutting down of the station's externals while they were outside. "Sorry," he said.

"That's okay. We had to postpone one burn, but we got a new solution and did it five minutes later. No problem." She didn't seem to be in any hurry to leave. She was holding a wall strap, her body hanging out from the wall at about a forty-five-degree angle, looking quite content to stay there and chat with him. "Anyway," she went on conversationally, "it isn't the first time. We've been having glitches for the last day or two. Have they been bothering you?"

He shook his head, aware that he was staring at her. He couldn't help it. The fact that she had been pregnant at one time certainly didn't change anything, not to mention the fact that it was just as certainly no business of his. He felt impelled to say something, and tried, "If these glitches kept happening, how much trouble are we going to have with the communications?" he asked.

She shrugged. "Nothing serious, if they don't get worse," she said. "A pain in the ass, yes, but we're okay. It looks to me as though there's some bad code in the repeaters, so if we isolate the reception from the station circuits we should be able to track down whatever went wrong pretty quick. Then restoring the remote displays will take more time, but we can get along without them forever if we have to." Then she twisted herself around to confront him more directly. "Dekker? Is something on your mind? You keep looking at me as though I had two heads."

He flushed. "I apologize."

"Damn you, Dekker, don't apologize. Just say what you want to say."

He hesitated, then took the plunge. "Annetta, when you had your accident—"

"Yes?"

"Well, you were pregnant, right?"

She stopped, hanging to a wall hold, and stared at him. She didn't seem offended at first. If anything, peculiarly, she seemed almost relieved. Then her expression changed. "Hell. Somebody's been gossiping about me."

He apologized. "I know it's none of my business—"

"Damn straight it isn't!"

He swallowed and took the plunge. "I just wondered if Pelly Marine was the father."

She gave him a hostile look. "Is there any reason I should discuss my private life with you?" He shook his head, and she relented—minutely. "Remembering that it's none of your business, just like you said, and there's no reason I have to tell you anything—well, yes. I did have a duty mate then, and it was Pelly Marine."

"I see."

"I doubt that."

"All right," he said, beginning to be irritated, "then I don't see. Forget I asked." He considered turning away and leaving her; there was just so much of this Earthie game-playing he could take. If she'd been a Martian she would have answered at once—or, more likely, he would never have had to ask, because she would have mentioned it long ago.

"Don't get hostile, Dekker," she said. "I guess it's just that I don't like being reminded. You see, Pelly and I were *ex*–duty mates at the time. It was over between us before my accident. We just hadn't made it official. I got pregnant, and—we had a big argument about it." She shrugged. "I wanted to have the baby."

"And I guess he didn't?"

"He *positively* didn't. Listen, Dekker, I don't hate the man. I didn't hate him then, but we agreed to break it up—and then I had the accident, and a miscarriage, and there were problems from that that they couldn't handle here. So I got sent down, and that was the end of it. If McCune hadn't decided—" She stopped herself. "Well, never mind that part. She sent him down, so he's gone. It doesn't matter, though. If he was still here we wouldn't be getting together again anyway."

She stopped there. Lacking anything better to say, he offered, "I'm sorry."

"What's to be sorry about?" she asked. "I'm all recovered, and Pelly's history."

That seemed to be the end of it, or should have been, except that she was still looking at him in a—what would you call it?—an appraising way. Not *sexually* appraising. If Dekker had learned anything from Ven Kupferfeld, it was what the look of Earthie-female sexual speculation was like. Annetta's was different, almost as though there were something else she wanted to say.

There was. "Dekker," she said finally, "as long as we're butting into each other's affairs, I have a question for you. Why haven't you seen Rima Consalvo?"

He looked at her wide-eyed. "What are you talking about? I *tried.* I couldn't ever find her in," he said, knowing he sounded aggrieved.

"Well," Annetta said, "I guess she was pretty busy at first. We all were, but she does sort of miss seeing you. I've heard her say so. And if you do want to see her—well, you know at least one place where she's going to be tomorrow, anyway, don't you? Like right here? Right around this time? When she'll be coming off her shift?"

40.

WHEN THE LITTLE whisper of music from his alarm woke Dekker the next "morning"—no more than his own personal "morning," of course, since Co-Mars Two operated around the clock—he was in the middle of a pleasing dream. It had a woman in it, of course. They weren't actively having sex. But the ambience of the dream contained the fact that they recently had, or undoubtedly would, and meanwhile were holding each other, naked and warm together, in that wonderfully acheless, strainless way that you could only find in zero gravity.

As Dekker untangled himself from his sleeping harness he could almost feel the woman's arms still around him. Or was that feeling nothing more than the gentle restraints of the harness, dream-translated into something more loving? And, for that matter, who, exactly, had the dream woman been?

He puzzled over that second question as he pushed himself down the yellow hall to the sanitary facilities. Then he had to abandon the thought, because he needed all his concentration for what he was doing. His skills at the zero-gravity toilets and the enclosed spray booths that substituted for showers on Co-Mars Two were still too rudimentary to maintain any other chain of thought while he was using them.

When he was back in his own room, hovering before his screen, the question came back. Had it been Rima Consalvo? Ven Kupferfeld? Either of them could certainly have been a likely candidate for an erotic dream of Dekker DeWoe's. But was either the one? Annoyingly, Dekker was quite sure that he knew the woman. He just didn't know who she was.

The important thing, though, was to see what the prospects were for adding the company of an actual, rather than a dreamed, woman to his life. Annetta Bancroft had told him where his best immediate prospects were, so Dekker settled down to the screen to check on Rima's shift assignment. He called up "current work assignments," then "comet control," and had the entire rotation displayed for him.

There were a lot of names on it. He had known there would be: Co-Mars Two kept two boards live at all times, two controllers on each board. The two teams took turns at active control and checking the other team's solutions, and each individual operator worked two hours on, two hours off, and another two hours on for a complete shift.

That used up a lot of people, so there were twenty full-time controllers in the rotation, plus a dozen or so fill-ins. Dekker found R. Consalvo's name just where Annetta had said it would be among the fill-ins. The timing was good, Dekker saw. He calculated that he would easily be able to put in his own day and be finished with time to spare before Rima would get off the second half of her shift. Then they would both be off duty for a good many hours. That would be plenty of time for a talk or a meal . . . or whatever.

While Dekker was at the screen he switched over to the news channels, conscious of a faint, warm glow of pleasure in his lower abdomen as he thought of that "whatever."

The glow didn't last. The news dispelled it for him soon enough. He quickly ran through the major headlines, all depressing and none, really, of any personal interest—what did he or any other real Martian care about Earthie strikes or financial crises?—and finally, three or four increasingly specific menus later, tracked down a brief report on the negotiations for the Bonds. What made it brief was that there was nothing to say; the negotiations were "proceeding" but no "resolution" had been reached.

At that point the image on his screen flickered out.

Surprised, Dekker reached for the keypad, but before his fingers got there the screen had flashed back on again, displaying the original main menu. He frowned at it before he turned it off. That shouldn't have happened.

It occurred to him that a glitch in the station's internal communications, even a tiny one, might still constitute some sort of emergency. If so, he might be needed. Accordingly he tried to call Jared Clyne at his office.

Clyne wasn't there, and the legend on the screen gave no hint of urgency. It was only the standard invitation to leave a message.

When Dekker had turned it off again he made up his mind what he would have to do. He would allow himself to take time for a quick breakfast, because there might not be any real urgency. But then he would go early to the office just on the chance that he might be needed. Probably he wouldn't. Certainly he hoped that was the case. He especially hoped that he would not be needed for anything that would prolong his working day—at least, not past the time when Rima Consalvo would be getting off shift.

Breakfast wasn't quick, though. The line was long, and by the time Dekker got to the end of it he found Toro Tanabe sweating and scowling as he handed out meal packets. "Oh, hello, DeWoe. Don't you start with me, please. All the timers went down and we had to reset everything by hand, so I know the service is slow, and if your omelet's too burned or too raw I'm sorry, but it wasn't our fault."

Dekker wedged himself with one foot and cracked the box open. "It looks fine," he reported. "So cheer up."

Tanabe looked up at him from under his glowering eyebrows. "You want me to cheer up," he said. "With all these people complaining, and the stock reports showing that all my father's holdings are under short-selling pressure, and my mother telling me I'm a fool and a disgrace to my family for working as a *cook* when I could be doing something useful and living like a king in Tokyo—and with fifty, count them, *fifty* lottery tickets in the last drawing and not one of them even coming close—with all that good stuff, you really want me to cheer up? Sure, DeWoe. I'll be glad to cheer up right away— if only you'll get the hell out of my way so I can get these people fed!"

Amused, but also slightly abashed, Dekker pushed himself away, clinging to his meal box and coffee bulb, and looked around for a perch. He saw Shiaopin Ye eating by herself in one corner of the room and floated over to join her.

When she looked up she nodded, but didn't look particularly

pleased. He snapped a strap to his belt and grinned at her. "Are they giving you a hard time, too?" he asked cheerfully.

She closed her meal box to prevent any of the little dumplings inside from flying away and finished chewing before she answered. "You mean about the communications loss," she said. "Yes. We are all blamed. But just over there, you see, is the head of the communications section, having a pleasant meal with Dr. Rosa McCune, so it must be so that he is right when he says there is really nothing to be concerned about."

"Ah," Dekker said, taking a pull on his coffee. "You don't sound as though you agree with him."

"You are correct," she said. She lifted the lid of the box and expertly pulled out another dumpling with her chopsticks. Dekker began eating, too, glancing over to where Toby Mory and the psycher were talking amiably together.

"He really doesn't seem worried," Dekker offered. "He must know what he's doing, Ye. He's the head of the section."

"Exactly," Ye said, nodding. "That is precisely what he told me, not ten minutes ago."

"But you don't believe it."

Shiaopin Ye looked at him for several seconds before answering. Then she closed her box and unsnapped her security belt. "DeWoe," she said, holding herself in place with one hand, "does this seem like a happy installation to you?"

"Happy?"

"I mean, do the people here seem comfortable in their work?"

He thought. "A little edgier than I would have expected, maybe. Some of them."

She nodded. "I would say quite 'edgy.' There is a tension on this station that I don't understand. I think things are being kept from us."

"By Toby Mory, you mean?"

"Not just by Toby Mory, but by him, too, yes. I am quite qualified in communications systems, DeWoe. You know that; we took the same courses. Yet when I begin to check the systems for myself Mory orders me to stop. He says he has done it himself."

Dekker scowled, trying to follow her logic. "If you're saying Mory really doesn't want the system fixed, that doesn't make any sense."

"It does not, but many things which do not make sense turn

out to be true anyway, don't they? That is why I am going to go back there when Mory is not around and run a check myself."

"What do you expect to find, for God's sake?"

"I won't know that unless I find it, will I? But I will check anyway."

Dekker caught at her arm as she started to leave. "If you do find anything, will you tell me? It might be a matter for the emergency service."

She thought that over, then sighed. "I like you, DeWoe. You have always seemed honest to me. Yes. I will come to your room or leave a note. I will not, though," she added, "use the communications screen."

The thing that made it hard to laugh at Shiaopin Ye's preposterous ideas, Dekker told himself as he headed toward Jared Clyne's little office, was that she wasn't a preposterous kind of person. She had always impressed him as about the calmest and most levelheaded person in his class.

That didn't prove that she might not be wrong in her suspicions. It didn't even prove that she couldn't be crazy, because Dekker had formed the opinion that any Earthie at all might have concentrated loopiness hidden under the most attractive exterior—witness Ven Kupferfeld. And he certainly had to agree that her observations were acute. The atmosphere around Co-Mars Two was tenser and stranger than he had expected: people disappeared from sight for days on end, things went wrong, puzzles weren't solved.

Yet when he reached the office, Clyne and Dzhowen Wang showed no sign of tension. The two of them were placidly going over the schematics for the air-circulation system, and Clyne looked up in surprise. "Hey, DeWoe," he said amiably. "You're early."

"I thought you might need me," Dekker explained. "Because of the communications problems, I mean."

"That's the kind of spirit I like," Clyne said, approving. "Communications aren't our worry, though, are they? We'll let the comm people take care of their own headaches." He nodded at the display on the screen. "As long as you're here, you and Joe can get started on pulling down those air pumps today." He paused, then twisted around to look at Dekker again, this time more carefully. "What made you think there was an emergency situation?"

"Well, I didn't, exactly, except—do you know Shiaopin Ye? She seemed to think there was a real problem. She even—" Dekker cleared his throat, embarrassed at the fantasy of what he was saying. "—she even thought that her boss was trying to cover it up."

Clyne looked at him in astonishment. "Toby Mory? Christ, no, DeWoe! I've known Toby for eight years! Ye's just new here; she just doesn't understand everything yet. I don't suppose she has any evidence to back up that kind of remark?"

"She might be getting some, I suppose. She said she was going to check it out for herself—when Mory wasn't around, I mean."

Clyne shook his head. "Jesus. I hope neither of you guys ever thinks you have to go behind my back like that. Anyway," he said heavily, "there's no emergency involved, so it isn't our problem. You'd better get on with those air pumps before they *are* an emergency."

Dekker felt himself rebuked. All the way to the pump room Dekker was conscious of Dzhowen Wang's curious looks, but Wang said nothing until they were there. The two of them had made all their routine checks before Wang offered, "Whatever it is, the air system's still intact."

Dekker shrugged in embarrassment, and Wang nodded to show the subject was closed. He let Dekker make the call to the station chief's office to request permission to switch to standby pumps. Then the two of them began dismantling the pump.

It was hard, hot work in the confined space of the pump room, especially with the problems of moving high-mass pieces of metal around in zero gravity; a Martian child could have pushed one across the room with one finger, but still if you got caught between one and a wall you would get hurt. Dekker was careful. He did his best to copy Joe Wang's practiced way of always having one hand or foot on a holdtight for leverage, and never letting go of a loose part of the pump until it was secured. And, actually, it was just the kind of thing he needed—real, useful, physical work, the kind he hadn't had since he left Mars.

They took time for a quick meal in the middle of the shift, but Wang was anxious to get the pump back on line. They didn't talk much, and they didn't dawdle. The suspect bearings turned out to look all right, but Wang said, "Let's put new ones in anyway." Dekker approved.

It was only at the end, when they were ready to request permission to switch back, that Dekker was reminded of the fact that there was some kind of a problem. It took a minute to get through to the station chief's office, and then the picture was only in monochrome. The internal systems were definitely over-taxed.

As they parted, Wang looked at Dekker soberly. "You know," he said, "as long as Pelly Marine was station chief we didn't have things going out like this. Maybe he was a doper after all—but I wish we had him back."

Dekker checked his watch. He was pleased to see that he had plenty of time to get there early to see Rima Consalvo.

He wanted to do that, but he also wanted to be reassured. So he used up a little of his time to stop by his quarters in case Shiaopin Ye had left a note—to admit, he was confident, that her suspicions had been unfounded, and no doubt to apologize for worrying him.

There wasn't any note under his door, though.

When he called her room there wasn't any answer, either, and when he decided to go one step farther and call the comm center the person he got was her boss. Mory didn't seem friendly, either, when he said, "No, she's not here, and we're kind of busy."

Dekker left for the control workstation, shaking his head. The way people disappeared on this little station! Of course, it was possible that in Rima's case she had simply kept out of Dekker's way because she was making up her mind about how much she wanted to get involved with him. That was actually a fairly cheering thought . . . but Ye?

When he got to Rima's workstation he was still early and she was busy at her work. When she saw him, she turned her head to whisper to her partner, then beckoned him in.

He let himself in apologetically. "I'm sorry if I'm bothering you," he offered. He was talking to the other woman, but Rima answered for both.

"Oh, hell no, Dekker. Myra doesn't mind, and I was expect-ing you."

"Get comfortable and watch," the other controller said hospitably. "There's not much to see. We don't have any more burns scheduled, anyway."

"Thanks," Dekker said, hitching his belt to a hook on the wall. They were simply rechecking trajectories, comet by comet; with each one the computer digested the orbital elements, factored in the gravitational pulls that would affect its course, and then laid the golden line projecting its arrival at Mars. Dekker's attention wandered between what they were doing at the board—and his wish that he were doing it himself—and the interesting view of the back of Rima Consalvo's neck—and his competing wish to explore that more thoroughly. Dekker had heard once of some Earthie woman, a celebrity of some kind, who had claimed she had fallen in love with her husband on first sight, although all she had seen was the back of his neck. That seemed illogical to Dekker; but just at that moment it didn't seem entirely impossible.

Rima turned for a moment to look at him. "You should've been here an hour ago," she offered. "We lost our feed for five minutes. Nothing on the screens at all."

"Not even at the backup station," her partner confirmed. "Scared the shit out of us."

Dekker nodded, wondering if he should share Shiaopin Ye's suspicions with them. He contented himself with saying, "They seem to be having communications problems." Then he leaned forward, staring at the board. "Hey! Is that 67-JY?"

Rima turned to look at him. "Yes, it is. Why?"

"Because it needs a burn, doesn't it?" It looked bad to him. Its golden projection funnel spread out to Mars all right, but just barely within the error probability.

"It does need a burn," Dekker said.

"It's not critical. No," Rima said.

He squirmed around to look at her. "What do you mean, no? It's an easy burn, and, look, Rima, that trajectory brings it pretty close to Earth. I know that comet; it's little, and it's been giving trouble all along."

"I know it, too," Rima said flatly, and then Dekker remembered. Of course she knew it. She had already told him that she was the snake handler who had threaded it out in the Oort. And who was sensitive about it now.

"Oh," he said. "Right."

She thawed slightly. "It already had one burn on this shift; the other board did it. So it's really all right, Dekker. If the next shift thinks it needs a burn, they can do it." She glanced over at the clock. "They're probably waiting to get in already," she said. "Take a look outside, will you, Myra?"

The other woman nodded and pulled herself out into the corridor. A moment later she peered back in and shrugged, signaling that they weren't in sight, then pointed down the hall and pushed herself away in that direction.

Dekker assumed she was heading for a lavatory, but Rima chuckled. "She's being discreet, I bet," she said, "in case we want to be private for a minute. Dekker? Why are you questioning an operator's decision?"

He said, "Well, I guess it's just that there are more things going wrong here than I expected."

"Like the comm systems?"

"For one thing, yes," he agreed.

"And that comet for another?" she asked. "Don't you think I know how to run a board—not counting that Myra's right here with me, and there are two other controllers on the other board?"

"No, of course you do. Only—well, there are people who might like the idea of diverting a comet. You've heard the rumors, haven't you?"

She was looking at him steadily. "What rumors are those?"

He shrugged to indicate he wasn't, actually, serious. "For instance, the ones about the habitats. I've heard it said that the people who are putting the farm habitats up would like a comet of their own—"

"And you think it might be 67-JY?"

"Why not?"

She was laughing at him. "Didn't you learn anything? Look at those trajectory elements."

He said huffily, "All right, I know what you're saying. If I were going to park a comet where the habitats could mine it I wouldn't pick this one. It's got far too much velocity to park it in an orbit they could use. But why else is everybody letting it go with that kind of CEP?"

"Maybe," she said kindly, "we don't know everything yet, Dekker. We're still beginners in this business, aren't we?" And before he could admit the justice of her argument, she added, "Anyway, here come Myra and the next shift. So I'm through here; how about a cup of coffee?"

* * *

It wasn't just the back of Rima Consalvo's neck that was attractive. As he followed her along the red corridor, the two of them pulling themselves from wall hold to wall hold, he found himself also intrigued by those long and unfortunately slacks-clad legs that were waving almost in his face.

The "cup" of coffee wasn't a cup, of course; it was a bulb, and the rec room was more crowded than Dekker would have preferred. The only wall holds they could find to tie to were next to a conversation about what was going on. One of the old hands was saying, "We've lost intrastation addressing facilities, so everything comes in on a single band. It's slowing down communications a lot. They've got somebody listening in and manually redirecting the traffic on each major incoming circuit—Co-Mars One, the Martian orbiters, Earth. We're not getting anything at all from ships in transit or the Oort cloud, though, and even the solar optics are out."

"Well, we don't need any of that, do we?" somebody else said. "For a while, anyway? It's a pain in the ass, but we're still operational and Parker will get it cleared up."

Rima looked at Dekker, then leaned over to the group next to them. "What's going on?" she asked.

The man looked surprised. "You haven't used a screen in the last few minutes? It's the intrastation communications. They're down to just the voice link."

"You can't get news from Earth at all," another one said. "We were watching it on the screen here, and it just went out. Damnedest thing you ever saw."

"It must have happened while we were on our way here," Dekker said to Rima Consalvo. She nodded, looking thoughtful but unsurprised. She looked at her watch instead of replying. But as he turned back to join in the conversation with the other group, she spoke up.

"Dekker," she said, lowering her tone so that the others couldn't hear. "I don't really want any more coffee, and I don't feel like talking about the station's problems right now. It's a little early, but—well, my room's just around the next intersection. Why don't we go there?"

She caught him by surprise. "Go to your room?" he repeated, as though that notion had never crossed his mind.

She nodded. "Yes. Go to my room. If you want to, I mean."

Of that there was no question at all in Dekker's mind. What he wished was that he could do both—maybe talk to these people in the rec room, maybe even tell them about what Shiaopin Ye had said, at least find out more about what was going on and whether, really, it wasn't his duty to get in touch with Jared Clyne and find out if his services were needed . . . and, if possible, at the same time take up the invitation he had been hoping for for some time.

Since he couldn't do both, there was not, really, any doubt about which to choose.

It didn't take long to get there, even less long for them to get inside and for Rima to close the door behind her. Then she smiled at Dekker. "I'm afraid I don't have a drink to offer you," she apologized.

"I don't drink much," he said—automatically and, he thought, a little inanely.

"It's just that it's more private here," she said, looking at her wall clock. "We've got a little extra time," she added, and then smiled at him. "Dekker? What do you think? Would you like to kiss me?"

There was only one answer to that, too, and then only one way for things to go after that. Things went that way. Very satisfactorily, although the fact that Dekker had had no previous experience of making love in zero gravity made him awkward, and made Rima Consalvo giggle.

But they managed it, by judicious use of all available limbs for clamping and holding. When they were finished they hung in midair, sweaty, relaxed, and naked, floating free of the holdtights and holding each other at an odd angle by their linked hands.

It was, Dekker realized complacently, very like his dream. The only difference was that this time he knew who he was holding.

Then there was another difference. He felt Rima move in his arms, craning her neck to look at the clock. "Oh, hell," she said. "How time flies. Dekker, I think we might want to put our clothes back on."

It was not a remark he had expected. "Why?"

"Because," she said, wriggling free and pushing against him to reach the wall, "we have company coming in about five minutes. I don't mind her knowing what we've been doing—but still. You might find it a little embarrassing."

"Who's coming?" Dekker demanded, grabbing a wall hold and reaching out for his floating shorts. "Why is it embarrassing?"

Rima paused in the act of wriggling into her underwear, and answered both questions at once. "It's Ven Kupferfeld," she explained.

When Ven arrived she seemed worried, but not so worried that she didn't take in the scene at once. She gave Rima a searching look. "You just couldn't wait to try him out for yourself, could you?" she demanded.

Rima looked complacent. "We had the time, so I thought we might as well get relaxed." Then, more sharply, "What's the matter?"

Ven Kupferfeld shook her head. "We had some trouble," she said, and didn't expand on the theme. Didn't have the chance, if she had intended to anyway, because Dekker had worked through a chain of reasoning and didn't like where it led him.

"Christ," he said prayerfully, "you two planned all this, didn't you?"

Ven opened her mouth, but Rima Consalvo forestalled her. "Of course we did, Dekker. Ven and I wanted to talk to you about something important—but, believe me, the other part was for fun. I do like you, Dekker."

"*Everybody* likes you, Dekker," Ven said savagely. "You and your mother. That's why we wanted to talk to you, one more time."

"What about my mother?" he demanded, still off balance.

Ven said, "She's a symptom of what's wrong with you people. She's a big wheel on Mars, isn't she? But right now she's down on her knees to the Japs, begging for crumbs. What's the matter with you Martians, Dekker? Don't you care that your planet's being stolen away from you?"

He was having trouble keeping up with her quick changes. He looked at Rima, who smiled politely but was no help. He said, "Mars isn't being stolen. It's a business deal; you people put up the money we needed, so of course we owe you something—"

"Christ!" Ven sounded disgusted.

"Hey," Dekker said, nettled, "which side are you on? You're an Earthie yourself!"

"I'm an *American*, Dekker," she said dangerously, "and don't you forget it. We're getting screwed, too. The Japs and the Europeans—but mostly the damned Japs—they've been selling off their Oort bonds all along, and we poor American suckers were left holding the bag, and your mother—" She paused, shaking her head in contempt. "She's getting raped, and all she wants is a pillow under her head."

"Now, listen—" Dekker began.

"No, Dekker, you listen. It's not just that my family's pretty near ruined, it's my *country*. Do you know that if the farm habitats go through, we Americans are going to have to buy food from the Japs? My grandfather would turn over in his grave, but he'd know what to do."

"Oh, hell," Dekker said, angry at last, "your grandfather was a *soldier*. He *killed* people."

She looked suddenly distracted, but kept on. "Right, he killed. There are times when killing's necessary."

"Or fun," he said bitterly. "Like your lion."

"Why not? Haven't you ever killed anything?"

"Of course not. For one thing, there isn't anything on Mars to kill—well, the fish and the meat animals, but nobody does it for pleasure."

Rima Consalvo stirred. "Ven," she said warningly. "Knock off that killing talk. Nobody's going to get killed."

Ven seemed to collect herself. "No, of course not," she agreed. "Dekker, do you remember—"

She had to stop there, because the comm system rattled into life. There was no picture on the screen, but Simantony Parker's voice came through, sounding tense.

"All personnel," the chief of station's voice said. "This is Parker. We have received relayed warning of a solar flare. The information was delayed, and the particles will arrive in about forty-five minutes. Safe all equipment, and everyone go to the flare shelter now."

"Hell," Dekker said wonderingly. "Listen, I'd better report to Jared Clyne—"

"No, you shouldn't," Rima Consalvo contradicted him. "You just go to the shelter, like everyone else, only you've got plenty of time. All the same, Ven, speed it up, will you?"

Ven nodded, her face grim. "What I'm asking you, Dekker, is do you remember the virt I showed you? The Battle of Seven Pines?"

"How could I forget it?" he demanded bitterly.

"I'm not talking about the killing; I know that upset your silly Martian conscience. What I'm talking about is the *strategy*. Lee *bluffed* the Yankees. He made a threat, and they fell for it."

"And a lot of people got killed," Dekker reminded her.

"Fuck the people who got killed! That was only a detail! Nobody *has* to get killed in a situation like that; if you deploy your forces right, the other side gives up. No bloodshed. So suppose there was a chance like that for Mars. Suppose—no, damn it, don't interrupt me! Suppose somebody could show you how you could use the *threat* of force to make the Japs and everybody else stick to the terms of the original agreement. What would you say?"

Dekker looked at her as he might at a staggering drunk or raving madwoman, but he considered her question. "All it would take would be a threat?"

"Right."

"But backed up by the possibility of actually doing some killing?"

"Well, of course, Dekker. What would you do?"

He nodded. "What I would do," he said, "is call up Dr. Rosa McCune and have that person certified and sent down. Right away."

Ven looked at him for a moment in silent revulsion. Then, shaking her head, she turned to Rima Consalvo. "I told you this would be a waste of time," she said.

Rima, surprisingly, looked smug. "Not for Dekker and me," she said complacently. "Anyway, Dekker, I guess you'd better get on down to the shelter—"

"No," Ven said.

"*Yes,* Ven. I'm sorry about the way this looked to you, Dekker, but I'm not sorry about anything we did. I hope we can do it again sometime—and we'll talk about it later."

In a space station where nothing is more than a couple hundred meters from anything else, forty-five minutes is a lot of time. Evidently Ven Kupferfeld and Rima Consalvo thought so, because they stayed behind when Dekker left them. Dekker thought so himself. It crossed his mind that he had time even to jump into a splash chamber and rinse himself off before going to the shelter; they would be in close quarters there for some time, and he didn't particularly want to advertise what he and Rima had been doing.

On the other hand, he needed all that time, because he needed to think.

He wondered if he actually should talk to Dr. Rosa McCune—or, perhaps even better, to the station chief himself.

The more he thought, the more that seemed his most practical option. His mind made up, he pulled himself rapidly along toward the logical place to find them, or anyone: the flare shelter. The difficulty, he told himself as he hurried along, was that he didn't know exactly what he would say when he found them. There was no doubt in his mind that Ven and Rima had been acting peculiarly—no, *ominously*, he corrected himself. But in Dekker's view Earthies always acted fairly oddly—not that such Earthified Martians as Jay-John Belster were much better; and what did that prove?

The problem disappeared when he reached the shelter. Neither Parker nor the psychologist was there.

As a matter of fact, less than half the station's complement was inside the shelter. Obviously a flare warning was old stuff to the personnel of Co-Mars Two. Dekker had passed more than a dozen others on the way to the shelter, none of them seeming particularly panicky, or even greatly concerned. He looked around for someone else to talk to, and found no one. Shiaopin Ye wasn't there, nor Toro Tanabe. Neither was his boss, Jared Clyne. Neither was Annetta Bancroft, Jay-John Belster, or the head of the communications section, Toby Mory; in fact, the only familiar face in sight belonged to Dzhowen Wang, idly playing with an unresponding screen on the wall.

The trouble was that Dekker really had nothing to say to Dzhowen Wang, and the people he most wanted to talk to were still outside somewhere.

The solution to that problem was clear enough. Dekker turned around to leave the flare shelter to look for them. The count-keeper at the door didn't like that. "You're supposed to stay inside," he told Dekker, sounding angry.

"I forgot something," Dekker said, pushing past him.

"Well, find it and get back here!" the man shouted after him. "You've got fifteen minutes, no more!"

Dekker waved to show that he understood. It occurred to him that what he was doing was not entirely sensible. Surely everybody on the station would sooner or later arrive in the shelter—well, all but the handful who would stay on duty at the control boards in the flare shadow—certainly *someone* he needed to talk to would. And if he failed to get back to the shelter in time—

He had a quick vision of those heavy ionized particles from the Sun sleeting through the station. Through *him*. He almost winced as he contemplated the storm of flare particles striking his internal organs, his eyes, his brain—striking a million individual cells and doing harm to each one.

It was not a cheering thought. He pushed it out of his mind and began a systematic patrol of the corridors leading to the shelter. A few more individuals and small groups were leisurely pushing themselves toward the shelter, taking their own sweet time about responding to the alarm. They looked at him curiously as he passed, but none of those faces were the faces he was looking for. He peered into a rec room, with its magnetic game tables and virtual bodysuits; no one there. No one in the dimmed-down private rooms whose doors stood open, either. The number of people still moving toward the shelter was getting sparser, too; time was passing.

When he finally did see two people he knew, they were only Ven Kupferfeld and Jay-John Belster, talking in low voices at a junction of red and yellow corridors. They were not the ones he wanted to see. He had nothing to say—yet—to the woman who had interrupted his rendezvous with Rima Consalvo, and nothing for Jay-John Belster, ever. He turned around and kicked himself down the yellow corridor.

As he passed the kitchens a face he did know popped out, peered at him, then pulled quickly back inside.

"Tanabe!" he called. The face cautiously reappeared as Dekker moved closer.

Tanabe looked worriedly up and down the hall. "Come inside quickly, DeWoe," he begged. "I don't want anyone else coming here."

Dekker did. As Tanabe was closing the door, he demanded: "Why aren't you in the flare shelter?"

"I will be," Tanabe said, "oh, yes, believe me; I will be there. But there is something I must do first. Can you help me?"

"Help you do what?"

"Open this freezer." Tanabe was tugging him over to the food-storage bins. One hatch had a seal on it, the kind that was used to protect valuable supplies; but it was strangely battered and scratched. "I want to see what's inside there. That asshole Belster came in with Chief Parker a while ago and chased everyone out of the kitchens; then when they let us back in my main freezer was sealed. I want to know what they put in it, so take that cleaver and help me get it open."

"Hold it! That's the station chief's seal!"

"I do not care whose seal it is. If you won't help me, then just go on to the shelter."

Dekker looked at the man, then at his watch. It was really about time to do that. And he certainly had more important things on his mind than Tanabe's curiosity. But still—

He surrendered. "I didn't say I wouldn't help you. You don't need to break it open, anyway—unless you've wrecked the lock already."

He was pulling his emergency override key out. "Ah, so," Tanabe said, thawing. "Yes, please, DeWoe, that would be much better! Then we can get out of here. Is the key working?"

It was—just barely. Tanabe's assaults had cracked the edge of the slot, but Dekker managed to slide his key in. On the third try the magnetic code caught and the seal opened.

Tanabe pulled it off, and grasped the freezer door handle. It slid wide. A dozen meal packets came floating out, evidently thrust in loose instead of being properly stored. And behind them was something that didn't belong there.

It was a human body, small, curled upon itself. Dead.

"Jesus," Tanabe breathed, appalled. "That's Shiaopin Ye!"

From the door Jay-John Belster's voice said, sharp and nasty, "What the hell are you doing here?" He was holding himself by the door frame, Ven Kupferfeld looking hostile beside him. He glanced at her. "I thought everybody would be in the shelter," he complained.

Dekker straightened to confront them. "What happened

to Ye?" he demanded, a moment before he observed that Belster was holding in his hand something that appeared to be—yes, definitely, incredibly, was—a *gun*.

Dekker faced an unbelievable fact. "You killed her," he said.

"No!" Ven cried. "Not on purpose; it was an accident."

"But," said Belster, grinning, "There may have to be a couple more accidents."

Ven turned and put her hand on his arm. "Damn you, *no*. We'll put them away somewhere—maybe up by the boards, so somebody can keep an eye on them."

"Why go to that trouble?" Belster asked in a reasonable tone. "Everybody else is safely tucked away in the shelter by now, so nobody's going to interfere. And we've already got one death."

"Because I say so!" Ven said harshly. They were paying more attention to each other than to their prisoners. Beside him Dekker heard a quick intake of breath from Toro Tanabe, and then the Japanese had launched himself, fast and hard, at Belster. The onetime Martian looked around a moment too late; Tanabe's head had driven into his belly. The gun went flying; Belster's knee came up as he squawked in surprise, and it caught Tanabe under the chin. The Japanese was knocked against the wall. He gasped once, and then floated limply away, unmoving.

The gun was drifting toward Dekker DeWoe.

Dekker didn't think about it. He simply pushed himself toward it, grabbed it, held it in his hand, loosely pointed toward Belster and the woman. He had never held a killing weapon before. It felt cold, hard, and unpleasant; the idea of touching it, much less using it, disgusted him.

Belster was slowly untangling himself, clutching his groin. Then he managed a wheezing laugh. "Hey, DeWoe," he said, sounding almost playful, "what the hell do you think you're going to do with that?"

"Stay away from me," Dekker said warningly.

"Now, why would I do that?" Belster was pulling himself along the wall, coming closer. "You know you won't shoot me, don't you? Just hand it over."

He reached out for it.

Dekker didn't hand him the gun. But when Belster's fingers closed over the barrel he didn't pull the trigger, either.

Then Belster's other fist smashed him in the face, and he tumbled away.

Belster had the gun. "Too much docility training, DeWoe," he said sagely. "And you didn't have enough time on Earth to get over it, did you? Well, Ven, I guess we can fit a couple more in the freezer—"

She looked up from where she was holding Tanabe. "He isn't dead," she objected. "I think he might have a fractured skull, though; he hit the wall pretty hard."

"That's easy enough to take care of," Belster said.

She glanced wildly at Dekker, then shook her head. "It isn't necessary. We'll tie them up somewhere. In a little while it won't matter anyway."

Dekker was holding his cheek. He felt the flesh around his eye swelling up, but some things he was beginning to see clearly. "There isn't really a flare, is there?" he asked. "You just wanted to get everybody out of the way so you could do something—" He stopped in the middle of the sentence. "That comet!" he cried.

"Intelligent man," Belster said admiringly. "Yes, we're going to do something with the comet, but there's nothing you can do about it, is there? Now move! We'll try it Ven's way, but don't try anything foolish. Do you understand me? Because the truth of the matter, DeWoe, is that I wouldn't mind killing you at all."

41.

YOU COULD DROP a comet on Mars without doing much harm, because there wasn't much on Mars to do harm to. The land surface of Earth, on the other hand, was vulnerable at every point. There was hardly a square kilometer of land left there that didn't have some human beings living on it, or building on it, or depending on it for something they needed for their lives, even if it was only forest cover that they needed to keep some otherwise useless mountainside from eroding down to choke their water supplies.

The impact blasts from the comets were only fireworks on Mars. On Earth they would be Hiroshimas or Colognes if they impacted on a built-up land area . . . and even if they struck the empty sea their impact would produce the vast, spreading ripples of ocean that would overwhelm the first coast they came to in the form of tsunamis—tidal waves—bores of water that would sweep away coastal homes, and drown buildings and people. A single comet fragment striking the Earth could kill millions.

42.

T HEY TIED DEKKER'S hands and blindfolded him, and then they plastered him, facedown, against a holdtight in a corner of the wall of the little air lock next to the control workstations. He didn't strive to get free. He might have done that, one way or another, but then what? He had too much to take in. He just listened to Toro Tanabe's ragged breathing, and to the conversations going on in the control chamber next to the lock, and he thought.

He didn't like his thoughts.

He could hear whisperings and murmurings as new people came into the room. He recognized some of the voices. Female voices. Annetta Bancroft's voice. Rima Consalvo's voice. Ven's voice. And the male voices of Jay-John Belster and Parker, the station chief.

He was not really surprised at any of the women; he had decided long since that Earthie women were a mystery past his understanding. What really astonished Dekker—shocked him—was that a Martian, a *Martian*, would so much as possess, much less ever threaten anyone else with, a *gun*. He could account for it in the case of an Earthified Martian like Jay-John Belster, perhaps, but even the station chief, even his boss, the very decent-seeming Jared Clyne—he didn't even count the Earthies like Ven Kupferfeld and Annetta Bancroft and the others—all of them seemed to take the use of a gun to keep Dekker DeWoe from doing anything they didn't desire as a perfectly normal exercise of authority.

When he felt a hand pulling him free, the next step, he expected, was to remove his blindfold and let him see again. It was. He blinked at the people before him. The station chief seemed to be gone, along with most of the Earthie men, but Belster and the three women were still there. "You're a pain in the ass, DeWoe," Belster said, reproaching him. "Why didn't you stay in the flare room the way you were supposed to?"

Dekker didn't answer that. Belster shrugged and passed the gun to Ven Kupferfeld. "He's all yours," he said. "We've got to get to the comm center."

"You heard the man." Ven grinned, waving the gun.

Dekker wasn't looking at the gun. He was looking at the two women he had made love with and the one he had known as a child. "You're crazy," he said. It wasn't a denunciation. It was the statement of a considered diagnosis.

"It's not what you think, Dekker," Annetta Bancroft said.

"I don't think it's just some simple cheating or selling test papers anymore, no," he agreed. "So what do I think, Annetta?"

She flushed. "Some violent scheme, I guess. Dropping a comet on Sunpoint or somewhere else on Mars—"

"No," he said positively, "I thought of that, but that couldn't be it. There are too many Martians here for that, and not even a psychotic like Jay-John Belster would do that. And it's not stealing a comet for the habitats, either, is it? So all that's left is that you're planning to bombard Earth."

"No!" Annetta said violently. "Nobody's going to get bombarded! Tell him, Ven."

Ven Kupferfeld shrugged. "Don't you think we've wasted enough time with this weakling?"

"Tell him!"

"Oh, all right. See, Dekker, I had hopes for you. You could have been useful to us," she said. "Not because of you. Because of that Queen Shit mother of yours; with you backing us up, it would have helped—afterward."

He looked around. Rima Consalvo was simply hanging there, apparently content to let the other two do the talking;

Annetta Bancroft was biting her lip. "After what?" he demanded.

"It's the Japs," she said simply. "You know they're the ones who are making the trouble with their damn habitats. For you as much as for us. Maybe it's not too late for you to show some sense yet, quite. Don't you think you ought to help us stop them?"

Dekker blinked at her. "Stop them," he repeated wonderingly. But in order to stop them—

He closed his eyes, trying to shut out the images that came to him. He was remembering the way Chryse Planitia had looked when the first cometary fragments struck—*empty* Chryse Planitia. His stomach convulsed when he thought of such terrible violence repeated on Earth—on cities, *human* cities, containing the defenseless flesh of human beings—men, women, babies, everyone—smashed or incinerated as the ground itself erupted and boiled away, with molten droplets falling like hell's own rain for a hundred kilometers around. "You'll kill a billion people," he whispered, his lips dry.

"Oh, Dekker," Annetta sobbed, almost laughing, "do you think we'd do *that*? We're not going to let the comet *strike*, are we, Ven?"

"Of course not," Ven Kupferfeld said soothingly. "It's a bluff, Dekker."

"A bluff?"

"A military ruse." She smiled at him. "They'll cave in, I promise."

"And if they don't?"

She hesitated, looked at her watch, then said, "Dekker, do you remember the virt of the Battle of the Seven Days?"

"You keep asking me that. I saw it."

"I know you *saw* it, for God's sake. I don't know if you *understood* it. See, Robert E. Lee was protecting Richmond—"

"Ven," Annetta protested.

"Shut up, Annetta. I'm trying to explain something to our friend here. The reason McClellan didn't take Richmond was that Lee outsmarted him. And how did he do that?"

Dekker shook his head, looking at the gun in Ven's hand. Would it be right, he wondered, to take it away from her? Would Rima or Annetta interfere? And if he did get possession of it, then what?

"Pay attention, damn you! Lee knew McClellan would fall for his bluff, because *Lee knew McClellan*. They'd served together and he knew his man. He knew McClellan wasn't going to throw his main force forward when his right wing was under heavy attack, and he was right. McClellan fought it out where he was until his losses began to discourage him, and then he gave up and went back to Washington. And, see, Dekker, it's the same here. I know these people. I know they'll cave in."

She seemed to be talking to Annetta as much as to him, Dekker thought. "And then what?" he asked.

Annetta answered for her. "And then they sign a treaty," she said proudly. "They stop building new farm habitats; the Oort project goes on; our investments are worth something again!"

"And if they don't?"

Ven looked him over thoughtfully. "Why then," she said, "things get really lousy, don't they? But they will. I promise."

He said only, "You'd better get Toro Tanabe to a doctor. I don't like the way he sounds."

"Shit," Ven said in disgust. "All right. Rima, do you want to stay with him?"

Rima Consalvo looked at him almost fondly. "I guess not, actually," she said.

"Then it's up to you, Annetta." Ven looked at her watch again. "Just keep him locked up. The other stations will start asking questions any time now, so Rima and I'd better get up there and help answer them."

His hands were still tied behind him, and the tie was strong and unyielding stickytape, but that wasn't Dekker DeWoe's real problem. From all the Earthie virts he had seen as a child he knew what you did about that; he painfully slipped his arms around his tucked legs so that his hands were in front, and when he found a reasonably sharp edge, at the neck of one of the spacesuits in the lock, he began rubbing the tape against it.

It didn't seem to cut through very quickly, but that wasn't the problem, either. The real problems were a lot more complicated. First, Toro Tanabe's breathing had eased a little, but the man was still unconscious—tied up, too, but definitely unconscious anyway. Second, there was the fact that he was locked in a room from which he saw no good way to escape. Finally—the *hard* problem—what he could do about what was going on if he did get free.

Of course, whispered a traitor voice in the back of his mind, it just *might* be that there was no reason for him to do anything at all. Ven had said they were fighting for the Mars project, and wasn't that what he wanted, too? And if you believed her, and believed that the bluff would work . . . why, then, you could believe almost anything.

Dekker did not believe the traitor voice. He rubbed harder and was still rubbing when the hatch to the workstation opened.

Annetta's face was there, looking in at him, seeing what he was doing. "You'll never get that off," she informed him.

He didn't stop rubbing, and she sighed. "Oh, hell," she said, and pushed a meal box into the hatch, setting it on a holdtight and moving away. "They brought me some food. I thought you'd need it more than I do."

"Tanabe needs a doctor."

"I'll get him one as soon as I can, I promise, but you probably need to eat."

He did. What he needed even more was something to deal with the thirst he had not been aware he had. His bound hands were of little use, but he pushed the lid up on the box and seized a bulb of liquid—it turned out to be coffee—and sucked on it thirstily.

Then he looked at her. "Thanks," he said.

She said doubtfully, "I don't see how you're going to manage eating this with your hands tied, but I guess you'll figure something out. I have to get back and watch the board."

"Wait a minute. No, really," he said more urgently. "I don't think you know what's going on."

"Oh, Dekker," she said patiently, "I've known all about this for a *year*. Do you think I haven't helped plan the whole thing?"

"Like getting everybody up here at the right time, and getting everybody out who might be suspicious, right," he said. "But when did you plan on murdering Shiaopin Ye?"

She was ready for him. "That was purely an accident. It couldn't be helped. Toby Mory was just trying to make her go away, but she resisted."

"Right," Dekker said, nodding. "Like Tanabe here."

"I told you I'd make sure he got a doctor!"

"Yes, Annetta, but he may not last that long, and anyway I don't believe what you tell me. Too much of what you people say is lies. See, I've been thinking. They're not doing this to save the Oort project, Annetta. Nobody could stop that now. There's too much invested. So it has to be for some other reason, and all I can figure is that they want to get the prices for the Bonds to go up again so they can get their money back."

"That probably will happen, too, yes. We've all—" She hesitated, then rushed on. "All right, we've all scraped up everything we had and sold farm-habitat securities short. I'll make some money out of it, I admit. What's wrong with that?" she demanded.

"I believe the part about the money, yes. The rest is all lies, Annetta. Either you're lying to me or they're lying to you."

"Nobody's lying!"

"Do you really believe that? Do you think that people who would do this would worry about a few lies?"

"We're doing the right thing!" she snapped.

"There isn't any real solar flare, either, is there?"

"That was the best way of getting everybody out of the way without hurting them, wasn't it? They've got food and water and air, and they'll be all right." She hesitated. "Oh, I'd rather have gone a different way, if we could. I don't like telling lies. I'm sorry for all those people, stuck there, not knowing what's going on. I don't like a lot of the other things that have happened, either—not just Ye's accident—well, I wish they hadn't framed Pelly with those drugs. He was a good man. But he wasn't the right kind of person to do this, so they had to get him off the station."

"And all the others? The ones Rosa McCune washed out of my class?"

She shrugged. "They had to make room so Jay-John and Ven and I could get here—there are only eleven of us. We had to do a lot of things just so we could get it set up in time, don't you see? This was our best chance. How often would we get just this right alignment of the planets, so the incomings for Mars would come so close to Earth?" She looked pensive. "It's too bad about their careers, but when the story comes out I'm sure they'll all be reinstated."

"Some of them won't be. They'll be dead, Annetta. One of the dead ones will probably be my mother."

She said furiously, "I told you, nobody's going to be *dead*." She slammed the hatch shut, and Dekker went somberly back to his rubbing.

* * *

He had just returned to the food box, his hands still tied tightly and beginning to hurt, when he heard the hatch opening again. Annetta was looking in on him.

"Just checking," she said. "Sorry you're having so much trouble."

He finished chewing the crumb of roll he had managed to bite off—the rest of it was floating somewhere in the room behind him—and said, "Are you willing to listen to me now?"

"No! I mean," she corrected herself, "I checked the board and there's nothing to do for a bit. I'm willing to talk to you for a minute. Not so you can convince me we're doing anything wrong, because we aren't. Just so you'll understand we're doing the right thing."

He said conversationally, "Murdering a lot of people can't be the right thing."

She looked at him with mixed anger and pity. "Damn you, Dekker! You keep saying that and we *told* you nobody's going to get killed."

"Except Shiaopin Ye, you mean. And maybe Tanabe."

"Belster says he'll be all right!"

He shook his head, and pointed out another fact: "You've still got that gun, too. What would you do with it if I jumped you?"

She pushed herself back a few centimeters. "You can't get out of there. Anyway, I wouldn't shoot to kill, just to stop you. I told you—"

He interrupted. "You told me the Japs would give in and promise to give up their habitats. Maybe they would; they'd probably promise anything right then. But what about after you've diverted the comet? How long do you think they'd keep that promise?"

She said with contempt, "Do you think we didn't plan for that? That's all taken care of, Dekker. There are *contracts* right there on Earth, ready to be signed. As soon as they see we mean business our negotiators are going to head for Tokyo and get them signed. They'll have penalty clauses and—what?"

He was trying to interrupt her. "You say they're *going* to head for Tokyo? You mean they aren't there already? Why aren't they?"

She looked at him for a moment. "That's the way we set it up, is all."

"No, Annetta, that isn't all. Think about it a little bit. The reason they aren't in Tokyo is that that's where the comet's going to fall. Right on Japan."

She shook her head. "Oh, no," she said positively. "You don't know what you're saying, Dekker. That's impossible."

He frowned at her. Was there something he had left out? "Why impossible? Do you think Co-Mars One might take over and divert it?"

"Of course not—not 67-JY. Rima and Berl Korman worked that one, out in the Oort, and they planted a command in it. The first thing we did was trigger it, and now it won't respond to any control but our own."

"Ah," said Dekker, the pieces falling into place. "That's why they picked a little one; it'll just destroy the place it lands on. And the place it's going to land on is Japan." He saw the expression on her face cloud over, and then he struck home. "Do you know why I'm so sure of that? Figure it out for yourself. How many Japanese are there on the station?"

"Why—?" She thought for a minute. "I think most of them got sent down," she admitted.

"Most of them?"

"All right, maybe all of them! How would I know? I don't keep the records!"

"I haven't seen any here, anyway. Except Tanabe, and he was the last Japanese in the class, and he damn near quit at the last minute. Why do you suppose that is?"

"You're *sick*," Annetta said furiously, "and I'm tired of listening to all this crap. Let me tell you what you ought to do. As soon as this is over you ought to go home, DeWoe. Plant some crops; take your mind off these crazy fantasies; marry some Martian woman and have a lot of children—and, most of all, don't bother me anymore!"

And she slammed the hatch again.

The fact was, Dekker acknowledged to himself as he went on rubbing against his bonds, Annetta was at least partly right. He was sick, all right. He was sick in ways he had never experienced before, because his whole concept of morality and social order was on the verge of collapse.

How could even *Earthies* do such a thing? Much less Martians?

Was it possible he could be wrong?

Dekker considered that possibility carefully, sawing away. It was true that he was under stress. He had never been confined against his will before.

It occurred to him that there was another side to the coin. He wasn't the only one whose judgment could have been clouded. Others had been subject to traumatic experiences, too. Dekker tried to imagine what it was like to be a rich Earthie who had lost all her wealth. A big shock? No doubt of that, he thought, remembering the spoiled young Annetta Cauchy of Sunpoint City, white dress, gold-spangled hair, unquestioned heiress to everything in sight. But was it a big enough shock? Could losing all that produce so lasting a hurt that it might only be healed by *this*?

Dekker couldn't answer that question. He didn't doubt that the acquisition of money was vitally important to Earthies; the evidence to prove that had been all about him for a long time. All the same, was it possible that they could have been so inflamed by their insensate passion for wealth as to commit this sort of bloody violence?

He had no answer for that, either . . . and then his train of thought was derailed as something in the vicinity of his aching wrists suddenly gave way.

It took a moment for Dekker to realize what it was. His persistent rubbing had begun to pay off. One strand of the sticktight had finally worn through. It didn't mean he was free. There wasn't much sensation in his hands now, except for pain, but when he tested his bonds, the remaining strands still held them fast.

They were, however, a little looser than they had been before, and that opened a new possibility, which Dekker began to explore. If he could just get his hands in *front* of him—

It meant twisting his spine in ways he had never tried before, and he knew they would all hurt. Painfully he arched his back, trying to slide his wrists down over his hips. It was not impossible anymore, he found. It was merely very painful, but he had the advantage of his lean anatomy; a slim

Martian body could bend a good deal more pliably than a stocky Earthie's. Even so, after he got his wrists down past his hams there was still the problem of getting past his long Martian legs.

That was harder. It took a long time, and a good deal of pain, for Dekker to forcibly twist one ankle enough to work the bound hands over one foot, then another.

But then his hands were in front of him.

The rest was only a matter of finding loose ends of the sticktight and tugging at them with his teeth until his hands were free. He flexed his fingers experimentally. Circulation was poor. The hands tingled painfully and did not move well, but he managed to push one hand into the pocket of the coverall and close the fingers on what they found.

The emergency override key was still in his pocket. It meant that he was no longer a prisoner.

He held the key in his teeth while he rubbed his wrists to restore circulation. Then he did what he had not done for a while and pushed himself over to where Toro Tanabe lay motionless and lashed to the wall. Dekker bent over him to see how Tanabe was doing.

Tanabe was no longer breathing.

When Dekker straightened up his face was drawn. He hung there in the air, by his dead friend, still absently rubbing his hands together. He wasn't mourning the death of Tanabe. There was no point in that; instead, Dekker was thinking through what he had to do. It would not be easy. There was a good chance that in the process he could get himself killed as well. But what choice did he have?

When Dekker appeared at the door of the workstation, tugging a spacesuit behind him, Annetta gasped and grabbed for the gun. She waved it toward him. "Get back in there! How did you get out, anyway?"

He didn't answer; his priorities went to more urgent questions. He pushed the suit in at her. "Put this on," he ordered.

She stopped the floating suit with one hand, blinking at him. "The hell I will! Look, Dekker, if you think I'm afraid to shoot you—"

He shook his head at her. "Tanabe's dead," he told her. Her face fell. "Oh, Dekker!" she whispered, stricken.

"Belster *promised* he'd get a doctor for him before it was too late."

"Belster lied," Dekker said, surprised he should have to say it. "He lied about everything; I thought you knew that by now. The question now is how many more people do you want to see die, Annetta? Me, for instance?"

"I never wanted to kill anybody!"

"Then," he said sensibly, "we need to get that comet out of the way before it hits Earth, don't we? There's still time for a few big burns to slide it away—"

"No!"

"Yes," he corrected her. "You don't have much of a choice, Annetta, because the only way you can keep me from doing that is by shooting me. Are you going to do that?" It was not a trivial question in his mind, but he was almost amused at the expression on her face. He added, "That comet isn't going to miss the Earth, you know. Not unless we make it miss."

"What's the use of talking about it?" she said wretchedly. "Even if you're right, it wouldn't work anyway. We can't do it. As soon as we started the course-correction burns they'd know in the comm room, and they'd be charging right up here to make us stop."

Dekker tried to be kind because she had said "we." "No, they won't be able to do that, Annetta. They won't be going anywhere; I'm going to make sure of that. But I don't have any more time to argue. So here it is: you can do one of two things. You can go ahead and shoot me if that's what you want. Or else you can just put that stupid gun down and start getting into this suit."

Whether Annetta was doing as she was told or not Dekker did not know. He turned away without waiting for her response. He felt a crawling sensation between his shoulder-blades as he returned to the lock, but he did not look around when he began the process of climbing into his own space-suit. He estimated that the actual likelihood that she would shoot him was low, but the decision was not his to make.

By the time the helmet seals were tight, the shot had not come, and a muffled clatter from the next compartment suggested that Annetta was in fact doing something with her

own suit. So far, so good, he congratulated himself; now it
was time to get to work.

He caught at the override key where he had left it floating
in the air and pushed himself over to the lock controls. He
didn't look at Tanabe's body. There was no point; Tanabe
was past all help, but the Earth was not. It was an awkward
job, fitting it into its slot with his still pained and now
gauntleted hands, but the procedure was just the familiar
fire-emergency blowout drill he had practiced so many times
on the hill, after all.

Just as in drill, as soon as he activated the locks for full
air blow, the take-shelter klaxons blared deafeningly from
all over the station.

The warning period they allowed was only ten seconds.
He hoped Annetta would have finished sealing her suit. He
did not want to take a life—even hers, though she had been
part of this deadly plan. Especially hers, he corrected himself, and wondered why.

Then the ten seconds were over.

That was when everything happened at once. Dekker
heard the grating, rumbling, crashing sound of every door
on the station simultaneously slamming shut. A moment
later the whole station shook as every outside lock flung
itself open to let the station's air pour out into the vacuum
of space. There was a harsh, hurricane scream of escaping
air, but that noise dwindled fast. In a moment there was no
longer enough air within the open spaces of the station to
carry sound, and Co-Mars Station Two lay airless and still
around him.

Anyone outside a closed compartment was now dead, he
thought, hoping no one had been so stupid. And everyone
within one would now stay there until he chose to fill the
corridors once more with air.

43.

WHEN DEKKER LET himself back into the control station
its internal air puffed out in a sudden blast. It almost
blew him away from the door, but he caught at a holdfast until
it was gone.

Annetta was waiting there inside. She was suited up, staring
whitefaced at him through the visor. He made a meaningless
gesture of reassurance in her direction but did not touch his
helmet to hers to speak. There was nothing to say and a lot
to do.

Dekker placed himself before the board, rehearsed for a
moment what he had planned, and then summoned up the
orbital elements of the comet on his screen.

When he keyed in the display of the comet's probability cone,
nothing had changed. The thickest part of the cone of golden
light was still centered precisely around the whole planet of
Earth.

That was what he had to alter. It was difficult to work the
controls with the gauntlets on, but he managed to set up the
integrals for a course correction and place his commands. As
soon as he had checked the computer's solution and found it
satisfactory he sent the command for the first long burn. It was
certainly going to be close, he thought.

Then he remembered to look around at Annetta. She was
watching him silently from beside the open door, and he could
see through her faceplate that she was weeping.

That didn't surprise him. It was a good time for weeping;
there was plenty of cause to go around. He wondered what
would happen to Annetta Bancroft. Something, he was sure of
that; vindictive Earthies would not let her go unpunished for
her part in the action. But nothing compared to what would
have happened to a good many million human beings if the
comet had been allowed to strike.

276

He turned back to the important job. The golden probability cone had begun slowly to slide across the screen as the simulation reflected the effects of the ongoing burn. Dekker studied the display carefully. The dot that was Earth still lay within the comet trajectory's probable error, but it was no longer directly in the center.

Dekker scowled at the display; it was going too slowly. He set up another course correction with a longer burn. The computer confirmed it, and he reached out a gauntleted finger to activate—

And paused, frowning.

He had felt another shudder in the structure of the station. A small one and brief, yes. But definitely something had happened, something that had made a thud somewhere in the station far away.

He stabbed the activation switch. It didn't matter. Someone had managed to open an airtight door perhaps, and the gas had slammed out. But no one was going to be able to move through the corridors of the station without a spacesuit.

It occurred to him that although the chances were very small that any of the plotters happened to have a suit available, they were not quite zero. He turned to the door.

Annetta was gone.

He frowned again, thoughtfully. That was not important either, though. There was no place for her to go, and, besides, he thought he knew what that unexpected thud had been.

He closed the door, and locked it with his emergency-override key, and returned to the board.

The long burn was still in progress. The comet's probability cone was now well clear of Earth, and inching farther away every second.

It was a terrible waste of a good comet, he thought. Mars needed those frozen gases.

Still, he thought, it would certainly make a remarkable spectacle from the surface of the Earth it was not, after all, going to strike. And it was almost time to begin the slow job of restoring pressure to the station from the reserve tanks.

44.

DEKKER WAS EXHAUSTED by the time he found Annetta Bancroft. He was not surprised to find her by the commroom because he had been pretty sure where she had gone. The surprise was that she was alive, waiting despondently to be discovered, with the bodies of the conspirators floating all about her.

"I was afraid—" he began, and didn't finish the thought.

She finished it for him. "You were afraid I'd kill myself, I guess. I thought of it, all right. Maybe I should have, but when I saw they were all dead, there just didn't seem any point to it."

"I'm glad you didn't," he said. "There are enough dead already." And there were. More than enough. Ven Kupferfeld's body was drifting no more than arm's-length away. Her hair was floating in all directions, her eyes were unseeingly open, and there was a froth of blood on her lips. He shook his head. He had been right about that little thudding sound that had shaken the station—when the conspirators had seen that they had failed they had opened the door of the commroom and let themselves die.

Inside the room the vanguard of the people he had released from the flare shelter were pushing past the bodies, making contact with all the alarmed incoming calls. Dekker shivered, cold for the first time in many weeks. The replaced air was chilly from its expansion from the reserve tanks.

"They weren't all Earthies," he said, mourning.

Annetta stared at him and he shook himself. He didn't want to explain his thought, but it stayed with him: Martians, not Earthies alone, had been part of this sad, terrible plan. The others were looking at her, silent and hostile, and he remembered that he needed sleep. He took Annetta's arm. "Come away," he said.

She didn't resist, but looked up at him inquiringly. "Are you arresting me?"

"Me? Of course not," Dekker said, astonished at the idea. "I'm not a Peacekeeper, though maybe when the ships get here—" Out of politeness he didn't finish the thought.

He didn't have to; Annetta knew very well what would happen when the ships began to arrive. She said morosely, "I'll be in Rehabilitation a long time, I suppose. But I'm not the only one. You people are still in trouble, too, Dekker. Do you think they're going to forget about the new terms for the Bonds?"

He shrugged, since he had been wondering about the same question.

"Well," she conceded, "maybe they will, at that. This time. With all the excitement and all. But what's going to happen a year or two from now, when everybody forgets what a wonderful person you were? Don't you see that nothing's really solved?" she demanded fiercely.

He looked down at her in surprise. "Nothing ever gets 'solved,' Annetta," he told her. "You just keep trying to make things a little better—for everybody, you see, and not just for yourself." He thought for a moment, and then added, "You do that if you can, I mean. And if you can't make them any better, then you just try to keep them from getting worse."

"That's all there is to look forward to?" she asked.

"What else could there be? But it's enough," he said. "You do what you can today, and then tomorrow, if you're lucky, maybe you can do a little more. We don't learn fast," he finished ruefully, "but maybe we will learn, sooner or later. At least we can hope, and what else do we need?"